IN LOVE WI

The way he looked at her made her feel lightheaded, like she was the most important person in the world to him. Like he didn't even know who Scilla Lambright was. Like Hannah was just as pretty as any girl in the whole *gmayna.* "Gingerbread . . ."—she cleared her throat—"gingerbread isn't hard to make, and it smells like Christmas. I hoped people would like it."

He reached out and wound an errant strand of her hair around his finger. "I wish I had your brain. You can make a batch of pretzels without a recipe, and you can paint or draw anything. I can't even do stick figures."

Hannah inclined her head. "You really don't need to know how to draw. It's not much of a skill. Besides, you're *gute* with numbers. That's a much more important skill."

"Tell that to my little *bruderen.* When they're hungry, they couldn't care less that I can multiply numbers in my head. They'd much rather have a donut than a math lesson."

Hannah watched as Benji popped the last bite of pretzel into his mouth and licked the cheese from the bottom of the cup. "They still adore you."

He gave her a wry twist of his lips. "Maybe, but they like you better."

"Maybe they do."

He ran his fingers through his thick auburn hair. "I get no appreciation around here."

"None whatsoever," Hannah said, when that wasn't true at all . . .

Books by Jennifer Beckstrand

The Matchmakers of Huckleberry Hill
HUCKLEBERRY HILL
HUCKLEBERRY SUMMER
HUCKLEBERRY CHRISTMAS
HUCKLEBERRY SPRING
HUCKLEBERRY HARVEST
HUCKLEBERRY HEARTS
RETURN TO HUCKLEBERRY HILL
A COURTSHIP ON HUCKLEBERRY HILL
HOME ON HUCKLEBERRY HILL
FIRST CHRISTMAS ON HUCKLEBERRY HILL

The Honeybee Sisters
SWEET AS HONEY
A BEE IN HER BONNET
LIKE A BEE TO HONEY

The Petersheim Brothers
ANDREW
ABRAHAM
HIS AMISH SWEETHEART

Amish Quiltmakers
THE AMISH QUILTMAKER'S UNEXPECTED BABY
THE AMISH QUILTMAKER'S UNRULY IN-LAW

Anthologies
AN AMISH CHRISTMAS QUILT
THE AMISH CHRISTMAS KITCHEN
AMISH BRIDES
THE AMISH CHRISTMAS LETTERS
THE AMISH CHRISTMAS CANDLE

Published by Kensington Publishing Corp.

His Amish Sweetheart

JENNIFER BECKSTRAND

ZEBRA BOOKS
KENSINGTON PUBLISHING CORP.
www.kensingtonbooks.com

ZEBRA BOOKS are published by

Kensington Publishing Corp.
.119 West 40th Street
New York, NY 10018

First Printing: July 2022

ISBN-13: 978-1-4201-4773-5
ISBN-13: 978-1-4201-4776-6 (eBook)

10 9 8 7 6 5 4 3 2 1

Printed in the United States of America

Chapter One

"It smells like something died down here."

Austin stood on the bottom step like he was too good or too clean to come clear down into the cellar, as if he might get bitten by a spider or eaten by a moth—fears Alfie and Benji had to face every day. Austin wouldn't be so high and mighty if he was the one who had to sleep in the cellar.

But Mamm would never make Austin sleep in the cellar. Austin was her favoritest son in the whole world. Austin *loved* making peanut butter. Austin was Mamm's best helper. Austin had never set anything on fire, as if that made him better than anyone else.

The cellar was for Alfie and Benji, two nine-year-olds who Mamm didn't think had any feelings. She didn't care that Alfie might die of a spider bite or get sick from a worm crawling down his throat while he was sleeping. It didn't even upset her that the cellar smelled like moldy socks and fermented pinto beans. And most people who knew what fermented pinto beans smelled like cared very much. But Mamm didn't.

Alfie couldn't stand the unjustice of it all. "If you think

you're so smart, Austin, you can sleep down here and Benji and I will take your room."

That didn't annoy Austin in the least. Austin was hard to annoy, even though Alfie tried real hard. Austin just laughed. "Even if you paid me a hundred dollars, I wouldn't sleep down here. It stinks."

Alfie eyed Austin. How much would they have to pay him? It might be worth selling all their worldly possessions to get out of the cellar. The only thing Alfie really cared about was their dog, Tintin, but surely they could get more than a hundred dollars for their other stuff like their clothes and books and bird nest collection. Mamm wouldn't be too happy if they walked around naked, and they probably wouldn't be allowed in school with no clothes. Alfie smiled to himself. All the better. He hated school. Except for recess.

Alfie glanced at his twin *bruder,* Benji. Benji was happily playing with the wooden train their *bruder* Andrew had made them. They could probably get ten dollars for that train, if Benji would part with it.

Benji didn't seem to care that Austin had just mocked their cellar, as if they belonged there like two orphan mice that nobody cared about. Benji was a *gute bruder,* but sometimes he just didn't care enough.

Austin stepped up to the second step. "Mamm says dinner's in ten minutes, and you better scrub your fingernails real *gute* or she won't let you touch the food."

What was it about Mamm and fingernails? Alfie and Benji had to keep their fingernails trimmed and clean, and the one time Alfie had put on fingernail polish, Mamm had nearly popped a blood vessel in her neck. Alfie had seen it bulging.

Alfie's blood boiled as he watched Austin run up the

stairs. Austin could escape from the cellar anytime he wanted, but Alfie and Benji were stuck here until Austin moved out of the house. Well, Abraham and Austin both had to move out, but Abraham was getting married next year, so they just had to find a way to get rid of Austin. They needed to find him a wife. But Austin was going to be real hard because Alfie didn't know of any girl who would take him.

Benji put the train in the bin Mamm had given them for their toys. "Let's go wash our hands. Mammi bought a special brush." Benji was a *gute bruder,* but sometimes he was too obedient and not angry enough.

"Benji, how can you think of scrubbing your fingernails at a time like this?"

"A time like what?"

"A time that we're still sleeping in the cellar."

"We have to sleep in the cellar. Dawdi had a stroke and now Mammi and Dawdi are living in Mamm and Dat's room. Mamm and Dat have our room, and Abraham and Austin share a room. There isn't room for us to sleep anywhere else."

Alfie growled. "I know that. That's why we have to get Austin out of the house. When Abraham gets married, Austin will be the only one left."

"Okay," said Benji, as if he already knew it all, which he did. They'd talked about getting their *bruderen* out of the house ever since they were eight.

"Benji, it doesn't seem like you care if Austin ever moves out."

Benji scratched his head. "I care. But I really want to eat dinner, and I have dog poop under my fingernails."

"Dog poop?"

"*Jah.* I was playing with LaWayne and accidentally put

my hand in his poop. I wiped most of it off on my pants, but there's still some under my fingernails."

Alfie pinched his lips together. No wonder it smelled so bad down here. "Before you scrub your fingernails, we need to talk about Austin. It's going to be real hard to find him a wife because he's cocky and proud and doesn't care that his little *bruderen* have to sleep in the cellar. And don't call our dog LaWayne. His name is Tintin."

"But Mamm said if we want to keep him, we have to change his name to LaWayne."

Alfie huffed out a breath. "We only have to call him LaWayne when Mamm is around. His real name is Tintin."

Benji almost nibbled on his fingernail but probably decided to wait until he scrubbed. "We don't have to find Austin a wife. I already know. He's going to marry Hannah Yutzy."

Alfie rolled his eyes. Benji was a *gute* partner, but he didn't know anything about love. "Austin won't marry Hannah. She's his best friend since first grade. He needs to fall in love with somebody."

"He's already in love with Hannah," Benji insisted. "He just doesn't know it yet."

"He is not," Alfie said. "He's more interested in Priscilla Lambright. She stares at him all the time in *gmay*."

"Even during the prayers?"

Alfie shrugged. "I don't know. I don't open my eyes."

"I'm going to look next time."

Alfie frowned. "The bishop will catch you."

"*Nae*, he won't. He never opens his eyes." Benji shifted his feet. "Probably."

"Even if Priscilla doesn't stare at Austin during the prayer, she likes him, and that's as *gute* as we're going to get because she's the only girl who might be willing to marry him. I have a plan, and we're going to make them fall in love. They'll get married, Austin will move out, and we'll get our room back. If we hurry, Austin and Abraham can have a double wedding. We'll kill two birds with one stone."

"We shouldn't kill birds. Mamm says they are Gotte's creatures and don't hurt a soul. Except sometimes they poop on people and eat their apricots."

Benji was a *gute* partner, but sometimes he had trouble concentrating on the plan. "We're going to make Austin fall in love with Priscilla Lambright, and we've only got a few weeks to do it if we want a double wedding."

"What's a double wedding?"

"It's when four people get married at the same time."

Benji squinted at Alfie. "To each other?"

"*Jah.* Priscilla works at the library. We should tell Austin to go check out some books."

Benji shook his head. "Austin is going to marry Hannah Yutzy."

Alfie clenched his teeth. He wasn't going to let Benji change the plan. "Priscilla is prettier than Hannah."

"She is not."

It was no use arguing about that. Hannah was prettier, and she smiled all the time. Priscilla never smiled, but Alfie wasn't about to admit it. "They are both as pretty as each other, but Priscilla knows how to make cookies."

"Hannah knows how to make donuts and pretzels."

"Priscilla is smarter," Alfie said. He didn't know if that was true, but it made a *gute* argument, especially since Priscilla worked at the library.

"Hannah knows how to quilt. And she laughs all the time. She thinks Austin is funny, and she's nice to the little kids."

Alfie pinched his lips together. Benji didn't know anything about girls, and he liked Austin too much. Nobody else liked Austin at all. "Benji, Priscilla is the only girl who might be willing to marry Austin. No one else will have him, especially not Hannah."

Alfie could usually talk Benji into anything, but Benji folded his arms and lifted his chin. "I want Austin to marry Hannah."

Alfie folded his arms too. He could be just as stubborn. "I want Austin to marry Priscilla."

"I won't help you spy on Priscilla," Benji said.

"I won't help you spy on Hannah," Alfie countered. "And I call the binoculars."

Benji squished his face until he looked like a prune. "Then I call the walkie-talkies."

Alfie didn't argue. You needed two people to work the walkie-talkies. Benji might as well throw them in the river for all the good it would do him. The binoculars were a much better idea. Besides, Benji wasn't as good a spy as Alfie. He'd be lost without Alfie's help. Alfie squared his shoulders. "I guess we're not partners anymore."

Benji sniffed and swiped his sleeve across his face. "I guess not."

It made Alfie kind of sad, the way Benji tried to be brave that they had broken up, but Alfie refused to shed a tear. Benji had made his choice, and he was going to lose for sure and certain. Alfie might as well start sending out invitations for Austin and Priscilla's wedding. Austin's bedroom was as good as his. And maybe if Benji asked real nice, Alfie would let Benji share it.

Chapter Two

Hannah Yutzy had mastered the art of being cheerful even when she wasn't. She could sing even when she cleaned toilets, smile when the donut fryer spit grease at her, and laugh when Austin Petersheim treated her like a potted plant instead of his best friend.

Austin had just arrived at the donut stand and was already restocking the table with Petersheim Brothers peanut butter while Hannah helped an Englisch customer.

Austin had smiled at Hannah's *bruder,* James, and waved to Hannah's sister, Mary, but had he even acknowledged Hannah's presence? Of course he hadn't. He was too busy with his peanut butter.

"I'll take six glazed and six chocolate and a couple of those pretzels," the Englisch woman said, smiling so wide Hannah could see all the fillings in her teeth.

How could Hannah not smile back at such a nice lady, even though she was out of sorts with Austin? "The donuts are nice and hot," Hannah said. "Just out of the fryer."

"Do you have a box?"

"*Jah.* Perfect for a dozen." Hannah snatched a piece of wax paper and started loading donuts into the box. "It looks like you've come from far away," she said. The woman and her husband had pulled up in a small RV with Colorado license plates.

The woman nodded. "Denver, Colorado. We're making a loop. Mount Rushmore, Wisconsin Amish country, maybe Chicago, but I don't think we can drive that thing into the big city. I'd love to go up in the Willis Tower, even though I'm afraid of heights."

Hannah laughed. "I don't know if I'm afraid of heights. The tallest thing I've ever been on is the silo on our farm."

The woman raised her eyebrows. "That's high enough. If that doesn't make you woozy, you're not afraid of heights."

"I've been up Timms Hill," Austin said, smiling at the Englisch woman and ignoring Hannah as if he hadn't seen her. "That's pretty high."

"The entire state of Colorado is higher than Timms Hill," the woman said. "We were at Timms Hill yesterday."

Austin set a jar of peanut butter on the counter. "If you're looking for something delicious to go with those pretzels, this is organic, one-hundred-percent-natural peanut butter, made right here in Bienenstock by me and my brothers."

Austin was a natural salesman. The woman picked up the jar and read the label. "How nice. I'll take it."

She tried to hand him some money, but he shook his head. "Just pay the girl in pink." He turned around to tend to his peanut butter, without even a glance in Hannah's direction. Didn't she even get a nod for being the girl in pink?

Why did Hannah let Austin bother her? Sometimes he treated her like a best friend. Other times he ignored her, as if she was a convenience instead of a person. Austin Petersheim was the stupidest boy in the world, except for her *bruder* James, who listened to rap music on his cell phone and smoked cigarettes behind the barn. James had an excuse for his stupidity because he was eighteen and in *rumschpringe.* Austin had no excuse at all.

He was the most self-centered, aggravating, lovable boy in the world.

Hannah gave the woman her donuts and smiled as if she was having the best day ever, even though Austin was ignoring her. And aside from Austin being himself, she really was having a pretty *gute* day. They'd sold a lot of donuts for a Monday, she didn't have to work at Aendi Linda's tonight, and an Englisch customer had told her that her dress was pretty. Besides, the sun was shining, and there was no rain in the near future. It was a wonderful *gute* day. If Austin would acknowledge her existence, it would be almost perfect.

"Here's your invoice, Hannah." Leaning across the counter, Austin handed Hannah a piece of paper and gave her that smile she'd been waiting for all morning.

Austin had very nice teeth, thick, beautiful hair, and the most handsome face Gotte had ever given a boy. And Hannah was completely in love with him. Not that she would ever tell him. If he suspected she had feelings for him besides that of a friend, he'd hightail it out of her life so fast, he'd fan up a stiff wind. Austin didn't want to be anything but friends, and Hannah would be wise to remember.

"Hannah?" More of that irresistible smiling.

Ach, she'd been daydreaming when she should have been planning how to yank Austin out of her life. "Austin Petersheim. It's been ages since we've seen your family. Ages."

He chuckled. "Well, yes, if ages means a day ago."

A ribbon of warmth threaded its way up Hannah's spine. They had seen each other at church yesterday, and their hands had accidentally touched when she handed him a bowl of peanut butter spread at the fellowship supper. She gave him a teasing grin. "Twenty-four hours is a long time, and I just adore Benji and Alfie."

He raised an eyebrow. "Would you like to adopt them? You can have them for free."

She reached across the counter and cuffed him on the shoulder. "Benji and Alfie are the sweetest boys in the world."

"Then you should definitely adopt them." Hannah loved the way his eyes danced when he teased her. "Last week, they washed the dog in the house when Mamm wasn't home. On Saturday, Alfie tried to set a library book on fire with a magnifying glass. He made a little brown spot on one of the pages. Mamm's making him pay the fine."

Hannah couldn't keep from laughing. "Sounds like he has a healthy sense of curiosity."

"He doesn't have any sense at all. Mamm makes him clean toilets as punishment, but he's been in trouble so many times, he's scheduled to clean toilets until next June."

"Poor boy. I should adopt him, if only to save him from a future of chappy hands."

Austin leaned against the counter and took her breath away with his smile. "He doesn't deserve you."

And there it was, the thing that kept her hoping. That look of unbridled affection she craved so much. Austin could be so attentive one minute and so thick-headed the next. What was a girl to think? How was a girl to even want to look at another boy?

Deciding she'd done quite enough pining for one day,

she pulled her gaze from his face and studied the invoice. "Did we really sell twenty jars last week?"

"*Ach, vell.* You've been carrying Petersheim Brothers peanut butter for three weeks. Word is starting to get around."

Hannah leaned closer and lowered her voice. "Since Glick's Amish Market refuses to sell your peanut butter, we've gotten more of their business." She giggled. "But don't tell. Raymond Glick would be angry if he knew, and then the sin would be on my head."

Austin laughed. "It's Raymond's sin if he gets angry. But I won't tell. I'd rather not see Raymond turn red. Or green with envy."

"I'm not sorry Raymond Glick isn't buying your peanut butter anymore, even if I'm sorry about how it all happened. It's Raymond's loss and our gain."

Several weeks ago, Austin's *bruder* Abraham had slugged Perry Glick because Perry had gotten fresh with Abraham's fiancée, Emma Wengerd. Raymond hadn't taken kindly to Abraham hitting his son, and he'd quit buying Petersheim Brothers peanut butter that very day.

"Raymond Glick won't allow any Petersheims in his market, but thanks to you, we've sold almost as much peanut butter as ever."

Hannah nodded. "I'm still allowed in the market, but the Glicks don't like the Yutzys either. Raymond says we take business away from his market, even though they don't sell donuts or pretzels."

"Even if they did, they'd never be as good as Hannah and Mary's donuts."

Hannah's sister, Mary, finished frosting a batch of donuts and wiped her hands on a towel. "*Denki.*" She giggled and handed Austin a glazed donut hole. "It's an old family recipe."

Hannah scrunched her lips to one side of her face. "Mamm got it out of an old Betty Crocker cookbook."

Austin laughed. "Why change a *gute* thing?" He popped the donut hole into his mouth. "*Appeditlich.* There's nothing like a Yutzy donut."

"It's one of the reasons the Glicks don't like us," Mary said.

Austin brushed the sugar off his hands. "The Glicks have a long list of people they don't like. They avoid the Petersheim family, don't speak to the Kanagys, despise all the Honeybee Sisters, and walk the other way when they see Bitsy Weaver coming."

"*Ach,* I know," Hannah said. "It must be exhausting to carry so many grudges."

Austin motioned for Hannah to follow him. "Have you got a minute? I want to talk to you about something."

The donut stand was enclosed by chest-high counters on four sides with a short swinging door on the back side. Hannah tapped the door with her knee and pushed it open, then followed Austin to his open-air buggy and flat wagon.

"I need some advice," Austin said. "And I always thought you were kind of smart."

"Only kind of smart?"

He grinned. "*Ach, vell.* Okay. Very smart. Maybe as smart as me."

"You were better at math. I was better at spelling. You're kind of smart too."

His lips twitched wryly. "Okay. Whatever." He leaned against the buggy. "I need your help."

"What help?"

"I need to sell more peanut butter. My *dat* and Andrew just finished expanding our peanut butter factory, but the grocer in Milwaukee has stopped selling our peanut butter because Skippy is cheaper."

Austin was very dedicated to the peanut butter, and if he wanted to call that room where they made peanut butter a factory, Hannah wouldn't begrudge him.

"So you need more places to sell it."

"Either that or we need to sell more of it. I can't figure out why we don't sell five hundred jars a week," he said. "It's the most delicious spread in the whole world."

Hannah smiled to herself. Austin was very dedicated to the peanut butter. "It wonders me if we could sell more here if we put up a sign."

"Andrew thinks I should advertise on the Internet."

"That might work, but I don't know anything about the Internet."

"Neither do I," Austin said. "But I guess we could learn."

That was another endearing and aggravating thing Austin did. When he said, *I guess we could learn,* he was automatically including her in the details of his life, as if she naturally belonged there. Like a *fraa.*

Or a best friend.

She didn't want to be the best friend anymore.

"Yoo-hoo, Austin."

Austin and Hannah turned at the same time. Priscilla Lambright stood not five feet away, waving at Austin as if trying to get him to notice her from a hundred yards. Priscilla had to get close like that to get anyone's attention.

To Hannah's irritation, Austin lit up like a candle. "*Hallo,* Scilla. *Vie gehts?*" He had the nerve—or maybe the *gute* sense—to take a step away from Hannah. Lately he'd been determined to let everyone know that he and Hannah were just friends, not dating, not sweethearts, just friends. And he seemed the most eager around Priscilla.

"Hannah and I were just talking about peanut butter. Nothing special."

Scilla almost smiled, which was about as close as she ever got to looking happy. "For sure and certain, Petersheim Brothers peanut butter is the only kind I eat."

Austin looked at Priscilla as if she was a bucket full of peanuts already shelled. "*Denki.* We use organic peanuts yet."

Priscilla nodded her approval. "Of course. If everybody went organic, all our diseases would disappear. In your own small way, you're saving the world."

Austin's smile was sickly sweet, like a bowl of maple syrup sprinkled with sugar. "I do what I can."

If Hannah stuck out her tongue and made gagging noises, would he stop smiling like that? What did he see in Priscilla that he couldn't see in Hannah?

Plenty.

Priscilla was a petite girl with soft chestnut curls that nobody ever got to see because she had to keep them under her *kapp.* At least that's what she told any of her friends who would listen, when they could hear her at all. Scilla was soft-spoken, so much so that even people who weren't hard of hearing had to ask her to repeat herself when she said anything.

Priscilla might have been soft-spoken, but she wasn't shy. Her favorite activity was pulling one or two friends aside at gatherings and gossiping mercilessly about everyone else. Hannah and Scilla used to be better friends, but whenever they were in a group of three, Scilla had the habit of whispering to one friend and leaving the other one out. It was better to be with Scilla one-on-one if you didn't want to feel like you were being excluded from her conversation.

And Hannah didn't especially like listening to Scilla's

gossip. Scilla was quite harsh when she thought someone wasn't strictly following the Ordnung. Scilla gossiped about everybody, which always made Hannah wonder what Scilla was saying about her when she wasn't around. Scilla was nice enough, but Hannah wanted to include everybody in her circle of friends and never liked it when someone got left out.

"I saw you from the library window," Scilla said, sidling closer to Austin and speaking to him as if Hannah was standing in another state. It was wonderful annoying, but Hannah couldn't take offense. It was how Scilla usually behaved. "Marva said I could come out and say hello, but only for a minute because I have to shelve the books."

It was unfortunate that their donut stand was just a few hundred feet from the library and equally unfortunate that Scilla worked there.

Austin propped his foot on the spoke of his wheel and leaned his hand awkwardly against the buggy. Well, not awkwardly, exactly. Nothing Austin did was awkward. He was broad-shouldered with strong arms and a trim waist. Every movement he made was athletic, as if motion was his natural state. Hannah was rarely able to pull her eyes from him.

Much to her aggravation.

"I'm *froh* I was here," Austin said. "And I'm *froh* you saw me. I was having a very bad day, but it's so much better now I've seen you."

Really?

Hannah wanted to smack Austin upside the head. He'd been perfectly cheerful with Hannah and Mary before Scilla had shown up. Hannah didn't know whether to feel offended, insulted, or depressed.

She was so annoyed with Austin that she had to be extra

nice to Scilla to make up for it. "Would you like a donut, Scilla? Fresh from the fryer. You can have it for free for working so hard at the library."

Scilla drew her brows together. "Do you have whole wheat ones?"

"*Nae,*" Hannah said, doing a very *gute* job of keeping the aggravation out of her voice. "No whole wheat."

Austin gazed at Scilla as if very concerned for her health. "They're smothered with sugar. And they're not organic."

"*Ach, vell,* I already knew that," Priscilla said. "Most people don't believe in organic like you and I do." She and Austin looked at Hannah as if she was an Englischer who didn't follow the true gospel and wouldn't be allowed into Heaven.

Hannah gritted her teeth.

Austin's face lit up with a wonderful *gute* idea. "I'll buy you a jar of my peanut butter. You can take it home and put it on your whole wheat bread."

Scilla seemed to like the idea as much as Austin did. She actually smiled. "How thoughtful of you."

Austin turned to Hannah as if remembering she was standing there. "My peanut butter is organic and made with sea salt."

As if Hannah didn't know that already. That bragger. Why in the world did she even give Austin the time of day?

"*Cum,*" Austin said, motioning for Scilla to follow him. "Pick any jar you want, and I'll pay Mary." He and Scilla walked away without another word to Hannah, as if she was a mailbox with no letters in it.

Hannah was usually a cheerful person, who laughed too loud and genuinely liked just about everybody, but Austin had pulled her out of her good nature today. He was *dumm* and insensitive, and she was determined not to like him one little bit ever again, even if he was too handsome to resist.

Hannah may not have been petite or soft-spoken or organic, but Austin wasn't any kind of friend, and she wasn't going to let him upset her. There was a quilting frolic tonight at Gingerich's, and she was going to spend the rest of the day looking forward to that. Scilla could go home and eat her organic peanut butter and develop a peanut allergy, all in the pursuit of Austin Petersheim.

It didn't make Hannah upset in the least.

Chapter Three

"*Ach, du lieva!*" Mammi said, in that voice she used when she saw a mouse in the house or when one of her grandsons stunk really, really bad. "What kind of a book is that, Alfie Petersheim?"

Austin was so used to that voice, he barely got concerned anymore. Poor Grandma Martha was anxious and worried and appalled at just about everything that went on in the Petersheim household. And she was kind of driving Mamm crazy.

Grandma and Grandpa or Mammi and Dawdi had moved in over a year ago after Dawdi had a stroke. Mammi tried to run the household as if it was hers, and Mamm was torn between being kind and loving to her mother-in-law or moving out of the house to live with the squirrels in the forest. The only thing that saved Mamm from a life in the forest was the fact that Mammi Martha loved to shop, and she spent a wonderful amount of time at Walmart searching for things to make Mamm's life easier—even though Mammi's "gifts" usually made things worse.

Mammi stood in the kitchen glaring at Alfie and pointing to a book on the table as if it was a cow pie. "Alfie, that is not any kind of a book for a child to read."

"But, Mammi Martha, you said we needed more books for family reading time," Alfie said, not seeming all that upset that Mammi had caught him with forbidden reading material.

"Family reading time is for reading uplifting and inspiring stories, not stories about murder and knives sticking out of people."

"But it's about animals," Alfie protested, still not quite as upset as Austin would have expected.

Mammi's description of Alfie's book made Austin curious. Murder and knives sticking out of people?

"Let me see, Mammi," he said, pretending to be as concerned about Alfie's reading material as Mammi was. He strolled into the kitchen and picked up Alfie's book. *The Story of Wolverine. W*olverine was one of those superheroes the Englischers liked so much. Austin had seen three Wolverine movies plus all the Avengers films. They were *gute.* He wouldn't mind reading that book after Alfie was finished with it.

But he could see why Mammi would be alarmed. The cover showed a very angry man with bared teeth and three steel spikes sticking out of his knuckles. Probably not what Mammi had in mind for family reading time.

But Austin admired Alfie for trying to get it past Mammi.

Mammi had started family reading time several months ago, and Alfie and Benji hated it. When it came to that, Austin hated it too. Mammi made them all sit down together and read, sometimes for a whole hour. Austin liked to read, but Mammi made them read depressing books like

The Bloody Theater or *Martyrs Mirror of the Defenseless Christians* or *Tongue Screws and Testimonies.*

Austin respected and revered the martyrs as much as anyone, but reading about them over and over again sure put a damper on his evenings. The only thing that got him out of family reading time was going to a gathering or a *singeon.* Austin went to a lot of *singeons,* but Alfie and Benji couldn't get out of it unless they were sick or throwing up. Alfie once tried picking a scab to get out of family reading time. It hadn't worked on Mammi.

Austin should probably humor Mammi. When Mammi was happy, things went better for everybody. "This looks like a pretty violent book," Austin said.

"A very violent book," Mammi insisted. "Soon you'll be robbing banks and missing church. No grandson of mine is going to read a book like this."

Alfie looked anything but contrite. "Don't you want me to learn about animals?"

"This book isn't about animals, young man. Don't think you can fool your *mammi.*"

Austin felt sorry for Alfie, even though he didn't have much patience for either of his little *bruderen.* Alfie didn't think things through like a normal person and got himself into all kinds of trouble. He should have known Mammi would never approve of such a book.

Alfie stuck out his bottom lip and looked at Austin with those fake puppy dog eyes that didn't fool him one bit. "Will you take me to the library so I can give back the book?"

"And find another one more suitable," Mammi said.

"To find another one more suitable," Alfie repeated.

"You can walk," Austin said. He had more important things to do than drive his *bruder* to town.

Alfie didn't even argue. He slumped his shoulders and dragged his feet to the front door. "Priscilla Lambright said not to pick this book. I should have listened."

Priscilla Lambright! What was Austin thinking? Priscilla worked at the library.

Priscilla Lambright wasn't one of those girls Austin usually took notice of. At gatherings she was like a mouse, going off to the side and whispering with one or two of her friends. No boy was ever going to disturb two girls whispering with each other. Besides, Scilla had always seemed like a girl who wasn't inclined to have fun, which was why Austin had barely noticed her over the years.

That had changed a few months ago when Priscilla had started coming to the house faithfully every week and buying three jars of peanut butter.

Three jars.

Every week.

She loved peanut butter and especially Petersheim Brothers peanut butter. After the second week of three jars of peanut butter, Austin began to take notice. Priscilla was obviously very smart with *gute* taste and more than her share of common sense. She had beautiful chestnut brown hair and light blue eyes that seemed to pierce right through Austin when she looked at him—as if she was looking right into his heart in hopes of finding a piece of it for herself.

He used to think Scilla was short. He was at least a foot taller than she was. But now he realized she was just petite. And what boy didn't want a petite girl? And pretty. Priscilla was pretty as a picture, and she really liked peanut butter. There was so much to like.

Alfie had just given him a wonderful *gute* excuse to see Priscilla today. "Okay, Alfie," Austin said, drawing out his syllables as if reluctantly giving in. "I'll drive you. But you had better take your time picking out a *gute* book."

Alfie went from fake dejection to utter happiness in half a second. "I will. I'll take as much time as you want."

Austin wasn't sure what Alfie meant by that, but he wasn't going to argue. The more time Alfie spent picking a book, the more time Austin might be able to spend with Priscilla.

Benji came in the back door just as Alfie was about to open the front one. "Where are you going?"

Alfie's smile looked almost like a taunt. "Austin's taking me to the library to get a better book."

Benji looked as if he was concentrating very hard. "I want to get a better book. And a donut."

Austin groaned. He couldn't flirt with Priscilla Lambright with two little *bruderen* in tow. One *bruder* was bad enough. "You don't need a donut, Benji. Dinner is in an hour."

"I could eat a carrot," Benji said. "Hannah has the best carrots in Bienenstock. A carrot won't ruin my dinner."

"He doesn't need a carrot," Alfie said.

"You don't need a carrot," Austin said.

Mammi folded her arms and cocked an eyebrow. "Both boys need more broccoli and spinach. Does Hannah have spinach?"

Austin was not going to run errands for the entire household. "No spinach, Mammi." Come to think of it, he didn't even need Alfie along to take that book back. He could go by himself and maybe steal a moment or two alone with Priscilla. "I'll return the book by myself. You don't need to come, Alfie."

"I have to come. I need to choose a different book."

"But wouldn't you rather stay home and play with Benji?"

"I don't play with Benji anymore," Alfie said, sticking out his bottom lip.

"Of course you play with Benji. You're best friends."

Alfie didn't have an argument, but he looked at Benji as if he didn't know him very well. "I'm coming. I want to find something for family reading time."

"I'll choose a book for you," Austin said. He squatted to Alfie's eye level and went into the babyish, patronizing voice he used when he wanted to convince Alfie or Benji to do something. "How about *Bible Stories for Children?* It has pictures."

Alfie never fooled Austin with his fake tears, and Austin wasn't going to fool Alfie with his fake consideration. "I've read it five times," Alfie said. "I'm coming with you."

"So am I," Benji said. "I want to pick a book too. And I want to say hello to Hannah. She's the nicest girl in the whole world. And the prettiest."

"She is not the prettiest," Alfie said.

Benji looked up at Austin. "Don't you think Hannah is pretty?"

Austin shrugged. For sure and certain Hannah was pretty, but why did Benji care? "I'm going by myself."

Mammi pulled some things from the fridge. "See if they have *Light from the Stakes.*"

Alfie wouldn't give up. "Priscilla told me to be sure to come again. She'll be mad if I'm not there."

Austin paused. It might look a little suspicious if he showed up at the library without Alfie. And if Alfie took a long time picking a book, it would give Austin a reason to stay even longer. "Okay. You can come."

Alfie jumped up and down and clapped his hands.

"Me too?" Benji said.

Two *bruderen* might be even better than one. Girls thought the twins were cute, and Benji would take even longer choosing a book than Alfie would. "You might as well come too."

"Okay," Benji said, just as happy as Alfie was about going to the library.

Alfie deflated like a balloon, but he didn't argue as both boys followed Austin outside and climbed into the buggy.

When they entered the library, Priscilla stood behind the reference desk reading a Bible propped on the counter. She looked up and gave Austin a smile that made his heart do a somersault. She must have liked him okay. Priscilla hardly ever smiled. She had a more serious nature, as if she always had serious things on her mind like the Scriptures and how to avoid sin.

"Austin, I saw you from the window. It's wonderful nice of you to visit."

Alfie and Benji came in a few seconds behind Austin because they had some sort of argument about who should get out of the buggy first. Priscilla's smile faded to nothing. "*Ach.* You brought the twins."

Austin mentally kicked himself. Priscilla wasn't happy to see the boys. He should have left them home, even if they had been a *gute* excuse for coming. Still, her reaction gave him hope that maybe she wanted to be alone with him as much as he wanted to be alone with her.

He showed her the Wolverine book. "We need something that won't shock my *mammi.* Maybe something with baby animals or Baby Jesus on the cover."

Scilla nodded, not at all surprised and maybe a bit disappointed. "The little boys try to get away with reading the trashy stuff, and Marva lets them check out whatever they want."

Alfie reached up and spread his hand flat on the counter. "Do you have any new Tintin?"

Austin grinned. He had read *The Adventures of Tintin* when he was Alfie and Benji's age. He would sneak them home from the library and hide them under his pillow so Mamm wouldn't know he had them. She probably knew all about his books, but hiding them from her made him feel like he was getting away with something, even if he wasn't. Lots of Amish boys read adventure books. *Wolverine* was a little extreme, but all but the most rigid Amish *mamms* approved of Tintin. It was harmless.

"I like Scooby-Doo," Benji said. "Or do you have *The Kid Who Only Hit Homers?*"

Scilla sighed. "Now, boys, those are foolish books. Let me show you a book of Bible stories with pictures. You'd like that, wouldn't you?"

Scilla sounded a lot like Mammi. Austin tried not to think about that too hard. She was only concerned for Alfie and Benji's well-being. There was nothing wrong with that.

Both boys grumbled under their breath as Priscilla led them to the religion section of the library. She pulled a few books off the shelf for them to look at, smoothed her hands down her apron, and smiled at Austin. They went around the corner out of sight of his *bruderen* to a short round table in the children's section. Austin made sure not to pick the chair right next to Priscilla. He didn't want her to think he was forward.

"It was wonderful nice of you to bring your *bruderen,* even though they've been naughty," she said so quietly that Austin had to lean very close to hear her. So much for appearing forward.

Austin wasn't entirely satisfied with her compliment.

He had only driven Alfie and Benji here because he wanted to see Priscilla. "What kind of *bruder* would I be if I made them walk all this way by themselves?"

"I would have made them walk. Children will only learn appropriate behavior if you don't coddle them."

Maybe his first thought to make Alfie walk hadn't been such a bad idea. Maybe Austin wasn't such a bad *bruder* after all. The boys certainly hadn't learned any lessons riding in the buggy. "You're right. I'll make them walk next time."

Priscilla fingered the wisps of hair sticking out from under her *kapp* at the back of her neck. "It gave you a reason to come in for a visit."

Austin smiled. "I'm *froh* for that."

She reached out and touched his arm, then glanced behind her as if something had startled her. "Hush. You can't talk that loud in the library."

Austin couldn't hide a frown. It was as if he was eight years old again being chastised by his teacher. "*Ach.* Okay. Sorry."

"They have very strict rules about noise, and you can't bring food in here because it ruins the books."

"I'll remember," was all Austin could think to say. How long had it been since anyone besides his *mater* had scolded him like that?

But it was wonderful *gute* that Priscilla wanted to follow the rules. Austin always tried to follow the rules too. Mostly. Unless Matt Gingerich wanted to race buggies or do donuts in the parking lot. But mostly Austin tried to follow the rules. He and Priscilla were in perfect agreement. He was definitely making Alfie walk next time.

Priscilla smiled as if she hadn't meant to scold him. "You know what I like best about your peanut butter? It has just the right amount of salt. Not too much, not too little."

Austin couldn't help but burst into a smile. Just in time, he remembered to keep his voice low. "We're very careful about our salt. Too much ruins the flavor."

"I like that I have to stir it before I use it. That's how I can always tell it's fresh. And organic."

"*Jah.* You never have to stir a jar of store-bought peanut butter. It doesn't seem right."

"I couldn't agree more." She leaned closer. "Is it just me, or does it feel like we agree on most everything? Like our thoughts are in complete harmony with each other."

Austin's heart beat faster. Her gaze turned toward him as if she thought he was the smartest boy in the world. Well, he was pretty smart. He knew how to make peanut butter with just the right amount of salt. It was a real skill.

Austin and Scilla pulled away from each other as Benji came around the corner carrying three of the thickest books Austin had ever seen. "We're ready to go," he said, obviously struggling to heft the heavy books. "Alfie won't pick so I picked three for him. These will take a long time to read, and he won't have to come back to the library for years and years."

Priscilla furrowed her brow. "He'll have to bring them back in six weeks or renew them. You can't keep a library book forever."

Alfie's voice floated across the library from about ten shelves away. "I don't want those books."

Priscilla frowned at the noise but didn't say anything.

Austin looked through the books in Benji's pile. "Alfie's not going to read these. This one's in German."

"Everyone should learn high German," Scilla said. "It's the language of the Bible."

"They're *gute b*ooks," Benji insisted. "This one is a Bible, and it has pictures." He nudged Austin with his elbow, almost dropping his books. "Let's go. I want a donut."

Austin wasn't about to leave. He hadn't spent enough time with Scilla. They hadn't said all he wanted to say about peanut butter. "Go look again, Benji. Find something you can actually read."

"Shh," Priscilla hissed. "You're being too loud again."

Austin huffed out an impatient breath. Benji was ruining everything.

"I want to read these books."

"What about those books I showed you?" Priscilla said. "Those are good ones for little boys."

"I'm not a little boy," Benji said, straightening to his full height. "I'm nine, and I want a donut."

Alfie came from the other direction carrying a two-foot stack of books. "Okay. We can go now. I want these." He set his extensive reading material on the table next to Scilla.

She picked up the book on the top of Alfie's stack. "This will never do." She showed it to Austin. The Hulk was on the cover holding a car in one hand. "I'm sorry, Alfie, but as your *bruder*'s friend, I can't let you check this one out."

Alfie looked a little too smug for his own good. "The Englisch lady at the counter already checked them out for me."

Austin sighed. "Alfie, Mammi will never let you keep that one."

Alfie curled one side of his mouth. "We'll have to bring it back tomorrow."

Austin never would have thought that Alfie could be so tricky, but Alfie acted as if he and Austin were in on a secret, and that secret was that Austin was interested in

Scilla and wanted to see her again. Was Alfie really that smart, or did he just want to irritate Austin?

It seemed Alfie was that smart. He turned to Scilla. “Are you working tomorrow?”

“*Jah,* but only from three to six.”

“We can come right after school,” Alfie said, smiling mischievously at Austin.

“I’m coming too,” Benji said, still holding those impossibly big books.

“You don’t need to come,” Alfie said. “It’s just for me and Austin.”

Benji finally set his books on the table. “I’m going to check out Captain America.”

Alfie made a face at Benji. “Mammi doesn’t care about Captain America.”

“Maybe she does and maybe she doesn’t,” Benji said, disappearing between two shelves. He wasn’t going to find Captain America down that row. It was called Women’s Studies.

Priscilla frowned. “He didn’t reshelve his books. Though he shouldn’t have taken them out in the first place. Patrons aren’t supposed to reshelve their own books.”

Alfie leaned his elbow on the table and looked at Priscilla. “So. Austin has really *gute* hair, don’t you think? Even though it’s a little bit red.”

“Shh, Alfie. You really need to keep your voice down or I’ll have to kick you out of the library.”

Alfie seemed unmoved. “Well, do you like his hair or don’t you?”

Scilla sort of batted her eyelashes as if she was looking at Austin from under them. “I do like it.”

"Austin's a hard worker, and he's not a picky eater," Alfie said. "He eats asparagus sometimes."

Priscilla approved. "Asparagus is good for you."

"Mamm says a *fraa d*on't want a husband who's a picky eater. Do you think you might want to marry Austin?"

If Austin's face was anywhere near the color of Priscilla's, his was bright red. He jumped to his feet. "Let's go get a donut."

They found Benji with an even bigger stack of books. Austin's *bruderen* were a nuisance, but maybe he could get rid of them and get some time to talk to Priscilla in private. "You boys go get a donut. I'll check out these books and meet you at the buggy in fifteen minutes."

Benji didn't seem to like that plan at all. "It doesn't take that long to check out a book."

"You picked a whole pile of them. It will take me long enough."

It was out of the ordinary for Benji to be so unhappy and so uncooperative. "Don't you want to say hello to Hannah?"

"I can say hello to Hannah any day."

"*Jah,*" Alfie said, almost taunting Benji. "He can say hello to Hannah any day."

Scilla leaned over and whispered in Austin's ear. "Hannah laughs too much, don't you think? She sounds like a goose."

Hannah liked to laugh, but Austin never thought she laughed too much. Her happiness just seemed to overflow from her mouth. He frowned. He'd always liked the sound of Hannah's laughter. Did she sound like a goose?

Benji was a very persistent nine-year-old. "I'd think you'd want to say hello to your best friend in the whole world."

Austin glanced at Priscilla. "Andrew and Abraham are my best friends."

It was true, but Andrew and Abraham were also his *bruderen.* It almost didn't count. But he wasn't about to admit that Hannah was his best friend while trying to make hay with Priscilla Lambright.

Besides, it was an old friendship. For sure and certain he and Hannah would drift apart in a few more years. He couldn't associate with Hannah if he was dating Priscilla. The thought made him a little sad, so he brushed it aside. Hannah was his closest friend, but he wouldn't need her once he found a wife.

And she wouldn't need him. No doubt she'd find a husband right quick. She was old enough, and about six boys in the district had their eye on her. Hannah was a real catch, with her blue-green eyes and lighthearted disposition. She laughed easily and often and never failed to make Austin feel better about himself when she was with him.

The only reason she wasn't already engaged was because she showed no interest in any of the boys in the district and had turned down several invitations to drive her home. Austin was glad she was so picky. She needed to wait for someone good enough for her.

He handed Alfie the money and scooted his *bruderen* out the door. Finally he and Priscilla would have a little time to themselves. He grinned at her. "Can I check out these books?"

"Well, I don't approve of Benji's choices, but I don't suppose your *mammi* will let him read them anyway." Priscilla went behind the counter, scanned the books, and put a card in each one that said when they were due.

Austin propped his elbow on Benji's stack of books.

"This is going to make a lot of extra work for you when we bring these books back tomorrow."

Scilla gave him that coy little smile he was beginning to like very much. "I don't mind, as long as you come with them."

"You can be sure of it. I think that's why Alfie picked the books he did. He wants to come back."

She blushed. "Maybe he has a crush on me."

"Maybe he does."

Scilla seemed a little breathless. Austin's mouth went dry. He'd never been so grateful that his *bruderen* were always making trouble.

Austin slowly walked from the library. After Scilla had scanned Benji's books, they'd spent all of a minute gazing at each other before Marva needed Scilla to enter some returned books into the system. Austin couldn't very well have stayed unless he wanted Scilla to get fired. But it was a *gute* visit. Tomorrow, maybe he'd come right as Scilla got off work and drive her home.

Wouldn't that be something?

Benji and Alfie were sitting at the picnic bench next to the donut stand talking to Hannah. Hannah was so kind to his *bruderen,* Austin suspected she liked the twins more than he did—which she probably did. Austin loved his *bruderen,* but sometimes he didn't like them very much.

Benji's face lit up when he saw Austin. "Sit by me, Austin."

"Where are our books?" Alfie said.

"I put them in the buggy."

Benji motioned to the pile of donut holes on the table.

"Hannah gave us a dozen donut holes for one dollar. And she gave me a Band-Aid."

Hannah giggled. "The Band-Aid was free. He had a paper cut."

Austin held out his hand. Alfie knew what he wanted. "Can't I keep the rest of the money? I need it for emergencies."

"What emergencies?"

Alfie popped a donut hole in his mouth. "Lotps a stumpf."

Austin smirked. "That doesn't sound like an emergency to me."

Alfie moaned and reluctantly handed him his change. Austin sat down and stole a donut hole.

Hannah gave him a teasing smile. "Be careful, Austin Petersheim. Those things can kill you."

Austin chuckled. Hannah liked to remind him how *dumm* he was sometimes. Maybe he had been trying a little too hard to butter up Scilla the other day. Hannah never let him get away with anything. "It's not organic and it isn't whole wheat, but the Yutzys make the best donuts in Wisconsin, without a doubt." He stuffed the whole thing in his mouth. "Their pretzels are pretty *gute* too, even though they're not gluten-free."

Hannah's eyes sparkled. She wasn't susceptible to flattery, but she knew a sincere compliment when she heard it. "This morning one of my customers said a pretzel with Petersheim Brothers peanut butter was the most delicious treat she'd ever tasted. She bought four jars."

"Four jars? You are a wonderful *gute* salesman."

"We give samples, and the peanut butter sells itself." Hannah licked a napkin and wiped a smear of chocolate from Benji's face. "That's what they do at the Costco in

Bellevue. You can get a whole lunch if you go at the right time."

"More people will buy if they can taste it."

Hannah concentrated very hard on her napkin as she smoothed it out flat on the table. "Benji says you got him some books."

"Me too," Alfie said.

Benji held up his bandaged finger. "I got a paper cut from the Bible."

"Maybe Derr Herr is trying to tell you something," Austin said.

Hannah tapped Benji's straw hat. "Just turn the pages more carefully next time."

Benji nodded. "I didn't mean to. I was in a hurry."

Alfie swiped his hand under his nose and sniffed loudly in Benji's direction. "Austin almost has a girlfriend."

"He does not," Benji said.

Hannah squeezed the napkin between her fingers as if she was strangling it. "You almost have a girlfriend? That sounds interesting."

Austin didn't know why he suddenly felt uncomfortable. Hannah was his best friend. She already knew about Scilla. Or, she *should k*now. She went to the same gatherings Austin did. For sure and certain she'd seen him flirting with Scilla. "Alfie doesn't know when to shut up, and I don't have a girlfriend yet."

"Yet?" Hannah huffed out a loud breath and looked away for a second. When she turned back to him, she gave him a real smile, one that didn't look like it was stapled on. "It sounds promising though."

"Nobody thought Austin could ever get a girlfriend because he's so *dumm,* but he's almost got one because Priscilla Lambright might be willing to take him."

Hannah formed her lips into an "O." "Alfie has a very high opinion of you, Austin." She giggled. "Do you think Priscilla will take pity on you and agree to ride home with you some evening?"

Austin folded his arms and leaned back. "Of course. I'm very handsome."

"He's not handsome," Alfie said, "but Priscilla doesn't care."

Benji gave Alfie a sour look. "Yes, he is handsome. His teeth are really white. Don't you think he's handsome, Hannah?"

Hannah tapped her chin as if she was thinking about it very hard. "*Ach, vell,* my opinion doesn't really count. Austin and I are just friends." Her words thudded to the ground like bricks. Didn't she like being his friend?

Benji got more animated. "He can throw a baseball really far, and he has a pocketknife that you can turn into a flashlight."

Hannah gave Austin a secret smile, crinkling her nose like she often did. "Everything a girl wants in a husband."

Austin pulled out his pocketknife. "You can also start a fire and open a can with it."

"Hmm," Hannah said. "Your value as a potential husband is going higher all the time."

Benji tugged on Hannah's sleeve with his sticky hand. "Would you marry Austin if he asked?"

Hannah turned to Austin, and her smile nearly blinded him. It was playful and teasing and beautiful all at the same time. *Whoa.* It was like getting knocked over by a train. He wasn't used to being knocked over by his best friend. "I don't know, Benji," she said. "He's tall enough. He has a flashlight pocketknife, and he could make me peanut butter whenever I wanted it. I might consider marrying him if nobody else asks me."

Benji's eyebrows nearly flew off his face, then he glared at Alfie. "I told you."

"You didn't tell me anything," Alfie said.

Benji suddenly lost his enthusiasm. "But probbally ten or seven boys are going to ask."

Alfie looked at Benji as if he felt sorry for him. Benji looked so dejected, Austin felt sorry for him too. "I told you, Benji," Alfie said. "Everybody wants to marry Hannah, and nobody wants to marry Austin."

"Hey!" Austin said. "There are lots of girls who like me."

Alfie rolled his eyes. "Not really. But you can get Priscilla."

Austin shoved Alfie off the bench with the palm of his hand. "Don't ever say marriage or girlfriend or sweethearts or anything like that in front of Scilla again. You embarrassed her."

Alfie gave Austin a nasty look, then stood and brushed off his pants. Austin hadn't shoved that hard. "Can't I even say the words when you get married?"

Austin glared at him. "Not even then. Not ever. Keep your nose out of my business."

Hannah giggled. "Oh, stop it, Austin. Don't be so touchy. Your *bruderen* are curious, that's all. Like all the rest of us." She gave Austin a penetrating look, as if waiting for him to tell her all his secrets.

"There's nothing to be curious about. Me and Scilla talked about peanut butter. And I got too loud, and she told me to be quiet." Austin frowned to himself. He hadn't really liked that part, even though it was his own fault. What was Scilla supposed to have done?

"*Jah,*" Hannah said with a smirk. "Scilla loves to whisper."

"What do you mean by that?"

"Nothing," she said, her eyes dancing.

"Don't say *nothing.*"

"I would never say anything bad about your girlfriend." Hannah made a big show of locking her lips and throwing away the key.

"Come on, Hannah. What were you going to say?"

Hannah pretended she hadn't heard him. "*Cum,* Alfie, Benji, you both need a wet wipe. We put extra sugar on our donuts. Your hands get extra sticky."

She went inside the little enclosure of the donut stand and grabbed a wipe for both his *bruderen.* Alfie and Benji wiped their hands, and Hannah took another wipe and cleaned their faces. Then she handed Austin a wipe because she was thoughtful like that, even though he didn't need one.

Alfie shook Hannah's hand. "We have to go now."

"But we'll see you tomorrow," Benji said.

Hannah kept hold of Alfie's hand and took Benji's hand too. "If you boys bring me your tomatoes, I can sell them."

Benji jumped up and down. Alfie whooped. "There's almost a bushel on the vines. We'll bring some tomorrow."

"*Gute.* Everybody likes homegrown tomatoes. It won't take me long to sell them. Then I'll give you the money."

The boys skipped to the buggy, for sure and certain imagining what they could buy with all that tomato money.

Austin could be as persistent as Benji. He wrapped his fingers around Hannah's wrist. "What were you going to say about Scilla?"

She crinkled her nose and looked at him sideways. "*Ach,* Austin, I was just teasing. It was nothing."

"I want to hear. If Scilla is going to be my girlfriend, I should know what you think about her."

Hannah pressed her lips together. "You really like her."

He shrugged. "I guess. She's pretty and nice."

"She is very pretty, but you're kind of tall for her."

Austin grinned. "Maybe she can buy some Englisch high heels."

Hannah laughed so loudly, Scilla could probably hear her in the library. "I'd like to see that."

"So, what do you think about her? You always give me *gute* advice."

Hannah folded her arms and leaned against the counter. "I can't give you any advice about this."

"But what were you going to say."

Hannah sighed in surrender. "It isn't nice to talk about anyone behind her back, so shame on you for making me tell."

Austin grinned. "You can't resist my charm."

"Maybe." She cleared her throat. "Scilla is a horrible gossip. That's all."

She was right. She should have kept that to herself. "What a mean thing to say. I've never heard Scilla gossip."

"I tried to warn you that you didn't want to know."

"But it's gossip to even say that. You're being a hypocrite." That was a little harsh, and Austin knew it, but he was just getting to know Scilla. Why would Hannah poison the waters for him like that?

"I suppose I am a hypocrite, but you wouldn't stop asking."

"Even if she is a gossip, nobody's perfect, Hannah. We all have faults. You laugh too much."

Austin immediately regretted that. The light completely went out in Hannah's face. "Your *bruderen* are waiting." She made a feeble attempt at a smile. "You better go before they get tired of waiting and drive the buggy home without you."

Austin didn't know how to apologize for saying something so stupid, so he threw his wet wipe in the garbage and jogged to the buggy without saying good-bye.

He didn't know about Hannah, but he wouldn't be able to laugh for the rest of the day.

Chapter Four

Hannah hated, *hated,* setting foot in Glick's Amish Market, but sometimes she unexpectedly ran out of supplies at the donut stand, and she had to pick something up to tide them over until they could get to Walmart in Shawano or the Amish market in Bonduel.

As it was, she sneaked around Glick's Market trying not to be seen until she actually had to pay for her purchases. Raymond Glick said the Yutzys stole business from his market and restaurant with their donut stand. He pinned Hannah with a nasty look every time he saw her in his store. Perry and Peter James Glick, two of Raymond's sons, were almost as bad as their *fater.* Perry skulked behind her in the aisles as if making sure she didn't steal anything, and Peter James would admonish her to repent every time he checked her out. Paul Glick, another son, was the worst of all. He liked to blame everyone else for his problems, and he would often lecture Hannah on why her family's donut stand was ruining his life.

Hannah would much rather take the hour buggy ride to Walmart, but today they needed yeast, and there was no time for Walmart.

Hannah opened the door as gently as she could so the bell wouldn't tinkle when she walked in. Perry Glick was at the counter ringing up something for Sol Nelson. She quickly ducked into the nearest aisle, hopefully without being seen. At least half a dozen other shoppers milled about the market. Perry probably wouldn't even notice her until she actually had to pay.

"Wait a minute. I know you!"

Hannah's heart jumped about ten feet in the air until she realized that unless Perry could see through a three-deep row of cereal boxes, he was talking to someone at the counter. He didn't sound happy.

Hannah peeked between the All-Bran and the Lucky Charms to see who Perry was talking to. Her heart jumped higher this time. Benji Petersheim stood at the counter holding some money in one hand and a package of AA batteries in the other. It was a well-known fact that the Glicks hated the Petersheims more than just about anybody in the whole world. Ever since Abraham Petersheim had hit Perry Glick, Perry wouldn't let anyone forget it.

"I need to buy these batteries," Benji said. He didn't seem to have any idea of the malice Perry Glick held for the Petersheims.

Perry narrowed his eyes until they were mere slits in his chubby face. "You're Abraham's *bruder,* aren't you?"

Benji nodded eagerly, unaware what he might be getting himself into. "Abraham is getting married."

Hannah let out her breath as Perry reached over the counter, took the batteries from Benji, and pushed some buttons on the cash register. Thank Derr Herr, it seemed Perry knew better than to pick on a little boy, even a Petersheim.

Perry handed Benji his change, then came around the

other side of the counter. "Will you give something to your *bruder* for me?" Perry said.

Benji looked up trustingly at Perry. "Which one?"

Hannah gasped as Perry grabbed Benji at the crevice between his neck and his shoulder and pinched hard. Benji cried out, and Hannah shot around the aisle like a bullet from a rifle.

"Perry Glick," she yelled, not caring if everyone in the market and the restaurant next door heard her. "You let go of him."

Perry, obviously surprised he got caught, let go of Benji like a hot coal and quickly put himself behind the counter, as if that would stop Hannah from tearing him apart. She wouldn't really tear Perry apart, but she sorely wanted to punch him in the nose. Now she knew exactly how Abraham had felt that day a few weeks ago.

She ran to Benji, knelt down, and took him in her arms. "Are you okay?"

Tears poured down Benji's cheeks as he laid his hand over the skin where Perry had pinched him. "I just needed some batteries," he wailed.

She gently lifted Benji's hand to see what Perry had done. A purple-and-red welt the size of a quarter had already appeared on Benji's shoulder, and there were three deep imprints from Perry's long fingernails. One of Perry's claws had drawn three tiny dots of blood. Oy, anyhow. Perry had squeezed hard.

"What happened?" Edna King and Serena Beiler appeared from around the end of the aisle. Reuben and Dorothy Zook came up behind them.

Hannah couldn't remember ever being so angry. Barely able to speak, she pointed at Perry. "He pinched Benji in the neck."

Perry's gaze darted from one person to the next. "He tried to steal some batteries, and he'll get worse if he ever comes in here again."

"I did not steal," Benji cried, more distraught than ever. He held up the receipt that was crinkled in his hand. Good, smart boy!

"I saw him buy the batteries myself," Hannah said, spitting out the words at Perry like venom.

"*Ach, du lieva,*" Edna whispered.

Reuben frowned and folded his arms across his chest. "What have you got to say for yourself, Perry?"

Perry's face turned bright red. "His *bruder* hit me."

"That is no reason to hurt Benji," Serena said. "You should be ashamed of yourself." She drew near and examined Benji's wound. "Put some witch hazel on that, and you'll feel better right quick." She planted a kiss on Benji's cheek, gave Perry an angry look, and walked out of the store.

"He pinched me," Benji said, as if he couldn't believe anyone could be so mean.

Edna had a cart full of groceries. "It wonders me if I should do my shopping somewhere else." She left the cart at the end of the row and walked out of the store.

"The bishop will hear about this," Reuben said. He walked out the door, and everyone else left in the store followed him except Hannah and Benji.

Hannah had one more thing to say. "You're despicable, Perry Glick."

Perry's expression was a mixture of deep embarrassment and unbridled anger. "Don't preach to me. He got what was coming to him."

Okay, maybe two more things to say. She stood and laid a hand on Benji's shoulder, giving Perry a look that could have taken down a sycamore tree. "If you ever touch Benji again, I'll make you very sorry." She didn't go as far as to threaten violence because the Amish didn't believe in violence, and she probably shouldn't either, but she hoped to scare him anyway.

If it worked, Perry didn't show it. "Don't come in my store again," Perry said. It wasn't really his store, and Raymond might not be happy to know how many customers he'd lost today, but Hannah left anyway, with Benji in tow. The sight of Perry Glick made her want to throw up.

She wouldn't be making pretzels today.

Hannah took Benji's hand, and they walked to the donut stand, Benji sniffling all the way. "You're wonderful brave, Benji," she said. "I bet that hurts."

"It hurts more when people are mean."

Benji didn't know how right he was.

Mary and James were frying donuts at the donut stand, but Mary came out and met them when she saw them coming. Either Benji's tearstained cheeks or the storm cloud on Hannah's face clued her in that something was wrong. "*Ach,* Benji. What happened?" She pulled a tissue from her apron pocket and started mopping up the moisture on his face.

Benji's bottom lip quivered.

"He went into Glick's to get some batteries, and Perry pinched him."

"Because Abraham hit Perry," Benji said, tears springing to his eyes at the very thought.

Mary took a look at Benji's shoulder and clucked her tongue. "We have some Band-Aids."

"She said I need witch hazel."

Mary nodded. "Well, a Band-Aid will make it feel better until we can get some witch hazel."

"Okay," Benji said.

Hannah led Benji to the picnic table near the donut stand. "Did you come to town by yourself, Benji?"

"*Nae.* Austin and Alfie went to the library. I told them I was going out to run an errand."

The library. Hannah used to love the library. Now she hated the very thought of it. How many books would Austin check out today? A tiny shard of glass had lodged in her heart ever since he'd told her she laughed too much. It was going to take some time to work the shard out of there. There weren't tweezers strong enough.

Mary brought a donut to the table. "Will a chocolate donut with sprinkles make you feel better?"

"*Jah,*" Benji said. "But I don't have enough money."

"It's free," Mary said. "Because you were so brave."

Benji nibbled on his fingernail. "I wasn't brave. I yelled real loud."

"That was the best thing you could have done," Hannah said. "If ever you're in trouble, you yell as loud as you can and someone will come to help you."

Benji smiled. "You helped me."

Hannah took what felt like the first normal breath since she'd gone into the market. "I'm glad I was there. And Serena Beiler and Edna King and the Zooks were there too. They're all *gute* helpers."

Mary peeled the paper off a Band-Aid and put it on Benji's shoulder. "Did that hurt?"

"*Nae.* The chocolate worked."

Hannah hadn't realized how shaky she felt until she stood up. She'd probably be trembling for hours. "*Cum,* Benji. Let's go find Austin. I want him to take you home so your *mamm* can look at your shoulder."

"I'm not done with my donut."

"Bring it with you. Austin will want to see this."

She took his hand, and they strolled to the library, Benji chattering away about his dog who they called Tintin unless their *mamm* was around and then they called him LaWayne.

Scilla stood at the checkout counter pressing her fingers into her forehead as if trying to keep her eyebrows from falling off. Alfie held a stack of books, and it looked as if he wanted to check them out.

"Thank Derr Herr," Scilla said, when Hannah walked in. "You wouldn't mind taking Alfie away and feeding him, would you? I'm very busy, and Alfie won't stop talking."

"I need to check out these books," Alfie said. "That's your job. To check out books for me."

Scilla pursed her lips as if barely tolerating Austin's little *bruder*. "Yes, Alfie, but you check out ten books every day and then bring them back the next day, and I have to reshelve them over and over again."

"But Austin likes it when I check out books."

Scilla expelled a long breath. "You pull fifty books from the shelves before you pick ten. Why don't you just pick one and leave the rest in peace?"

Alfie shrugged. "Mammi gets madder the more books I bring home."

Scilla flicked her gaze at Hannah. "Can you see what I have to deal with?"

Hannah couldn't feel any sympathy for Scilla. According to Alfie, she was almost Austin's girlfriend. She was the envy of every girl in the *gmayna*.

Scilla finally noticed the donut in Benji's hand. "No food in the library. It ruins the books."

At the moment, Hannah didn't care if Benji got chocolate on every book on the shelves. "Where's Austin?"

"*Ach,* he took something to the post office for me. He was trying to be nice, but now I have a splitting headache."

"Okay," Hannah said. She wasn't going to waste any more time in the library. "We'll go back to the donut stand. Tell Austin we need to talk to him as soon as he gets here."

Scilla cleared her throat in that high-pitched voice she used when she wanted to get someone's attention. "Take that one with you." She pointed to Alfie. "No unattended children allowed in the library."

Alfie drew his brows together. "But I want to check out these books."

"We can do that another time, and you'll be much happier outdoors."

"Look, Alfie," Benji said, pulling off his Band-Aid so Alfie could see his bruise. Hannah smiled to herself. Band-Aids never lasted very long on children.

Alfie's eyes got wide. "What happened?"

"Perry Glick pinched me."

"For reals?" Alfie said.

Benji nodded, the excitement and innocence back in his eyes. "For reals."

For a nine-year-old, it didn't take long for a traumatic experience to become an adventure, something he could tell his friends about, and if he was lucky, the bruise would last for weeks to make it that much more exciting.

"Were you being naughty in the market?" Scilla said. "Did Perry have to pinch you to make you behave?"

Hannah looked at Scilla in bewilderment. "You never pinch a child, even if they are naughty."

"Spare the rod, spoil the child," Scilla said, as if that explained everything.

Ach, Hannah hated that expression. The people who used it didn't even know what it really meant. "A rod is what shepherds use to guide their sheep, not hit them. And sometimes they use it on a wolf, if they have to."

Alfie did a thorough examination of Benji's wound. "It looks really bad. Wait until Max Glick sees what his cousin did."

"Serena says to put witch hazel on it."

Scilla's eyes pled with Hannah. "Please," she mouthed.

"Alfie, leave your books here and come get a donut. We can wait for Austin while you eat."

It didn't take Alfie much time to decide between a stack of books and a donut. He set his books on the nearest table. "Have Austin check these out for me," he said.

Scilla didn't make a commitment one way or the other.

Hannah and the boys walked back to the donut stand. Well, Hannah walked. Benji and Alfie bounded as if their joy could not be contained. Why wouldn't they be happy? Alfie was getting a donut, and Benji had a wound to show all his friends. It had turned out to be a *gute* day for both of them.

Austin took his sweet time and showed up about fifteen minutes later. He said hello to James and Mary and sort of glanced in Hannah's direction. Either he couldn't really care one way or the other about her or he felt bad for what he'd said to her and couldn't meet her eye. Or maybe he was just being Austin, self-centered and aggravating.

Why did she like him so much?

Hannah felt compelled to stop making donuts and join Benji and Alfie at the picnic table. Someone needed to make sure Austin got the full story because it was for sure and certain Scilla hadn't given it to him.

Frowning, Austin slid next to Benji on the bench. "Scilla says you were making trouble at Glick's Market."

Jah. Scilla had no idea what had really happened at

Glick's Amish Market. And it made Hannah angry all over again.

"It wasn't Benji's fault," Hannah snapped. She didn't care if Austin wouldn't believe anybody but his dear Priscilla. She was going to cram the truth down his throat.

Austin looked at her like she was some crazy person.

"Benji went to the market to buy batteries," Hannah said.

Austin pinned his *bruder* with a serious look. "You know you're not allowed to go in there. Mamm said."

"I needed batteries," Benji said. "It was an emergency."

"You think it's an emergency when the chickens run into the road," Austin said.

Hannah had never cared about tiptoeing around Austin's feelings, and she didn't now, even if he liked Priscilla more. "Will you shut up and listen?"

Austin leaned back as if she'd shoved him. "Okay. Okay. Don't get so touchy."

"I was in the market because we had a yeast emergency."

Austin cocked his eyebrow. "Yeast emergency?"

"You know I never go in there unless it's urgent. Benji bought some batteries and then Perry came around the counter and pinched him."

Benji nodded. "He said to give it to Abraham, but I'm not going to."

Austin's mouth fell open. "He pinched him? Is that a joke?"

Hannah didn't even blink. "I'm not laughing."

Austin studied her face, shut his mouth, and looked down at his hands. "I'm . . . I'm sorry. I didn't mean that." He looked at her. The regret in his eyes was obvious. "I didn't mean any of it."

She wasn't about to let him get off that easily. "We're

talking about Benji and Perry Glick. Perry pinched Benji. Hard. Benji yelled and about seven people came running."

Austin looked at Benji as if he didn't quite understand. "He really pinched you?"

"He told me to get out of his store and never come back because he hates the Petersheim brothers. Then Hannah yelled at him and told him if he ever pinched me again, she'd beat him up. And he won't because Hannah looked wonderful scary."

That wasn't exactly the way Hannah remembered it, but it did make the story better and made her sound like the meanest, toughest Amish girl in the district. Benji could tell the story that way if he wanted to.

Austin gazed at Hannah in awe. "You told him you'd beat him up?"

"I said I'd make him very sorry."

He flashed a brilliant smile, and she instantly forgave him for everything. Well, almost. She wasn't about to forgive him for taking a fancy to Priscilla Lambright. "Oh, Hannah, I love you."

He didn't really mean *love* love her, but it was nice to hear all the same. She smiled. "Nobody hurts my boys without hearing from me."

Benji turned and pulled down his collar so Austin could see the bruise. Hannah winced. It was now the size of a half-dollar and turning black-and-blue.

Austin drew in a sharp breath as his expression darkened like midnight. "I'm going over there." He swiped his hand across his mouth. "I'm going over there right now."

"*Nae,* you're not."

"He's going to think Abraham's punch was nothing when he feels mine."

Hannah reached out and snatched Austin's wrist before

he could stand up. "No good will come of it, Austin. Perry picks on people weaker than himself. You are not like him." She emphasized the last five words while squeezing his wrist to make him stay put.

Something almost imperceptible changed in his expression, and he came to rest like a spent thunderstorm. He wrapped his arm around Benji. "Does it hurt?"

"Not as much anymore."

"I'm *froh.*" He glanced at Hannah. "I'm still going to talk to the bishop."

"You should. But I don't know if it will make any difference."

"It will make me feel better."

She nodded. "It will make me feel better too. I'd hate to have to carry out my threat."

A smile grew on Austin's mouth like a sunrise. Then a laugh escaped from his lips. "I'd like to see that."

Even though his laughter was infectious, she resisted joining in. "I bet you would."

Benji took the last bite of his donut. He'd made it last a long time. "Can you take me home, Austin? I want to show Max Glick my scar."

"It's not really a scar, Benji. It will disappear in about a week."

Benji narrowed his eyes as if thinking hard about it. "Then we better hurry."

"Will you boys give me a minute? I need to ask Hannah something."

"Okay," Alfie said, "but hurry. We want to show Max before dinner."

Austin chuckled. He stood and motioned for Hannah to follow him away from the donut stand and toward the library, but not too close. He suddenly looked very uncomfortable, and she might have felt sorry for him, but he couldn't just hurt his best friend's feelings without suffering the consequences. He needed to say the words.

"Hannah, I'm sorry for what I said. I was irritated and just sort of let my mouth walk ahead of my brain."

"It's not like it hasn't happened before."

He nodded vigorously. "You know. We've been friends long enough that you know what I'm like. You know how I say *dumm* things and how I don't mean them and that I'm really a nice person even when I say *dumm* things."

She loved Austin's complete sincerity. If he made a mistake, he was more than willing to own up to it—usually after he'd thought about it for a few days. "It's okay, Austin. I shouldn't have said anything about your girlfriend. You got defensive."

"She's not my girlfriend yet, but if Alfie keeps checking out books, it won't be long." He couldn't have known how his enthusiasm hurt her or maybe he would have tempered it. "Hannah, I love how you laugh. You laugh just the right amount, and I don't want you to stop laughing."

She gave him a wry smile. "Don't flatter yourself. Nothing you could say would persuade me to laugh less."

"I'm sorry I said it."

"You were just repeating what Scilla told you. You've got to think for yourself more often."

He furrowed his brow. "How did you know that?"

"Because you don't usually say things like that. And I know Priscilla thinks I laugh too much. She told Mandy Gingerich."

"I think she was just . . . just trying to . . ."

Hannah giggled. "You can't dig her out of her own hole. Keep your shovel for your own digging. You need it."

He smiled. "You're right. What I really need is a new shovel. My old one is wonderful worn down."

"Whatever you do, don't get it at Glick's."

"They don't sell shovels."

"Lucky for you."

They both laughed at that. It was nice to be on familiar ground, even if Austin wasn't going to stay there very long.

Hannah caught her breath as an amazing, *wunderbarr* idea hit her in the head. "Austin, I know how you can sell more peanut butter."

Chapter Five

Family reading time. The worst thirty minutes of the day. Sometimes the worst hour of the day if Mammi Martha was feeling especially zealous.

Sometimes Mamm put her foot down and only made them read for twenty minutes, but she had to put her foot down often with Mammi and she probably figured she wouldn't put her foot down when she absolutely didn't have to. Like for family reading time.

Mammi and Dawdi sat on the sofa next to Dat. Mamm was in her rocker, and Austin took the recliner Dat usually sat in. Alfie and Benji sat on two folding chairs next to Austin. It was almost painful to watch Alfie and Benji try to sit still. Fidgeting got the evil eye from Mammi plus a stern rebuke that wasn't worth the trouble of misbehaving for. Three hours of church was hard enough for any nine-year-old boy. Another half hour every night must have been pure torture.

Abraham was away visiting Emma tonight. Austin envied him. It might be worth getting a fiancée if he could miss out on family reading time. He smiled to himself. Maybe he would have a fiancée if everything went well with Priscilla. She seemed to like peanut butter more and more every day.

What would Hannah think if Austin and Priscilla got engaged? She didn't seem to like Priscilla very much. *Ach, vell.* Once she got to know Scilla better, Hannah would be fine. Hannah liked just about everybody except Perry Glick. And Raymond Glick. And probably the entire Glick family except for Martha Glick. Hannah and Scilla could be *gute* friends if Hannah put a little effort into it.

Hannah still hadn't told Austin her idea for selling more peanut butter, as if it was some big secret. She could be funny like that sometimes. Hannah liked to make a big fuss about things, and she was probably planning some grand surprise announcement with donuts and party favors. Hannah could make even the simplest events seem special. It was one of her best qualities.

Mamm had taped a big gauze pad to Benji's neck. His bruise hadn't needed a bandage, but Austin could tell it had made Mamm feel better. Then she had yelled at Alfie and Benji for almost ten minutes, warning them that if they ever set foot in Glick's Market again, she'd give them both the spatula. It was obvious she was angrier with Perry Glick than she was at Alfie or Benji, but the boys would never know. Neither would they know that she'd taken Dat and gone to see the bishop that very night.

Alfie giggled quietly.

Mammi looked over her glasses at Alfie. "Would you like to tell us what is so funny in your book?"

"*Nae,* Mammi." Alfie pressed his lips together and went back to reading. He and Benji were more dedicated than usual to their reading tonight. Maybe they had realized they weren't getting out of family reading time no matter how much they complained about it.

Or maybe not. Austin studied the book in Alfie's hands. Alfie clutched it close to his chest as if it contained some secret code he didn't want anyone else to read. Austin waited for a few minutes, watching Alfie out of the corner of his eye. When Alfie relaxed his grip on the book, Austin stole a look at the page and almost laughed out loud. The dust jacket said, *Children's Bible Stories,* but that wasn't the book inside. Alfie was reading *Tintin.* Austin craned his neck to catch a glimpse of Benji's book. He was reading a baseball story, even though his cover said, *Amish Faith, Journey for the Young Reader.*

Had Austin been that clever when he was nine? *Nae.* He wasn't even that clever now. Why hadn't he ever thought of switching covers on his books?

Ach, vell, maybe because it was a little deceitful, but surely what Mammi didn't know couldn't make her mad. And a little *Tintin* never hurt anybody. Mammi could rest easy in ignorant bliss. At least her grandsons were improving their minds by reading, and wasn't that the main goal of family reading time?

Actually, Austin wasn't sure what the main goal of family reading time was, unless it was to torture everybody.

Someone knocked on the front door. Clutching their books carefully in their hands, Alfie and Benji jumped to their feet and ran to the door. An interruption was the most exciting thing that ever happened at family reading time.

Austin's heart leaped in his chest. Scilla Lambright stood on the porch with a plate of cookies, or something resembling cookies. Alfie beamed. Benji slumped his shoulders—not the normal reaction of a boy who'd just been given a reprieve from family reading time.

Normally when there was a pretty girl on the porch,

Mamm would race to the door with boundless enthusiasm. Mamm loved visitors, and a girl of marriageable age was her favorite kind of visitor. Mamm's goal in life was to get all her sons married off. With Andrew married and Abraham engaged, she was doing a *gute* job so far. Austin's pulse sped up. He was next, and Priscilla might be the one.

Except Mamm didn't leap from the sofa like Austin would have expected her to. He'd seen her do it when Emma used to come over to see Abraham. Tonight she saved her place in her book with her finger and cocked her head to one side, as if only mildly curious about who had interrupted family reading time. As if she wanted to get back to her book as soon as possible.

"Scilla Lambright," she said, as if commenting on the weather. "How are you?"

Scilla had a pretty, small kind of smile. Austin loved that she was so modest and demure. "I hope I'm not interrupting."

Mamm just sat on the sofa like moss on a log. "We're having family reading time."

"*Ach,*" Scilla said. "I can come back later."

What was Mamm thinking? They always jumped at any excuse to cut family reading time short. Austin didn't care how *gute* Mamm's book was. Scilla was at the door. For sure and certain she'd come to visit Austin. What more could Mamm want?

Austin would have to do it himself. And come to think of it, maybe that's what Mamm was waiting for. He strode to the door and opened it wider. "*Cum reu, cum reu,* Scilla."

Scilla's gaze flicked hesitantly from Austin to Mamm. "I don't want to get in the way of family reading time."

"Who is that?" Mammi Martha said.

"It's a girl here to see Austin," Dat replied.

Mammi Martha reacted with a little more enthusiasm than Mamm. She didn't jump from the sofa, because it took her a long time to go anywhere, but she slowly got to her feet and clasped her hands together. "How nice. Come in. We're finished with family reading time." The only person more eager than Mamm to get Austin a wife was Mammi.

Alfie and Benji jumped up and down as if they'd been let out of school early. Alfie nearly dropped his book. Austin was overjoyed. They hadn't been reading but ten minutes. He should ask Scilla to come over every night.

Scilla handed Austin the plate of cookies. They looked like miniature cow pies, but it didn't matter what they looked like. Scilla used whole wheat and organic ingredients. For sure and certain they'd taste *wunderbarr.* "I came over to see how Benji is feeling. I got a little busy yesterday and didn't get a chance to examine the sore." She gave Alfie a pat on the head. "How is your neck?"

Alfie and Benji were identical twins, and some people had a hard time telling them apart. It was a common mistake, even if Benji had a huge gauze pad on his neck.

Alfie made a sour face. "I'm Alfie."

Scilla frowned and turned to Benji. "How are you feeling?"

Benji fingered the tape at his neck. "It's okay. But Max Glick said it was just a little scratch."

"Don't fuss with it, young man," Mamm said. "It will come off."

Scilla took the plate from Austin and pushed it in Benji's direction. "I made you some cookies to help you feel better."

"That's wonderful nice of you," Austin said. Scilla had to be one of the most thoughtful girls in the *gmayna.*

Benji wrinkled his nose and tried to smile. To a nine-year-old, those cookies probably didn't look very *gute.* "I'm feeling much better. You didn't need to bring me anything."

"It was no trouble at all." Scilla peeled the plastic wrap from the plate, picked up a cookie, and handed it to Benji. "Try one. They're called BM cookies."

Benji knew his manners, especially with Mamm sitting not six feet away from him. He studied the cookie then gingerly took a bite. While Scilla watched, he chewed it for what seemed like three minutes and finally swallowed. He smacked his lips and gave Scilla a polite but painful smile. "I need some milk." He turned around and marched into the kitchen.

Austin glanced at Scilla and forced a carefree laugh. "Cookies go better with milk."

Scilla hadn't seemed to notice that Benji had practically gagged down her cookie. "Is it raw milk?"

Austin nodded. "From our cows."

Scilla picked up another cookie and held it out to Alfie, who had backed against the wall as if he'd been cornered by a bear. "Alfie, I don't want you to miss out on all the fun. They're whole wheat made with honey and molasses."

"Yum, honey and molasses," Mammi said.

Mamm remained silent. Was she deliberately trying to hurt Austin's chances with Scilla, or was that book really that interesting?

Alfie liked Scilla. He talked about her all the time. He loved going to the library with Austin to visit her. But he'd never been as polite as Benji, and he obviously wasn't about to take one of her cookies. "I'm full," Alfie said, pressing himself against the wall as if trying to get to the other side by going through it.

Austin would have to be the one to set a *gute* example. "Well, I want one," he said, scooping the biggest cookie from the plate.

Scilla seemed pleased, though she didn't smile. "Of course you do. They're whole wheat." She looked at Alfie. "They're *gute f*or you. I would think you'd want to eat something that helps you grow big and strong."

Austin grinned at Alfie and took a hardy bite of his extra-large cookie. It was like biting into a dirt clod, clay soil. He didn't change his expression as he tried to chew it, but it was quite a workout for his jaw. He did his best to smile at Scilla while he chewed. It really didn't taste too bad—like sawdust and mud sweetened with molasses—but he could sure use a big glass of cold, wet milk right about now.

He finally swallowed his bite. "*Appeditlich,* Scilla. The molasses really give it a flavor." He turned to his parents and grandparents and held up the rest of his cookie. "Everybody needs to try one of these cookies." He glanced at Scilla. "I'll get some milk." Maybe he was being a little too enthusiastic, but since no one else but Mammi was helping, he had to be enthusiastic enough for all of them. Maybe Dawdi shouldn't have a cookie. He'd been doing really well with eating lately, but Austin didn't want him to choke yet.

Benji came from the kitchen with half a glass of milk and no cookie. It was a *gute* guess he hadn't eagerly finished his cookie in the privacy of the kitchen. Austin didn't even have to check the trash can to know where Scilla's cookie had ended up.

Well, Austin wasn't a coward. He liked Scilla and that made her cookies taste delicious to him—kind of like how

Jacob worked seven years for Rachel and it only seemed like a day because he loved her so much. Without a glass of milk, he took another bite of Scilla's cookie and swallowed it down cheerfully. And it didn't even lodge in his throat.

But maybe he'd get a glass of milk. Cookies always tasted better with milk.

"I'm having seconds, for sure and certain," he said as he strolled into the kitchen. He poured himself a generous glass of milk and gulped it down. His tongue plumped up again just fine.

Austin poured milk for the rest of his family. Benji came into the kitchen and helped Austin carry cups to the living room and hand them out.

Going around the room, Scilla handed out cookies to everybody, practically shoving one into Alfie's hand. She tilted her head in dejection and showed Austin her empty plate. "I'm sorry. You won't get another one."

Austin slumped his shoulders and tried to feel profoundly disappointed. "Nobody wanted to miss out on your whole wheat BM cookies."

"It's okay," Scilla said. "I'll make another batch tomorrow, and you can have a whole plate to yourself."

Austin glanced at Alfie, still plastered against the wall with a cookie in his hand. "Take a bite, Alfie. You'll like it." Okay, that was a lie, but Scilla was looking at him as if he were an angel. He couldn't disappoint her. Besides, it would be rude for Alfie not to eat the cookie.

Alfie took a drink of milk then a small bite of his cookie. Another drink of milk, another miniscule bite. He managed to get through ten percent of his cookie that way, at least until Austin stopped watching him. Alfie just couldn't appreciate health food.

Austin and Scilla stood by the front door and watched everyone enjoy Scilla's cookies. "You're so thoughtful, Scilla," he said. It wasn't the taste, but the thought that really counted. "I don't think I've met someone as nice as you. It's wonderful thoughtful of you to come and check on Benji."

Scilla looked down at her hands and the empty plate. When she raised her head, the admiration in her eyes took his breath away. "You're the thoughtful one, Austin. You're so kind to everybody, even people who don't deserve it." He had to lean in close to hear her.

Alfie was still working on that cookie. He wasn't making much progress. Benji nudged Alfie with his elbow and whispered in his ear. Both boys strolled into the kitchen. "We're getting more milk," Benji said, to no one in particular.

Austin knew right where that cookie was going.

Scilla gazed in the direction of the kitchen and gave Austin a sympathetic smile. "I know how hard it is with your *bruderen,* but you're so patient with them. For sure and certain they'd drive me crazy, especially the way your *mater* lets them run wild."

Austin frowned. Mamm didn't let the boys run wild. They found their own trouble. "They're wonderful annoying," he said. "But I guess I was that way when I was nine."

Scilla shook her head. "*Ach.* You weren't anything but nice and well-behaved, even back then."

Scilla didn't have a very *gute me*mory.

Austin just smiled, as if the compliment she'd given him was the absolute truth. She admired him. He wouldn't do anything to burst her bubble. "What does BM stand for?"

"What?"

"You said they are BM cookies. What does that stand for?"

Scilla moved closer and lowered her voice even further.

Austin's pulse sped up when her sleeve grazed his hand. "BM stands for bowel movement. They're called Bowel Movement cookies because if you're plugged up, they'll help you have a *gute* bowel movement. And after what happened at the store yesterday, I knew your *bruderen* needed some. Little boys tend to misbehave when they're constipated."

Austin didn't quite know how to respond. First, there was that part about the boys misbehaving at Glick's Market yesterday. Benji hadn't done anything wrong. Did Scilla think he had? Second was the fact that Scilla had said the words *bowel movement* in his living room. Of course, she'd said it really softly, but it didn't make it sound more pleasant. Thirdly, Austin suddenly felt the need to oversee Alfie and Benji's eating habits. Did they need more roughage in their diet? Should he talk to Mamm about it?

Or Mammi?

If Mammi knew, she'd buy a case of bran and have everybody taking it twice a day. Maybe he wouldn't tell Mammi.

Oh, *sis yuscht.* He'd eaten a whole BM cookie. He might be up all night.

Alfie couldn't sleep. Not after eating a half of one of Scilla's cookies. Not after having to go to the bathroom two times in the night. Not after realizing that he had been wrong. Alfie hated being wrong, so he always tried to be right. But this time, Benji had been right, and it made Alfie so mad. Benji was a *gute* partner, but sometimes he made Alfie look bad.

Alfie sat on the air mattress in the cellar staring at the rows of canned turkey and salsa and spaghetti sauce. It had been a *gute* harvest, and Mamm had spent the whole month canning with Aendi Beth. Well, good for them. Bad for Alfie. It had been more than a year, and Alfie and Benji were still sleeping in the cellar, and it was getting more crowded all the time. Mamm had canned pickles this year. Hundreds and hundreds of pickles. Now the cellar smelled like vinegar, as well as mold, dirty socks, and dead spider bodies. It made it worse that they had to go upstairs to use the bathroom, and sometimes you had to go real bad.

Benji turned over. "Alfie, turn off that lantern. Mamm says it's for emergencies."

"This is an emergency." Alfie was about to admit he was wrong. Of course it was an emergency. Might as well get it over with. He needed Benji's help, and he couldn't get it unless he owned up to his mistakes. "Benji, I don't want Austin to marry Priscilla."

Benji propped himself on his elbow. "Why not?"

"Because she is the worst cook in the world. If he married her, she'd make us eat BM cookies every day, and we'd have to do it because Mamm says we have to be polite."

Benji grimaced. "It's really hard to be polite sometimes."

"She likes Austin, but she hates us."

"She doesn't hate me," Benji said, sitting up and leaning against the wall.

"*Jah,* she does. She smiles when Austin comes to the library, but she frowns at us. I try to talk to her and she tells me to sit quietly and not to pull out any books because she doesn't want to reshelve them. She said I was naughty four times. I hate it when she calls me naughty. She talks in a baby voice."

"I like Hannah better," Benji said.

Alfie couldn't stand it anymore. He burst into tears. "I'm sorry, Benji. I was wrong, and I should have listened to you. You're my partner, and if I ever have to eat another BM cookie, I'm going to choke."

Benji wrapped his arms around Alfie and patted him on the back. "It's okay. I don't mind."

Benji was the best partner. He never said things like, "I told you so," or "You're so *dumm,*" or "You shouldn't have set that on fire." He just listened and tried to make it better.

"We should work together," Benji said. "I can't talk to myself on the walkie-talkie. Well, I *can,* but it's not very fun, and they squeak if I get them too close to each other."

"I need your help. We have to trick Hannah into marrying Austin."

Benji smiled. "I like Hannah. She doesn't make us eat BM cookies. And she doesn't get mad when I lick my fingers and don't use my napkin."

"Everybody likes Hannah. That's the problem. She could have any boy she wants. But we've got to convince her to marry Austin. I'm not staying in this cellar for another year. Mamm will probably put up cabbage next year, and I'll die from the smell."

Benji scrunched his lips together. "We need some helpers."

"Max Glick can't keep a secret. I'm not asking him."

"*Nae,*" Benji said. "We need girls."

Alfie drew back in horror. "Girls? I don't want girls. They're stupid."

"Not just any girls. We need Ruth Ann and Dinah Yutzy."

"Ruth Ann and Dinah? What for?" He knew the answer as soon as the question was out of his mouth. Ruth Ann and Dinah were Hannah's cousins, and Hannah sometimes worked as a mother's helper for their *mamm.* Hannah went to their house almost every day after working at the donut stand.

"They can help us," Benji said. "They're Hannah's cousins."

It was a terrible idea. A really *gute,* terrible idea. Alfie got the creepy-crawlies even being around girls, but if anybody could get them closer to Hannah, it was Ruth Ann and Dinah. Alfie hated the thought of it, almost as much as he hated BM cookies.

But if he truly wanted to get out of the cellar, he had to make the hard sacrifices. If he wanted Austin to have any chance with Hannah, Ruth Ann and Dinah were their only hope.

His stomach hurt. It was either the thought of having to talk to the girls, or those BM cookies.

Oy, anyhow. This plan had better work.

Chapter Six

Ruth Ann Yutzy and about five other girls usually spent recess huddled on the merry-go-round giggling and whispering to each other. Girls were so *dumm.* Didn't they think other people might want to use the merry-go-round for twirling instead of giggling?

Alfie took a deep breath and thought about Austin, about how *dumm* he was and how he'd never get married because he was so *dumm* and how they needed Ruth Ann's help to get Hannah and Austin together so Benji and Alfie could get out of the cellar. It was a lot to think about, but it gave him the courage to talk to Ruth Ann at recess.

Well, maybe it wasn't courage he needed, because he wasn't scared. But Ruth Ann was ten and Alfie was only nine. The older girls always thought they were too *gute* for Alfie, even though he was the one who was too *gute* for them.

Benji hooked his elbow around Alfie's and pulled him right up to the merry-go-round. Suvie Nelson and Eva Zook looked at them as if they had boogers sticking out of their noses, but Ruth Ann had her back turned and didn't see them.

"*Hallo,* Ruth Ann," Benji said, as if Ruth Ann was his best friend and he didn't even care that she was ten.

Ruth Ann turned around and propped her lips to the side of her face like she had no idea why a nine-year-old would even be talking to her.

"We need to ask you something," Benji said. He motioned for her to get off the merry-go-round.

She made another face but said something to her friends and climbed down from her perch and folded her arms. "What do you want? I don't talk to boys."

"We need your help," Benji said. "And Dinah's."

Ruth Ann tightened her arms around her waist. "With what?"

"Just a minute." Benji ran to a group of kids playing tag, leaving Alfie standing all by himself with Ruth Ann, who was looking at him the way Scilla Lambright sometimes did. He wasn't even going to try to fill the uncomfortable silence.

Benji came back with Dinah. Dinah was six and seemed to like boys just fine. "We want our old room back," Benji said.

Dinah smiled and nodded, while Ruth Ann's lips puckered into a deeper scowl.

Benji was a *gute* partner, but sometimes he didn't explain things very well. Alfie would have to take over. "We have to sleep in the cellar because our Dawdi had a stroke, and he has to live with us now. Austin and Abraham are sleeping in our room, and if we can get them out of the house, we can have our old room back. We want to find a wife for Austin so he'll move out."

Dinah giggled into her hand. "Austin is wonderful handsome."

Ruth Ann narrowed her eyes. "So what if Austin is

handsome. You don't think Dinah should marry him, do you?" This sent Dinah into a fit of laughter like Alfie had never seen before. It wasn't funny, and girls were so *dumm.*

"We want Hannah to marry him," Benji said.

"But she can marry anybody she wants, and Austin is a *dummkoff.*" Alfie shouldn't have said that. The girls might not help if they knew it would be hard to get Hannah to say yes.

Ruth Ann glanced at Dinah. "You want us to help you get Hannah and Austin together?"

Benji nodded. "She's your mother's helper."

"And she makes us dinner sometimes," Dinah said. "I like Hannah. And I like Austin too."

Ruth Ann pressed her lips together. "Dinah and I need to talk about it. Will you give us some privacy?"

"Uh, okay."

Ruth Ann tugged Dinah around the corner of the schoolhouse where Alfie and Benji couldn't see them.

Benji stuck his hands in his pockets. "Some girls think Austin's handsome."

"Girls don't know anything."

Dinah stuck her head around the corner of the schoolhouse and crooked her finger, bidding Alfie and Benji to come. They went.

Ruth Ann leaned against the school. Dinah stood next to her. "We've decided to help you," Ruth Ann said. "But you have to do two things for us."

"What?" Alfie asked. He'd do just about anything to get out of that cellar, except maybe eat more BM cookies.

Ruth Ann held up one finger. "Our *mamm* needs a new wheelchair."

Benji frowned. "We don't have any extra wheelchairs. Dawdi is still using his."

"We don't want you to steal your *dawdi*'s wheelchair. Just get our *mamm* a new one. Hers creaks, and it's hard for her to push by herself. And it makes her achy yet."

"How are we supposed to do that?" Alfie asked. He only had about twelve dollars in his piggy bank.

Ruth Ann turned up her nose. "I don't know, but that's what we want."

"Will you help us get Hannah and Austin together first?" Benji said. "It will take months to save enough for a wheelchair, but Hannah buys our tomatoes at the donut stand. We'll save all our money for a wheelchair." Benji was a *gute* partner and wonderful smart sometimes.

Ruth Ann thought about it and nodded. "I guess that will be okay. Let's shake on it."

She held out her hand and shook Benji's hand first and then Alfie's. Dinah did the same.

"What's the other thing you want us to do?" Benji said.

"You need to give me a kiss." Ruth Ann tapped her cheek with her index finger. "Right here."

Dinah giggled.

"Me?" Benji said.

Ruth Ann raised her eyebrow. "*Nae.* Alfie."

Alfie's stomach jumped into his throat. "I'm not kissing you."

Ruth Ann folded her arms again as if she wouldn't move from that spot for a hundred days. "Then we won't help you."

Alfie groaned. He wanted out of the cellar so bad, he thought he might die. But if he kissed Ruth Ann, he'd probably catch a disease and die anyway. He shuffled his feet to Ruth Ann, got on his tiptoes, and gave her a kiss right on the cheek. Then he drew away and wiped his lips across his sleeve about seven times.

"Will you help us now?" he said, scowling. He wiped off his tongue for good measure.

Ruth Ann seemed satisfied. *Gute,* because he was never, ever doing that again. "Okay. We'll help you. What do we need to do?"

"We have a plan," Alfie said.

Benji leaned in to whisper. "And we have walkie-talkies."

Chapter Seven

Austin pulled the buggy up to the old, abandoned house sitting back from the main road. Of all the places he could have met Hannah, she had chosen here?

"This looks like a place where ghosts live," Benji said from the back seat.

"Or bears," said Alfie. "One time we found three rats in that old barn by the Nelsons' house. Remember?"

Austin turned to look at his *bruderen.* "You've been to that old barn?"

Alfie faked a casual smile. "Who wants to know?"

Austin growled. "I want to know. You shouldn't go in that old barn. You could get hurt."

"We won't get hurt," Alfie said. "Tintin can protect us." Tintin, or LaWayne as Mamm insisted they call the dog, sat between Alfie and Benji and wagged his tail enthusiastically enough to fan up a breeze. Mamm was getting soft. She never would have let Austin and his older *bruderen* have a dog, and she certainly never would have let it ride in the buggy.

"If you fall and break your neck in that old barn, the

only thing Tintin would be able to do is pull your dead body home to Mamm."

Tintin barked as if pulling Alfie's dead body out of the rubble of a collapsed building sounded like the best adventure in the world. Austin reached back and scratched behind Tintin's ears. It was a very *gute* thing the boys had a dog. Tintin might very well keep them out of the worst kinds of danger.

Austin hadn't wanted to bring Alfie and Benji, but he couldn't very well be out here alone with Hannah. It wasn't proper, and she knew it. Why in the world had she told him to meet her out here? The donut stand would have been a *gute* place to talk about ideas for his peanut butter.

Austin set the brake, and he and his *bruderen* and Tintin jumped out of the buggy. The house looked at least a hundred years old, but it was made of brick and probably had at least another hundred years ahead of it. It had a huge front yard and a wide porch that looked to be overpopulated with cobwebs and dead leaves. There were two big windows at the front of the house. One of the windows had a large crack in it, but the other window was intact.

Hannah pulled up in her buggy and waved to him. He waved back with a question in his eyes. *What are we doing here?* She simply smiled and slid out of the buggy with two of her little cousins close behind her. Hannah was a mother's helper for her *aendi* Linda, who had been bound to a wheelchair for almost a year. Ruth Ann and Dinah were two of Linda's children, and they spent a lot of time with Hannah at the donut stand when they weren't in school.

"Aw," Alfie moaned. "Why did she have to bring them?"

Austin looked at Alfie. "Don't you like the Yutzy girls?"

Benji scrunched his lips together. "He doesn't like Ruth Ann because she made him kiss her."

"Benji!" Alfie hissed.

The laughter exploded from Austin's lips. "You kissed her?"

Benji shrugged. "He had to do it, even though he didn't want to. We have a plan."

"What kind of a plan involves kissing?"

"A secret plan," Benji said, before Alfie shoved him and nearly made him fall over.

Austin looked sideways at his *bruderen.* He didn't understand half of what they said.

"Hannah!" Benji ran to Hannah and gave her a big hug. Hannah hugged him right back. Someday, that's how his *bruderen* were going to feel about Scilla. And maybe she'd even hug them back.

Ruth Ann, the older of Hannah's cousins, looked at the house and wrinkled her nose. "*Ach,* spider webs." She gave Tintin the same reaction when he tried to jump on her. "Go away, dog," she said.

"Can we go in there?" Alfie asked.

"*Nae,*" Austin said. "It's not safe." That house looked like tetanus, a broken neck, and the plague all waiting to happen.

"It's okay," Hannah said, pulling a key from her apron pocket. "I've been in there." She handed the key to Alfie. "Don't trip on anything. And don't go down the stairs because it looks like there's some sort of critter living in the basement."

Alfie's eye got wide. "You mean like a wolverine?"

"I mean . . ." Hannah glanced at Austin. "*Jah,* probably like a wolverine. You don't want to get attacked. And you don't want Tintin to get in a fight."

"Okay," Alfie said. With Tintin hot on their heels, he and Benji ran like the wind straight up the porch steps.

Alfie unlocked the door, and they disappeared into the house.

Dinah followed after them, although her legs weren't long enough to keep up. Ruth Ann folded her arms and watched the house, as if she was too grown up or too sanitary to be exploring.

Austin glanced at Hannah doubtfully. "Are you sure they'll be okay?"

Hannah laughed. "For sure and certain. There aren't any broken windows, and it's only been vacant for a couple of years. There's at least one mouse in the basement, but as long as Alfie thinks it's a wolverine, he won't go down there. It's too dark for them to see their way safely." She shaded her eyes with her hand and pointed to the south. "Listen."

"I don't hear anything."

"It's the highway, silly. It's five minutes from here. Easy on. Easy off. That's what the Realtor said."

"That's very interesting, Hannah, but what does it have to do with peanut butter?" Austin said.

Hannah smiled. It was one of those smiles that made him feel warm all over, like a beautiful sunrise that he wanted to look at all day. No one made him feel quite like Hannah could when she got excited about something. "Austin, I think you should start your own Amish market. Right here."

"My own . . ."

"It's close to the highway, so tourists can get on and off easy. We can put up a sign so they know where to find us. You could sell peanut butter. I could make donuts and pies. We could give people another choice besides Glick's Amish Market. Their price on cheese is wonderful steep."

"I could make bread," Ruth Ann said. "Mamm says I'm her best bread maker."

Hannah draped an arm around Ruth Ann's shoulders. "Ruth Ann could make bread. Bitsy Weaver could sell Honeybee Sisters honey here."

Austin was truly speechless. He'd never even considered the possibility of opening his own store to sell Petersheim Brothers peanut butter. "But. Hannah. I'm not smart enough."

"You're more than smart enough. I'll help you, and I'm sure Andrew and Abraham will help. You know enough about running a business. You've been running the peanut butter business. My *dat* knows the accountant at the cheese factory. I'm sure he'd help us." She wrapped her fingers around his arm. "Austin, don't you see? It's perfect."

"I don't know what to say."

Her eyes sparkled. "It would have the added benefit of making Raymond Glick wonderful irritated."

Austin grunted. "I wouldn't have to spend near this much money to irritate Raymond. I can do that just by walking into his market."

Hannah laughed. "Okay. We'll leave Raymond Glick out of it. *Cum.* Let me show you the house. The Realtor says we can get it for cheap. We would have to ask the town to rezone it, but the mayor doesn't want a junky old house bringing down property values. It shouldn't be a problem."

Austin shook his head slowly. "I can't do this. I didn't even understand half the things you just said."

"I only know stuff because I sat down with the Realtor. She can educate you on everything." She took hold of his hand with both of hers and pulled him up the steps of the house. Ruth Ann followed them. "It's wired for electricity. Of course, we'll have to get permission from the bishop, but it's also ready for a phone. There's trash everywhere, but it won't take but a minute to clean it up."

The house smelled like cigarettes and bleach, as if someone had been trying to hide the cigarette smell. The front room was tiny, with brown, filthy carpeting and walls riddled with nail holes and dings.

"The only carpet is on this floor," Hannah said. "Once we pull it up, most of the cigarette smell will disappear. And there's a wood floor underneath." The kitchen behind the front room took up the whole back half of the house. There were old newspapers and other junk scattered over the floor and an old mattress in the corner.

Austin tiptoed around the trash as the children stomped around upstairs and Tintin barked above their heads. The stairs sat on one end of the kitchen against the wall. Ruth Ann took a tentative step up to the second floor. "Go ahead," Hannah said. "You can help us decide what room the quilts will go in." Ruth Ann seemed to like that idea. She bounded up the stairs without another second's hesitation. Hannah tapped on the wall between the front room and kitchen. "If we take out this wall, we'll have this whole space. You can put shelves everywhere, and people can watch us make pies over here by the sink. We could do cooking demonstrations. Wouldn't they think that was fun?"

Hannah's excitement was infectious. "*Jah,*" Austin said. "I think they would."

"Andrew could help us with the walls." She slid her foot across the dusty floor. "It wonders me if this won't be beautiful once Andrew refinishes it."

Austin knelt down and ran his hand along the planks. They were dotted with pockmarks and lined with all sorts of scratches. "It's in bad shape."

"But won't it look nice when we sand and polish it?"

Austin loved that Hannah could see the possibilities, even if it meant a lot of work. He loved that she wanted to help him, as if it was her project as much as his. He wouldn't be alone. "How much are they asking for the house?" He swiped his hand across his forehead. "*Ach, du lieva.* I can't believe I'm considering this, Hannah. It's so big. It's too big."

"It's not too big. I've already talked to my *dat.* This is a better location to sell our donuts, so we can draw people in. Tourists will pass here before they drive into town. And this place is just as close to most of the neighbors as Glick's Market is."

Austin's heart was thumping so loudly, Hannah could probably hear it. "Do you think . . . do you think it would really work?"

"If I didn't think we could do it, I wouldn't have shown you the house."

"Let's go see the rest of it."

By the time Hannah had taken him through the rooms upstairs, Austin was already planning where he would put the Amish handicrafts. And they'd need to sell groceries so people wouldn't have to make an extra trip to Glick's for things they couldn't find at Austin's store.

The basement had more than enough room for storage, and there was a small shed in the back if they needed more. It was almost too *gute* to be true. Austin gave Alfie his flashlight and let the four children explore the basement while he and Hannah went upstairs to measure the space.

Hannah held one end of the tape measure as he took notes on the back of a receipt he found in his pocket. He hadn't come prepared to start a business. Was he ever going to be prepared? Hannah helped him measure the wall he wanted to take out, then the weight of what they were considering fell on him. How much did one sheet of drywall cost? How many jars of peanut butter would he have to sell to pay for it?

He blew a long breath from his lungs, shook his head, and plopped himself down on the bottom step of the stairs. Hannah sat next to him. "I can't even begin to guess how much money this is going to take. We have to buy food and merchandise and redo the floor and the walls and build shelves yet. That's before we can start to sell anything. I'm sorry, Hannah. You got me really excited, but we both know this is a *deerich* dream."

Hannah laughed and slapped his knee. "I've never known you to be the cautious type."

"I'm not always cautious, but I don't want to be reckless either."

"What have you got to lose?" Hannah was loud and kind of boisterous. Her voice echoed all through the empty house.

"A lot of money," he said.

She stood up, looked at him straight on, and grinned like a mischievous cat. "What's the worst that can happen?"

That coaxed a smile from his lips. It was a game they had played when they were younger, usually when Hannah tried to talk him out of doing something stupid like bungee jumping from the bridge or building a makeshift zipline between the barn and his house. She certainly wasn't demure like Scilla, but it was funny that even though Hannah was loud and unembarrassed, she had always been a calming presence in his life. She made him stop and think about things instead of diving headlong into something dangerous or stupid. Now he was making her think.

"The worst that can happen is I borrow all this money

and the store fails," he said. "The worst is if I have to take up truck driving to repay my loan or go into the army or ask Raymond Glick for a job."

She giggled. "I think I'd rather join the army."

"Me too."

She propped her foot on the bottom step. "What's the best that can happen?"

He smiled reluctantly. "The store is a huge success, Perry Glick never pinches my *bruder* again, and I sell a hundred jars of peanut butter every day."

Hannah's lips twitched in amusement. "Peanut butter always figures into your plans somehow."

"It's my life."

A sudden, ear-piercing scream rose from the basement. And not just one. At least three of the four children down there were screaming and Tintin was barking. Austin leaped to his feet, but before he or Hannah could run down the stairs, Alfie, Benji, Dinah, and Ruth Ann emerged from the basement, panting and fussing like they'd just seen a ghost.

"What happened?" Hannah said, wrapping her hands around Dinah's upper arms.

"We saw a snake," Ruth Ann squeaked.

Benji wrapped his arms around Austin's waist. "A really big one."

Alfie was the last to come up the stairs, and he was as calm as a summer morning. "It wasn't a snake."

Dinah spread her arms as wide as they would go. "It was this long, and it slobbered on me."

"It was a hose, and you stepped on it," Alfie said.

Alfie's explanation was more likely, but they had found evidence of some mice living in the basement, so it was possible there was a snake. Although, if there was a snake, he'd get rid of the mouse problem right quick.

Benji took in a quick breath. "We left Tintin down with the snake." Unmindful of his own safety, Benji ran back down the stairs to save his dog.

"It wasn't a snake," Alfie called.

Hannah was always game for an adventure. "Let's go down and see."

Ruth Ann shook her head. "I'm not going down there."

Hannah took Dinah's hand, and they started down the stairs together. Dinah looked over her shoulder at Ruth Ann. "If you stay up here by yourself, the rats might eat you."

Ruth Ann squeaked. "Don't leave me."

They all tromped down the stairs, and Alfie shined the flashlight into the corner where Benji stood with Tintin. Austin's heart did a somersault. Tintin was sniffing at a long snake on the floor. Or at least it looked like a snake until Austin got closer and realized it was a curvy stick. But it was a very convincing snake from far away.

"I told you," said Alfie.

"No snakes in this house," Hannah said, though nobody could be entirely sure of that. Snakes were sneaky.

Alfie shined his flashlight around the unfinished basement. "I like this house. You could have a store upstairs and live down here." He nudged Benji. "We might not need our plan."

Was that the plan that involved kissing Ruth Ann?

Ruth Ann folded her arms. "We still want a wheelchair."

"A wheelchair?" Hannah said.

Alfie stepped in front of Ruth Ann and laughed nervously. "What do you think, Austin? Do you want to live here?"

"Not yet. It's got a lot of work before anyone can live

here. Getting the water turned on is about step two hundred and seventeen."

Alfie didn't like that answer. "You could dig an outhouse and move in next week."

Austin laughed. If only it were that easy.

And it wouldn't be easy.

Nope. He wasn't going to do it—dig an outhouse or buy this run-down house or start his own store.

It was too much of a risk. Even for him.

Chapter Eight

Benji tiptoed his way across the floor to Hannah. She was impressed with his concern, even though he didn't need to be so careful just yet. They'd only just removed most of the old varnish. "Do you need help?" he said.

"Help with what?"

"Ruth Ann told Alfie to tell me to ask you if you needed help with the scraping."

Hannah smiled. "Why, *denki,* Benji. That's very thoughtful of you to ask, but I'm doing fine." As much as she loved Benji and that impish grin of his, the last thing she needed was a nine-year-old trying to help her scrape the finish off the edges of the wood floor. "Aren't you and *die kinner* working on cleaning out the basement?"

"*Jah,*" Benji said. Without another word, he tromped down the stairs, his errand upstairs obviously finished.

Hannah picked up the file and sharpened her scraper. The sander Andrew had rented did most of the floor just fine, but it couldn't reach the narrow strip of varnish around the edges and in the corners. That had to be done by hand, and it was tedious, difficult work.

She turned as she heard much bigger boots tromping

up the stairs. Austin appeared, his face covered with a light layer of dust. He wore a pair of work gloves, some heavy-duty kneepads, and a wide smile. She really loved that smile, especially when he gave it to her and only her.

"You were humming again," he said.

"Was I?" Hannah had a habit of humming to herself when she baked or put together a puzzle or cleaned the house. Mamm called it her "busy noise." She did it almost unconsciously. Austin thought it was wildly funny.

"Alfie says you need help."

Hannah curled her lips. The message had obviously gotten mixed up. "I said no such thing."

He sat down on the floor next to her and took her scraper, eyes flashing as if he was stealing a cookie from the jar. "I'm going to help anyway. You're doing the hardest job."

Hannah leaned back on her hands to give her knees a rest. "And I'm slow."

"You are not. You've done more work on this floor than I have."

She gave him a teasing grin. "*Denki* for noticing. I slave away every day while you clip your toenails and read *The Budget.*"

He laughed. "I haven't had time to clip my toenails for two months. They're wonderful long."

"Just don't catch those long toenails on anything. You'll rip off a nail."

"It's not safe to go barefoot anymore." He started scraping where Hannah had left off.

"*Ach,* remember when you went barefoot and stepped on that rusty nail and you hid it from your *mamm* because you didn't want to get a shot?"

He blew a puff of air from his lips. "And you came to

my house and put me in a chokehold until I told Mamm everything."

The laughter bubbled out of her throat. "I was your best friend, so I wouldn't tattle on you. I had to make you do it yourself."

Austin put his hand to his throat. "You saved my life by almost killing me."

"It wasn't a real chokehold. You could breathe the whole time."

He made a face. "You don't know that. It's only because you didn't hold on long enough to find out if I would have died. I was only ten."

"I saved your life by seeing that you got a tetanus shot. That's all I cared about."

He grunted in mock disbelief. "I'm sure it was."

She laughed. "Well, that and making sure you were nice to people."

"I was always nice to people."

"Only after I made you be nice."

He raised his eyebrows. "I was nice. You only had to make me be nice a few times. You baked a pie and made me take it to Treva Nelson. Who gives someone a pie to apologize?"

"A pie is better than a plate of cookies. It takes more work so the offended person knows you really care."

Austin shook his head. "She beaned me with a snowball and stuck out her tongue at me so I tripped her on the playground. She started it. She didn't deserve a pie."

"You tripped her, and she scraped her face on the ice," Hannah said. "I didn't want all the girls to hate you for the rest of eternity, so I baked her a pie and asked you to take it to her as a gesture of repentance."

"You didn't ask. You commanded me to take that pie to Treva or you'd tell my *mamm* what I'd done."

She curled her lips mischievously. "I wouldn't have really told your *mamm.* One little chokehold and you would have confessed everything."

He grinned and yanked one of her *kapp* strings. "I would have apologized eventually, without a pie."

"I know."

"I did feel bad about Treva's face, even though she's always been a pill. But you were tricky with that pie."

Hannah couldn't help but laugh at the memory. "I thought the hearts cut into the crust were a nice touch."

"Because of those hearts, she thought I was in love with her. She wouldn't stop following me around for the rest of the school year."

"It was better than if she hated you."

"I don't think so," he said. "She wrote me love notes and chased me and tried to kiss me at recess."

"Girls always do that at recess. It's a time-honored tradition."

"I was thirteen!"

Hannah laughed at the thought of Treva Nelson chasing Austin around the playground. "She was taller than most of the boys, but thankfully, she wasn't very fast."

"Fortunately for me."

"You did get a lot of exercise that year."

"Ha!" He twirled the scraper in his fingers. "But I learned my lesson yet."

"Not to trip girls?"

"*Nae.* Andrew taught me how to get out of a chokehold."

Hannah threw back her head and laughed. "A wonderful *gute* lesson." She reached out and brushed some dust from

Austin's face. He had such a nice smile. It was a shame to cover it up. He playfully tapped her hand away, and his face turned red under all that dust. "I had a talk with Treva," Hannah said.

"You did?"

"I couldn't stand watching her torture you anymore. I told her to leave you alone or I'd trip her myself."

Austin gasped. "You didn't."

"I'm joking. I told her to leave you alone, but I didn't threaten violence. The whole thing was sort of my fault since the hearts on the pie were my idea."

Austin snorted. "I'm glad you're finally taking responsibility."

"She wouldn't listen at first, and I had to be blunt, but she finally understood I was serious. She was pretty mad, but she left you alone after that. For months afterward, she turned and walked in the other direction whenever she saw me coming, and if she was in town, she'd cross the street to avoid the donut stand." Treva and Scilla had started whispering behind Hannah's back. Of course, Hannah hadn't taken it personally. Scilla whispered behind just about everybody's back.

Austin gave her a sympathetic grin. "I'm sorry she was mean to you."

Hannah shrugged. "Treva's kind of mean to everybody, except maybe the bishop's and ministers' families, so it's not like I'm eager to be her best friend."

"You already have a best friend." Austin's smile sent a ribbon of warmth threading down her spine. She savored and resisted that feeling. It was so foolish to fall more in love with Austin. Priscilla Lambright had him *ferhoodled.*

Austin cleared his throat, pulled his gaze from her face, and started scraping the varnish. It came off a lot easier for him than it had for Hannah. His arms were so toned, his muscles had muscles. "We need to get you some gloves and kneepads. I'll put that on my list."

"It's okay, Austin. I don't want you to run out of money."

He flashed a grin. "And I don't want you to run out of knees."

Hannah should have thought to buy her own kneepads the last time she was at Walmart, but everything had happened so fast, she hadn't had much time to think of anything before Austin and his *bruderen* had started on the house.

Her heart galloped around the room when Austin laid his gloved hand over hers. "This is all your doing, and I'm wonderful grateful. *Denki* for talking me into it."

"I just talked. You've taken all the risks."

"You came with me to the city council meeting. That was pretty risky." He smiled. "It's going to work, Hannah. We're going to have a store."

Hannah melted like warm chocolate on a hot day. Austin should always be this happy. Despite all his misgivings, he had met with the Realtor and the banker the day after Hannah had shown him the house. They had explained the financing to him so he wasn't so frightened of his ignorance.

It bolstered Austin's resolve when Perry Glick started spreading the story that he had pinched Benji because Benji had tried to steal some candy from Glick's Market. Injustice was a powerful motivation.

Two weeks later, Austin and Hannah had appeared in front of the city council to get the property rezoned. Hannah could hardly believe that an Amish girl like her could have done such a brave thing. After they'd gotten approval from the city, Austin had made a low but reasonable offer on the house, and the eager owners accepted it in less than an hour. A week ago, Austin had closed on the house, and he and his *bruderen* got to work.

Since then, the house had been a constant beehive of activity. The day after closing, Andrew, Austin, and Abraham had knocked out the wall between the front room and the kitchen, measured for shelves, and started building a shed for the solar water heater.

Now that the crops were in, many neighbors came to help because they were less busy on their farms. They'd cleaned and painted, repaired squeaky floorboards and stairs, swept and hauled garbage away. The Honeybee Sisters had been there along with their husbands. Bitsy and Yost Weaver were there almost as much as Austin was, and Hannah's *bruder* James, and her sister, Mary, had come too. Mary had scrubbed the sink in the kitchen until it sparkled pearly white. Hannah smiled to herself. Pretty soon, they wouldn't have to close the donut stand because of cold weather. They could make donuts all year round in Austin's warm house—complete with a new pellet stove.

Tonight, everybody but Austin and the twins and Hannah and her two cousins had gone home for dinner. Hannah wanted to finish the floor before she left, although right now, it was Austin doing the floor for her. "If you need to do something else, Austin, I can finish."

"I don't need to do anything else but help you. You've worked so hard, and Alfie said you were tired."

Hannah cocked an eyebrow. "I'm not sure where Alfie is getting his information, but I'm fine." But it was nice to know that Austin cared about her.

Someone knocked softly at the front door, and since Austin was occupied, Hannah jumped up to get it. She wished she hadn't bothered. Priscilla Lambright stood on the porch with a huge picnic basket draped over her shoulder. "*Ach,* Hannah," Scilla said. "I didn't expect to see you."

"I'm just working on the floor," was all Hannah had to say. She hadn't expected to see Scilla either, and her arrival put a damper on Hannah's whole day.

As soon as he heard Scilla's voice, Austin leaped to his feet and pulled off his gloves. "Scilla! You came." He stepped in front of Hannah as if she was a hatstand in the entryway and took the basket from Scilla's arm.

"I was going to come earlier, but there was a field trip and I had to reshelve a hundred books. I don't like field trips."

"You must be exhausted," Austin said. He moved back, almost stepping on Hannah's foot. "*Cum reu.* Come see what we've done."

Scilla stepped into the house as if she was afraid it would collapse and bury her in the rubble. "*Ach, du lieva,* Austin. You said it was going to be a lot of work, but I don't think any amount of work is going to turn this into a nice place to sell things. It wonders me if you should have bought it in the first place."

Her criticism didn't seem to discourage Austin. "You should have seen it when Hannah first showed it to me. I thought she was crazy."

Hannah pressed her lips together and pretended to be the hatstand Austin obviously thought she was.

Scilla glanced sympathetically at Hannah and then made a slow circle around the space that used to be the living room before they'd knocked out the wall. "*Ach,* well, if anyone can make this place into something *wunderbarr,* it's you, Austin. You have a talent for things like this."

Austin smiled as if Scilla had just bought a whole case

of his peanut butter. “Look at the wood floors. They’re going to be wonderful pretty.” He held up the scraper. “We’ve been finishing the edges so we can stain it.”

“It wonders me if anyone can scrape edges like you can,” Scilla said breathlessly. She and Austin stared into each other’s eyes in a nauseating, private moment together. It was definitely time for Hannah to go. If she claimed a headache and slipped out the front door, would they even notice she’d left?

“I’m glad you came,” Austin said. “I’ve been wanting to show you this place for two months.”

Scilla smoothed her hand down her apron. “*Ach, vell,* I know how single-minded you are when you work. I didn’t want to get in your way.”

Hannah couldn’t resist. “You wouldn’t have been in anybody’s way. We all helped pick up trash.”

Scilla flashed a self-deprecating smile and tried to ignore Hannah altogether. “I really wouldn’t have been of much help. I’m not *gute* at heavy lifting like some girls.” Austin nodded as if he was in complete sympathy with Scilla’s limitations. Hannah wanted to put him in a choke-hold. “Besides,” Scilla said, “you said there were mice, and you know how I feel about mice droppings. And snakes. I don’t like snakes.”

Hannah wanted to ask if Scilla was also afraid of sticks that look like snakes, but she bit her tongue.

Austin took her elbow and led her to the kitchen area. “All the mice and droppings are gone. You don’t have to worry.”

Scilla rubbed her nose. “Are you going to be able to get rid of the smell?” she said, glancing at Hannah like she might be the source of the stink.

If only Scilla had been here two months ago, she’d

know it already smelled so much better. But if she'd come two months ago, she probably would have fainted and talked Austin out of buying the house.

Austin set the picnic basket on the kitchen counter and had the nerve to take Scilla's hand. *Ach, vell,* he had the nerve to do it in front of Hannah, but he had no idea of Hannah's true feelings for him. But he shouldn't have been holding hands with Scilla anyway. Surely it was against the rules. "Let me show you around. This is where the shelves with groceries will go." He pointed to the long back wall where the floor had been newly scraped of finish. "We are going to put a big fridge back here. One of those kinds with a glass door so you can see what's inside."

Scilla seemed mildly shocked. "With electricity?"

He glanced at Hannah and smiled. "*Jah.* We already got permission from the bishop, and he says we can have a phone. But the lights will be propane powered. The tourists want it to look authentic, like Amish people really own it."

"What a wonderful *gute* idea," Scilla said. "You're so smart, Austin."

"That was Hannah's idea. She's worked the donut stand long enough to know what the Englisch want."

Scilla seemed to back away from her praise. "*Ach.* Propane lanterns won't give you enough light. Maybe you'll need some battery-operated lights as well."

Austin nodded thoughtfully. "You're right. We need plenty of light. *Denki* for thinking of that."

Scilla seemed to soak up his gratitude like a sponge. "I know about light since I work in the library. The light has to be just right so people can read."

Austin was as excited as a little boy with a new dog. "*Cum* upstairs, and I'll show you where we'll put the quilts and Amish handicrafts."

Scilla slipped her hand out of Austin's. "*Ach.* Those stairs don't look very safe. Maybe I should wait until you finish them."

Hannah glanced at the stairs going up. Andrew had installed a new railing that they hadn't stained yet, but other than the finish, the stairs were done. Was Scilla really that touchy? Maybe she was just too lazy to climb the stairs. Maybe she feared an encounter with some mouse droppings.

Austin hesitated but must have decided not to try to persuade her. "Okay. We can go up there another day, but look here at the kitchen." He tapped his hand on the counter. "Hannah and her family are going to move their donut stand in here."

Scilla studied Hannah's face in puzzlement. "For good?"

"*Jah,*" Austin said. "They're going to close the one in town and move here. It's closer to the highway. Hannah's *dat* is paying to fix the gas oven, but the stove works just fine." He grinned at Hannah.

Despite herself, Hannah grinned back as a shiver of pleasure tingled up her arms. It was probably not a *gute* idea to tell Scilla, but they had found a squirrel nesting in the oven and three very big spiders making a home on the burner plates, not to mention that the oven had been a black, sooty mess. It had taken Mary and Hannah a whole day to scrub it clean. Tintin had chased the squirrel outside where, Lord willing, it had found a nice home in a nearby tree.

"Hannah is going to be working here?" Scilla said, fluttering her eyelashes as if she had something stuck in her eye.

"Me and Mary and James. And sometimes my *mamm* and *dat.*"

Scilla cleared her throat. "*Ach,* Austin, that will never do."

Hannah drew her brows together. "What will never do?"

"Austin understands the importance of organic food. Your donuts aren't even gluten-free."

Hannah had a strong feeling Scilla's objections had nothing to do with gluten. She acted as though she was jealous. Jealous? Of Hannah? That was impossible, considering how Austin ignored Hannah whenever Scilla was around. The truth was, Scilla liked to be the queen bee, and for some reason, Scilla thought Hannah's donuts and pretzels were a threat. Or something else stupid like that.

Hannah clenched her teeth and faked a smile that wouldn't have fooled anyone but Scilla . . . and Austin. Austin only saw what he wanted to see. "Not everyone is as healthy as you are, Scilla."

Austin nodded. "She's right, Scilla. You are very special that way."

It was all Hannah could do to keep her eyebrow from inching up her forehead. Oh, *jah.* Scilla was special. As special as a potato chip shaped like someone's head.

Scilla caught her breath and pressed her fingers to her mouth. "I just had the most *wunderbarr* idea."

"All your ideas are *wunderbarr,*" Austin said, and Hannah again wondered why she hadn't left yet to go throw up in private.

"Why don't you have an organic, gluten-free section in your store? The Englisch love organic yet."

Austin liked that idea so much, his hair practically stood on end. "They *do* love organic. What an excellent idea."

Hannah bit the inside of her cheek. Much as she hated to admit it, Scilla's idea was a *gute* one. Austin could get twice as much for a gallon of organic milk as he could for regular milk.

"I can make gluten-free bread and organic pies and BM cookies. Your *bruderen* love my BM cookies."

Austin seemed to hesitate, but the movement was so brief, Hannah might have imagined it. "Alfie and Benji love cookies. We could advertise them as a way to help constipated children," he said.

Scilla clapped her hands. "*Ach,* Austin. Isn't it *wunderbarr?*"

He looked at Scilla the way Hannah always wished he'd look at her. "What would I do without you?"

"Your *bruderen* would be plugged up, that's for sure and certain."

Austin laughed and lifted the picnic basket from the counter. "What's in here?"

Scilla beamed. "I brought you dinner."

"You did? How nice. I've been so busy, I hardly get a chance to eat ever."

Scilla laced her fingers together. "I thought we could spread out a tablecloth on the floor and eat a picnic. Pretend we're under the shade trees in my backyard." She looked at Hannah as if just noticing she was in the room. "But . . . but I only brought enough for the two of us."

The look Scilla gave her made Hannah feel about as low as a pile of mouse droppings. It wasn't fair. Scilla had just gotten here. Why did Hannah feel like the intruder? She had half a mind to plant herself on Scilla's picnic blanket and watch the two of them eat, just to make herself annoying. But she didn't need the aggravation or the heartache, and she certainly didn't need to apologize. Watching Austin and Scilla fall in love from a distance was painful enough.

Austin drew his brows together as if he felt bad about leaving her out. "You can share my portion."

Hannah swatted away his fake concern. "I've got to get the girls home for dinner."

"Girls?" Scilla said.

"Ruth Ann and Dinah are downstairs," Hannah said. She shoved back the smile that wanted to crawl onto her face. "And Alfie and Benji."

Scilla seemed to wilt like a dandelion sprayed with Roundup. "Alfie and Benji are here?"

Hannah nodded enthusiastically. "They're downstairs cleaning up the mice droppings. And the sticks."

"Oh," Scilla said, trying valiantly to add some lilt to her voice. "I don't think I made enough for your *bruderen.*" Her eyes actually pooled with tears. Hannah suspected the disappointment had to do more with the fact that Alfie and Benji were going to ruin her romantic picnic than the fact that she hadn't brought enough food.

Austin saw the tears too. "Hey," he said softly, "Hey, Scilla, don't cry. There's a whole bag of trail mix downstairs. The boys can eat that for dinner."

Considering that Scilla was into health food, the boys would probably rather eat trail mix for dinner. *Ach, vell,* that was Austin's problem. Hannah was getting out of here. Let Austin and Scilla finish the floor together. Of course, knowing Scilla, she'd watch Austin finish while she praised his scraping and kept a sharp lookout for mice.

The stairs down sat directly underneath the stairs up. Hannah started down the stairs only to find her cousins and the Petersheim twins perched on the third and fourth steps like a gaggle of geese. Ruth Ann and Dinah squeaked like piglets when they saw Hannah, and all four of the children ran down the stairs as if she was chasing them. Alfie had a pair of binoculars around his neck, and Benji and Ruth Ann carried what looked like old cell phones.

Hannah followed them down the stairs. "What are you four up to?" she said. Certainly not cleaning, although she couldn't fault them for that. They'd been working hard ever since school got out. If they wanted to spy on the people on the main floor, they had earned a few minutes of fun.

Benji slipped the cell phone into his pocket. It beeped, and Hannah realized it was a walkie-talkie. They really had been spying. "We was just looking around," Benji said.

Dinah scratched the side of her nose. "Are you going to marry Austin?"

Hannah laughed hard so they wouldn't know she was hurting. "Of course not. Why would you say that?"

Ruth Ann looked at Alfie. "See?"

"I'm sorry," Benji said. "You must be so sad."

Yep. She was pathetic. Even the little kids felt sorry for her.

Hannah reached out for Dinah's hand. "It's time to go. I need to check on your *mamm* and get dinner on."

"Can't you stay?" Benji said. "Scilla is here, and she doesn't like us."

"*Nae,*" Hannah said. "She brought dinner for Austin. They're going to have a picnic." Hannah hated to break the news to them, but somebody had to do it. She tried to put some excitement into her voice. "You get to have trail mix for dinner."

"We know," Alfie said. "We heard."

Benji nodded. "We've been spying."

Alfie gave his *bruder* the stink eye, then bent over and picked up the trail mix bag. It was empty. "Austin and James ate it," Alfie said. "I guess he forgot."

Austin was forgetting a lot of things lately, like Hannah's existence. She clenched her teeth. Again, this was not her problem. Let the lovebirds figure out how to feed Alfie and Benji. She had her own chores to worry about.

Holding Dinah's hand, Hannah climbed the stairs. The other children followed her. Upstairs, Austin and Scilla sat on a charming red-and-white checkered tablecloth with the picnic basket next to them. Scilla was pulling food from the basket and laying it at Austin's feet. When the children got to the top of the stairs, Scilla leaned over and whispered something in Austin's ear.

Austin gave Scilla a half smile, stood, and put one brotherly arm around Alfie and one around Benji. "Scilla and I are having a picnic. You boys need to stay downstairs and not bother us. There's a whole bag of trail mix you can have for dinner. It has chocolate chips in it."

Alfie pulled the crinkled trail mix bag from his pocket and handed it to Austin. Austin studied the bag as if he didn't quite know what to do with it.

Benji slid out of Austin's grasp and stepped on the tablecloth. "What are you having for dinner?"

Scilla seemed hesitant to answer. For sure and certain the boys would want to share her precious meal, and it was plain she didn't want them to touch it. "Well, um, well, okay. There's not enough for you. I'm sorry."

"Did you bring BM cookies?" Alfie said.

"Um, well, *nae.* I brought black bean veggie burgers and roasted cauliflower." She smiled up at Austin. "And a chocolate cake made with white beans instead of oil. It's better for you even though it's not gluten-free." She turned her gaze back to Alfie. "But there's not enough for everybody."

Benji made the face Hannah's *bruder* James usually

made when he was about to throw up. He took Hannah's hand in both of his. "Please, Hannah. Can we eat at your house?"

Austin mussed up Benji's hair. "Hannah has to go. You two go downstairs, and when I'm finished, I'll take you to the gas station for chips and ice cream."

Austin must have been desperate to stoop to bribery.

Hannah half expected Scilla to disapprove of feeding the boys something so unhealthy, but she nodded eagerly. "Yum," she said. "You'd like that, wouldn't you Alfie?"

"I'm Benji."

Alfie wasn't having any of it. "We'll get sick. Like when we ate those BM cookies." He nudged Benji. "We're staying here."

"*Jah,*" Benji said, following Alfie's lead. "We're going to watch you eat."

Scilla stood up and laid a hand on Hannah's arm as if they were friends. "Could you take them home? I'd be so grateful. I just don't have enough food."

Austin gave Hannah that look she couldn't say no to. "You don't mind, do you, Hannah?"

Hannah's heart sank to the floor. Of course she didn't mind taking the boys with her, but she hated the thought of making things easier for Scilla. Or Austin. But there was nothing else to do. The boys were hungry, Ruth Ann and Dinah needed to get home, and Hannah needed to fling herself on her bed and have a *gute* cry. "Okay," she said.

Austin gave her a grateful smile. She ignored it. She sent the children out the front door and followed them to her buggy, not turning around once to look back at the house or the stupid man inside.

He had no idea how much he had hurt her. He had no idea how sorry he should feel.

Lord willing, black bean veggie burgers would be punishment enough.

Chapter Nine

Austin couldn't wait to see the look on Hannah's face when she saw the floor. It was beautiful. Especially the edges.

Austin stepped out onto the front porch while he finished rolling the last coat of sealant on the last section of the floor. Hannah had picked a stain that brought out the natural wood grain and wasn't oppressively dark. Scilla had preferred a dark chestnut stain, and Austin had been inclined to go with Scilla's choice, but his entire family had sided with Hannah. She'd done research at the library and said the store would look brighter and airier with a lighter stain. Mamm had practically broken a blood vessel in her neck lecturing Austin on being practical instead of just going along with what his girlfriend wanted. Dark chestnut, she had said, would show every speck of dust and would have to be swept four times a day.

As much as Austin wanted to please Scilla, Mamm and Hannah had been right. Honey pecan was a perfect color. The floor was so beautiful, it felt like a sin to walk on it.

Scilla had only been slightly offended. She had given

Hannah the cold shoulder for a couple of days, but at least Scilla was still talking to him.

Austin put the lid on the jug of sealant that sat on the porch, pulled the roller off the handle, and wiped down the handle. Now they just needed to let the floor dry, and they could start moving in shelves. It was a perfect day to finish the floor. Tomorrow was Thanksgiving, and Austin would make Mamm very unhappy if he had to finish the floor on a holiday. He felt much better about taking a day off because the floor had to dry anyway.

Hannah was going to be so excited that he'd finished the floor. She hadn't been able to come to the house today or yesterday because she and her sisters were baking about a hundred different dishes for Thanksgiving. He reassured her that she could spend a few days away from the house without the whole project falling apart while she was gone. She cared about the store as much as he did.

Austin shivered against the wind that blew across the porch. Even though Scilla wasn't happy about the floor color, he couldn't wait to show her the finished product. The walls had been patched and freshly painted. The stairs and bannisters were finished. The basement was free of spiders, mice, and those little worms that liked to crawl into abandoned spaces and die.

Since their first picnic here, Scilla had only come back twice because she was afraid of mice and afraid that the dust might give her allergies. Austin had made it a point of visiting the library almost every day to keep her updated on the store's progress and talk about organic food. Scilla had been so excited about the organic section of his market, he'd decided to put her in charge of it—which had been a nice thought but not a very *gute i*dea.

Scilla didn't know enough about business or Englischers or even organic food to put together a *gute* organic food section. So far, the only products she'd come up with were Petersheim Brothers peanut butter, gluten-free bread, and black bean veggie burger patties that she was planning to make herself. Austin hadn't had the heart to tell her that she'd need a food handler's permit and a health department–approved kitchen. He especially hadn't had the heart to tell her that nobody was going to buy those black bean burgers of hers. He felt disloyal even thinking the thought, but they tasted terrible. And Austin wasn't a picky eater.

Austin loaded his supplies in his wagon just as Gary Mast, the deacon of the district, pulled up in his buggy. He parked and climbed out, pulling the collar of his coat tighter around his neck against the wind. Gary was about seventy years old, with a salt-and-pepper gray beard and a round paunch that hung over his trousers like a muffin reaching over the edge of its paper.

Austin's gut clenched. Nobody especially liked it when the deacon paid a visit. He usually came to someone's house to call them to repentance or chastise them for doing something the church disapproved of.

Austin took a deep breath and tried to relax. The bishop had approved the store before Austin made an offer on it. Maybe the deacon was just interested in the project. Maybe he was paying a friendly visit to see how things were coming, to offer encouragement and tell Austin what a fine job he was doing. Maybe he wanted to look at the floor and encourage Austin to stain it darker. Maybe he wanted to share his opinion about black bean veggie burgers.

The deacon smiled and trudged toward Austin. The smile was comforting. Why would he smile if he was delivering bad news?

"Austin Petersheim. *Vie gehts?*"

Austin returned his smile and tried not to act suspicious. "I just finished the floor. Honey pecan. Do you want to see it?"

"I love pecans. Lois is making me a pecan pie for Thanksgiving, and I'm going to eat the whole thing." Gary laughed. He always tried to lighten the mood because people got understandably tense around him. The problem was that Gary thought he was funnier than he really was. Much funnier. Sometimes it was painful to be around him.

Austin laughed politely. "Who doesn't love pecan pie?"

The deacon stroked his hand down his beard. "They tell me you've done a lot of work to fix up the place."

Austin couldn't be comfortable. "*Jah.* Do you want to see?"

Gary's eyes twinkled in amusement. "I hear you had a squirrel in the oven. I've never had roasted squirrel. Was it good?" He threw back his head and laughed.

Austin didn't know what to do except pretend Gary was the funniest person he'd ever met. "Not as good as roasted wolverine."

The deacon laughed even harder. "I hope I never find out."

"We cleaned out the oven and the stove, and the basement is so clean, my *bruderen* think I should live down there. You should come and see."

The deacon seemed determined not to even so much as peek into Austin's house. "I'm sure the mice have all found new homes."

Maybe the deacon didn't have any particular reason to be here, and as much as Austin wanted to stand there all day and listen to Gary Mast try to make jokes, it was getting cold, and he needed to go home and milk the cows.

"It was nice of you to come by and see the house. We should be able to open in two weeks. Just in time for Christmas. Be sure to drop by."

"With all the work you've done, it wonders me if you won't be able to sell and make a *gute* profit."

"I'm . . . I'm not selling," Austin stuttered. "We're opening in two weeks, Lord willing."

The deacon lost his smile. Was he done cracking bad jokes? "Everything is going to be okay." He propped a hand on Austin's shoulder. "For sure and certain you'll land on your feet and be richer than when you started. Who wouldn't want that?"

Austin's heart lodged in his throat. "I don't understand."

"You'll need to put the house up for sale right after Thanksgiving. The bishop has withdrawn his permission for you to open a store."

Hannah was through with Austin Petersheim. Done. Finished. Giving up.

She chopped the carrots with so much spite, she sliced right into her finger. Hissing, she dropped the knife, cradled one hand in the other, and watched as blood pooled under the narrow slit in her index finger. Oh, *sis yuscht.* It hurt something wonderful, and it was Austin Petersheim's fault for distracting her. It was his fault for being stupid and *dumm* and too *wunderbarr* for words. It was his fault for making her believe she might have a chance. Everything in the world was his fault.

Austin was her friend when it was convenient, like when he needed her to get the squirrel out of the oven or scrape the wood floor or give him a free donut, but as soon as pretty, petite, uptight Priscilla Lambright showed up, it was as if Hannah turned into a piece of furniture.

And that's why she was done with him.

Hannah turned on the water and ran her finger under the faucet. Blood trickled into the sink. It always looked like more blood when you mixed it with water. She wrapped a paper towel around her finger and did her best to finish cutting the carrots. This cheesy carrot casserole wasn't going to make itself.

Aendi Linda slowly wheeled herself into the kitchen. "Is everything okay?"

"*Ach,* I cut myself. But it's not bad."

"I'm sorry. Do you need a Band-Aid?"

Hannah curled her fingers around the paper towel. "*Jah.* Once the bleeding stops."

"Let me see." Aendi Linda tried to maneuver her wheelchair closer. Hannah went to her. Aendi Linda's arms were as weak as a *buplie's*, and they were getting weaker all the time. About three years ago, she'd been diagnosed with Lyme disease, but the treatments hadn't worked and she'd started getting weaker and weaker. Soon it got harder for her to walk. Now she had a hard time lifting her arms. She needed one of those expensive battery-powered chairs. The *gmayna* could pay for part of it, but Aendi Linda and Onkel Menno still needed to come up with a great deal of money.

Hannah showed Aendi Linda her finger. "It's not too bad. I was distracted."

Aendi Linda raised an eyebrow. "Don't get distracted again. I wouldn't want you to lose a hand."

"Me either."

Aendi Linda studied Hannah's face. "Anything I can help with?"

She was so nice to ask, but Aendi Linda could barely hold a knife, let alone chop vegetables. "*Denki,* but I'm almost done. Then I can get these carrots in the steamer for the casserole." Hannah was making cheesy carrot casserole for Thanksgiving dinner tomorrow. She'd put it together here at Aendi Linda's house, then Ruth Ann or Onkel Menno could put it in the oven in the morning and bring it to Thanksgiving dinner at Hannah's house.

Aendi Linda gave Hannah a half smile. "I know I can't help with the carrots. It wonders me if I could help with the distraction yet."

Hannah felt her face get warm. "*Ach.* I don't think so. Don't worry. I'm done being distracted." Through with Austin Petersheim. Done. Finished.

"Okay," Aendi Linda said doubtfully. "If you need me, I'm just in here reading to Dinah."

Hannah usually loved that Aendi Linda noticed so much. If you were having a bad day, Aendi Linda wanted to hear about it. If you were sad about something, Aendi Linda tried to help. She always seemed to have plenty of time to listen to all your problems, even ones that might have seemed *dumm* to other people. But Hannah wasn't about to tell anybody about Austin, especially since she was through with him. Finished. Never wanted to see him again.

Which also meant she was done with the store. Let Austin's *bruderen* help him put up shelves and stock them and put prices on everything. Being done with the store also meant she was done with the donut business. She refused to go to the store every day to watch Scilla and Austin slobber all over each other. Mary and James would just have to make donuts and pretzels and goodies by themselves. To be truly away from Austin, Hannah would probably need to move to Montana and buy a log cabin with no indoor plumbing.

Maybe she could move to Colorado. They had indoor plumbing in the Amish communities in Colorado. At least that was what she'd been told.

Hannah sighed and went back to cutting carrots. She didn't really want to move to Colorado. She didn't know anyone in Colorado, and her family was here. She couldn't leave her family. Not even to get away from Austin Petersheim. But Colorado or not, she was done with him. She just didn't need the aggravation.

She tapped the cutting board so hard with her knife that the sound reverberated throughout the whole house.

"Is everything okay in there?"

"Just fine, Aendi Linda." The day after Thanksgiving, she was going to march straight to that house and tell Austin she was quitting. It wasn't like he was paying her or anything. It wasn't as if he showed any appreciation. And if he needed help, he should ask his precious Priscilla to paint and take out trash and kill spiders. Hannah would never lift another finger for Austin again.

She jumped as the back door flew open. As if he knew she'd been thinking bad thoughts about him, Austin came inside, his face as dark as a storm cloud. Sweat beaded on his forehead, and he breathed as if something was stuck in his throat.

Hannah momentarily forgot she was mad at him. She'd have plenty of time to stew after the holiday. "What's the matter?"

"Hannah," he said, wrapping his fingers around her arms as if she were some sort of lifeline. "They said I can't open the store."

"Who said? What are you talking about?"

"They want me to sell the house."

"Is that you, Austin Petersheim?" Aendi Linda called from the other room.

"It's him," Hannah called back, hoping Aendi Linda wouldn't try to wheel herself into the kitchen to greet him. Hannah had a feeling this was a conversation they needed to have in private.

"It's about time," Aendi Linda said. "Hannah's been distracted all day."

Aendi Linda saw too much, but Hannah couldn't worry about that now. She took Austin's hand and led him to a kitchen chair. Sitting down next to him, she laid her hands over his arm. "Who wants you to sell the house? What happened?"

He pressed his hand to his forehead and expelled a shuddering breath. "The deacon said the bishop changed his mind. He won't give me permission to open the store."

Hannah furrowed her brow. "But that's not fair. He already gave you permission. You got a loan. You put all that money down on the house. I don't understand."

Austin shot to his feet and paced around the small space between the fridge and the table. "It's more than unfair. It's wrong. We've already put so much work into it. I won't get my money out of it. Who else would even want to buy that house?"

"But why did he change his mind?"

"The deacon said Raymond Glick came to them last night. Raymond told them that if I opened another Amish market in town, it would compete with his Amish market and put him out of business. The deacon said it would be wrong to have two people in the same district competing against each other, and since Raymond Glick was here first, I have to sell." Austin's hands shook as he ran his fingers through his hair. Hannah's heart ached. He was barely keeping his composure.

"How could they do this to us?" Hannah murmured, even though she knew the answer.

Austin came to rest in the chair and shoved his hands through his hair again. "Raymond Glick is petty and small and resentful."

Hannah nodded. "But he's also a keen businessman. Maybe your market won't hurt Raymond's business, but Raymond isn't about to take a chance that it will."

"It doesn't help that Raymond hates our family almost as much as he hates the Honeybee Sisters. He probably feels justified in keeping me from opening my own store. It's just another way he can punish the Petersheims."

"Don't tell Abraham. He'll think it's his fault because he hit Perry Glick."

Austin frowned. "As soon as I tell my family, Abraham will blame himself anyway. But it's not his fault. Raymond would have objected to anyone opening another market in town. It's just sweet revenge on his part that it's me."

"It wonders me if he'll try to close down the donut stand next."

Austin closed his eyes and squeezed the bridge of his nose between his fingers. "I don't know what to do. Even if I sell the house, I'm up to my neck in debt. It will take years to pay off."

Every ounce of Hannah's righteous indignation bubbled to the surface. "Then the *gmayna* should pay off your loan. It's their fault. They gave you permission."

"They'd never do that." A moan came from deep in Austin's throat. He covered his eyes with his hand as great sobs wracked his body.

Hannah had never seen him cry before, and his raw pain

tore her apart. She wrapped her arms around his shoulders and pulled him close to her. Aendi Linda wheeled herself halfway into the kitchen. Hannah glanced in her direction, and understanding flashed in Linda's eyes. She wheeled herself back out of the kitchen, leaving Hannah and Austin to face their pain together.

Hannah pulled back as Austin lifted his head and swiped the tears from his eyes. "This is my fault. I was so excited about the store, but deep in my heart I wanted to get back at Raymond and his family for mistreating Benji and Emma and Abraham. Gotte saw what was really in my heart. He's punishing me for being so spiteful."

"The store was my idea because you wanted to sell more peanut butter." She gave him a half smile. "But the added benefit of irritating Raymond might have crossed my mind."

"It settled in my heart. I don't know how to forgive him."

Hannah took his hand. "You didn't borrow all that money, spend hours fixing up that house, or take a huge risk just because you wanted revenge on Raymond. Of course it was in the back of your mind, but that is not why you did it. And if Gotte punished us for all the bad thoughts or motives we had, we'd all be in a very sorry state."

He took a deep breath. "I really did want that house to be a nice place people could come to shop." A small smile flitted across his face. "I finished the floor this afternoon."

Hannah tilted her head. "How does it look?"

"Beautiful." He slumped his shoulders. "Maybe someone will want to buy it."

"It's in much better shape than when you bought it." It wasn't much encouragement, but it was something.

Austin scrubbed his hand down the side of his face.

"I don't know what to do. I feel hollow, as if a robber has come into my house and stolen my furniture."

"Then let's figure out what we can do to get your furniture back."

That coaxed a smile from his lips. "I might have to sleep on the floor."

"If you can sell the house, I still think the *gmayna* could be persuaded to pay at least part of your loan. At the very least, the bishop should feel very bad for what he's done to you."

"The deacon said the bishop thought I was only going to sell peanut butter. Raymond Glick couldn't object to that since he won't carry it in his market."

Hannah shook her head, remembering how she'd gotten the idea for a store in the first place. "Peanut butter and shovels. The Glicks don't carry shovels either."

"It wonders me if they sell black bean veggie burgers."

Hannah felt a rush of wind blow through her mind. She caught her breath. "You don't have to sell that house."

"I guess I could rent it to someone. I can't afford to live in it."

She grabbed his arm and yanked him toward her.

"Ouch!" he said. "What was that for?"

"The deacon said you can't open the store because it would be competing with the Glicks, right?"

"Raymond got to him. He's very forceful when he thinks he's right."

Hannah squeezed Austin's arm. "I know how to persuade the bishop to let you open the store."

The hope in Austin's expression made her heart pound against her chest. "But how?"

"We need to go see the bishop right now." Laughter

tripped from her mouth. "And we need to gather some friends right quick."

Austin raised an eyebrow. "What have you got in mind?"

"Raymond Glick has made his own bed. Now he can lie in it."

Chapter Ten

"This is a bad idea," Scilla said, wringing her hands as if she was trying to squeeze all the skin off them. "You should never go against the bishop."

Through the heavy snow, Austin pulled the buggy in front of the bishop's house and laid a hand over Scilla's laced fingers. He loved that Scilla was always so concerned about doing the right thing, even though her hesitation made her timid. "I'm not going against the bishop. We're just trying to get him to change his mind."

She wasn't reassured. "I shouldn't have come. The bishop is going to be irritated, and he's going to think I had something to do with it. If we all just obeyed the bishop, things would be so much better."

Austin tried not to be irritated. Scilla was a sweet, demure girl who didn't like conflict or bad feelings. "But you want me to open the store, don't you?"

She shifted in her seat. "I suppose. But not if it's going to get you in trouble with the bishop."

"It won't get me in any trouble. We're just going to have a talk."

Crist Stoltzfus wasn't one of those bishops who liked

getting people in trouble. He was fair and nice and didn't act like he loved being in charge like some other bishops Austin had heard about. Some bishops liked to have complete control of the district and were quite severe when someone broke the rules. Some bishops were so strict that people actually moved to other districts just to be away from them. Most bishops just wanted to preach the Bible on Sundays and lead the district as best they could without being so rigid they couldn't bend a little. Crist Stoltzfus was one of those bishops. He tolerated Bitsy Weaver's hair and her fingernail polish. He gave the children candy when he saw them on the street. He even approved special heaters for buggies because Wisconsin winters got wonderful cold and a buggy ride to church shouldn't give someone pneumonia.

But Austin couldn't be comfortable. The bishop's decision was still the final word on anything in the district. And if Crist sided with Raymond Glick, Austin was lost.

Another buggy pulled in front of Austin's. Bitsy and Yost Weaver got out. They were both wrapped tightly against the cold. Yost wore a hat with ear flaps, a heavy coat, and a thick red scarf. Bitsy wore a puffy coat and a pink scarf. A strand of purple hair peeked out from under her black bonnet. Bitsy Weaver was not a conventional Amish *fraa.* She had lived as an Englischer for over twenty years and hadn't altogether given up some of her old ways. She often dyed her hair strange and exciting colors, and sometimes she wore earrings and fingernail polish. But Bitsy was a dear and loyal friend to the Petersheims. When Andrew's wife, Mary, had returned to the community, pregnant and alone, Bitsy had taken her in. There wasn't a better example of Christian charity in the whole district, and Austin needed her help tonight. Bitsy was not afraid of ruffling the bishop's feathers.

Maybe because she always ruffled the bishop's feathers.

Scilla looked out the window and narrowed her eyes as Bitsy waved at Austin. She wrapped her arms around her waist. "I shouldn't have let you talk me into this. I'm staying in the buggy."

Austin gave her a warm smile. Scilla was delicate and easily distressed. He completely sympathized with her. She must have been terrified at the prospect of visiting the bishop's house. Austin had known her long enough to understand she needed a little reassurance, a tender reminder of what she meant to him. "You know I would never let anything bad happen to you, don't you?"

She seemed to loosen her grip around her waist. "You have always been my protector."

"I'm sure you're uneasy about this, Scilla. If you want to stay here, I understand. I brought some extra blankets. You should be warm enough, but I hate to leave you out here all by yourself. Why don't you come in? You won't have to say a word."

"Can't you take me home first?"

Austin's stomach sank to his toes. He'd be half an hour later than everyone else. That didn't seem like a *gute* way to start things out with the bishop. But if that was what Scilla wanted, he would do it for her. He didn't know a lot, but sacrifice seemed like something people did for love.

He gazed out the window. Big flakes of snow drifted to the ground, and the snow was starting to stick to the roads. It wouldn't be an easy journey there or back. "Okay. I will take you home."

Hannah appeared on his side of the buggy. With a wide smile on her face, she knocked on the window. "You coming?" she said, making her voice loud so he could hear her.

The weight on his chest got heavier. "Start without me."

Hannah frowned, then slid Austin's door open. "We can't start without you. You are the reason for the meeting."

He glanced at Scilla. Did he love her or not? "Scilla wants to go home. I'll take her and come right back."

"The storm is getting worse. We don't want to be out too late or we may never get home on these roads."

"I'll hurry."

Hannah's mouth twitched downward as her gaze flicked in Scilla's direction. Then in a second the expression was gone, and she smiled as if she couldn't be more overjoyed with the delay. "Okay then. We'll be waiting for you." She held up a large brown paper bag. "I brought donuts. No one can resist a donut." She leaned a little closer. "Except maybe Raymond Glick."

Austin chuckled as Hannah closed his door. He grinned at Scilla. "Hannah thinks her donuts cure disease."

Scilla pursed her lips. "They're not even organic."

"I guess not, but the bishop loves her donuts." Austin released the brake and reluctantly guided his horse back onto the road, reminding himself how much he cared about Scilla. No sacrifice was too great.

Scilla was stiff as a board, with her arms still clamped around her waist. "Why did she bring donuts? This isn't even her meeting."

"The meeting was her idea. And a wonderful *gute* one."

"It was her idea to get you in trouble with the bishop?"

Austin drew his brows together. "*Nae.* She wants to save the store. And she's brave enough to talk to the bishop."

Scilla looked at him as if he'd just insulted her black bean veggie burgers. "You don't think I'm brave?"

Austin didn't know quite how to respond. What exactly did Scilla want to hear? "Of course you're brave. You work at the library and talk to Englischers all day. And you reshelve books, even if you have to climb a ladder."

"But you think Hannah is braver?"

Austin felt himself stepping into a trap, but didn't know how to avoid it. "I never said that."

"Just because I don't want to get in trouble with the bishop doesn't mean I'm afraid."

"Of course not. You're delicate and shy, and you don't like confrontation. I like you just the way you are. But I need Hannah's courage tonight. She has a wonderful *gute* idea, and she's not afraid to talk to the bishop."

Scilla stuck out her bottom lip. "I have talents."

Uh, okay. "*Jah,* you do."

"Don't you think what I have to say is important?"

Austin didn't know what to do except be agreeable. "It's very important."

"Then turn around. I'm going to that meeting. I have some things I want to say, and I don't care if the bishop has me shunned."

Austin wasn't sure what to do. Maybe it would be better to take Scilla home. Just what was she getting up the courage to say? And would it ruin his chances of getting his store back? Shoving his misgivings aside, Austin turned the buggy around. He couldn't hesitate when he really needed to get to that meeting. Hannah could always keep Scilla quiet with a donut if they got desperate.

Ach, Scilla didn't eat Hanna's donuts. They weren't organic. But Austin still had a week-old BM cookie in his pocket. Maybe that would do.

Thankfully, Austin and Scilla weren't the last to arrive. Mayne, the bishop's wife, invited them into the living room and told them to sit wherever they wanted. Mayne didn't even look suspicious or curious as to why they were there. A lack of curiosity was probably a *gute* quality for a bishop's wife to possess. There was probably a lot less anxiety in not knowing and not having to care.

The house carried the sweet, tart smell of freshly baked apple pie. It was the night before Thanksgiving, and just like most of the *fraaen* in the *gmayna,* Mayne had been getting a head start on her baking. Austin loved Thanksgiving if for no other reason than the smells.

Hannah's face lit up like a lantern when Austin walked in. "You're back sooner than I'd hoped."

Scilla nodded decisively. "I have something to say." And it appeared she was going to say it right now. With feeling. "I have as much courage as anyone, and I think the bishop should let Austin open his store."

Hannah's smile faltered. "Okay. *Denki,* Scilla."

That was very nice of Scilla. Austin swallowed hard. Lord willing, she'd lose her courage before the bishop actually came in the room.

Hannah sat on a folding chair next to Ruth Ann and Dinah, Benji and Alfie. They had debated the wisdom of bringing children but had finally both agreed that *die kinner* might be able to help persuade the bishop. Bitsy and Yost Weaver sat on the sofa next to Dan and Lily Kanagy. Lily was one of the Honeybee Sisters. It had been Hannah's idea to ask them to come.

Hannah stood up, folded down the sides of her paper bag, and offered donuts to everyone. Everybody but Scilla took a donut, and Alfie tried to take two. "*Nae,* Alfie," Hannah said. "We've got to save some for the bishop."

Just as Scilla and Austin sat down, Mayne answered the door to Abraham, Austin's *bruder,* and Emma, Abraham's fiancée. Austin stood and shook Abraham's hand warmly. Abraham was thoughtful and quiet, and Austin knew how hard things like this were for him—sort of like they were for Scilla. Abraham didn't like to make waves, and he certainly didn't want any attention. He'd been mortified when he'd hit Perry Glick because that kind of thing definitely drew attention. Warmth spread through Austin's chest. Abraham had come because Austin needed him. And nothing else mattered.

Emma and Abraham each got a donut and sat down on the folding chairs on the far side of the sofa. They didn't touch each other, and it was supposed to be a secret that they were engaged, but anyone who saw them together could guess they loved each other very much. Austin loved the way Emma looked at Abraham and the way Abraham looked at Emma. Scilla often looked at him like that, as if the sun rose and set by him. Austin sat up a little straighter. Well, he was a *gute* catch. Any girl would be blessed to have him as a husband, and Scilla adored him. It was one of the things he liked most about her.

The bishop, Crist Stoltzfus, came into the room as if he'd been hiding just outside waiting for everybody to get there. Austin's face got warm. Lord willing the bishop hadn't heard Scilla trying to be courageous. They needed to handle this very carefully if they were going to get his approval.

Crist wasn't yet sixty years old, but his beard was nearly as white as the snow on the ground. His face was deeply lined, especially around his mouth, and Austin had never seen him without that look of worry in his eyes. That was what came of being a bishop for two decades. The years of solving problems, preaching sermons, and making hard decisions had taken their toll. Lord willing, Austin would never be bishop. Or minister. And most hopefully not deacon.

The bishop couldn't have been happy to see any of them, having a pretty *gute* idea of why they had come, at least why Austin had come. But he was kind enough to shake hands and give everyone a genuine smile. It seemed genuine. Maybe it wasn't, and he'd simply had years of practice making it look so. His smile sort of froze when he caught sight of Bitsy and her purple hair, but he shook her hand warmly with both of his. "It is *gute* to see you, Bitsy and Yost. I hear you're going to plant some cherry trees."

Bitsy nodded. "A half dozen. Bees like cherry blossoms, and they bloom at a different time than the apples."

Bitsy loved coloring her hair and keeping bees. She'd do just about anything for her bees.

"They're going where some of the soybean crop used to be," Yost said.

The bishop knelt down to be eye level with Ruth Ann and Dinah and the twins. "Are you excited for Thanksgiving?" he asked.

Alfie nodded. "Mamm made three kinds of pie."

Austin half expected Scilla to mention that pie wasn't nutritious, but she didn't make a peep. Her lips were pinched tightly together, and her hands were clasped securely in her lap. The bishop's presence seemed to have rendered her mute. Austin breathed a sigh of relief. Scilla had lost her courage.

"Alfie doesn't like stuffing," Benji said. "But I do. Mamm says I can eat as much as I want."

The bishop nodded. "I like stuffing too. And yams."

Benji made a face. "I hate yams, but I can eat them if they have sugar and marshmallows." He furrowed his brow. "But it's okay if you like them."

The bishop chuckled. "I'm *froh* you think so."

Hannah held out her bag. "I brought you some donuts."

The bishop lit up like an electric bulb. "Chocolate?"

"Of course."

He reached into Hannah's bag, pulled out a chocolate donut smothered with chocolate frosting, and took a big bite. "I'm going to get fat."

Bitsy held up what was left of her donut. "But what a way to go."

Everyone except Scilla laughed. She was probably afraid the bishop would disapprove of her laughing during such a solemn occasion.

The bishop took another bite, looked around the room, and sank into the empty recliner. No one had sat in that recliner. They all instinctively knew it belonged to the bishop. "So, Austin Petersheim, I was expecting a visit. I wasn't expecting you'd bring all your friends and neighbors."

Austin felt Scilla tense beside him. Nope. She wasn't likely to say anything. "I suppose you know what I want to talk to you about."

The bishop braced his hands on the armrests. "I suppose I do."

At Linda's kitchen table earlier that day, Hannah had given Austin some very *gute* advice. Everyone wanted to be heard and understood. Even the bishop. Austin folded his hands in his lap. "Can you explain why you made the decision you did? About not letting me open my store?" He kept his tone neutral so the bishop wouldn't think he was being accused.

The bishop raised his brows and studied Austin's face. He obviously hadn't been expecting that question. "As I told Gary, I'm concerned that another market in town would create too much competition that might put you both out of business. And it would not be *gute* for harmony in the *gmayna* if you and the Glicks are competing with each other. The Glicks have had that market and restaurant for over thirty years. It wouldn't be fair for you to open a market to compete with theirs."

Austin bit his tongue on the tart reply that wanted to escape his mouth. Even though Raymond Glick was spiteful and selfish, Austin could tell the bishop was trying to be fair, even if his decision would ruin Austin financially. The bishop probably didn't understand that everything Austin had was tied to that house.

Austin nodded thoughtfully. "So is your main concern about my store competing with Glick's Amish Market?"

"*Jah.* The whole district will take sides."

Surely the bishop knew that the whole district had already taken sides. Austin leaned forward and propped his hands on his knees. "I have a proposal for you, a way to still open my store without competing with Raymond Glick. Could I share it with you?"

The bishop didn't seem all that eager to hear what Austin had to say, but he nodded his head.

Austin motioned toward Abraham. He'd already warned his *bruder* that it might get uncomfortable for him, but Abraham had been more than willing. He was loyal to a fault. "As you know, Abraham punched Perry Glick last summer when Perry kissed Emma without her permission."

Both Abraham and Emma turned a darker shade of red, but neither said anything.

"That is water under the bridge," the bishop said. "Everyone has forgiven and forgotten."

Well, Raymond hadn't done either, but Austin wasn't going to argue with the bishop about it. "Now Raymond refuses to buy our peanut butter."

The bishop stroked his white beard. "I'm sorry to say it, but I can't blame him."

"I can't either," Austin said. "I might have done the same thing if someone smacked one of my *bruderen.*"

The bishop seemed pleased with that answer. "I'm *froh* you can understand."

Austin pointed to Lily Kanagy. "Will you tell the bishop what happened between you and Paul?"

Lily gave Austin a sweet smile. His heart swelled. Some of Lily's past experiences with the Glicks had been very painful, but like Abraham, she had set her own discomfort aside to help Austin. She would never know how much he appreciated it.

"I know what happened between Lily and Paul," the bishop said. "It's all water under the bridge."

"If you'd just listen," Austin said. "I'm trying to help you see why it might be okay for me to open a store."

The bishop shrugged.

"As you know," Lily said, "Paul was quite hurt when I called it off with him and married Dan. But that wasn't all. He had been taking advantage of our family and paying me half of what our honey was worth." Lily looked around the room. "I've never told anybody but Bitsy, and there is no need to spread any of this outside of this room. Benji, Alfie? Ruth Ann and Dinah? Do you understand?"

All four children nodded, though it wasn't likely that

anyone but Ruth Ann had any idea what Lily was talking about.

Bitsy grunted. "When Lily broke up with Paul, the Glicks stopped buying our honey and refused to let us buy anything in their store. I don't want you to think it was a bad thing they stopped buying our honey. We're getting twice as much for it from a store in Shawano."

"I'm *froh* to hear it." The bishop was obviously uncomfortable with all this dirty-laundry airing, even though for sure and certain he'd heard all of it before.

Dan Kanagy chimed in. "Raymond Glick thinks my *dat* cheated him out of some property years ago. He won't let my *dat s*hop there either. And since I married Lily, the whole Kanagy family has been banned from setting foot in the market."

The bishop must have heard enough. He pinned Austin with a serious eye. "What is all this leading to?"

Benji pulled his collar down and tilted his head, though the bruise Perry had given him had long since disappeared. "Perry Glick pinched my neck. I got a big bruise."

"I have talked with Perry Glick about hurting little children," the bishop said. "He won't do it again."

Austin mussed Benji's hair. "My *mamm* won't allow them to go back anyway."

The bishop sighed. "I'm sorry that all these things happened, I truly am. But what does this have to do with your store?"

Austin looked at Hannah. It was her turn. She was better at this kind of thing than Austin ever could be. "First of all, Bishop, the people who are not allowed to shop at Glick's Market need a place to shop."

The bishop sat up as if he'd just started paying attention. "You're right about that. If Raymond's is the only store in town, then he shouldn't be allowed to ban certain people from coming in." He bounced his fist on the armrest. "I will have a talk with him. If he refuses to serve everyone in the *gmayna,* then Austin should be allowed to open his store."

"And parents need to feel confident that if they send their children to the store, they won't come home with bruises." Hannah said it cheerfully enough, but the power of her words seemed to strike the bishop right between the eyes.

"I'll make it clear to the entire Glick family."

Austin's heart beat faster. Hannah had convinced the bishop to consider another point of view, to consider that maybe Raymond Glick hadn't exactly been taking the high road. He could have kissed her—but not really because the only girl he wanted to kiss was Scilla.

Hannah didn't smile, but her eyes danced with brilliant fire. "Secondly, Bishop, if Austin sells his peanut butter at his new store, that wouldn't be competing with the Glicks because they don't sell Petersheim Brothers peanut butter."

The bishop had taken to tugging at the hairs of his eyebrow. "That's true."

"And if he sells Honeybee Sisters honey at his store, that wouldn't be competing because Raymond won't sell Honeybee Sisters honey in his store."

"People around here have to make a special trip to my house if they want to buy it," Bitsy said.

Hannah laced her fingers together. "So, would there be anything wrong with Austin selling only things in his store that people can't get at Glick's?"

The bishop nearly yanked out an eyebrow hair. "I don't know."

"They don't sell carrots," Benji said. "Or cabbage."

"Or organic," Scilla squeaked. It was so soft, the bishop probably hadn't heard her, but Austin gave her credit for trying. And she was right. As far as he knew, the Glicks didn't sell anything organic in their store.

Hannah gave Austin a private smile that sent his blood pulsing through his veins. She truly was remarkable. "We are moving our donut and pretzel stand inside Austin's store. We plan on making bread and pies and cakes that will directly compete with Glick's Restaurant, but we have always sold baked goods at our donut stand, so it seems fair to let us keep on doing it. And the Zooks and Beilers feed tourists at their homes when Englischers pay for a tour. Glick's don't seem to be concerned about that competition."

The bishop frowned. "*Ach,* they're concerned all right."

Austin was suddenly more sympathetic to the bishop than he had ever been. How many complaints from Raymond Glick had he fended off?

"Glick's Restaurant isn't going to suffer just because the Beilers and the Zooks feed tourists to bring in a little extra income." The bishop had obviously had this conversation before.

Hannah must have anticipated all of Raymond's objections beforehand. "It will be even better for Raymond when we move out of the center of town because the donut stand will be farther away from his restaurant and less likely to compete."

"They don't sell cherries," Ruth Ann offered.

Alfie slumped his shoulders. "They sell dog food."

"It would be a *gute* place to sell Andrew Petersheim's

furniture and woodwork," Dan said, "because of course, Glick's won't sell it in their store."

"They have clocks," Dinah said.

The bishop had fallen silent several seconds ago. He held his beard in two hands like he was holding on to two handles. Benji opened his mouth to say something, but Alfie poked him with his elbow. Alfie was a smart one. Some moments were better blanketed in silence. Every eye focused on the bishop. Austin held his breath.

The bishop looked at Bitsy, then at Hannah, and then at Austin. "Okay, Austin," he finally said. "You've got your store."

The children seemed to erupt from the sofa. Benji, Ruth Ann, and Dinah joined hands in a circle and danced around the room. Alfie pumped his fist in the air and yelled happy things to the sky.

The rest of them had a more quiet celebration. Bitsy and Yost were all smiles, and Dan laughed. Scilla nodded in satisfaction, and Hannah clapped her hands. Her smile took Austin's breath away. He'd been in the depths of despair only a few hours ago, and now he felt like floating to the ceiling. It was all because of Hannah.

"Alfie, Benji, settle down," Austin said. "You're in the bishop's living room."

The bishop seemed happy and troubled at the same time—probably wondering how he would break this to Raymond Glick, although the bishop seldom delivered bad news to anyone. That was what the deacon was for. "Please remember the conditions, Austin. You can't sell anything in your store that Raymond carries in his."

Hannah put her arm around Dinah. "Would it be fair to clarify that Austin isn't allowed to sell anything the Glicks have in their store *today?* Because much as I respect Raymond," she said with a straight face, "I'm afraid that when he hears our agreement, he'll start stocking all sorts of things on his shelves he's never had before."

"Like carrots," Benji said.

"That seems fair to me," the bishop said, standing up. He probably wanted all these people out of his house. "We'll talk to Raymond after Thanksgiving."

And by "we" he most likely meant Gary Mast.

The snow was falling in thick white clusters when they left the bishop's house. Austin shook so many hands, he probably shook a few twice. He even shook Hannah's hand when he really wanted to give her a hug. He smiled so hard, his cheeks ached. But it was a *gute* ache, and Hannah smiled back at him. "I can't believe it. My store is back in business!"

Hannah raised her face to the sky, caught some snowflakes on her tongue, and cheered at the top of her lungs. "This is the best day ever."

"I couldn't have done it without you." Austin looked around at his family and friends. "Any of you."

"He was doubly convinced when I mentioned organic," Scilla said.

Austin laughed at the pure joy of the moment. "*Jah,* he was." And because he wanted to be encouraging, he said, "You were very brave. *Denki.*"

Scilla smiled. "I was, wasn't I? It's all thanks to you, Austin. You have a way of making me believe I can do anything."

Austin loved the way Scilla looked at him, like he was the smartest, most important person in the world. Like he was a slice of whole wheat, organic bread slathered with homemade organic raspberry jam.

He would have liked to stand gazing into Scilla's eyes

forever, but it was cold out here and he had to get Scilla and the boys home. Hannah had been kind enough to pick up the boys and bring them, but even though he wanted to be alone with Scilla, Hannah shouldn't have to go out of her way to take his *bruderen* home.

He pulled his gaze from Scilla. "*Denki* for everything, Hannah."

But she wasn't there.

He frowned at Bitsy. "What happened to Hannah?"

"She left with the little girls," Bitsy said, glaring at Austin as if it was his fault. She looked up. "Dear Lord, please give Austin Petersheim some brains before it's too late."

Austin had no idea what she was talking about, but everybody knew Bitsy prayed right out loud and said things no one could understand. He wasn't going to worry too much about it.

"We're still here," Alfie said, with a smug twist of his lips. "And we're riding home with you and Scilla."

"I call front," Benji said.

Austin looked around as if Hannah was hiding behind a bush waiting for him to find her. Had she really gone like that without even saying good-bye? She always said good-bye. Was she worried about the snow?

All of a sudden, irritation just bubbled up inside him. Had she been in such a hurry that she couldn't even say one final congratulations before she left?

What was her problem?

Chapter Eleven

"I'm not going in there," Ruth Ann said, folding her arms like she always did when she was being stubborn. "Perry Glick will pinch me."

"He will not," Alfie said, with more confidence than he felt. "The bishop told him not to pinch people anymore."

Tintin showed his agreement by barking and licking Alfie's hand. It was nice to have someone around who understood Alfie so well. Tintin would never let him down. That was why Alfie had brought Tintin with them, just in case any pinching happened.

Dinah's eyes got big. "Will he pinch me?"

Ruth Ann nodded. "Perry likes to pinch little kids. He got Benji right on the neck."

Benji pulled down his collar, showing Dinah the place where it had happened.

Alfie held tightly to Tintin's leash. "It's better now, and the bishop told Perry to be nice."

Ruth Ann shuffled her feet, her boots crunching in the snow where she stepped. "Then why don't you go? We'll stay out here and watch."

"I can't go in. They'll get suspicious. And we can't take a dog into the store."

Dinah's lower lip trembled. "You have to come. You need to protect us."

Benji put his hand on Dinah's shoulder. "I'll protect you."

Benji was a *gute* partner, but sometimes he didn't think. "Benji, you can't go in there. Mamm said."

Benji looked very unhappy. "I'm sorry, Dinah, but Alfie is right. Mamm has forgiven us from going in Glick's Market ever again."

"*Forbidden* us, Benji. Not forgiven."

"*Jah,*" Benji said. "She yelled at us, even though I was the one who got a bruise. She should have yelled at Perry."

"Well," Ruth Ann said, leaning against the telephone pole that was just across the road from Glick's Market, "we're not going in there if you're not. We don't want to get pinched. We'll stay out here with Tintin."

Alfie groaned. "*Ach,* come on. It's too cold, and don't you want your *mamm* to get a new wheelchair?"

Ruth Ann stepped forward and narrowed her eyes as if she was trying to see into Alfie's brain. "How are you going to get our *mamm* a new wheelchair?"

Alfie held Ruth Ann's stare, just so she thought he had everything under control. "We have to concentrate on one problem at a time, and right now, we need to get Hannah and Austin to marry each other."

Ruth Ann didn't even blink. "You don't have a wheelchair plan, do you?"

Much as Alfie hated to admit any such thing, he also didn't want to lie. "I'm working on Hannah and Austin first."

Ruth Ann looked at Alfie like he was a pile of mice

droppings. "How will spying on the Glicks make Austin and Hannah fall in love?"

"We're not spying on the Glicks. We're spying on the store. We've got to tell Austin what they don't have so he can put it in his store. If Austin can open his store, he and Hannah will see each other almost every day, and he'll never see Scilla because she works at the library. For sure and certain Hannah and Austin will fall in love."

Dinah stepped behind Ruth Ann. "I'll get pinched."

"You won't get pinched."

Benji put his arm around Dinah and talked to her in a baby voice. "It's okay. We'll go in with you." He looked at Alfie. "Mamm never has to know."

"Mamm always knows." But they'd have to take the chance of getting found out. The girls weren't going to go in unless Benji and Alfie were there to protect them. He might as well get used to it. Sometimes girls just needed boys. "Okay," he said. He looped Tintin's leash around the telephone pole and clipped it to itself. Tintin whined and showed Alfie his sad eyes, but Alfie couldn't help it. He hated leaving Tintin out in the snow, but Perry would definitely pinch them if they brought their dog in the store.

Alfie pulled his walkie-talkie out of his pocket. "Benji, you and Dinah go first. Take your walkie-talkie, but only use it in an emergency. Me and Ruth Ann will come in second. We're looking for things that the Glicks don't have in the store."

Benji frowned. "How can we look for things that aren't there?"

Alfie sighed out his irritation. "Just do it, Benji."

Benji shrugged. "Okay. Come on, Dinah." He took Dinah's hand, and they walked across the road together and into the store. Dinah laid her free hand over the right side of her neck for a little extra protection.

"Okay," Alfie said. "Let's go."

"I want to hold the walkie-talkie," Ruth Ann said.

"*Nae.* That's the boy's job."

"You're making that up. It can be the girl's job too."

Alfie ground his teeth together. They never should have asked Ruth Ann and Dinah for help getting Austin married. Girls were nothing but trouble. "Okay. You can hold the walkie-talkie, but don't push any buttons. They make noise."

Ruth Ann looked disgusted. "I know."

He handed her the walkie-talkie and started across the snowy road. Ruth Ann just stood there like a bump on a log. "Are you coming?"

"Aren't you going to hold my hand?"

Alfie had never been more disgusted. "Of course I'm not going to hold your hand."

"Benji held Dinah's hand."

"Dinah's a little kid." Alfie crossed the road, not even waiting to see if Ruth Ann followed. He wasn't going to hold her hand, and if she didn't like it, she could just stay out here with Tintin and freeze to death.

By the time Alfie got to the door, Ruth Ann was right behind him. It was *gute* she had come, mostly because she had the walkie-talkie. You never knew when you were going to need a walkie-talkie.

The front counter with the cash register faced the door. Paul Glick was helping two Englisch customers and didn't even see Alfie and Ruth Ann come in. They quickly ducked behind the first aisle. Paul probably wasn't a pincher like Perry, but it was *gute* they didn't have to find out.

Alfie and Ruth Ann walked up one aisle and down another. When they met Dinah and Benji in an aisle, they turned around and walked the other way as if they didn't know each other. Dinah giggled every time they saw each other down one of the aisles, but other than that, they tried to be completely silent. Alfie had warned everybody that really *gute* spies were as silent as bobcats. They were a lot less likely to get caught or pinched that way.

Alfie and Ruth Ann strolled down the aisle with the small plastic bins of candy lining the shelves. This was Alfie's favorite aisle—any kind of candy you could want in every color imaginable. Ruth Ann picked up a tub of lemon drops, shook it softly, and put it back. "I don't know what they don't have," she said. "It looks like they've got everything in this store."

"Check to see if they have peanut clusters."

Ruth Ann rolled her eyes and picked up the tub right in front of her. "Of course they have peanut clusters. And those disgusting licorice things."

Alfie caught his breath as he heard Benji's voice plain as day coming from what sounded like the direction of the front counter. "Do you have potato chips?"

Ruth Ann's eyes nearly popped out of her head. She'd heard him too. They sneaked past two aisles and peeked around the corner of the end aisle. Benji and Dinah bravely stood at the counter looking up at Paul Glick as if they were sure he wasn't going to pinch them, even though Dinah's hand rested protectively over her neck.

Alfie held his breath as Paul Glick looked down at Benji as if he was a fly pooping on Paul's counter. "Do you have money?"

Benji answered the question without really answering it. "We get money every summer when we sell tomatoes."

"We don't have potato chips," Paul finally answered, as if it was really a trial to be talking to a couple of kids.

Alfie's heart raced. They didn't have potato chips! Austin could make a lot of money just selling potato chips.

"Do you have candy bars, like Snickers?" Benji said.

Paul scowled. "We've got candy on aisle three. Go find what you want and quit bothering me."

No candy bars. This day was just getting better and better.

To Alfie's surprise, Dinah spoke up. "Do you have books?"

Ruth Ann tensed beside him. She was nervous for Dinah, but she didn't need to worry. Benji would protect her little sister.

Paul looked at Dinah as if trying to figure out why a six-year-old was asking him a question. "We don't have books. That's what the library is for."

Benji and Dinah smiled at each other. Alfie smiled with his heart. They didn't have books, not even Wisconsin travel books. Englischers loved books about Wisconsin. And Amish people.

Austin was going to be rich.

"Do you have soda pop?" Benji said, though Alfie had no idea why he would ask that. Mamm wouldn't let them drink soda.

Paul started growling. "Are you going to buy something or not?"

Alfie saw Benji flinch, but he never lost his courage. He slid his finger into his pocket and pulled out some money, though where he'd gotten it, Alfie had no idea. "What can I buy for this much?" Benji said, laying his coins on the counter.

Paul was quickly losing his patience. His face got red.

"Thirteen cents doesn't buy anything in this store. Go away and quit bothering me."

"Not even a gumball?" Benji said, widening his eyes like he did when he wanted people to think he was just a sweet little kid.

Paul clenched his teeth. "We don't have gumballs."

Benji gave Paul the biggest smile Alfie had ever seen. Alfie couldn't believe how brave Benji was acting. "No gumballs? That's wonderful nice."

Paul slapped his hand on the counter. Dinah jumped. Benji took her hand. "Get out of my store. I don't have time for this."

"But the bishop said you can't kick us out," Benji said, still with those big eyes that usually got grown-ups to do exactly what he wanted.

Paul wasn't budging. He leaned over the counter. "I told the bishop I would let the Petersheims shop here, but I didn't say I'd let them loiter around my store and stir up trouble."

Alfie didn't know what *loiter* meant, but it sounded bad, and if Paul told Mamm that he and Benji had been loitering, she might give them the spatula. It was time for them to go, even though they hadn't finished their mission. Alfie grabbed Ruth Ann's hand and pulled her to the front counter. Then he grabbed Dinah's hand, and since Benji was holding her hand, Alfie managed to get all of them at once. He pulled them out the front door, and then letting go of hands, they breathlessly raced across the road. Tintin barked and licked Alfie's face when he rested his hand against the telephone pole and doubled over to catch his breath.

He looked up. Ruth Ann was smiling at him as if she'd won a contest or something. "You held my hand," she said.

He made a face. "I had to rescue you."

Ruth Ann propped her hands on her hips and studied his face. "I didn't need rescuing, and you know it. Why did you hold my hand?" She got that weird glimmer in her eyes like girls did when they wanted to chase you on the playground.

Benji hugged Dinah, then bent over and hugged Tintin. Tintin wasn't easy to hug. He got so excited he nearly knocked Benji to the ground. "Did you hear, Alfie?" Benji said. "They don't have gumballs."

Alfie forgot about stupid Ruth Ann Yutzy. "They don't have gumballs or potato chips." He laughed. "You two were so brave."

Ruth Ann hooked her arm around Dinah's shoulder. "So brave."

Dinah grinned. "We couldn't find anything they didn't have, and Benji said, 'Let's go ask.' I was scared, but I didn't even get pinched."

"But, Benji," Ruth Ann said. "You left your money."

Benji frowned. "I guess Paul can have it. Maybe he won't tell Mamm we were here."

Ruth Ann pulled a small notebook and pencil from her coat pocket and started writing. "Okay. No gumballs, no potato chips, and no soda pop."

"Or books," Dinah added.

"Good, Dinah. No books."

Even though he wished he hadn't invited the girls, Alfie had to appreciate that Ruth Ann had thought ahead. They needed to keep a list so they could tell Austin what they had learned.

Ruth Ann wrote more notes. "They don't have penne

pasta. You can make a lot of salads with penne pasta. Austin should know."

Even though he didn't like girls, Alfie had to appreciate that Ruth Ann had *gute* ears, and that she knew what penny pasta was.

Benji reached down and patted Tintin's ears. "You know what else they don't have? Ice cream."

Dinah's eyes lit up. "We need to tell Austin."

Alfie's heart raced. Austin could sell gallons, *gallons,* of ice cream in double-decker cones. It was going to be the best summer ever.

Ruth Ann tore the page out of her notebook and handed it to Alfie. "Give this to Austin immediately."

Alfie nodded. There was no time to waste.

Benji unhooked Tintin from the telephone pole. "We have to go, Alfie. Mamm will be mad if we're late for dinner."

"We don't have to go home yet," Ruth Ann said with a smirky look on her face. "We're going to the library."

"The library?"

Dinah giggled. "We're going to take all the books off the shelf and make Scilla mad. That was Ruth Ann's idea."

Ruth Ann nudged her little sister. "We don't want anybody to know."

"We're *gute* spies," Benji said, "and *gute* spies never tell."

Alfie beamed at Ruth Ann. Maybe she really did want to help Alfie and Benji get out of the cellar.

Maybe girls weren't so bad after all.

He watched as Dinah and Ruth Ann ran in the direction of the library. It was too cold to stay outside very long. Unfortunately, Alfie and Benji still had a half-hour walk home. "Come on, Benji. Mamm will be suspicious if we show up late for dinner."

They decided to take the shortcut behind Glick's Family Market and into the vacant lot and pasture beyond. The snow was deep, but cutting across the pasture was the quickest way home. They both had *gute* boots, and Tintin could dig them out if they got stuck in the snow.

Once they got through the pasture, the going was a little easier. The dirt road had some ice puddles, but if they stayed in the tire ruts, they didn't have to walk in the snow. About halfway home, they passed a huge motor home parked off the road behind some trees. Tintin started pulling at his leash and barking at the motor home. He almost pulled Benji off his feet.

"Home is this way, Tintin," Benji said, trying to tug Tintin back, but Tintin wouldn't stop barking at the motor home.

Alfie sighed. "Benji, you've got to do that patting thing Abraham showed us."

"I can't," Benji said. "He's pulling too hard."

Alfie sighed again and took hold of the leash. He pulled back with all his might, but Tintin was slowly dragging both of them toward the motor home. When Tintin got his mind on something, he was hard to manage. He pulled against his leash until he yanked it out of Alfie's and Benji's hands and ran like a crazy badger straight for the motor home. Well, Alfie wasn't sure if badgers could even run, but Tintin sure looked crazy.

Benji took off after him. "Tintin, come back, boy."

"He probably saw a squirrel," Alfie said, shielding his eyes from the bright sun. They had to get home soon or Mamm would start asking questions.

Tintin ran right up to the motor home and jumped and barked as if hoping someone would open the door and let him in. Benji caught his leash, but he couldn't get Tintin to leave the poor motor home alone. Tintin suddenly stopped barking and scratched at the door. He really wanted to go in there. Maybe they were cooking steak. Alfie sniffed the air but couldn't smell anything, but Max Glick said that dogs could smell food from ten miles away.

With a tight hold on Tintin's leash, Benji went to the front of the motor home and stood on his tiptoes to peek into the window. "I can't see anything." A line appeared right across his forehead. "Something's wrong, Alfie. I think we should knock."

"It doesn't look like anybody's home. Let's go."

Benji gazed into the woods. "Maybe they got lost in the forest."

Alfie sighed. Benji was a *gute* partner, but sometimes he got distracted. "We have to get home. We can't be late for dinner or Mamm will know we were spying at the market."

Benji stared at the door on the side of the motor home. "She won't know that."

"Mamm knows everything."

Without stopping to consult him, Benji knocked on the motor home door. He knocked softly at first, but when no one answered, he knocked loud seven times. No answer.

"They're not home."

"Tintin's worried," Benji said. "I think we should go in."

Alfie growled, let go of Tintin's leash, and started walking away. Maybe if Benji thought Alfie was going to leave, he'd give up trying to get in the motor home. Of course, there was still the problem of convincing Tintin to go along with it, but Benji had to cooperate first.

Alfie took about ten steps away but turned around when Benji didn't even try to follow him. Benji glanced at Alfie, then reached up and turned the doorknob.

"Benji, nooo," Alfie yelled, but the door was already open. Tintin jumped into the motor home and disappeared. Ignoring Alfie, Benji stuck his head in the motor home to look around, hesitated for only a second, and climbed in after Tintin.

Alfie's heart jumped up and down like a rock skipping over the water. He ran to the motor home and climbed in. Mamm would make Benji clean toilets for a year if he got caught in someone else's property.

Tintin was barking like a crazy dog. He jumped up on Alfie, then hopped out of the motor home, only to return a second later and jump on Alfie again. It took a minute for Alfie's eyes to adjust to the dimness, but he could see a man probably as old as Dawdi sitting on a padded bench with his head cradled in his hands. Alfie wrinkled his nose. The man had thrown up, and there was a disgusting, smelly mess on his pants and on the floor. An Englisch woman was asleep on the bench across from him, and she looked even older than the old man.

Benji didn't seem to notice the throw-up all over the floor. He bent over next to the man and patted him on the shoulder. "Are you okay?"

The man just moaned and rocked back and forth as if he was getting ready to throw up again.

Benji looked at Alfie and then at the woman on the bench. "We need to wake her up."

Alfie shook his head. He knew better than to wake an old person who was trying to take a nap. Mammi had scolded him enough times for being too loud while Dawdi was sleeping.

"Wake her up," Benji snapped.

Alfie stepped back in surprise. Benji never talked to him like that. Benji was the nice one, always trying to help people and never getting angry. It was as if Perry Glick was right there in the motor home with them. Alfie was about to argue when he realized that maybe Benji knew something Alfie didn't. Benji noticed things, and he never got mad unless it was important. Besides, Tintin was acting strange too. Something was definitely wrong, and Alfie was smart enough to listen to Benji when he acted like this.

With shaking hands, Alfie lightly tapped the woman's shoulder. She didn't move. He grabbed hold of her shoulder and shook her. "Lady? Lady, your husband is sick, and you need to help him." Because Alfie wasn't going to clean up this mess. The woman didn't open her eyes or move a muscle. Alfie's stomach sank to his toes. He looked at Benji. "Is she dead?"

Benji pressed his lips together as lines appeared on his forehead. "I don't know, but we've to get them out of here. I think they've got carbon monoside poisoning."

"What's that?"

"Mamm and Aendi Beth were talking about it, and it's real bad. They said you have to get out of the house or you will die."

"It's cold out there." Still acting like a crazy dog, Tintin clamped his teeth down on Alfie's trousers and pulled hard in the direction of the door. Alfie caught his breath as his heart lodged in his throat. "He wants us to get out."

Benji nodded. He wrapped both hands tightly around the old man's arm and pulled. "Come on, mister. We have to get you out."

"What about the old lady?"

"It will take both of us to carry her out," Benji said. "Let's get him out first."

Alfie thought his heart was going to jump out of his throat. "We can't carry her."

The old man groaned but wouldn't stand up. He seemed confused, like he didn't even know where he was. Alfie had to be brave. He stepped right on the throw-up on the floor and grabbed the man's other arm. He and Benji yanked the old man to his feet. They led him to the door, and he sort of tripped out of the motor home. Alfie and Benji had a tight hold on his arm, and they tried to lower the man to the ground gently. He was so heavy that when he started going down, they couldn't slow him very much. He fell to the ground but didn't fall hard. The snow crunched and sort of padded his landing.

Tintin sniffed at the old man as he lay in the snow, then ran back into the motor home.

Alfie and Benji were both breathing hard. "How are we going to get the lady out?" Alfie said. He was usually the one who had a plan, but he couldn't think straight, and Benji knew more about carbon monoside.

Benji jumped back into the motor home. Alfie followed. "Pick up her feet, and I'll get her head," Benji said.

"She's too heavy."

"We just need to slide her off the bench and then we can drag her out."

It didn't seem very nice to drag her across the floor, but it was better than dying. Alfie wound his arms around her legs, and when Benji gave the signal, they pulled her off the bench. There was a very loud thud when she hit the floor. A gasping sound came from her mouth. She was alive, but she didn't wake up.

"Help me," Benji said, lifting one of her arms and pulling hard.

Alfie took her other arm, and they managed to pull her

across the floor and out the motor home door. Tintin barked wildly as they climbed from the motor home and dragged the old lady down with them. Her body hit the snow like a brick, but there was nothing else they could have done about it. If she wasn't dead, they might have just killed her. Alfie was going to be sick.

But *nae,* she started coughing. And kept coughing. There was nothing else to do but keep going. They dragged her next to her husband. "Help her sit up," Benji said, "and pound on her back."

"Pound on her back?"

Benji's eyes flashed with fear. "When I had pneumonia, Mamm pounded on my back to help me breathe."

That actually sounded like a *gute* idea. They pulled her to a sitting position. Benji held her up by one arm while Alfie pounded on her back. She kept coughing. Alfie kept pounding until she threw up all over herself. Alfie tried to avoid it, but some of it splashed on him. Mamm was going to be suspicious when he came home smelling like vomit.

The old man was more awake than his wife. He sat up, but he held his head in his hands as if it weighed too much to hold up. "Do you have a phone?" Benji asked. He glanced at Alfie. "We need to call the police." The old man looked at Benji as if trying to figure out who he was. He nodded slowly and pulled a cell phone from his shirt pocket. Benji let go of the woman's arm, and she sank to the ground. But at least she was still breathing. Benji took the phone and touched the screen. "I need your thumb."

Hannah's *bruder* James had a cell phone, and he had shown them how to use it. Sometimes he let them listen to music on his phone, but they never told Mamm. She said it was devil's music.

Benji took the old man's hand and helped him press

his thumb to the phone. A new screen came up. "Do you remember how to make a call?" Benji said.

"I think so." Alfie took the phone. He pushed a few wrong buttons until he found the little keypad with numbers and dialed 911.

He heard a lady's voice on the other end. "Nine-one-one. What's your emergency?"

"My name is Alfie Petersheim."

"What is your emergency, Alfie?"

"We found a motor home with a dead lady in it. And there was throw-up everywhere."

The woman on the other end paused. "You say someone is dead?"

Alfie's hand shook so hard, he nearly dropped the phone. Benji gave him a reassuring look. "She's not dead anymore. We think she has carbon monoside poisoning."

"What is your location?"

Alfie looked around. It was a road they didn't often take. "I don't know."

"I see that this phone belongs to Hilda Burnham. Are you a friend of hers?"

"No. We found this motor home, and our dog started barking." Alfie looked at the old woman. She was almost as white as the snow around her. His whole body shook. "I think they're going to die."

"Alfie," the woman said, "stay calm. You are doing just fine. I am going to send someone to help you, but I need better directions. Can you see any street signs or other buildings?"

"There are some beehives under the trees."

"Anything else?"

Benji nudged Alfie's shoulder. "Tell her to go to Glick's Market and up that road behind the pasture."

"Do you know where Glick's Market is?" Alfie asked.

It sounded like the woman was talking to three people all at once. "In Bienenstock?"

"*Jah.*"

"Yes. I know where that is."

"If you go through the pasture behind Glick's Market, there is a road on the other side. We are on that road by the beehives."

"Do you know what direction from Glick's Market? North, south, east, or west?"

Alfie looked at Benji, mad at himself that he didn't know his directions better. Every good spy should know his directions. Benji shrugged. He didn't know his directions either. "I think it's north," Alfie said, because he remembered that Mamm had once said they lived north of town. "It's halfway between our house and Glick's Market."

"Where is your house?"

Alfie hesitated. If he told them where his house was, the police might go there and tell Mamm. He looked at the old woman. Her eyes were open, but it didn't look like she was looking at anything. "450 State Road 87."

"Very good, Alfie," the woman said. "Someone is headed in that direction right now. The policeman is going to turn on his siren. Tell me when you hear it."

"Okay."

"You said you think it's carbon monoxide poisoning," the woman said. "You need to open all the windows."

"We dragged them out of the motor home. The lady is laying in the snow."

"Can you find a blanket or something to keep her warm?"

Alfie nodded to Benji. "Go find a blanket."

Benji frowned, as if he was mad at himself for not thinking about that sooner. He took a deep breath, held it, then jumped back inside the motor home. He came out with a whole pile of blankets so tall he couldn't see where he was going and almost fell out of the door. With the phone still in his hand, Alfie ran to help him. They spread three blankets over the woman and put one over the old man's shoulders while Alfie held the phone to his ear.

Then he heard it. The best sound in the whole world. A police car. "I hear the siren," he said into the phone.

"Good," the woman said back. "Listen carefully. Is it getting closer or farther away?"

"Closer."

"Okay. Tell me if it gets softer."

Alfie's heart clattered against his chest. In the distance, a police car turned onto their road and started coming in their direction. "It's here!" Alfie screamed.

Tintin barked and jumped for joy. Benji cheered. Alfie started breathing again. A policeman was coming. Benji ran to the middle of the road and waved both hands above his head. The policeman turned off his siren and honked twice. He'd seen them.

The policeman was talking into a walkie-talkie attached to his shoulder as he got out of the car. He knelt down next to the man and woman. "You pulled them out of the RV?" he said.

Alfie nodded and handed the policeman the phone. He didn't want anyone to think he'd stolen it.

The policeman's walkie-talkie beeped. "Are either of you hurt?"

"I stubbed my toe coming out the door," Alfie said.

The policeman nodded. "Okay, you boys move back a little while we take care of these people." A red truck and an ambulance rolled down the road.

Alfie and Benji sat on their haunches and hugged their

dog while the men in uniforms quickly loaded the two old people into an ambulance. The ambulance driver drove off in a very big hurry to get to the hospital. Alfie would have liked to ride in an ambulance like that. It looked like there were a lot of interesting things in the back.

The policeman picked up the blankets and went inside the motor home. After a few minutes, he came back out to talk to Benji and Alfie. "You boys were very brave," he said. "How did you happen to find these people all the way out here?"

"We was taking a shortcut," Benji said. "We're late for dinner."

Alfie's stomach felt like he'd eaten a bag of rocks. Mamm was going to find out about the spying. "We better go. Mamm will be mad."

The policeman smiled. "I don't think your mom will be mad. You saved those people's lives. They have a portable gas heater in there that wasn't working right. If it weren't for your quick thinking, they'd be dead. How did you know it was carbon monoxide poisoning?"

Benji patted Tintin's head. "One time, Mamm and Aendi Beth were whispering so I sneaked behind the table and listened. They said an Amish boy in Wautoma died from carbon monoside poisoning. He fell asleep and never woke up."

Alfie gazed at Benji in surprise. Benji was a better spy than he thought.

"It's really cold out here," the policeman said. "Do you want me to give you a ride home?"

It was tempting, but if Mamm saw the police car, she wouldn't stop asking questions until she got the whole story. "We better walk," Alfie said.

The policeman gave them a wonderful nice smile. "I

can drop you off down the road so your mom doesn't even see me."

"Can we bring our dog? I don't want him to walk by himself. He'll get lonely."

"Of course."

Benji glanced at Alfie. Alfie glanced at Benji. They smiled at the same time. "Can I hold your gun?" Benji said.

"Nope. But I'll let you listen to the radio."

Benji nodded. "Okay. I call front."

Chapter Twelve

"Do you like lavender ice cream?" Benji said, wrinkling his nose at the very thought.

A smile tugged at Austin's mouth. He'd never tasted lavender ice cream, but he couldn't resist teasing Benji. "We should sell it in the store."

Benji made a face and stuck out his tongue. "No one will buy it. It tastes like you're eating grass."

Austin stared at the crumpled paper Alfie had given him.

Ice cream, candy bars, potato chips, books, soda pop, gumballs.

"You could make a hundred flavors," Alfie said. "Like pistachio and bubble gum."

Benji nodded. "I like bubble gum but not lavender. Or Rocky Road. It has too many things in it."

"I like strawberry," Alfie said. "Double-decker."

Austin couldn't help but be touched by the lengths his *bruderen* had gone to to get this list. "So you sneaked into Glick's Market."

"Don't tell Mamm. She told us not to go in there ever again, even though Perry doesn't pinch people anymore."

Austin smiled. The list was fairly useless, but the boys had been very brave to get it for him. Maybe he underestimated his *bruderen.* "I won't tell Mamm. It was wonderful nice of you to go look."

"We wasn't afraid of Perry," Alfie said, puffing out his chest as if that were really true.

Benji looked at Alfie sideways. "But we're afraid of Mamm."

Alfie didn't lose his swagger. "I'm not afraid of Mamm, but she'd worry about us if you told her."

Benji leaned his hand on the railing. "The girls were afraid, but we protected them."

"What girls?"

"Dinah and Ruth Ann," Benji said. "They're our partners."

Alfie narrowed his eyes at Benji. "They just helped us look around the store."

"Then we almost died," Benji said, almost as an afterthought.

Austin raised an eyebrow in amusement. "You almost died? How did that happen?"

Alfie glared at Benji, smiled at Austin, and laughed nervously. "We didn't almost die."

Benji returned Alfie's glare. "Mamm never found out because we wiped off the throw-up in the snow."

"Throw-up?"

Alfie sort of pushed Benji away. "Did you see we have gumballs on the list? You can buy gumballs in a hundred flavors too. You could have a hundred flavors of ice cream and a hundred flavors of gumballs. You could be the Hundred Store."

Austin decided to ignore Benji's comment about nearly dying. Nine-year-olds tended to exaggerate. He wasn't going to lose any sleep over whatever mischief Alfie and Benji had gotten themselves into. He smoothed the list with his fingers. "This is a *gute* list. It will help."

The front door opened, and Hannah and her cousins, bundled like snowmen, came in with the wind, carrying a long, oval piece of wood at least four by six feet. The sign. Hannah carried one end, and Ruth Ann and Dinah were straining to hold it up on the other end. Austin bolted to the door. "Benji, Alfie, help."

Benji and Alfie cupped their hands under the middle of the board to hold it off the ground. Austin took Ruth Ann and Dinah's end. It was a wonder they hadn't already dropped it as heavy as it was.

"Ruth Ann, grab a towel," Hannah said, huffing and puffing as she spoke.

While they held the board, Ruth Ann ran to the kitchen area, took a towel from the drawer, and spread it on the floor next to the wall.

"Now, lay it on the towel and we'll lean it against the wall," Hannah said. They set it down gently on the towel. Austin smiled. Hannah was careful about the floor, probably because she'd scraped most of the edges.

Dinah shut the door on the wind and sighed. "That was heavy."

"What is this?" Benji asked, stepping back and gazing at the white words painted on the red board.

All Austin could do was stare.

Hannah beamed like a ray of sunlight. Austin loved that smile. When Hannah smiled like that, Austin knew everything was going to be okay. "This is the sign I painted for the front of the store."

"Whoa," Alfie said.

There really were no other words. Austin tried anyway. "It's perfect, Hannah."

Hannah's smile got wider. "Do you like it?"

Austin stepped back to get a better look. In big white letters, it said, PLAIN AND SIMPLE COUNTRY STORE. Hannah had painted the outline of a yellow oval encircling the words, and below the words she'd painted some simple yellow and orange flowers. "It's exactly what I wanted."

Hannah brushed her hand along the front of the sign. "I love the country red. I think you should paint the shutters out front the same color. Tie everything in."

Benji knelt down to get a better look at the flowers. "Are you going to hang it over the door?"

Hannah nodded. "But we'll have to get Abraham and Andrew to help us. It's heavy, and it needs to be secure so it doesn't fall down."

Alfie squinted at Hannah. "You should write 'One hundred ice cream flavors' on the sign. Then more people will come."

Hannah grinned and messed up Alfie's hair. "That is an excellent idea. But maybe we could put signs on either side of the front door advertising goods depending on the seasons since we probably won't be selling ice cream all year. The ice cream sign could go up in the summer. Maybe a special Christmas sign could go up right now. We'll still have two weeks before Christmas when the store opens."

Austin's heart raced with the possibilities. "I like it."

"I put four coats of sealant on it. It shouldn't fade for a few years at least. And I made a smaller sign we can put up near the highway exit. Ben Natzke said we could use his property. He's going to check with the city about the rules."

"You've thought of everything. Where in the world would I be without you?"

Her face seemed to glow. "Lord willing, it will attract a lot of attention. In the summer, we can set rocking chairs and tubs of petunias and chrysanthemums on the porch. Davie Helmuth wants to sell his chrysanthemums here." Her eyes sparkled with amusement. "The Glicks don't carry chrysanthemums or petunias. And we should plant flowers around the outside of the store. Don't you think that would be beautiful?"

"Beautiful." Austin was already excited about the store, but Hannah had whipped him into total euphoria. This was going to work, and probably only because Hannah was involved. She never did anything halfway.

She slid her hand into her coat pocket and pulled out a stack of papers. "I made some quarter-page flyers to advertise the opening. I thought maybe Alfie and Benji could help us pass them around town."

It was just getting better and better. Why hadn't he thought about flyers? "That would be *wunderbarr.*"

"Aw," Alfie moaned. "Do we have to?"

Ruth Ann gave him a disgusted look. "Of course you don't have to. You *get* to. Don't you want to help Austin and his store?"

Alfie exhaled a deep breath. "I guess."

Benji scratched his nose. "Can we bring Tintin?"

"Is he here?" Hannah said.

"He's at home in his doghouse. It has a solar heater. Abraham put it in for us."

Hannah gave Benji a sweet smile. "I'd like to go now before it gets dark. We won't have time to get Tintin. He can come next time."

"Next time?" Alfie raised his eyebrows.

"We're not going to be able to get it done today. There are a lot of houses in Bienenstock."

"Aw," Alfie whined, slumping his shoulders so low his knuckles nearly dragged on the floor.

Ruth Ann rolled her eyes. "Alfie, don't you want to help Austin and his store?"

"I guess."

Austin chuckled. "Go downstairs to storage, and you can each pick out a piece of candy before you go." All four children cheered with delight and clomped quickly down the stairs. "Only one each," Austin called. *Die kinner* would clear out his whole inventory if he let them.

More groaning from Alfie.

"I don't know which to pick," Benji said. "He's got about a hundred candies down there."

The candy had also been Hannah's idea. They were old-fashioned candies to put in glass jars and set on the counter by the cash register. Hannah said they'd go *gute* with the wood floors and the Amish quilts.

Austin ran his hand over Hannah's sign again. "This is wonderful *gute,* Hannah. I always wished I had your talent."

"Maybe you weren't so keen on my talent when Treva Nelson told the teacher I was drawing graven images."

Austin grimaced. "Treva Nelson always fancied herself so righteous, like she had to personally make sure everyone was following the Ordnung."

Hannah gave him a wry smile. "Poor girl hasn't changed a bit."

Austin nodded. Treva Nelson had been wonderful unkind to Andrew's wife, Mary, when she'd first come back to the community. Treva had thought it was her job to remind Mary of her sins and punish her for them. Andrew had chastised her in front of half the *gmayna,* which had only made her behavior worse. "The teacher fed more than one of your drawings to the woodstove. I'm sorry."

"It wasn't your fault. And Teacher was right. I just needed to use my talents in a better direction. I didn't have to draw people to do that. I like making signs and flyers and painting milk cans."

They both caught their breath at the same time. "You can paint milk cans for the store," Austin said.

"Or decorative plates. Englischers would like that." He loved Hannah's laugh, as if everything in her life was a sheer delight. "It wonders me if Treva would have a problem with painted rocking chairs."

"Probably."

"Treva means well," Hannah said. "And Sol isn't nearly as severe. He's the reason we're friends."

"Who's the reason you're friends?"

With his back to the door, Austin hadn't even heard Scilla come in. She was bundled in a heavy coat with a black bonnet covering her head and a knitted scarf over her black bonnet. Fat snowflakes sat atop her scarf like a layer of dust on a table. Austin's heart skittered about like water on a hot skillet. Scilla looked like a snow angel, with her blue eyes and rose-petal lips. "Scilla, it's so *gute* to see you. It must be snowing."

"*Ach.* It's a blizzard out there." Scilla looked at him as if he was a slice of organic chocolate cake made with beans instead of oil. "Nothing but seeing you could tempt me to come out in a storm like this."

Austin glanced out the window. Snow fell gently to the ground. It wasn't that bad, but it was comforting to know that had it been a blizzard, Scilla still would have come. She adored him that much.

Scilla removed her scarf and shook off the snow onto Austin's new wood floor. Then she took off her bonnet and set it on the empty shelf where the peanut butter and honey would go. Austin helped her off with her coat and hung it on the hook for the homemade aprons they were going to sell.

Hannah went behind the counter, grabbed another towel, and started wiping up melted snow puddles from the floor.

Scilla looked at Hannah, her smile tight. "I hope I wasn't interrupting a private conversation."

"Not at all," Austin said, leaping at the chance to explain himself. Scilla had no reason to be suspicious or jealous or whatever it was she seemed to be feeling. "We were just talking about how we got to be friends."

"I know why Hannah wanted to be friends with you," Scilla said, batting those big, beautiful eyes at him. "You were always the handsomest boy, even in grade school. All the girls had a crush on you. And you are wonderful nice to everybody, no matter if they take it the wrong way."

Scilla always had a way of making him feel ten feet tall. "*Denki.*"

She drew her brows together. "But I never understood why you wanted to be friends with Hannah."

Austin glanced at Hannah. Scilla didn't mean that the way it had come out, but Hannah's face was turned toward the wet floor, so he couldn't really tell how she felt about it. "Everybody wanted to be friends with Hannah, except Sol Nelson. He and Matt Gingerich and some of the other boys had a secret hideout in the pasture behind the school. It was an old abandoned storage shed, and we liked to go there after school."

Scilla pinched her lips together. "I remember that hideout. Treva and I sneaked in there once, but it was damp and stinky. We didn't go again."

Hannah looked up and grinned at Austin as if she couldn't help it. "The boys liked that smell. They thought it was manly."

"We used to sit in there hoping the smell would absorb into our skin."

Hannah crinkled her nose at the very thought of it. "It did. And it was sort of amazing that anybody else even wanted to be around you."

Austin grunted. "Everybody wanted to be around me no matter the smell."

"*Jah,* they did," Scilla said.

Hannah's lips twitched. Was she amused or annoyed? "I wanted to join Austin's hideout gang, but Sol Nelson was the boss, and he said no girls allowed. But Austin talked him into it. He told Sol I could be the cook."

Austin had to laugh. "And then you refused to cook anything."

"Of course. I wanted to have adventures, not be stuck in that smelly shed fixing peanut butter and jelly sandwiches for you stupid boys."

Austin winced. "You thought we were stupid, but you still wanted to join us?"

Hannah giggled. "I can't explain it. I was eight. What did I know?" She finished wiping the floor and stood up. "I could run as fast as the boys and climb trees in a dress, and Austin watched out for me, even though I didn't need him to."

The way she looked at him sent a ribbon of warmth trickling down his spine. Sometimes he'd been considerate of Hannah, and sometimes he'd been as selfish and insensitive as most eleven-year-old boys. It was nice Hannah remembered the good parts.

"That doesn't explain why you became friends," Scilla said.

Actually, Austin thought it explained everything pretty well. But there was one more thing. "One day we were all standing outside the old shed because it really was stinky, and sometimes we just had to get fresh air. Hannah ducked into the shed to get something, and I followed her in. There was a long, thick snake curled up against one of the walls taking a nap."

Scilla gasped. "What did you do?"

Austin didn't want to dampen her opinion of him, but he was too far into the story to back out now. "I screamed so loud I'm sure the nearest cornstalks dropped their corn. Hannah wasn't scared. She poked at the snake with her finger, and it slithered under the wall and out of the shed."

Scilla's eyes looked like big, round saucers. "That was wonderful *deerich,* foolish, Hannah. It could have bitten you."

Hannah shook her head. "It was just a garden snake. I've found dozens of them in our yard."

"Sol and the boys ran into the shed when they heard the screaming, and Hannah acted scared and let them believe she was the one who'd done the screaming." He smiled in Hannah's direction. "She saved me from a lot of teasing. I've been grateful ever since."

Scilla's brows almost touched together on her pretty face. "Hannah shouldn't have lied."

"I didn't lie," Hannah said. One corner of her mouth curled upward. "They just assumed it was me, and I wasn't about to tell them who'd really done the screaming."

"Well," Scilla said, smoothing her hands down her apron. "It was a nice gesture, but it seems like such a small thing for all the gratitude he's given you over the years."

Austin was taken aback. He hadn't known Scilla to be petty. Of course, he didn't know her as well as he knew Hannah, but Scilla was too righteous and pretty to be small-minded like that. Maybe she didn't like that Austin was friends with a girl. Maybe she wished it had been her. Maybe she didn't like Hannah.

Hannah's gaze flicked in Austin's direction. "It's . . . it's not gratitude. We've just become *gute* friends. That's all," she said.

Austin didn't know what else to say. He'd have to explain to Scilla that he wouldn't be friends with Hannah when he and Scilla got married. But he couldn't say the word *marriage* until he was sure that was what he wanted. It would be a tricky conversation and one he'd rather postpone for as long as possible.

Scilla seemed to tire of the conversation or just didn't want to talk about it anymore. She pointed to Hannah's sign. "What's this?"

Austin smiled at Hannah. "It's the sign Hannah made for the store. We're going to hang it above the first-floor eaves. Isn't it *wunderbarr?*"

"Hmm," Scilla said. "I would have used blue."

It seemed Scilla wasn't going to give Hannah any credit today. Maybe she was just in a bad mood. "I think the red really makes the sign stand out," Austin said. "And the yellow and orange."

Hannah's face brightened. "I went to the library and did some color research. Red is supposed to get people's attention. And yellow is so cheerful."

"When did you go to the library?" Scilla asked. It almost sounded like an accusation, as if no one was allowed to go to the library without her permission. "I didn't see you there."

"I went on whatever day it is you don't work."

Another time, Austin might have laughed. Scilla didn't

know Hannah well enough to pick up on the tease in Hannah's voice. But there was no laughing today. For some reason, Scilla was out of sorts, and he instinctively knew that now would not be the time to laugh. She'd think he was poking fun at her.

"Do you like the name of the store?" Austin said.

Scilla turned her doting attention back to him. "I love it. Plain and Simple Country Store. It's perfect. You're so smart, Austin."

"It was Hannah's idea."

Hannah shook her head. "We both had the idea. When people see the word 'plain,' they think Amish, so we don't actually have to come out and say it."

Scilla fingered the hair at the nape of her neck. "It's too long." She glanced up at Austin, maybe to see if he agreed with her.

His heart sank. "You think it's too long?" Would Englischers think the same and not stop to shop?

Concern filled her eyes. "It's okay, Austin. You can't change it now anyway. I'm just saying you should have asked my opinion first."

Austin nodded. He should have talked to Scilla about the name of the store. She was his girlfriend after all. "You're right. From now on, I'll get your opinion on all the important decisions."

Scilla tilted her head to one side and stared at the sign. "You need to add 'organic.'"

Hannah bent her head closer. "What?"

Scilla pointed. "Right there, underneath the flowers, you need to write 'organic.' Everyone should know that you sell organic here. Twice as many people will stop."

Austin frowned. He liked the sign just the way it was.

Hannah folded her arms across her chest. "We can advertise organic somewhere else. I think the sign is perfect. It's clean and bright, and it isn't cluttered with extra words. It doesn't need to be changed."

Scilla pinched her lips together. "Only Gotte can create perfection. Beware of pride."

A hint of red overspread Hannah's cheeks, and she forced a laugh. "It *is* a sin to be proud, but it's not a sin to say I'm very happy with the way the sign turned out. And it's not a sin if I don't want to do it your way." The scold in her tone was evident. Should Austin be annoyed that Hannah was chastising his girlfriend?

Scilla seemed annoyed enough for both of them. "You don't have to get mad. It was just a suggestion. I think we should let Austin decide. It's his store and organic is going to be a big part of it."

Both girls turned to look at him, Scilla adoring and smug, Hannah hurt and defensive. Austin's throat went dry. He would lose no matter what he decided.

Austin had never been more grateful for his *bruderen* than he was at that moment. The four children were sufficiently loud as they stamped up the stairs and invaded the main floor. "Look what kind I got," Benji said, his eyes alight and his hand open. "Root beer." As soon as he'd shown his candy to Austin, he popped it into his mouth.

Alfie unwrapped a blue candy. "I got blueberry."

Dinah was already sucking on her candy, but she didn't seem to be enjoying it. "I got horehound, but it's icky."

"I told you not to get that one," Ruth Ann said.

Hannah giggled. "Horehound is an old-fashioned candy they used to make because they didn't have sugar. Some people like it."

"I don't," Dinah said. She blinked back tears of disappointment.

Hannah held out her hand. "Here." Dinah spit her candy into Hannah's open hand. Hannah threw the candy into the trash can and wiped her hand with a paper towel. She curled one side of her mouth and raised an eyebrow in Austin's direction. "Can Dinah go pick a different piece of candy?"

Austin was about to say yes when Scilla clicked her tongue. "She wasted the candy she chose. I don't think she deserves another one." She looked to Austin. "It's a hard lesson learned about choosing wisely."

"Um, well, sure, but Dinah didn't know and—"

Growling in disgust, Hannah shoved her hand into her coat pocket and pulled out a dollar bill. She pressed it into Austin's palm. "I'll pay for Dinah's extra piece."

She didn't need to do that. She'd painted the sign for free. She'd scraped his wood floor. He owed her hundreds of dollars he'd never be able to pay back. He tried to give her money back. "You don't need to pay me for an extra piece of candy."

Hannah pretended she didn't hear him. She grabbed Dinah's hand and led her down the stairs while the twins and Ruth Ann stared silently after them as if something serious and important had just happened. Alfie glared at Austin, then the three of them scooted to the other side of the room, probably to look at Austin's new fridges.

Scilla cupped her hand in front of her mouth and whispered to Austin. "We can't blame Hannah for the way she was raised. Her parents were never strict with any of their kids, and look where it's got them. Her *bruder* James listens to wild music, and there's a rumor he's going to buy a car.

That's what comes of spoiling your children instead of letting them suffer the consequences of their actions."

Austin frowned. He'd never known Scilla to be so judgmental. James listened to strange rap music and sometimes he sneaked a cigarette behind the barn, but he was a hard worker and respectful to his elders and worked tirelessly at the donut stand and on his *dawdi's* farm. And Hannah, well, there was no better person than Hannah Yutzy. If her parents had failed, then there was no hope for any Amish family in Wisconsin.

It wouldn't be the end of the world if James bought a car. That was something *die youngie* did when they were in *rumschpringe.* Some parents even encouraged it. That way they didn't have to hire a driver every time they went somewhere.

He didn't know what to say. He wanted to be agreeable, but she was wrong about Hannah and about the candy. Candy seemed like a safer topic. "I don't mind if Dinah chooses another piece. We all make mistakes."

To his relief, she seemed to concede. She didn't smile, but the hard lines around her mouth relaxed. "You're so nice, Austin. It's one of your best qualities."

He bloomed into a smile. They agreed on so much. He shouldn't let a small piece of candy come between them. "*Denki,* but don't be too impressed. I'm not perfect. I still find my *bruderen* annoying."

She nodded. "Me too. But you treat them better than they deserve. That's what worries me. You've got to be more strict with *die kinner.* If you hand out candy to every pouty child, you'll go bankrupt and everyone will be forced to shop at Glick's again. You don't want that, do you?"

"*Nae.*" Austin didn't know why the irritation bubbled up inside him. What Scilla said made perfect sense.

Hannah and Dinah came up the stairs holding hands. Dinah wore a closed-mouth smile, obviously enjoying whatever flavor she'd finally chosen. Hannah was also smiling, but her smile looked to be pulled across her face like a rubber band, as if it would snap at the least provocation. "Okay, children," Hannah said. "Let's go pass out some flyers before it gets dark."

Alfie and Benji grabbed their coats and hats from the counter and put them on. Alfie dragged his feet, but he followed Benji and the others out the door.

Austin nudged Hannah on the arm as she passed him. "*Denki* again for the sign. It's beautiful."

She gave him a tentative smile, maybe a little more sincere this time, and slid on her gloves. "It will look wonderful nice on the house." She left without another word, before he even thought to thank her for passing out flyers. It was probably just as well. He had so much to thank her for he barely knew where to start.

When Hannah shut the door behind her, Scilla folded her arms and stared after her. "It looks like someone needs to work on her humility."

"She's happy that I like the sign. I don't think there's any pride in it."

Scilla gave him a conciliatory nod. "I know she's been a wonderful helper here at the store, but you don't have to make excuses for her. Pride has always been one of Hannah's weaknesses. It's why she's so loud. She likes the attention."

That wasn't the reason, was it? He didn't want to argue with Scilla, but Hannah wasn't like that and Scilla should know so she didn't think badly of his best friend. "Hannah likes to have fun. I don't think she craves attention as much as she sees happiness in everything. Sometimes her joy just overflows loudly."

Scilla didn't seem convinced, but she didn't argue with him. "Okay. But watch out for her. She likes to get her own way."

"I don't know if that's true."

"Did you see how she fought me about the sign? She's proud of it and doesn't want it to be changed, but anybody can see it would be a thousand times better if you wrote 'organic' at the bottom. You're going to attract so many more customers that way, and I should know because my *dat's* second cousin owns a store in Appleton. You shouldn't lose business just because Hannah is too proud to change the sign."

Austin liked the sign, but it was more important to make Scilla happy. Wasn't that what love was? Sacrificing your own needs for someone else's? Besides, her third cousin owned a store. She knew more about this than he did. "You're right. I'll ask Hannah to paint 'organic' on the bottom."

"Better to do it without telling Hannah. She'll try to talk you out of it, and I know how tenderhearted you are. It's something everybody likes about you, but it's also one of your weaknesses. You tend to let people walk all over you."

Austin swallowed at the lump in his throat. Did he really let people walk all over him? Of course he did. If it hadn't been for Hannah coming to his rescue with the bishop, he wouldn't even have a store now. Hannah wasn't going to be happy about the sign, but he had to stop letting people take advantage of him, even Hannah. That thought made him feel even worse, and he didn't want to talk about the sign anymore. He pasted a smile on his face. "I'll bet you didn't come here to talk about the sign."

Scilla's eyes lit up like a lantern. "For sure and certain. I've got *gute* news. I've done some experimenting, and I can now make three different flavors of BM cookies, and they're organic."

"*Ach.* That's really something, Scilla."

"I'm going to make three batches a day for you to sell here at your store. One kind even has organic chocolate chips. Isn't it *wunderbarr?* People are always looking for a delicious way to stay regular."

Austin was without words. He could only clap his hands in delight and nod enthusiastically.

Every store owner wanted regular customers.

Chapter Thirteen

Hannah finished sprinkling the cinnamon sugar mixture, then carefully rolled the dough into a long cylinder. "It smells *appeditlich* already," she said.

Austin's *mamm,* Rebecca, brushed her hands down her apron. "This is my best recipe, except for my peanut butter bars. I'll teach you how to make those next."

In addition to donuts and pretzels, Hannah and Mary had decided to turn the kitchen in Austin's store into a full bakery where customers could buy bread, cinnamon rolls, cakes, pies, and donuts and pretzels of course. Rebecca had graciously offered to show Hannah how to make cinnamon rolls. This close to Christmas, they were sure to be popular at the store.

One of the only things they wouldn't be making at the bakery was dinner rolls, because Raymond Glick had put his foot down with the bishop about dinner rolls. Dinner rolls were a specialty at Glick's Restaurant, and Raymond had convinced the bishop not to let Austin sell them in his store.

But that didn't stop them from making cinnamon rolls, especially since they would be Rebecca Petersheim's famous cinnamon rolls, which Raymond Glick would never dream of selling at Glick's Family Market.

Rebecca opened one of her kitchen drawers and pulled out some dental floss. She handed it to Hannah. "Get a nice long piece."

Hannah giggled. "Do I have something in my teeth?"

Rebecca's glasses lifted off her nose when she smiled. "Dental floss is my baking secret."

"Okay," Hannah said doubtfully. "What do I do?"

"Get a long piece and slide it under the rolled-up dough. Then pull the strings up, cross them, and pull the floss through the dough. The floss cuts the dough, and each individual roll doesn't get pinched at the ends, like happens when you use a knife to slice them."

Hannah slid the floss around the roll and pulled it through the dough. It made a nice, straight cut without smashing the dough on the end. "Very clever," she said.

Rebecca grunted. "I'm not the clever one. I learned that trick from my *mater.* Except she used thread, but you can't find *gute* thick thread anymore. So I use unflavored dental floss. It's strong and sanitary." Hannah finished cutting the rolls, and Rebecca placed them in a casserole dish. "We have to put them in a deep dish because when they're done rising, we pour heavy cream over the top just before baking. It makes them extra gooey." She leaned toward Hannah and lowered her voice. "That is the secret to my cinnamon rolls. Don't tell anybody."

"I'll take it to my grave." Hannah pretended to lock her lips.

"I suppose you can tell your sister Mary and your *mamm,* if they are going to help you with the baking."

"They are."

"And you'll have to tell the customers because some of them might be lactose intolerant."

Hannah laughed. Heavy cream wasn't much of a secret ingredient after all. "The Englischers will love them."

Alfie and Benji came storming in the back door, their cheeks bright red with the cold.

"Don't let the door—" Rebecca said, right before the screen door slammed loudly behind them.

"Sorry, Mamm," Alfie said. "We was in a hurry. It's zero degrees out there."

Rebecca propped her hands on her hips and pinned the boys with a stern look. "Zero degrees?"

Alfie scrunched his lips to one side of his face. "That's just an expression people use when they mean it's really cold."

Benji nodded. "An expression. The thermometer says thirty."

Rebecca lifted her eyebrows as if she wouldn't be convinced. "No expression can justify slamming the door. Don't let it happen again. Are the cows milked?"

"Abraham's finishing the last one," Alfie said.

"*Ach, vell,*" Rebecca said. "*Denki* for that. You're *gute* boys, even if you like to slam the door."

"We don't like to slam the door," Benji said. "We just forget. There are too many things to remember, but we get in trouble when we forget."

Rebecca nodded thoughtfully, a twinkle of amusement in her eyes. "I'll take that into consideration the next time you slam the door."

The boys ran down the stairs. Their bedroom was in the cellar, which Hannah wouldn't like at all if she had to sleep there. Too many spiders and strange noises.

Rebecca set the pan of cinnamon rolls on the counter

to rise. "I saw the sign you painted for Austin's store. It's *wunderbarr.*"

Hannah lowered her eyes, determined not to be proud about the sign and give Scilla any reason to admonish her. "I hope it brings in many customers for him."

"I don't wonder but it will." Rebecca started wiping flour off the table. "*Denki* for helping Austin with his store. He couldn't have gotten this far without you, even if he's too busy to realize it."

It felt like a shard of glass lodged in Hannah's throat even while a bolt of pleasure zinged through her chest. Hannah both loved and hated thinking about Austin. She was mad at him one minute and madly in love with him the next. She couldn't think about anyone else, but her heart broke every time they were together. She had no idea what to do with all these conflicting emotions. Moving to Colorado was still a very real option. Hannah cleared her throat. "It will help my family too if the store is successful. We can sell baked goods year-round. It will be a more consistent source of income."

Rebecca peered over her glasses at Hannah as if she was looking right into her heart. "We both know that's not why you're helping Austin." She washed her hands at the sink. "You're a loyal friend, Hannah." She emphasized the word *friend* as if that word meant so much more.

Hannah's mouth went dry. Did Rebecca know how Hannah felt about Austin? Of course she knew. The knowledge was written all over her face. Hannah swallowed hard. She'd have to guard her feelings more carefully. No use being made a fool in front of Austin's entire family. "Austin has always been a *gute* friend to me."

"Huh," Rebecca said, expelling a puff of air from between her lips. "I can't figure out that boy. He's a *gute* son and a hard worker, but self-centered. Heaven knows I've tried to convince him he's not the center of the universe, but it's hard not to be full of yourself when you're so handsome."

"He is handsome." Hannah suddenly felt the need to defend Austin, even though she had no idea why. Wasn't she ferociously angry at him? "He's got many other *gute* qualities yet."

"*Ach,* I know he does. I'm his *mater* and I love him more than anybody, but I'm not blind to his failings. He can be ungrateful, and I can't figure out why he is so determined to like Scilla Lambright when that poor girl doesn't have a good-natured bone in her body. It's like she drinks sour milk every morning for breakfast."

"Organic sour milk," Hannah added, unable to keep her lips from curling upward.

Rebecca laughed so hard she snorted. "You'd think with all the BM cookies that girl eats, she'd be a little less uptight."

Hannah burst into laughter, then clamped her lips together and looked behind her to make sure no one else had heard her laughing at Scilla's expense. It probably wasn't nice, even though it was wonderful funny. Bless Rebecca for brightening her day. "I've never eaten one of those famous BM cookies, but Alfie and Benji start trembling whenever Austin mentions them."

Rebecca threw up her hands. "What's the use of nutritious food if you can't bear to eat it?" She shook her head. "I'm sorry that Austin isn't thinking straight. He's been busy getting the store ready and trying to impress Scilla."

"Scilla is very pretty." Hannah tried to hide the catch in her breath.

"Pretty is as pretty does," Rebecca said. "Besides, you're

every bit as pretty as Scilla on the outside and a thousand times prettier on the inside. Once the store opens, Austin will come to his senses. And if he doesn't, he'll hear it from his *mamm* till the cows come home."

"*Ach,* please don't say anything. I'd hate for anyone to be browbeaten into noticing me."

Rebecca opened her eyes wide in mock surprise. "Me? I don't browbeat people. But I have been known to knock a few heads with my spatula."

Hannah laughed. Rebecca threatened her boys with the spatula every day, but it was a rare occasion when she actually used it. As far as Hannah knew, the last time she'd used it on any of her boys was when Austin pushed a girl at school when he was six years old.

A loud knock came at the door. Rebecca hissed. "I wish people would knock quieter. Dawdi David needs his nap."

Hannah followed her to the door, and her stomach sank to her toes.

Raymond Glick stood on the porch with his arms folded across his chest and an unyielding scowl on his face. "Rebecca, I would have a word with Benaiah."

Rebecca didn't seem at all impressed by Raymond's harsh manner or rigid bearing. "He's not here," she said, offering no other explanation, as if she didn't think Raymond deserved one. Hannah's pulse beat double time. She had to admire Rebecca. Nothing seemed to intimidate her. Maybe it was because she had five sons. She was tough and didn't back down from anybody.

"I need to talk to Benaiah," Raymond said. "When will he be home?"

Rebecca acted as if she didn't notice Raymond's irritation. "He took his *mamm* to Walmart. It could be hours.

When Mammi Martha gets it in her head to shop, there's no telling how long she'll take. Would you like to wait?"

Raymond acted as if it was a preposterous question. "I can't wait. I need to get back to my store. You know, the one your son is trying to destroy."

Rebecca spoke calmly, even though Hannah sensed Rebecca's rising tension. "*Ach,* Raymond. No one is trying to destroy anything of yours, and if that's what you came to talk about, you might as well not bother. Benaiah works too hard on the farm to fret about what goes on with his sons."

It was true. Austin's *dat* was a dear man, but he didn't like conflict and he left the discipline to Rebecca. Did Rebecca ever resent that? Or was she happy to run things her own way? Whatever the case, everybody knew if you had an issue with one of the Petersheim boys, you took it up with Rebecca.

The lines on Raymond's forehead bunched together. "Your boys need the firm hand of discipline."

"I already told you, Raymond. Austin is not trying to hurt you or your family. He just wants a place to sell peanut butter."

Raymond's face turned bright red. "He's selling more than peanut butter."

"I suppose he is."

Raymond marched into the house. Rebecca and Hannah stepped back to let him in, then Rebecca shut the door. Might as well not heat the entire outdoors. "While I find Austin's behavior vengeful and petty, that is not what I came to talk to Benaiah about," Raymond said.

"What do you have to say, Raymond? I will pass it on to Benaiah when he gets home, if you like."

Raymond took off his hat but left his coat zipped.

Much to Hannah's relief, it didn't look as if he was planning to stay long. He lifted his chin. "Your twins won't stop harassing me and my family."

Rebecca tilted her head as if she hadn't heard him correctly. "My little nine-year-old boys are harassing your family?"

"They're not as innocent as you think. They come into my store, run around, and don't buy anything." Raymond pinched his lips together. "When they came into the store last week, they wouldn't leave Paul alone. They asked him question after question, and he didn't have time to tend to our other customers. Then they threw coins all over the floor, and Paul had to clean them up so people wouldn't trip."

Rebecca's expression grew darker with every passing minute. "Did he pinch them to make them behave?"

Raymond hesitated, as if reluctant to admit anyone in his family was to blame for anything. He cleared his throat. "Perry will not pinch anyone again, even if he is unjustly provoked."

"That's wonderful *gute* news."

"I am here to demand that you keep your twins out of my store."

For sure and certain, Rebecca was annoyed. She peered at Raymond through half-lidded eyes and pasted an *I'm-barely-putting-up-with-you* expression on her face. "The bishop said you agreed to let everyone come into the store, even people who have not been allowed in before."

"I will not tolerate harassment or mischief. Those boys are not allowed in my store. The bishop will agree with me, especially since the Petersheims are out to destroy us."

Ach, du lieva, Raymond Glick was an angry, unreasonable man.

Another knock at the door. This one didn't seem angry. They could only hope. Hannah opened the door. A policeman and an Englischer in a white shirt and tie stood outside. Hannah's heart thumped against her ribs. Raymond Glick was an irritation, but the sight of a policeman was absolutely terrifying. The man in the tie looked familiar, but Hannah couldn't put her finger on where she'd seen him before. "We're looking for Alfie and Benji Petersheim," the policeman said. "Is this where they live?"

"Um, yes, come in please."

Rebecca seemed more annoyed than shocked at the sight of a policeman. She'd probably had dealings with the police a few times over the years. Andrew had gotten into trouble for knocking over someone's outhouse when he was a teenager. And last year, Alfie had gotten stuck in one of Bitsy Kiem's trees, and they'd had to call the fire department. "What did they do?" Rebecca said, a tinge of resignation in her voice.

Raymond's look of surprise was soon replaced with a smug sneer. "Looks like your boys can't stay out of trouble."

The man in the tie seemed friendly and eager. "Are Alfie and Benji here? We have something to tell them."

Rebecca sighed loudly. "You'll have to get in line." She turned to Hannah. "Would you be so kind as to fetch my little angels from the basement?"

Hannah quickly went down the stairs. Alfie and Benji sat on their air mattress studying what looked like a map. Alfie shoved it under his pillow when he saw Hannah. "There's someone to see you upstairs," she said, not daring to tell them it was the police for fear they'd try to escape out the window.

Alfie drew his brows together. "Who is it?"

"*Cum* and see."

The boys followed her up the stairs with no clue she was leading them to their doom. They stopped short when they laid eyes on the policeman.

"Hello, Officer Branson," Benji said, obviously surprised but not in any way upset.

Benji knew the policeman? That couldn't be good.

Alfie frowned as if he were very annoyed. He looked around the room, seemingly unfrightened by the presence of a policeman or Raymond Glick. "You said you wouldn't tell."

The policeman knelt down next to Alfie. "I'm sorry, Alfie, but everybody should know what happened."

Rebecca gave Alfie and Benji the evil eye. "Yes. Everyone should know. Especially your mother."

"We almost died," Benji said, as if it was the most mundane thing in the world, like *We found a shiny rock* or *We ate chicken for dinner.*

The look from Rebecca could have seared a hole through Raymond Glick's hat. "You almost died?"

The policeman stood up. "Mrs. Petersheim, Alfie and Benji saved a couple from carbon monoxide poisoning. They had parked their motor home along Old Haul Road, and their heater malfunctioned. The husband was delirious, and the woman was unconscious. Alfie and Benji pulled that couple out of the motor home and called the police. They saved their lives. Ma'am, these boys are heroes."

The man in the tie stepped forward and shook Rebecca's hand. "I'm Hal Peters, the mayor of Bienenstock."

The mayor. Hannah had seen him at the meeting when she and Austin had gone to request that the house property be rezoned.

The mayor's moustache bobbed up and down when he spoke. "The city council would like to give these boys the Brett Favre Memorial Award for Bravery at our next city council meeting."

The mayor probably could have knocked Rebecca over with a feather. "Carbon monoxide?"

"Thanks to their quick thinking, the Burnhams are alive today. And very grateful. We all are."

The mayor nodded. "I don't like it when people die in my city."

The policeman stood and patted Benji on the shoulder. "With your permission, we'd like to present the award on December eighth at the city council meeting. We know you don't allow photographs, but the newspaper wants to report on it."

Rebecca still looked a little bit stunned. "We don't mind photographs before baptism, but the bishop would have to approve of it. We don't want to encourage pride."

Raymond's face looked like a looming storm. "These boys don't deserve an award. They should be arrested for being nuisances."

The policeman peered at Raymond as if he'd just said something really *dumm*. "We don't arrest children for acting like children."

"You should. These boys harass people's families and enter stores when they aren't welcome." Raymond's agitation could have fanned up a breeze. "Someone has been sneaking lemon drops from one of my bulk candy bins. I don't wonder but it's the Petersheim boys."

What a horrible accusation to hurl in a moment of irritation.

Alfie shook his head.

"We didn't," Benji said.

Rebecca's eyes flashed with raw anger. "Are you accusing my boys of stealing?"

Raymond realized his mistake. He raised his hands and took a step back, no longer on the offensive. "I didn't say that."

Rebecca wasn't about to let him get away with it. "*Jah,* you did." She advanced on him as if she was a cat about to pounce. "My boys may get into their share of trouble, but they are not thieves, and nobody, I mean nobody, questions their integrity or the integrity of this family."

Bullies tended to back down if someone stood up to them, and Raymond seemed to shrink under Rebecca's withering stare. "I'm only saying that someone needs to take those boys in hand before they get into real trouble."

Rebecca pointed to the door. "I'll thank you to leave my house immediately. And don't come back until you can bring a humble and sincere apology."

Hannah's heart wanted to explode from her chest. In her fierce loyalty, Rebecca was awesome and terrifying. Hannah wanted to be just like her someday.

Raymond shoved his hat onto his head, glanced at the policeman, and stormed out of the house, pretending to go because he wanted to leave, not because he was forced out by a mother bear protecting her cubs.

The mayor valiantly held on to his smile when Raymond slammed the door. He probably had to smile through a lot of unpleasant encounters in his job. "What do you say, Mrs. Petersheim. Can we count on you coming to the city council meeting?"

Rebecca tried to regain her calm, but her glasses sat askew on her face and her breathing was labored and noisy. "Let me talk it over with the bishop and my husband. Give me your phone number, and I'll call you."

The mayor patted his pockets. "Do you have a piece of paper?"

Hannah went into the kitchen and found paper and pencil in the drawer.

The mayor wrote his number on the paper and handed it to Rebecca. "Please call me. We want to give these boys the recognition they deserve. They are an example to all little boys everywhere."

Rebecca scrunched her lips. "Indeed."

The policeman opened the front door. "We'll be seeing you, Alfie and Benji. Stay out of trouble."

"We will," Benji said, giving the policeman the thumbs-up sign. Hannah nearly laughed out loud. Where had he learned that?

"And tell Tintin I said hello."

Rebecca gave the boys a stern look. "His name is LaWayne."

The policeman bent closer. "Whose name?"

"The dog." Rebecca folded her arms. "The dog used to be named Tintin, but the boys agreed to call him LaWayne as a condition of keeping him."

The policeman nodded. "Oh, I see. Well, we hope to hear from you soon. Alfie and Benji deserve an official congratulations."

The mayor followed the policeman out the door. Rebecca exhaled deeply, as if she'd been holding her breath for an hour. She glanced at Hannah, then gasped. "We've got to get those cinnamon rolls in the oven or they'll be a crispy mess. Come on."

Smiling uncomfortably, Alfie grabbed Benji's arm as Rebecca headed for the kitchen. "We'll go outside and clean something."

Rebecca stopped in her tracks. "You'll stay right there, young man. And don't move a muscle until I come back."

"But, Mamm."

Rebecca shushed him. "You use a hundred muscles when you talk. Don't talk. Sit on that sofa and think on your sins until I get back."

Benji and Alfie slumped onto the sofa. Hannah wasn't even sure what they were in trouble for, but it was obvious they were anticipating some sort of punishment or chastisement from Rebecca.

Rebecca stood at the counter studying her cinnamon rolls. "They're ready to bake, so we've got to hurry. Preheat the oven, and I'll warm the cream."

Austin walked in the back door just as Hannah turned on the LP gas oven. Her heart never failed to hammer against her ribs at the sight of him. His auburn hair and ready smile were two of Hannah's favorite things. He was so handsome and so lovable, and she felt like a melty puddle of salted caramel every time he walked into a room. "Are the boys in trouble again?" he said, smiling as if he found that thought amusing.

Rebecca loudly rearranged pans in her cupboard before pulling out a small saucepan and slamming the cupboard door shut. "Why do you ask?" she said snidely, almost as if she was daring Austin to make a fuss about it.

"A police car just pulled away from the house."

Rebecca slammed the pan down on the stove. "Oh, there's trouble all right. Stick around and you'll get an earful of it." She pulled the cream from the fridge, poured it into her pan, and turned on the burner. She turned to Hannah and smiled as if nothing bad had ever happened in the world ever. "You warm the cream so the rolls will keep rising during baking. If the cream is too cold, the rolls will stop rising."

While Rebecca stirred the cream in the pan, Austin turned to Hannah. "So, how was your day?"

Hannah grinned at the playful twinkle in Austin's eye. His curiosity was evident, but he knew his *mater* well enough not to ask questions about the police, especially not while she was baking. "It was a *gute* day. I cleaned Aendi Linda's house and took care of *die kinner.* Your *mamm* is teaching me how to make cinnamon rolls for the store."

He looked at her as if she was the Queen of Sheba. "*Denki,* Hannah. The Englisch will love them. My sister-in-law Mary had a wonderful *gute* idea, but I wanted to see what you thought. She used to work at an Englisch bakery and people would call in and order cakes and bread and such. Do you think we could take bakery orders over the phone?"

"That is a *wunderbarr* idea. We could do special orders for Thanksgiving pies and Christmas cookies."

He leaned against the counter and studied her face. "It would be more work for you."

"More work and more money and more people coming to the store. I'll ask my *bruder* and *schwester,* but I think they'll like the idea. It's better to make baked goods that already have a buyer. They spoil fast."

"What would I do without you, Hannah?" His grateful look made her knees weak, even though she tried to ignore it. Austin liked her as a friend, but she'd never be pretty enough or demure enough or *gute* enough for him. He was only being nice when he asked what he would do without her. He'd get along very well without her. Scilla was everything Austin wanted. Hannah would never be enough.

Rebecca took the pan off the stove. "I was just telling Hannah how much I like the sign she painted. Have you hung it yet?"

Austin's smile faded to almost nothing. "Andrew and Abraham will hang it tomorrow, Lord willing."

Hannah couldn't make out his expression. Had he changed his mind? Didn't he like the sign anymore? "Do you want something different? I can repaint it if you don't like it."

"Of course I like it." He cleared his throat. "But I wanted to tell you—"

"*Cum,* Hannah, I'll show you how to pour the cream." Rebecca instructed Hannah how to pour the cream over the rolls. Then they slid the rolls into the oven and set the timer. "Twenty minutes," Rebecca said. "That will give me barely enough time, if I talk fast." She wiped her hands on the towel hanging from the fridge handle. "Come in the living room, Austin, if you want to hear about the policeman."

Austin and Hannah followed Rebecca into the living room, where Alfie and Benji were still sitting on the sofa awaiting their fate. Alfie chewed his fingernails, and Benji pulled at a small hole in one of his pant legs.

"Benji, stop that," Rebecca said. "If you make that hole any bigger, your underwear is going to show through. The girls will laugh at you, and you'll get a spot of frostbite on your leg."

Alfie slid so his bottom was only halfway on the sofa. "Mamm, we don't have time to sit here. We need to go clean the spiders out of our cellar before it gets dark."

"Stay where you are, young man."

"But, Mamm, if we don't clean out the spiders, they will bite us and we will die down there and you won't find our bodies until morning."

Rebecca's gaze could have pierced a hole through a milking pail. "Alfie Petersheim, what have you got to say for yourself?"

"We was only trying—"

"I don't want to hear it. I made it perfectly clear that you two were not allowed in Glick's Market ever again."

"But the bishop said—"

"I don't care what the bishop said," Rebecca growled. "I have the last word, even over the bishop, and I told you never to go in there again. Even if the bishop had a talk with Raymond Glick."

Hannah stifled a giggle. Only Rebecca would be bold enough to rank her word over the bishop's. Hannah gave Austin a secret smile. He smiled back, his eyes alight with amusement. Oh, *sis yuscht,* she would be so much happier if she didn't like him so much.

Benji scratched his cheek. "We was just looking."

"I don't care what you were doing." Mamm narrowed her eyes and pointed at the twins. "You are not to go into that store again, even if you need batteries. Even if you're bleeding and need a Band-Aid. Even if you need to go to the bathroom so bad you can't hold it for another minute. Do you understand me?"

Benji's eyes got wide. "But you told us never to go to the bathroom in the bushes."

Rebecca fairly exploded. "Never go to the bathroom in the bushes. You just have to plan ahead. Or run to the library. They have nice bathrooms in the library."

Alfie frowned. "We can't go at the library. Scilla hates us."

Austin drew his brows together. "She doesn't hate you."

Hannah wanted to set Austin straight about that, but now wasn't the time. Rebecca hadn't finished her lecture yet, and the boys were worried about having to go to the bathroom in the bushes.

"I don't care if Scilla hates you. Better to go in the library than at Glick's Market. Have I made myself clear? Don't ever disobey me again."

That was like asking Tintin to quit wagging his tail, but Rebecca wasn't going to budge.

"We'll try, Mamm."

Rebecca seemed to lose a little of her steam. "It's for your own safety. Raymond is mad, and I wouldn't put it past him to make up stories about you. You don't want to do anything to jeopardize Austin's store, do you?"

"Can we spy in the window?" Benji asked.

"No spying." Mamm grabbed a ball of yarn and some scissors from her basket next to the sofa. She measured a length of yarn about ten feet long and cut it off the ball. "Stay this far away from Raymond's store. No exceptions."

Rebecca handed Alfie the yarn, and he stuffed it into his pocket. "We was just trying to help Austin's store."

Rebecca wasn't having any of it. "Austin's painted himself into a corner, agreeing not to sell anything Raymond does, but it's his corner and he's got to paint himself out."

Concern spread over Austin's features. "You think I've painted myself into a corner?"

Rebecca waved him away. "There's always a window to crawl out of. Don't worry about it."

Alfie slid off the sofa. "Okay, Mamm. We won't go in there again. *Denki* for the talk." He pulled on Benji's arm. "Come on. Let's go."

"Not so fast, young man. Sit down."

Alfie groaned and slinked back to his seat.

Rebecca, it seemed, had just been saving up her true righteous indignation. She paced back and forth in front of the sofa. "What were you doing, sneaking around other people's motor homes? The Petersheims do not sneak."

"It wasn't our fault," Alfie said. "Tintin started barking at the motor home, and he wouldn't stop until we went inside."

Rebecca raised an eyebrow. "Without knocking?"

"We knocked, but they didn't answer."

Austin looked at Hannah. "What's going on?" he whispered.

Hannah tilted her head in his direction, catching a whiff of new wood and fresh paint that hung about him. "Benji and Alfie pulled two people out of a motor home so they wouldn't die of carbon monoxide poisoning. The mayor wants to give them an award."

"*Ach, du lieva.*"

Alfie had his fingers tightly curled around the sofa cushion. "Tintin kept barking, and Benji was sure something was wrong so we went in without being invited. She was asleep, and the man threw up all over the floor."

Benji nodded. "It was carbon monoside poisoning, so we dragged them out of the motor home. We had to pull real hard, and I think the lady got a scrape on her bottom, but I didn't look."

Rebecca's outer shell softened for a fraction of a second as she gazed at her twin sons. "I see."

"I'm sorry we scraped her," Benji said.

No-nonsense Rebecca came back full force. "Why didn't you tell me? *Mamms* are supposed to be the first to know, not the last. I shouldn't have to hear a wild story like this from strangers, especially not the police."

"We didn't want you to find out that we went to the store."

"Don't go in there again," Rebecca snapped. "And another thing. Your dog's name is LaWayne. It's a nice, sensible name that will help you think of your *dawdi* every time you say it."

Alfie nibbled on his bottom lip and dared to touch his foot to the floor. "Can we go now?"

"Not yet." Alfie pulled his foot back. Rebecca knelt down and spread her arms. "Come here right now." The twins slid into their *mamm's* arms, and she pulled them in for a tight, fierce hug. "What a brave, brave thing you did," she said, her voice cracking in a hundred different places. "You saved two lives when you could have died yourselves. I'm so proud of you. So, so proud."

Benji buried his face into his mother's neck as a sob parted his lips. "We didn't want them to die."

"Of course you didn't. You did the right thing, even if you went into the motor home uninvited. Sometimes you have to follow what your feelings tell you, even when it may be against the rules or you might get into trouble. You are smart, *gute* boys. And don't you let Raymond Glick or anyone else tell you otherwise."

Both boys were crying at the end of that speech, but they were good tears. Hannah wiped a few from her eyes too.

"Tintin . . . LaWayne wouldn't give up until we went in there," Alfie said.

"I never thought I'd say it, but may Derr Herr bless that dog," Rebecca said.

Austin chuckled and glanced at Hannah. "I never thought she'd say it either."

"I guess Alfie and Benji's inclination to get into trouble was a *gute* thing this time. They're *gute* boys, you know."

Austin nodded. "*Jah,* I know. They've helped at the store more than just about anybody, and they went into Glick's as a favor to me. They're still wonderful annoying, but I haven't appreciated them near enough."

Someone else knocked at the door. It was a busy day at the Petersheims'. Austin was closest to the door, so he opened it. It felt like a big rock sat at the pit of Hannah's stomach. Scilla Lambright stood on the porch with a plate of dog poop. Okay, it probably wasn't a plate of dog poop, but that was what it looked like.

Austin glanced back at Hannah, as if he wished she wasn't there. Well, too bad. Rebecca had invited her, and she was learning how to make cinnamon rolls for the store. If he and Scilla wanted to be alone, they could go freeze on the porch.

Scilla came into the house as if she belonged there and handed Austin her plate of poop. "They said the police were just here. Is everything okay?"

"*Jah,*" Austin said. "They wanted to talk to the boys."

Scilla nodded as if that didn't surprise her. "I thought so. So I brought some BM cookies. Constipated boys tend to misbehave."

Alfie and Benji pulled out of Rebecca's arms and ran down the stairs without even asking Rebecca's permission. Hannah had never seen them move so fast.

Chapter Fourteen

Matt Gingerich and Sol Nelson seemed sufficiently impressed as they gazed around Austin's store. "It looks like that floor took some time," Matt said. "Hannah tells me she did a lot of scraping."

Sol fingered the hats on the shelf against the wall. "It smells new. Like pine and varnish." He turned and set a plastic garbage bag on the counter. "Here's the quilt from my *mamm.* She's says to tell you she's got two more almost ready."

Austin pulled open the edges of the bag. A stunning combination of orange and red fabrics met his eye. Erna Nelson made exquisite quilts. One had sold at auction last year for eight hundred dollars. "And she's okay to work on consignment?"

"*Jah.* Pay her when you sell the quilt. She's *froh* to have a place to sell them besides at auction. They sell for more money in a store."

Austin nodded. "*Denki.* I hope we sell every quilt she wants to make."

Matt Gingerich showed Austin his box. "It wonders me

if you would want to sell these ornaments. The Englischers love a souvenir for their Christmas trees."

Austin reached into the box and pulled out a little black buggy molded from clay, complete with Amish people looking out the window. "I like this," he said. Another clay ornament was an Amish girl holding a basket of apples. "These will be *wunderbarr* for the Christmas season."

Matt burst into a smile. "I mold them, and my *schwester* Mandy paints them."

"It wonders me if you will let me take them on consignment." Austin didn't have enough money to buy the Amish handicrafts outright. He barely had enough to stock regular grocery items. Even with the relatively short list of things the Glicks didn't sell, it had taken a great deal of money to put goods on the shelves.

"For sure and certain," Matt said. "I made two copies of my list. You pay me for what you sell, and I'll come get the rest after Christmas."

"And you'll be sure to bring more if I sell out?"

"*Jah,*" Matt said, grinning at the thought of selling out.

Austin did a quick look about the store. All the shelves were up and most of the merchandise was on the shelves. Hannah and James had draped pine boughs with red ribbon over the windows and doors and up the stairs. It looked and smelled like Christmastime. "On opening day, Hannah and Mary Yutzy are baking gingerbread cookies free for every customer." Then the store would really smell like Christmas. Austin's heart thumped inside his chest. They opened in five days.

Sol's eyebrows bobbed up and down. "I hear Priscilla Lambright is very interested in your store."

Warmth traveled up Austin's neck. "She's helping me with my organic section."

Sol grinned. "You're working on more than the organic section together. They say she likes you."

Matt Gingerich set his box on the counter and eyed Austin curiously. "*Ach.* I wish she liked me. She's wonderful pretty."

Sol smoothed his hand along the counter. "Do you know how many boys envy you?"

"Covetousness is a sin," Matt said, "but I'm jealous. Scilla is so pretty, and I hear she's a wonderful *gute* cook."

Matt probably hadn't tasted Scilla's BM cookies.

"Tyler Kauffman has been trying with Scilla for two years, and then you come along and it takes you about three days. How did you do it?"

Austin shrugged. "I'm irresistible."

"Ha," Sol grunted. "I don't think so."

It was probably wrong to revel in their envy, but Austin could have floated off the ground. Having a pretty girlfriend won him a lot of admiration.

Sol nudged Matt. "We've got to go. I'll bring more quilts when Mamm finishes them."

"Will you come to the opening on Tuesday?"

"Wouldn't miss it," Matt said. "I like gingerbread. And it will give me a chance to see Hannah Yutzy. Maybe *I'll* have a pretty girlfriend by New Year's."

Matt Gingerich wasn't someone who usually annoyed Austin, but Austin was annoyed all the same. Matt shouldn't come in here on Tuesday expecting to flirt with Hannah. She was going to be wonderful busy baking cookies and selling donuts. Matt had better not distract her.

"See you on Tuesday," Matt said as he and Sol opened the door and braced against the cold wind.

Austin's gut tightened for about the tenth time today. Five more days. They still had so much to do. They needed to hang the special battery-powered lights and stock the refrigerators with food. The Yutzys were bringing in their deep-fat fryers tomorrow and hooking them up to the generator. The bathroom faucet needed to be replaced, the windows needed to be washed, and the cash register wasn't hooked up yet. There was so much to think about, Austin couldn't think at all. He pulled Alfie and Benji's list from his pocket and read through it one more time. It had become a reminder that if all else failed, his family still loved him and there would always be someone to buy his ice cream.

Andrew and Abraham came in and stamped their boots on the rug just inside the door.

"*Ach,*" Abraham said. "It's cold today."

His *bruderen* took off their coats and hung them on the hooks by the door. Andrew peeled off his gloves. "The sign is up and secure. The house will probably fall down before it does."

"What's that?" Abraham said, drawing closer and setting his drill on the counter.

"Alfie and Benji sneaked over to Glick's Market to see what's on their shelves. They made me a list of things Glick's don't have."

Andrew raised an eyebrow. "That was brave. Or stupid. I'm never sure with those two."

Austin handed the list to Andrew. "It's a nice thought, but I can't carry just gumballs and Doritos."

Abraham read over Andrew's shoulder. "There are ten different kinds of Doritos."

Austin chuckled. "Everybody loves Doritos."

Andrew's lips twitched as he read through the list again. "Nothing on this list will meet with Scilla's approval."

Austin stiffened. There it was again, that twinge of

something annoying and unpleasant every time he thought of Priscilla. "Not unless it's organic or whole wheat."

"Scilla doesn't approve of much of anything, so there's really no use trying to please her." Andrew was teasing, but Austin didn't feel like laughing.

Abraham studied Austin's face and punched Andrew lightly on the arm. "Don't talk about his girlfriend that way."

Andrew rolled his eyes. "I'm sorry if I hurt your feelings, Austin."

Austin exhaled a long breath. "It's not that."

Andrew tilted his head as if to get a better angle on Austin's face. "What's going on? You two lovebirds having a spat?"

Austin couldn't help but laugh. "Since when do you use words like 'spat'?"

"It sounds nicer than a fight or a disagreement. Mary likes to call it a spat."

Austin leaned against the counter. "I shouldn't feel this way, not when things are going so well."

"Feel what way?" Abraham said.

"I don't even know what's bothering me."

Lines formed across Andrew's forehead. "About Scilla?"

Austin shrugged. "Since we met with the bishop, she comes to the store almost every day after she gets off at the library. She brings me taste samples of things she thinks we should sell in the store. She's really excited about our organic section."

Abraham made a face. "How many black bean veggie burgers have you eaten?"

Austin cleared his throat. "I'm really starting to enjoy them." He said it with a straight face, so Andrew and Abraham didn't dare contradict him. Nobody insulted the girlfriend's cooking. "Scilla feels a certain responsibility for the store because she sees herself as the one who convinced the bishop to let me open it back up."

Abraham laughed out loud, which was rare for him. He was usually so reserved. "She thinks she convinced the bishop? I don't think she said one word to the bishop that night."

Austin scrubbed his hand down the side of his face and half smiled. "I don't mind if Scilla thinks she's responsible for the bishop's change of heart. It makes her happy, so I'm happy."

Andrew grunted. "I hope you're happy about the sign. She ruined it yet."

A yawning pit opened up in Austin's stomach. Hannah hadn't seen what Scilla had done to her sign. It looked terrible. *Ach,* people made a lot of sacrifices for love, but he wasn't even sure he loved Priscilla that much, and now his sign was ruined. "She didn't ruin it. And now people will know we have organic." He paused too long. "I like the sign." It wasn't exactly a lie. He loved the sign, especially if he closed one eye and pretended Scilla hadn't painted the word *organic* on it.

"So what's bothering you?" Andrew said.

Austin squirmed. How could he explain something he didn't understand himself? "I don't know. Scilla is pretty, but she never smiles. Maybe I don't really know her. Maybe she doesn't really know me. Maybe I'm bothered that Alfie has lost interest in checking out books. Maybe it's because she looks at me like I'm one of the blessed saints, even when I say something *dumm.*" Austin stretched his torso across the counter and thumped his forehead on the hard surface. "Maybe I don't really like black bean veggie burgers," he groaned.

"That's seems like a pretty good reason," Andrew mumbled.

Abraham patted him on the arm. "It's obvious she adores you."

Jah, adoration bordering on worship. Austin had never thought it would get old, but now he wasn't so sure. He tiptoed around everything he said to her just so he wouldn't risk damaging her opinion of him. Austin stood up straight and pressed his hand to his slightly aching forehead. "I know she likes me, but I can't figure out why I'm not head over heels in love with her yet. She has everything I've ever wanted in a wife. She's wonderful pretty."

Andrew smirked. "That's the only thing that ever gets your attention. Some people might call you shallow, but I would never be one of them."

"*Denki,*" Austin said. Andrew was a loyal *bruder.*

Andrew tapped his chin with his index finger and squinted. "You're more self-centered than shallow."

"Thanks a lot," Austin said, giving Andrew a healthy shove. "That's not the only reason I like Scilla. She's reserved and modest, and she's well liked. She has lots of friends. She's one of the most devout girls in the *gmayna.* She can quote dozens of Bible verses by heart, and her *bruder* is a minister in Bonduel."

Andrew's eyes lit up mischievously. "A minister *bruder* is a wonderful *gute* reason to marry somebody."

"It's not the only reason," Austin protested, "but it makes everything else about her that much better."

Andrew looked as if he was on the verge of laughter again. "I suppose it does."

Abraham furrowed his brow. "So there are a hundred reasons to like her, but you don't?"

"I like her," Austin said. "I really do, but something's not right. When she comes to the store, Alfie and Benji run upstairs and make funny noises at the top of the stairs when we're trying to talk."

"They like Hannah better," Abraham said.

Austin grunted. "They like Hannah better because she gives them free donuts. Scilla doesn't believe in donuts. She brings BM cookies, and the boys don't like them."

Andrew folded his arms. "BM cookies?"

"Don't ask."

Abraham slid his hands in his pockets. "Hannah doesn't seem to like her all that much either."

That was the most discouraging thing of all. Hannah was Austin's best friend, and he trusted her judgment over just about anyone else's. He wasn't entirely sure how Hannah felt about Scilla, but it was obvious that Scilla didn't have many nice thoughts about Hannah. "I know you think I'm shallow—"

"Self-centered."

"I know you think I'm self-centered, but I like that Scilla is pretty. I've always wanted to marry the prettiest girl in the *gmayna*."

"Was that a New Year's resolution?" Andrew said.

Austin ignored the amusement in Andrew's voice. "Just when it seems I might get my wish, I'm having doubts. I don't know what to do."

Abraham thought about that for a minute. "Emma is the prettiest girl in the *gmayna,* but Scilla can be second if you want."

Andrew laid a hand on Austin's shoulder. "Why don't you find someone who's not quite as pretty but is a really *gute* cook? Or someone whose *dat* is a bishop or uncle is a deacon? Or someone pretty who has false teeth and snores at night?"

Austin slapped Andrew's hand away. Now it was getting ridiculous.

Andrew laughed. "I'm sorry, *bruder,* but the answer has been staring at you for a decade."

Austin narrowed his eyes. "A decade? What are you talking about?"

Andrew folded his arms and shrugged. "I always thought you'd marry Hannah."

"Hannah? She's my best friend."

"So?" Andrew said. "Why can't she be your girlfriend?"

Abraham shook his head adamantly. "Hannah would never marry Austin. She knows him too well."

"What is that supposed to mean?" Austin snapped.

Abraham talked to Andrew as if they were the only two in the room. "Don't steer him toward Hannah. She's got five or six boys interested, and he'd only get his heart broke yet."

The lines on Andrew's forehead deepened. "Maybe you're right. Hannah knows what Austin's like. But she's put up with him for a lot of years."

Austin opened his mouth to protest but decided it would do no good. His *bruderen* sure enough didn't have a very high opinion of him.

Abraham looked at Austin. "I'm not saying you should settle for just anybody, but Hannah will only break your heart. And Scilla really likes you."

Austin simultaneously wanted to agree and disagree. He'd never thought about dating Hannah, but that didn't mean Hannah couldn't be convinced to marry him if he asked. Those five or six other boys weren't good enough for Hannah, and Austin was a real catch. Just ask Scilla. He clenched his teeth. Abraham was right. Hannah knew Austin too well to fall in love with him.

"It's okay, Austin. It's just a case of cold feet, that's all." Abraham was a *gute bruder,* always trying to make things better for his siblings. "You've been looking for reasons not to like Scilla. That's what happened with Emma and me. She wanted to keep flirting and having fun at gatherings, so she started making up reasons not to like me."

"But she finally figured it out," Austin said, rolling that thought over in his brain.

"Maybe you're so worried about the new store and making sure everything goes well that you're pushing Scilla away with your thoughts."

That made sense. "You're right. I just need to give it more time. I've been interested in other girls, and there was always a point where I soured on them. Do you think I'm afraid of marriage?"

"Of course not," Andrew said. "But you might have to go through a lot of girls to find the one you really want to marry."

Austin wasn't sure what to believe. "Maybe I'm being too picky. I feel like running away from marrying Scilla, and she's all I ever wanted in a *fraa.*"

"That doesn't mean you don't want to get married. It just means you don't want to marry Scilla."

"But I do want to marry Scilla," Austin said. Plain and simple, he was just trying to run away from marriage. He'd never been afraid of marriage before, but that seemed the only explanation that made sense. The only cure for cold feet was to push through, because when he married Scilla, he'd be the happiest man alive. He'd be a fool to throw away a good thing just because he was afraid of it.

Andrew frowned. "There's still the problem of black bean veggie burgers. If you marry Scilla, you might die of starvation."

"He can eat dinner at Mamm and Dat's," Abraham said.

It was a nice thought, but it wouldn't work. Scilla would suspect Austin didn't like her cooking if he went to his *mamm's* house for dinner every night.

Andrew picked up his drill. "I still think he should take another look at Hannah, even if she breaks his heart. That or face fifty years of black bean veggie burgers and fake turkey for Thanksgiving."

Austin deflated like a balloon. "It's called Tofurky." And he was going to cry.

Someone knocked on the door as if the store was a house. Austin strode to the door and opened it. A tall Englischer with a short, dark beard and a bright orange beanie stood on the porch. "Are you Austin Petersheim?"

"I am."

The Englischer stuck out his hand. "I'm glad to finally meet you." His grip was firm, even wearing thick gloves.

Austin wasn't sure what to think, but nobody, not even a mountain man or a biker gang member, should be left standing outside on a cold day like this. "Come in," Austin said, stepping back so the Englischer could come into the store.

"Thanks a million. It's cold enough to make even me doubt global warming." The Englischer took off his gloves and beanie, revealing a bun fashioned at the back of his head. Austin's brows inched together. He'd seen that hairstyle before. Hannah called it a man bun. Austin just called it strange.

The Englischer was as tall as Andrew and as skinny as a walking stick. His beard was chestnut brown, and his hair was a lighter brown, with streaks of blond that didn't look like they were completely natural. Well, Bitsy Weaver colored her hair, and she was about the most dependable, no-nonsense person Austin had ever met. The man looked young, probably not much older than Austin.

The Englischer took off his coat and hung it next to Andrew's, as if he'd done it a dozen times before. "I'm glad you're here. I tried calling the number she gave me, but I guess it hasn't been hooked up yet."

Item number 327 in Austin's list. Get the phone working.

Instead of wiping his feet on the mat, the Englischer untied his boots and took them off, as if he meant to stay awhile. His stockings were bright, fluorescent blue. Would walking be more enjoyable in fluorescent blue stockings? After taking off his stockings, the Englischer stuck out his hand again, as if forgetting they'd already shaken hands not two minutes ago. "I'm Will Williams."

"Will Williams," Austin repeated, shaking his hand while trying hard to keep a straight face.

Will smiled wryly. "My parents have a cruel sense of humor."

Austin relaxed into a smile. "Sometimes I can't figure out what parents are thinking."

"My dad thought it would be a cool name for a professional baseball player. My mom just kind of went along with it. It turns out I don't even like baseball. I'm more of a tennis guy." Will moved past Austin to Andrew and Abraham. He stuck out his hand. "Will Williams."

Andrew and Abraham shook hands with him while Abraham kept a close eye on the man bun.

Will let his gaze roam around the store. "This is really nice. It feels homey and Amish. I'm guessing that's what you were going for."

"Yes. I want to attract tourists, but Lord willing, I'll have a lot of Amish business too."

Will's face lit up. "You have a kitchen." He marched to

the kitchen area, leaving Austin no choice but to follow. Abraham and Andrew followed too. "These are nice fridges. The sliding doors are convenient. Do you power everything with liquid propane?"

"For the oven and fridges. But we have solar for the water and two pellet stoves for heat."

Will nodded enthusiastically. "Good for you. I'm almost a hundred percent solar at my place."

Austin didn't want to be rude, but they'd been in conversation for five minutes, and he still had no idea who Will was or what he wanted. "So, our store opens on Tuesday. If you come back then, you can get a free gingerbread cookie."

The bun on Will's head bobbed up and down when he laughed. "I'm sorry. You're being so polite and have no idea what I'm doing here. I guess I should have led with that." He folded his arms and leaned against the counter. "I've got a farm about an hour west of here. We've owned it for three years, and we're one hundred percent organic. We've been experimenting with ways to help the topsoil and make our crops more nutritious." He waved his hand in the air. "Anyway, that's more than you wanted to know. I need a place to sell my milk and eggs and beef and chicken. That little market in town"—he waved his hand toward the south—"that other Amish market isn't interested because organic is expensive, but here's the thing. They're not only organic, but my chickens and cows are pasture fed. Do you know what that means?"

Austin raised an eyebrow. "You feed them in the pasture?"

Will grinned. "True enough. Most cows and chickens are fed soybeans and corn, and it's not as good for you. And don't get me started on Roundup. Anyway, I've built quite a following on my website, and people are looking for a place to buy without having to drive all the way out to my place. Right now, they come to the farm, but it's out in the middle of nowhere, and I don't want to get into the retail business. If you sell my products here, I can post your location on my website, and you'll get customers from all over."

Austin's heart skipped a beat at the possibilities. Will's milk and eggs would bring people into the store who normally wouldn't come, and if he advertised on his website, surely that would bring in even more customers. And best of all, Will had already been to Glick's. Raymond couldn't complain about Austin selling something Raymond had refused to sell. He looked at Abraham and Andrew.

Andrew smiled and nodded. "It sounds like a *gute* idea to me."

"Me too," Abraham said. "But I hope you'll still buy Emma's eggs."

Austin turned to Will. "Abraham's fiancée has chickens. They're exotic, and they lay multicolored eggs."

"Okay," Will said. "I don't want to take anything away from your fiancée, but I think you will be able to sell both without them competing against each other. I'll advertise on my site about the multicolored eggs. People like those."

Austin smiled. "I don't see any reason why we shouldn't do it. We have plenty of fridge space, and if it doesn't work out, we can mutually agree to part ways."

"It's going to work out," Will said. "There's more demand than you can imagine. And it's growing all the time."

They shook hands. "How did you hear about my store?" Austin said.

"I was in the other Amish market a few days ago, and some Amish girl heard me talking with the owner. I think his name was Raymond. He wasn't interested. Anyway, when I left the store, she followed me and told me about your store. Said I should come check it out."

"What girl?"

Will pressed his knuckles to his forehead. "I can't remember her name. But she was pretty, and she wore a blue dress."

"Was it Scilla?" Though what Scilla had been doing in Glick's Market was anybody's guess.

"I don't know."

"Hannah?" Andrew said.

Will sighed. "I really can't remember."

Austin had to know. "Could it have been Priscilla?"

"It might have been."

He felt the warmth of it right in the middle of his chest. The mystery girl had been Scilla. He just knew it. And it was another reason he wouldn't give up on her. It wasn't a small thing for a single Amish girl to talk to an Englisch man like that, especially not for Scilla. She was making sacrifices for love too.

Will opened and closed Austin's fridges, then stepped back to get a good look at the whole kitchen. "If you'd like to do business, I'll come back tomorrow with a pricing sheet and delivery schedule. How does that sound?"

"I'd like that very much," Austin said.

He and Will shook on it. All four of them laughed when Will shook hands with Andrew and Abraham all over again. Will put his coat and hat on. "I'll see you tomorrow then. And I'll see that your opening gets on my website."

Austin handed him one of Hannah's flyers. "Here is the information if you need it. Remember to tell them that everybody gets a free gingerbread cookie just for coming in."

Will grinned. "I will. People will always show up for free food." He sat down on the floor and put on his boots.

"My wife can make gluten-free pies for your Christmas customers, if you want."

Austin didn't know if he liked that idea or hated it. He'd tasted some of Scilla's gluten-free bread, and he'd just as soon pass. "I don't know how many people will want gluten-free pies."

Will wasn't offended. Instead, he laughed. "I say 'gluten-free' and people think 'disgusting.' But they're really good. We can talk about it tomorrow. You could put up a sign-up sheet at your store opening, and then my wife can make the pies and have them here before Christmas."

Austin rubbed his hand down the side of his face. "I guess it couldn't hurt." Scilla would probably order a gluten-free pie. But since she fancied herself such a *gute* cook, she might want to make one herself, just so she could prove she could do it better than any Englischer.

"Okay." Will opened the door, and frigid air blew into the store. "I'll bring a sign-up sheet. We'll see you tomorrow. Is two o'clock okay?"

"I'll be here," Austin said.

Will shut the door behind him, and Austin immediately moved to the pellet stove to borrow some of its warmth. "Every time that door opens, the whole store freezes."

"I could build an atrium extension out on the porch," Andrew said. "It would cost some money for the wood, but it would definitely make the store a more pleasant place to be in the winter."

"How much?" Austin tried not to clench his teeth. It felt like he was shoveling money into a big hole.

"I'll figure it out," Andrew said. "If you don't want it to look makeshift or stupid, that will probably cost more."

"Whatever you do, don't make it look stupid."

Andrew laughed. "Good to know."

The front door opened again, and Hannah walked into the store carrying a box wrapped in shiny red paper with a silver bow. The box was bright and cheery, but Hannah's face was anything but. She looked as if her dog had run away or her *mamm* had contracted the flu or her donut stand had burned down.

Or her sign had been defaced.

Ach.

Austin's stomach plummeted to the floor. He had meant to tell Hannah about the sign, but he hadn't gotten the opportunity yesterday because of the police and Raymond Glick and the cinnamon rolls that had nearly burned in all the confusion.

"Hannah," Andrew said, rushing to her side. He shut the door and helped her off with her coat. "It's wonderful *gute* to see you. You look so pretty today, well, like you do every day. Austin for sure and certain appreciates all you've done for him and his store."

Austin pressed his lips together. He was grateful to Andrew for trying to smooth things over with Hannah, but no amount of flattery was going to fix her sign. Or maybe Andrew was just trying to butter Hannah up so she'd notice Austin and maybe want to marry him. Why did his heart race at that possibility? He was dating Scilla, and Hannah would never be interested in Austin. Hadn't both Andrew and Abraham said so?

Hannah wasn't usually one to beat around the bush, but she didn't even look Austin in the eye when she handed him her box. "This is for you," she said halfheartedly, "to celebrate the opening of your store."

She didn't sound like she wanted to celebrate. He'd gotten himself into this mess, and he'd have to be a man and get himself out of it. At the very least, he had to see Hannah smile. She just wasn't herself without a smile. He took the box from her and fingered the ribbon. "This is beautiful, Hannah."

"Okay," she said, taking her coat from Andrew and pulling it on. "It's a gift so you can let Scilla repaint it if you want."

The tinge of bitterness in her voice sent Austin reeling. He had known she wasn't going to be happy about the sign. Maybe he hadn't realized how much. Or maybe he hadn't wanted to think about it. He grabbed her gloved hand and pulled her back before she opened the door. "Don't you want to see me open it?"

The pain in Hannah's eyes was raw and uncommon. "Not really. You won't like it, and Scilla will hate it."

Andrew and Abraham glanced at each other. "We should see how that paint is drying downstairs," Andrew said.

Abraham nodded. He grabbed his tape measure from the counter and followed Andrew down the stairs at a brisk clip.

Austin didn't know if it would be better to have his *bruderen* here defending him or face Hannah alone. But he wasn't about to call them back. No one could explain this better than he, and no one could smooth things over with Hannah the way he could, or at least like he used to be able to do. "I guess you saw the sign."

"I guess I did." Hannah fixed her gaze on the basement stairs, probably trying to decide if Austin's *bruderen* were spying.

"Do you want to go upstairs?" Austin said. He didn't want his *bruderen* overhearing them either, just in case he made a real mess of things.

"Not really. I just want to go home."

"Hannah, you're not being fair. I want to talk without my *bruderen* listening in."

Her face turned bright red. "*I'm* not being fair. Isn't it just like you to blame everything on me."

His throat went dry. Hannah was madder than he would have thought. But what could he have done differently? Scilla had been insistent about the sign, and he'd been forced to choose between the two of them. "Please, Hannah, can we just go upstairs and talk about it?"

Hannah glanced again at the stairs to the basement. "I've got to get home."

"It's not that urgent, or you wouldn't have bothered to come today."

She lifted her chin and clamped her lips together. *Ach.* He knew better than to antagonize her right before he tried to apologize. He motioned for her to go first and then followed her up the stairs with the festive box tucked under his arm. He was going to gush shamelessly over whatever was in this box, even if it was a plate of BM cookies.

Austin got a great deal of satisfaction when he went upstairs. It was the one place in the store that was completely ready for customers. A long hall ran down the middle of the second floor opening to three bedrooms with a bathroom at the end. Each bedroom was filled with Amish-made handicrafts of every variety imaginable. Hannah, Abraham's fiancée, Emma, and Andrew's wife, Mary, had decorated every square inch with garlands of fruit and leaves, ornate lanterns, and homespun ribbons. In one room sat an entire dining set made by Andrew, plus three stunning quilts hung on the walls. Mandy Gingerich had hand-painted a set of dishes with delicate flowers on the edges, and Serena Beiler had sewn potholders and table runners that rested in a basket by the door.

Andrew's other woodwork was scattered around the second floor, as were more quilts and wall hangings. They had Amish *kapps* and hats and Christmas tree ornaments. The Englisch were going to love exploring.

Hannah walked about halfway down the hall, stopped, and studied his face, obviously waiting for him to explain himself.

He swallowed hard. Might as well be straightforward and contrite. "I'm sorry about the sign."

A deep line appeared between her eyebrows. "*Nae,* you're not."

She wasn't going to make it easy on him, that was for sure and certain. "I'm sorry you feel bad about it."

"Why should you care how I feel?"

It was an accusation, not a question, and an irritating one at that. Why was she being so unreasonable? "Of course I care how you feel, Hannah, but I didn't want to hurt Scilla's feelings either."

Hannah grunted her disapproval and rolled her eyes. "Oh, yes, because Scilla's feelings were sooo wounded by my sign."

"I just thought . . . I mean . . . she has a cousin or an uncle or something who owns a store, and she knows about things like this—about how to attract customers."

"That's why you changed my sign, because you think it will attract more customers?"

"Well. Yes." That was probably why he had changed it.

"You're a liar, Austin Petersheim."

Austin stepped back. "How could you say that? We're best friends."

"Are we?"

Oy anyhow.

Hannah pinned him with a piercing gaze. "Look me in the eye and tell me you like the sign better this way."

He wouldn't have answered that challenge for all the peanut butter in Wisconsin. He didn't owe Hannah an explanation about something that was between him and his girlfriend. "If Scilla says it will bring in more customers, I trust her. Don't act like you know anything about opening a store, because you know even less than I do."

She reacted as if he'd slapped her. "I guess I don't."

"I didn't mean that," he said, realizing too late how mean that sounded.

"Of course you did."

"I did not. And you know it."

Hannah looked at him as if he'd said something ferociously stupid. "This is not my fault, Austin. At least own up to it."

"It's your fault you're so upset."

She opened her mouth and closed it again. In one moment, she seemed to come to rest, like a tornado that had blown itself out. "You're right."

He forced a playful grin onto his face. "I'm right? How nice of you to finally admit it."

She didn't laugh. She didn't smile. There wasn't even the hint of amusement in her eyes. She took a deep breath and shook her head. "You're right, Austin, and I'm sorry for questioning your judgment."

He wasn't exactly satisfied with that, but he didn't know how to argue with her when she didn't seem to want to put up a fight. He felt as low as the floorboards at his feet.

"This is nothing I don't already know and haven't already accepted," she said, more to herself than to him.

"I really liked your sign," he said weakly, as if that made everything okay.

She didn't respond. Without warning, she scooted past him and headed down the stairs. "Good-bye, Austin. I'll see you on Tuesday."

"Hannah, wait." He quickly followed her down the stairs and nearly dropped the present when he stumbled over the last step.

She didn't even pause, storming out the door, then slamming it behind her.

Austin was tempted to run after her, but it was cold out there and despite what she'd said, she was still wonderful mad. It wouldn't do him any *gute* to apologize *again* until she had cooled off.

He'd never be able to figure out girls and why they overreacted to everything.

He might as well open Hannah's present. He wouldn't even have to gush shamelessly because Hannah wasn't there to see it. Austin set the wrapped box on the counter and untied the bow. He carefully peeled back the paper and took the lid off the box. A shovel head without the handle sat cushioned in a bed of white tissue paper. Austin caught his breath. On the back of the shovel, Hannah had painted a picture of Austin's store beneath a brilliant turquoise sky with puffy clouds floating by. She'd added a small replica of the sign she'd painted for the front of the store, plus bunches of purple, blue, and yellow flowers along the foundation. A rocking chair sat on the porch with a pot of yellow chrysanthemums next to it, and a buggy was parked in front of the store with a dog that looked suspiciously like Tintin lounging next to it.

Over the painted sky, she'd written *Plain and Simple Country Store* with the year and Austin's name in bright orange.

It was extraordinary.

A little card sat on top of the white tissue paper.

Dear Austin,

I wanted to give you this gift before things got too busy around here. I hope you like it. A painted shovel might seem like a strange gift, but the idea of a shovel is what got you started down this path, so I thought it was appropriate. Denki for listening to me, for making me laugh, for standing up for me. I am blessed to call you my true friend.

Sincerely,
Hannah

P.S. Don't worry about your store. You are going to be amazing, as you always are. But don't let it go to your head.

Austin closed the card and wiped his eyes. He'd never felt so low in his entire life.

Chapter Fifteen

Hannah had finished blubbering by Monday morning. Then she'd made sixteen dozen gingerbread cookies without crying. She'd cut out those cookies without once wishing she could throw them at Scilla Lambright, and by Tuesday morning, she'd stopped caring about Austin at all.

Forever.

Never again.

And so on.

Even if she was just pretending not to care, it was a *gute* first step.

And it was still okay to be mad about her sign, even if she had pretended to forgive Scilla and Austin and everybody who liked organic food.

She found herself wishing she had a cell phone, just this once, so she could have taken a picture of her sign before Scilla had scribbled on it. Maybe this was what came of being proud. Maybe this was Gotte's way of telling her to give up painting and art and Austin altogether and focus her attention on caring for Aendi Linda's children and making donuts. And maybe moving to Colorado.

She obviously hadn't learned her lesson about Austin,

because here she was again, standing at the front door to his store with a basket full of gingerbread cookies. It was half an hour before opening, and they would have barely enough time to set out their cookies and arrange the other baked goods in a pleasing display before people started coming—or at least they hoped people would come. Andrew had built a shelf to sit on the counter that held bread, cinnamon rolls, cookies, and whatever else they wanted to display there. Mary had made bread dough this morning that they could pop into the store oven immediately. The store would smell like baking bread and gingerbread cookies when customers walked in the door.

"Are you going to go in?" James said.

Hannah sighed and turned the knob. "Of course. I'm just gathering my wits before things get busy."

Austin had his back to the door when Hannah, James, and Mary walked in. He turned and burst into a heart-melting smile when he saw them, specifically when he saw Hannah. He didn't even look at James and Mary. He rushed over and offered to take Hannah's basket. "It's not heavy," she said.

He slid it off her arm. "Heavy enough." They followed James and Mary to the kitchen. "*Denki* for coming, Hannah."

"Did you think I wouldn't?" She'd practiced her casual smile a hundred times yesterday. It still felt foreign on her face.

His smile was so warm, she could almost believe he was happy to see her. "I prayed very hard that you would."

"Of course. If I hadn't shown up, you wouldn't have any gingerbread cookies to hand out. People would have accused you of false advertising."

He didn't take it as the joke she'd meant it. "That's not it at all, Hannah. I don't care about the cookies. I mean, I'm grateful, but I wanted you here with or without cookies. You know that, don't you?"

She didn't want to ruin such a nice moment, so she told him what he wanted to hear. "I know you're glad I'm here."

Austin set the basket on the counter. "*Cum,* I want to show you something."

"We don't really have time. . . ."

He took her hand. Actually took her hand. Right in front of Mary and James and Andrew and Abraham and Emma who were dusting shelves and making sure everything was in place. "It doesn't matter. I need to show you."

She let him pull her along, mostly because she couldn't have been more shocked if he'd given her a kiss right on the lips—which she in no way wanted him to do because that would be very improper and she wouldn't be able to think straight for the rest of the day.

He led her back to the front door and pointed to the wall to the right of the door. "Look."

The shovel head she'd painted was mounted right next to the door as sort of a welcome to people who entered the store. She hadn't even seen it when she came in. Her heart skipped inside her chest like a skater bug over the water. "It looks nice."

"Emma helped me hang it. I wanted to make sure people know it's special."

She couldn't resist asking, even when she knew what he was going to say. Maybe she just wanted to hear him say it. "Do you like it?"

"I love it."

"I tried to make it look just like the store." Her tongue went dry. "If you want me to put 'organic' on the sign, I think I could do it with a white Sharpie."

"*Nae, nae, nae,*" he said, shaking his head adamantly.

He nudged her arm so she would turn to face him, then curled his fingers around her shoulders. "I made a real mess of my apology. Will you let me try again?"

One side of Hannah's mouth involuntarily twitched upward. "I don't know. Are you going to make a mess of this one too?"

He smiled. "Probably. But I have to try anyway. Hannah, I'm sorry about the sign. I was trying to make Scilla happy, even though I liked the sign the way it was. Then I snapped at you because I wanted to justify myself."

"I understand," she said, and she truly did. Austin loved Scilla, and Hannah would have to accept it. And probably move to Colorado. Boys did stupid things for love, like ruin perfectly *gute* signs and eat black bean veggie burgers. Hannah didn't like it one little bit, but she understood why Austin had done it.

Unfortunately, it was a really good apology, so she couldn't use it against him on the days she tried to talk herself out of liking him. But there were other reasons not to like Austin, and the biggest one walked through the door just then, giving Hannah a *gute* excuse to step away from Austin before she did something stupid like believe he could ever love her.

Scilla kicked the door shut with her foot because her arms were full of packages. Hannah's gaze flicked to the door. Scilla's shoe had made a nice black scuff at the bottom. Hannah sighed inwardly. Maybe she could scrub it off.

"*Hallo,* Scilla," Austin said, moving away from Hannah as if he didn't like the way she smelled.

Scilla stopped just inside the door, right next to Hannah's shovel head, and peered at Hannah as if she'd never seen her before. "What are you doing here?"

Really? *What are you doing here?* It was opening day, and Hannah was in charge of the gingerbread and the entire bakery. What did Scilla think she was doing here? With every last ounce of willpower she had, Hannah smiled as if she was delighted to see Scilla. "Mary, James, and I came early to get everything set out. We made two hundred gingerbread cookies."

Austin's eyes got as round as saucers. "Two hundred?"

"*Nae,*" Scilla said. "I meant, what are you doing *here?*" She drew a little circle in the air with her finger, as if pointing out the territory Hannah wasn't allowed to set foot in.

Austin smiled uncomfortably. "I was just showing Hannah where I'd hung the shovel she painted for me. See? Isn't it *wunderbarr?*"

Scilla eyed Hannah's shovel with intense interest. "We should write 'organic' on the little sign to make it match the real store."

It probably wasn't Christian to claw Scilla's eyes out, so Hannah kept her smile glued to her face and put her hands behind her back. "I like it just the way it is," she said. "But Austin can do what he wants."

Take that, Austin! If he were as sorry as he said he was, he wouldn't let Scilla touch that shovel.

Austin took Scilla's bags from her. "What did you bring?"

The coward. But the fact that he wouldn't stand up to Scilla gave Hannah another *gute* reason not to like him.

Scilla preened like a cat and turned away from Hannah's shovel. "Two loaves of whole wheat bread I made yesterday and three dozen BM cookies. I would have made more, but I had to work. But I specially asked for the day off today so I could be here in your time of need."

"*Denki* for coming," Austin said. "There's so much to do, I'm not even sure where to start."

Scilla patted him on the arm. "Don't you worry. I can help you with everything. I'm *gute* at counting money, and I know how to make change. And I'll refill the candy if it runs low."

This seemed to make Austin ecstatically happy. "You are so thoughtful, Scilla. There will be plenty for everybody to do. Mary and Andrew are here as well as Abraham and Emma. Mamm and Dat will bring the boys over after school. I know Mary and Hannah will need help keeping the kitchen clean."

Scilla pinched her lips together. "Cleaning gives my hands a rash, but I'll do anything you need me to, Austin."

Cleaning gave Scilla's hands a rash? *Ach.* She was going to be a lot of fun today. And no help at all. Not that Hannah cared. She would much rather Scilla stayed out of the kitchen and away from the food. She could stand in the far corner and try to sell her BM cookies.

Leaving Austin and Scilla to fawn over each other, Hannah preheated the oven and put the loaves of bread in to bake. In addition to the gingerbread cookies and the bread, they'd brought three dozen cinnamon rolls and dough to make donuts and pretzels. They had decided to put the deep fat fryer outside so it didn't stink up the entire store. It sat on a folding table under a small canopy they used in the summer at their donut stand. James was the designated donut cooker. The house sheltered him from the wind, he wore a coat and two oven mitts, and he stood over the fryer, so he was plenty warm.

At ten o'clock, Hannah's *mamm* and *dat* arrived, along with about ten other neighbors and six or seven Englischers. Ten minutes later, Will Williams, the Englischer

Hannah had met at Glick's Market, came in the back door with a wagon full of milk. Better late than never. He put his milk in the refrigerators, then went back outside for eggs and butter. Hannah was wonderful glad she'd suggested Will contact Austin. He could advertise Austin's store on his website and bring in more business with his milk and eggs.

The morning flew by. Almost every one of their neighbors from the *gmayna* stopped by to have a look at the store and eat a cookie. Some of them even bought groceries. Almost all of them bought a jar of Petersheim Brothers peanut butter to show their support. But the Englischers were the best customers. One of them bought the rocking chair Andrew had built, and another one spent seven hundred dollars on one of Lily Yoder's quilts. Mary and Hannah made pretzels and frosted donuts and sold all the cinnamon rolls before noon.

Austin was happier and more nervous than Hannah had ever seen him. He walked around the store, telling people about the merchandise, but mostly he ran the cash register while Scilla stood next to him and acted like she was in charge of something.

At about two o'clock, when they had a lull and there weren't any customers in the store, Hannah and Mary cut a pretzel in four pieces and shared it with Austin and James. Scilla refused to eat Hannah's pretzels because they weren't whole wheat, but that didn't stop the rest of them from enjoying a piece. "Try this hot mustard, Austin," Hannah said. "It's *appeditlich* on a pretzel."

Austin dipped his pretzel in the hot mustard, took a bite, and coughed as if he were choking. James pounded him on the back until he stopped coughing. "That is hot," Austin said, gagging and gasping for air.

Mary laughed. "Englischers love it."

"It's *gute,*" James said. "You just don't want to breathe in when you take a bite."

Austin went to the kitchen sink and took a drink straight from the tap. "Thanks for the warning." He wiped his face on a napkin. "Did you see we sold that blue and green quilt Lily Yoder made?"

Hannah nodded. "And most of the organic, pasture-fed milk."

Austin leaned against the counter. "Someone wanted to buy your shovel head, Hannah."

Hannah hadn't expected that. "They did?"

"I told them it wasn't for sale, but they said they'd come back and maybe give you a special order. I hope you don't mind."

"Mind?" Hannah said. "I'm thrilled someone likes my art."

Scilla was sort of dusting the cash register with one of Hannah's dishtowels. "Now, now, let's not let our pride run away with us."

Hannah was too happy to let Scilla's petulance bother her. Very much. They paid Austin a percentage of everything they sold in their little bakery, but most of the money went to them, and they'd made a *gute* amount this morning. It was satisfying after a full day of baking yesterday and a busy morning today. The Englischers loved the donuts, as usual, and they'd gotten orders for four dozen cinnamon rolls. For sure and certain more orders would come in this week. So many people threw Christmas parties this time of year.

Scilla's loaves of whole wheat bread had sold, even though they looked like poky lumps of cow manure. But she hadn't sold any BM cookies, because they looked even worse. Hannah tried to muster some pity for Scilla, but she couldn't do it. Hannah's donuts were simply better than Scilla's BM cookies, and that was a fact. Scilla would just have to get over it.

"It wonders me if we should whip up another batch of cinnamon rolls," Mary said, "for the crowd that's sure to come tonight."

"*Gute* idea," Hannah said, dabbing her hands with the napkin. "I'll grab more flour from the basement."

"I'll get it," Austin said, already heading toward the stairs.

Scilla glanced at Hannah. "You have more important things to do, Austin. James can get it."

"I don't mind." Austin smiled warmly at Hannah, sending a zing of electricity right to her heart. "After everything the Yutzys have done for me today, the least I can do is some fetching and carrying."

Scilla frowned at Hannah as if everything in the world was her fault. "I'm coming with you."

Austin shrugged. Scilla followed him down the stairs. James made a face. "She's a little tense."

"And grumpy," Mary added in a whisper.

Hannah giggled. "She needs to eat more BM cookies."

By five o'clock, the rolls were in the oven, and Hannah and Mary were readying a batch of pretzels. The rest of the Petersheim family was coming for a dinner of pretzels and peanut butter, and so were the Gingeriches and two or three other families in the *gmayna.* Scilla was going to be appalled at such an unnutritious dinner, but it was a special occasion, and the Yutzys often ate leftover pretzels and church spread for their evening meal.

Alfie, Benji, Ruth Ann, and Dinah burst into the store and ran straight for the kitchen. Rebecca and Benaiah

Petersheim followed after them. "Slow down," Rebecca called. "You are not a herd of buffalo."

Benji came around the counter and gave Hannah a hug. "We're going to the city council meeting tonight to get a prize."

Alfie rolled his eyes. "We're getting an award, Benji, not a prize."

"Oh," Hannah said. "I wish I could be there."

Benji shrugged. "It's okay. Mamm doesn't want anybody to come. She says our heads will explode."

Alfie groaned. "She doesn't want us to get big heads, Benji. They're not going to explode."

Ruth Ann pushed between Alfie and Benji. "Me and Dinah are going because we're Alfie and Benji's partners."

Alfie winced. "We are not partners. We're just helping each other."

"You're not helping very much," Ruth Ann said, giving Alfie a private look that Hannah couldn't begin to interpret.

Hannah slid her hands down her apron. "Are you getting your picture taken?"

"*Jah,*" Benji said. "The bishop said they can take our picture, but they aren't allowed to use it in the newspaper. But he's going to let them put Tintin's picture in the paper. Tintin will like that. Mom let us tie a ribbon around his neck. He's waiting for us in the buggy."

Mary put four pretzels on four paper plates. "Do you want a pretzel?"

"*Jah,*" Benji said. The other children nodded eagerly.

Hannah handed out napkins. "*Cum.* Sit at the counter. We've got seven kinds of dipping sauce. Melted cheese, peanut butter spread, honey butter, yellow mustard, hot mustard, and marinara sauce."

Dinah made a face. "What is mariner sauce?"

"It's like spaghetti sauce."

"Can you say the choices again?" Benji asked.

Hannah ran through the dipping sauces two more times before each child made a selection. Alfie and Dinah wanted two sauces each, and Hannah finally gave them a cup of everything except the hot mustard so they could try it all.

Rebecca looked around the store, then scooted over and gave Hannah and Mary a hug. "It smells like you girls have been baking all day."

"We have," Hannah said. "We've sold just about everything we brought this morning. Your cinnamon rolls were gone in about two hours."

Rebecca smiled. "They're your cinnamon rolls now. I just helped with the recipe."

Scilla approached them with a plate of her BM cookies. She'd taken them out of the package. "Rebecca, would you like a free BM cookie? I'm giving out free samples because I think people will buy a package if they know how delicious and nutritious they are."

Rebecca's smile looked as if she'd fastened it there with two thumbtacks. "*Denki,* Scilla, but I've already tasted your BM cookies. What a *gute* idea to try to give them away for free."

Scilla seemed pleased. "I told Austin I have several wonderful *gute* ideas for the store. It was my idea to put 'organic' on the sign outside. People need to know."

Rebecca nodded, still with that tight smile in place. "Don't feel bad that your lettering is a little clumsy. We can't all be as artistic as Hannah."

Hannah nearly hugged Rebecca again, but then felt wicked for gloating over Scilla's lack of ability. Could Scilla help it if her printing looked like something Alfie might have done with his eyes closed?

The store door opened again, bringing a gust of cold air

and seven Englischers with it. One of them was the mayor. He spread out his hands as if giving the other six people a tour of the store, even though to Hannah's knowledge, he had never been in the store before. "Look at what they've done to this old place? It's a credit to our fine city."

The six Englischers with the mayor nodded their agreement, and Hannah finally realized they were the Bienenstock city council. Austin immediately moved to greet them. He shook the mayor's hand. "*Hallo.* Welcome to Plain and Simple Country Store."

The mayor looked extraordinarily pleased with himself. "We've already got a picture of your store on our town website under 'Attractions.' Now that we have two Amish markets, a library, and a gas station, we're going to start our very own chamber of commerce. Thanks to you."

Austin smiled tentatively. "Thank you." He didn't know what a chamber of commerce was. Hannah certainly didn't, and it was a *gute* bet Scilla didn't either, even if her third cousin twice removed owned a store.

"Now, I know you don't want to be photographed," the mayor said, "but can we take a picture of the city council here in the store? Maybe put it in the town newsletter?"

"Of course."

Hannah smiled to herself. More free advertising. They could use all they could get.

"Randall, will you take a picture?" The mayor handed his phone to a short, balding man with a spindly moustache. The mayor glanced around the store until his gaze landed on Hannah's shovel. Her heart skipped a beat as the mayor stepped up to get a closer look. "Get us standing in front of this painted shovel. A picture of the store *in* the store. This is a very nice rendering."

"It's not exact," Scilla mumbled. Hannah ground her

teeth together. Gotte had put Scilla in Hannah's path. He must have really wanted her to learn patience and long-suffering.

"Is this shovel painted by someone Amish?" the mayor asked Austin.

"Yes," Austin said, practically bursting with excitement. He pointed to Hannah with a look that could have warmed a snowman's heart. "My friend Hannah painted it."

Scilla stiffened beside Hannah. Hannah was too giddy to care.

The mayor eyed Hannah. "We've met before, haven't we?"

"Yes. At Alfie and Benji's house."

He nodded. "I remember. You're a very fine artist." He turned to a woman bundled in a pink coat. "Wouldn't it be something to hire Hannah to paint all the attractions in Bienenstock on shovels and hang them at city hall? Like a memorial."

The woman crumpled her brows together. "I guess, but we don't have many attractions."

The mayor frowned. "Maybe we need to find a few. Pensaukee River could be an attraction. There's good fishing. And one of the Green Bay Packers got gas at our station once." The mayor gathered the council members around him, making sure not to block the shovel, and Randall snapped a few pictures. Once the mayor was satisfied, he turned and shook Austin's hand again. "We're honoring your brothers tonight at city council meeting. I'll be sure to mention that you've opened a store."

"*Denki.* I would appreciate that."

The mayor zipped up his coat. "We just stopped by to take a look before city council meeting, but I'm sure we'll be back. I'd like to buy some Christmas goodies for the family."

Austin's face fell. He was obviously hoping someone on

the city council would buy something. "*Ach, vell,* thank you for coming. We will see you soon, Lord willing."

The mayor inclined his head in Austin's direction. "Lord willing," he stuttered before he closed the door behind him.

Austin looked at Hannah and shrugged. "They didn't buy anything."

"They didn't even stay long enough for me to offer them a BM cookie," Scilla said.

Thank Derr Herr for that.

"They really liked your shovel." Austin seemed genuinely happy that the mayor paid special attention to her shovel painting.

Rebecca's gaze flicked from Hannah to Austin. "Scilla, why don't you show me your organic section? Austin says you've been working hard on it."

Hannah couldn't tell if Scilla was pleased or put out by the request. "I'd like to, but I need to keep handing out BM cookies."

"I'll take care of it," Mary said, taking Scilla's plate without waiting for her to agree. Mary was clever. She never said she'd hand out the cookies, which was a *gute* thing because Mary wasn't one to lie. But as far as Hannah could tell, everyone but Scilla felt the same way about her BM cookies. Mary might toss them in the garbage when Scilla wasn't looking, but she wouldn't hand them out. As she said, she'd take care of it.

"Okay," Scilla said. "Would you like to see the refrigerated organic foods first or the non-refrigerated?"

"Refrigerated."

Scilla and Rebecca wandered to the refrigerators while Scilla explained to Rebecca what *organic* actually meant.

Hannah brushed a piece of lint off Austin's shoulder. "How does it feel to be a store owner?"

"It feels like I'm on one of those wild roller coasters at Wisconsin Dells."

"You're doing very well. But you need to stop acting so sad when a customer doesn't buy anything."

He sighed. "Is it that obvious? I'm just so eager to make the store a success."

"I know, but if you're too eager, you'll drive customers away. If they think you're disappointed in them, they won't come back. Just be glad they've come in. They might not buy anything the first time, but they'll buy eventually. Let them browse without you following them anxiously around the store. They'll tell all their friends about your pretty store and what a nice feeling there is here. If they don't feel pressured to buy something, they'll keep coming back."

Austin squared his shoulders. "I can do that. I think."

"Of course you can. Just be your own friendly, chipper self. They'll love you."

He raised his eyebrow teasingly. "Chipper?"

She giggled at his comical expression. "It's a *gute* word."

"I don't even know what it means."

"You do too."

He pointed to Mary. The BM cookies had mysteriously disappeared, and she was walking around the store offering gingerbread cookies to the shoppers. "The gingerbread cookies were the best idea. It gives people a *gute* feeling about our store, whether they buy anything or not."

The way he looked at her made her feel lightheaded, like she was the most important person in the world to him. Like he didn't even know who Scilla Lambright was. Like Hannah was just as pretty as any girl in the whole *gmayna.*

"Gingerbread . . ."—she cleared her throat—"gingerbread isn't hard to make, and it smells like Christmas. I hoped people would like it."

He reached out and wound an errant strand of her hair around his finger. "I wish I had your brain. You can make a batch of pretzels without a recipe, and you can paint or draw anything. I can't even do stick figures."

Hannah inclined her head. "You really don't need to know how to draw. It's not much of a skill. Besides, you're *gute* with numbers. That's a much more important skill."

"Tell that to my little *bruderen.* When they're hungry, they couldn't care less that I can multiply numbers in my head. They'd much rather have a donut than a math lesson."

Hannah watched as Benji popped the last bite of pretzel into his mouth and licked the cheese from the bottom of the cup. "They still adore you."

He gave her a wry twist of his lips. "Maybe, but they like you better."

"Maybe they do."

He ran his fingers through his thick auburn hair. "I get no appreciation around here."

"None whatsoever," Hannah said, when that wasn't true at all. He didn't know how much she appreciated his boyish smile or his bright, teasing eyes. And he certainly didn't know how much she appreciated his broad shoulders and chiseled arms. She even adored his aggravating confidence and his self-satisfied swagger. She especially enjoyed taking his bravado down a peg when he deserved it. And he almost always deserved it.

"Austin," Scilla called from the other side of the store. "Come tell your *mamm* about our ideas for an organic pet food section."

Austin eyed Hannah almost regretfully. "I've got to go."

Hannah tried valiantly not to laugh about organic pet food. "And I've got to take the cinnamon rolls out of the oven."

About half an hour later, Rebecca and Benaiah took Alfie and Benji, and Ruth Ann and Dinah to the city council meeting. Hannah really did wish she could have gone. Alfie and Benji were like her adopted *bruderen,* and she was exceptionally proud of what they'd done for those people in the motor home.

As Hannah was wiping up *die kinner's* sticky mess, Raymond and Perry Glick strolled into the store, looking as guilty as two foxes in a henhouse. They were certainly spying, but they had as much right to be here as anybody. Hannah caught Austin's eye and raised her eyebrows. Austin nodded but pretended not to see them, which wasn't too hard to do since there were about forty people in the store and he was busy helping customers.

Raymond's expression always looked like he was suffering from a sour stomach. He could ruin any Christmas party just by showing up, and he put a damper on any gathering he was in. Hannah lifted her chin. Raymond wasn't going to spoil Austin's grand opening, not if she had anything to say about it.

She grabbed the plate of gingerbread from Mary and confronted Raymond while he studied her painted shovel head by the door. "Raymond Glick, how nice of you and Perry to come celebrate with us!"

Raymond narrowed his eyes, immediately suspicious. Hannah couldn't blame him for that. She was only pretending to be happy to see him. "I didn't come to celebrate," he said. "I came to make sure Austin isn't breaking the rules set down by the bishop."

Hannah stretched her smile wider across her face. "Have a gingerbread cookie. Nothing says Christmas like a gingerbread cookie."

He pinched his lips together. "How much?"

"They're free, just to thank you for coming in."

Raymond didn't quite seem to believe that Hannah was telling the truth. "No, thank you. I'd rather eat a roll at Glick's Family Restaurant."

Hannah turned her smile to Perry, though she really couldn't stand him. "Would you like a cookie, Perry?"

"For sure and certain," Perry said, grabbing a handful of cookies from the plate. Hannah decided not to mention that the cookies were supposed to be one per customer. If Perry ate his weight in gingerbread, he was less likely to make trouble.

Raymond scowled at his son. "We're here to inspect the store. Put those cookies back."

With a look of deep regret, Perry reached out to return his cookies, but Hannah pulled back the plate. "It's okay, Perry. Please eat them. Everybody who comes in here deserves a thank-you cookie. We're just so grateful you came to see the new store and wish us well."

Raymond turned his scowl to Hannah. "We didn't come to wish anybody well. We came to make sure Austin follows the rules." He pulled a small notebook from his pocket along with a pencil. "I see that he is selling milk. We sell milk at our market. He is not allowed to sell it here."

Hannah didn't want to argue. Would it do any good to try to set Raymond straight? "Actually, that is organic, pasture-fed milk from Will Williams. Do you remember him?"

"Why should I remember him?"

"He came to your store offering to sell you his milk.

You said you weren't interested, so I told him about Austin's store. Since you didn't want his milk, it seemed fair to let Austin carry it here."

Raymond pressed his lips into a rigid line, obviously realizing he would have to do better than that if he hoped for a victory over Austin Petersheim. Hannah didn't really care if Raymond went through the whole store with a fine-tooth comb. They'd been very careful about only carrying merchandise that Raymond Glick didn't. But she did care that Raymond stay away from Austin and not ruin his big day.

Maybe it would work to get the Glicks on a different floor. "We've got quilts and all sorts of Amish handicrafts upstairs," she said. "Would you like to have a look?"

"Maybe," Raymond said, peering toward the stairs as if the answer he wanted was up there.

When he hesitated, Hannah said, "Why don't you sit at the counter and have a donut? We have some maple bacon donuts that are *appeditlich.*" She looked at Perry. "They're a special price today."

"I'd really like one of those," Perry said, his mouth full of gingerbread cookie.

Raymond grabbed Perry's sleeve and pulled him toward the stairs. "We aren't here to eat donuts. Let's go upstairs."

Raymond and Perry climbed the stairs as if they were on an important secret mission. Well, Raymond did. Perry looked back longingly at Hannah's plate of gingerbread cookies.

While they were gone for a few minutes, Hannah could figure out how to get rid of them entirely once they came back down. And maybe there was a way to take care of two nuisances at once. She handed Mary the plate of gingerbread cookies. "Mary, where are Scilla's BM cookies?"

"You're not thinking of handing them out, are you?"

"I want Raymond and Perry to have a taste."

Mary rolled her eyes. "Why did they have to come?"

"To make trouble," Hannah said.

Mary pointed to the fridge. "I almost threw them away but decided that might hurt Scilla's feelings. They're in there."

Hannah grinned. "*Denki.* They're going to be helpful." She retrieved the BM cookies from the fridge and then located Scilla standing next to Austin at the cash register. She caught Scilla's eye and motioned her over.

Scilla seemed reluctant to do anything Hannah asked, but she tore herself from Austin's side and edged closer to Hannah. "What do you want?"

"Raymond and Perry Glick are here."

"I saw them. I think it's nice they're showing some Christian charity by coming out to see our store."

"I don't think charity is what they have in mind."

Scilla looked down her nose at Hannah. "You shouldn't always assume the worst about people."

Hannah bit her tongue and nodded as if Scilla always said the wisest things. "They went upstairs to look at the quilts, but when they come down, I thought you might enjoy showing them around the store, especially your organic section. I think they'll be impressed."

Dislike for Hannah warred with vanity and self-importance on Scilla's face. "Okay. I'll show them. You'll see they have no ill will toward Austin."

Hannah gave Scilla the plate of BM cookies. "Perry loves cookies. He'll want to try these."

Scilla gave Hannah a smug smile. "I told you they're *gute.*"

Yes, fine. Anything you say, Scilla. Just go away and keep Raymond and Perry occupied.

Scilla didn't wait for Raymond and Perry to come downstairs. She went up after them, BM cookies in hand. Ten minutes later, the three of them descended to the main floor, and Scilla was talking a mile a minute. She'd already started the tour, and Raymond was stuck. He looked as if he wanted to run, but even he wasn't that rude, and Scilla was ready to tell him everything about the store. He wanted the information, so he was probably willing to put up with Scilla.

A Scilla-guided tour turned out to be one of Hannah's best ideas. Scilla took Raymond and Perry to the organic section first, and she talked while Raymond took notes. Raymond refused a BM cookie, but Perry wanted one. Hannah watched as he took a bite, then slipped the rest into his pocket. She smiled to herself. Not even Perry Glick could stomach a BM cookie.

After organic foods, Scilla led Raymond and Perry around the store, telling them where Austin had purchased everything and how much money he'd bought the house for. Hannah cringed with every word out of Scilla's mouth, but Raymond seemed to be soaking it in. *Gute.* If he was satisfied with the information Scilla gave him, he was less likely to make trouble.

After about fifteen minutes, Raymond and Perry said a cursory good-bye to Scilla and left. Hannah breathed a sigh of relief. Scilla had been a big help, and Hannah couldn't be ungrateful, no matter how much Scilla got on her nerves.

Soon, the store felt like a big party. Scilla's parents came as well as all of Bitsy Weaver's nieces and their families. Austin's two *aendis* and one *onkel* and their children stopped in. It felt as if the whole district was there, plus plenty of Englischers to make it exciting. Sometimes

Hannah wondered if the Englisch came to events like this just to get a peek at the Amish. The gingerbread cookies hadn't lasted long, so they'd started cutting cinnamon rolls into eighths and handing them out instead.

More than once, Austin glanced across the store, caught Hannah's eye, and smiled or winked. The smile was bad enough, but the wink was completely inappropriate and completely swoon inducing. How would she stand it when Scilla and Austin married?

About ten minutes before closing time, the store was still packed with people, who seemed to be having too good a time to go home. Hannah skipped down the stairs to fetch more paper towels. Austin and his *bruderen* had put up row after row of white wire shelving for storage, plus they had finished one small bedroom just in case Austin actually needed to sleep there sometimes—which had already happened five times.

Hannah grabbed three rolls of paper towel and turned to go back upstairs. She squeaked when she nearly crashed into Scilla. Scilla was so close behind her, she might have been Hannah's shadow. Hannah took a deep breath. "Scilla, you scared me. I didn't even hear you come down the stairs."

Scilla gave Hannah an *I-feel-sorry-for-you* look. "Along with everything else, you're hard of hearing too? You poor thing."

Scilla liked to feel superior, and if it made her feel good to think she had better hearing than Hannah, what did it matter? "Did you need help finding something?"

"I came to talk to you." Scilla glanced behind her toward the stairs. "In private."

Hannah tried her very best not to expel a long and loud

sigh right in Scilla's face. "Can it wait? There are fifty people up there."

"He's never going to love you," Scilla blurted out, as if she'd been waiting to say it for weeks and weeks.

Hannah swallowed hard. "What are you talking about?" she said, even though she knew exactly what Scilla meant.

"*Ach,* Hannah. Everybody sees it. You follow Austin around like a puppy, hoping he'll feed you some scraps or throw you a bone." Scilla placed her hand on Hannah's arm as if she cared about Hannah's feelings. "He's not going to, Hannah. For sure and certain you want more than friendship with Austin, and you're embarrassing yourself. Poor Austin doesn't know what to do with you."

Hannah couldn't speak past the lump in her throat. Was that really how Austin felt? *Jah.* If he loved Scilla, that was exactly how he felt.

"You've got to quit pestering Austin. We're both tired of it."

Hannah waited to speak until she felt confident she wouldn't burst into tears when she opened her mouth. "Did he . . . did he say that?"

"What are you going to do when we're married?"

She'd been expecting it, but the mention of Scilla and Austin getting married still felt like a slap across the face. She clutched the paper towels tighter. "Are you engaged?"

Scilla sniffed indignantly. "That's personal information. Neither of us are ready to tell people."

It felt as if Scilla had pulled Hannah's heart out of her chest and ripped it in half. "I hope you'll be very happy." It was a nice thing to say, considering she really wanted to tell Scilla to go away and never come back.

Scilla wasn't satisfied. "Thou shalt not covet thy neighbor's husband. That's what the Bible says."

Much as she hated to give Scilla any credit, it was something Hannah had already considered. "You think very poorly of me indeed if you believe I would ever covet another woman's husband."

"As long as you work at Austin's store, it will always be a temptation. I've read plenty of books about it."

Just what kind of books was Scilla reading? "Austin and I are just friends."

"Austin might consider you a friend, but you're in love with him and I won't stand for it, not in my store."

Hannah was squeezing the paper towel rolls so hard, they were nearly flat. "This isn't your store."

"It will be when I marry Austin."

And that was the raw and painful truth. Hannah couldn't deny it. If Scilla had seen how much Hannah liked Austin, everybody could see it. Hannah had never been one to temper or hide her emotions. Scilla would soon be in charge of Austin and the store, and Hannah would not be able to bear working here. She had to leave. Much as she hated to admit Scilla was right, Hannah had to cut Austin out of her life for her own *gute.* And for Austin's. No matter how hard she would try not to, Hannah would create a wedge in his marriage. If Scilla was to be believed, he already saw Hannah as a nuisance.

Hannah pressed the paper towels to her chest to stop the ache. She wasn't one to hang around where she wasn't wanted. Austin had made his choice, and she would have to live with it. But, *ach,* the thought of Austin and Scilla together made her want to cry. Or throw up. Or both.

Scilla rarely smiled, but her lips curled upward in a

smug grin. She knew she'd won. It was a painful defeat, but Hannah wasn't going to stand there and let Scilla lord it over her. Without another word, Hannah stepped around Scilla and ran up the stairs. She certainly wasn't going to cry in front of Scilla. She'd already wasted too many tears on Austin, and Scilla would only gloat at her heartache.

Maybe she'd have a *gute* cry when she got home. Maybe she wouldn't. And maybe the next time Matt Gingerich asked if he could drive her home from a gathering, she'd say yes.

The rest of the evening passed in a blur. After the customers left, Hannah, Mary, and James cleaned up the kitchen while Austin swept and dusted and straightened and restocked shelves. Scilla didn't do much of anything except follow Austin around, probably to make sure Hannah wouldn't try to get within ten feet of him. Twice, Austin tried to talk to Hannah, but she kept her head down and pretended she was extraordinarily busy and didn't have a minute to spare for chitchat.

At ten o'clock, James took out the last bag of garbage and hitched up the horse while Hannah and Mary finished cleaning. James came back inside and collected the bowls and baking sheets they'd brought with them. Hannah and Mary put on their coats.

Austin helped Scilla on with her coat. "Is your *dat* still coming to get you?"

"*Jah.* He'll be here in five minutes."

Austin patted James on the shoulder. "I can't thank you enough for your help today. I don't know what I'd do without all of you."

James nodded. "We sold everything we made, even the donut holes. It was a *gute* day."

"Everyone loved the cinnamon rolls," Austin said, grinning at Hannah. She looked away. That warmth in his eyes wasn't hers to enjoy anymore.

Scilla pinched her mouth into a frown. "I would have sold more BM cookies, but people were afraid to try them."

Austin smiled at her. "You'll sell more tomorrow for sure and certain." Austin was so kind, but it was plain that even he didn't believe Scilla would sell more BM cookies.

"But I sold all my gluten-free bread. Putting 'organic' on that sign outside really brought in a lot of customers. I knew it would."

A twinge of pain pinched at Hannah's heart. Oh, how she mourned her beautiful sign!

Austin glanced at Hannah. "Whatever it was, I'm glad people came. I had three people tell me they came for Will Williams's milk. It sold out too. And the mayor said he'd come back sometime. He sure enough liked your shovel, Hannah."

Hannah tried to not let his praise soften her up. "He was just being polite."

"He was not. You heard him. He wants more shovel paintings for city hall."

Scilla went around the counter behind the cash register and pulled a black Sharpie from the drawer. "It's a nice shovel, but it doesn't match the sign outside." She went to the shovel on the wall and took the lid off the Sharpie. "I'm going to fix it."

Hannah's heart jumped like a grasshopper. She sprang at Scilla, nudged her aside, and snatched the shovel head off the wall. Not even caring that it was Austin's gift, she wrapped her hands around it and marched out the door. Scilla was not getting her grubby little hands on it.

Austin called to her, but she didn't even pause as she stormed down the porch steps to the buggy. Mary and James must have sensed she meant business. They quickly followed her to the buggy. James snapped the reins, and they were off before Scilla could say "organic BM cookies."

Chapter Sixteen

Austin fired up the pellet stove in the basement before lighting the one on the main floor. No one wanted to freeze to death while they shopped. There were still three hours before opening time, but Mary and Hannah were coming early to make donuts and cinnamon rolls for what Austin hoped was the morning rush. This was only the second day for the store, so Austin wasn't even sure there would be a morning rush, but Lord willing, dozens of Englischers would want a cup of hot *kaffee* and a donut on a morning like this.

Mary and James walked through the door right on schedule. Mary carried a bowl of dough in her arms, and James clasped a paper bag in his hand. Austin took the bowl from Mary and set it on the counter. "You were up early, I see."

"I wanted to make the dough before I came," Mary said. "Get a jump on the baking."

Austin looked toward the front door, determined to be more attentive than ever to Hannah. She'd stormed out of the store last night with her shovel head, probably not trusting that Austin would have protected it from Scilla. She had obviously been tired and still irritated about her sign, but she shouldn't have doubted Austin. He wouldn't have let Scilla do anything to that shovel. Hannah had painted it especially for him, and Scilla would have listened to him if he'd asked her not to write on it.

Hannah wasn't on the porch. He gazed into the Yutzys' buggy. She wasn't in there either. "Where's Hannah?" he said, closing the door.

Mary barely spared him a glance. "*Ach.* She had seventeen orders for cinnamon rolls yesterday. She stayed home to bake them in our oven. It's bigger."

Austin's chest filled with the emptiness of disappointment. He wanted to talk to Hannah about the opening yesterday. He wanted to know what she thought and share his excitement with her. Most of all he wanted to see her smile and hear her tell him what a *gute* job he'd done yesterday. He needed her encouragement like he needed food. It had always been that way.

"When will she be coming?"

Mary didn't even look at him. Was she purposefully avoiding his gaze? "She might bring the rolls in later this afternoon yet. I don't know."

James reached into the paper bag and pulled out the shovel head Hannah had painted for Austin. "She wanted me to bring this back. She said it's your gift, and you can do whatever you want with it." He cleared his throat. "And you can let Scilla do whatever she wants with it too."

Austin took the shovel head and hung it back on the wall. "Tell her not to worry. I like it just the way it is. I'll tell Scilla."

James nodded curtly. "I'm sure you will."

What did James mean with that *I-don't-believe-you* tone? "Really, James. Scilla's not going to write on it."

"It doesn't matter," Mary said, sprinkling flour on the counter and dumping her dough out of the bowl. "Hannah understands."

"What does Hannah understand?"

Mary arched an eyebrow. "Nothing. It doesn't matter."

"What doesn't matter?" Austin said. Why was Mary acting so strange, as if Austin was her worst enemy and she was barely putting up with him? "Mary." At his insistent tone, she finally looked at him. "Tell Hannah that Scilla won't touch my shovel, okay?"

Mary punched down her dough. "I'll tell her. But it doesn't matter."

Austin wanted to growl. Mary was being purposefully obnoxious, and he didn't have time for it today. He'd talk to Hannah when she came in later this afternoon and set her straight. Had she no faith in him?

Sol Nelson came in the store. "*Hallo,* Austin. *Hallo,* James and Mary."

"*Vie gehts?*" James said, washing his hands at the sink.

Sol tried to smile, but the gesture didn't quite reach his eyes. "Did you sell my *mamm*'s quilt yesterday?"

"*Nae,* but we did sell one of Lily Yoder's quilts and a rocking chair. I had an Englischer ask me about your *mamm*'s quilt. She might come back this week and buy it. You never know."

Sol shuffled his feet. "It wonders me if I could take it back yet."

Austin frowned. "Take it back? You don't want me to sell it?"

Sol looked down at his feet. "Raymond Glick offered to sell it in his store for two hundred extra dollars. That's a lot of money."

Austin couldn't believe what he was hearing. "Raymond offered you more money for your *mamm's* quilt?"

"I'm sure you understand. It's not personal. Raymond said this is business. We're going to take our business to the highest bidder. You understand, right?"

A canyon opened up in the pit of Austin's stomach, but he didn't change his expression. "I understand," he said, even though two weeks ago, Raymond Glick couldn't have cared less about Erna Nelson's quilt.

"You don't mind if I take it now, do you?"

Austin waved his hand as if dismissing a stupid question. "Of course not."

Sol hesitated, then tromped up the stairs. If only Hannah were here. She'd need to redecorate the quilt room. Erna Nelson's quilt took up the entire north wall. It was a stunning sight when you first walked into that room. Now there would just be an empty space.

How could Sol do this to him?

That question was easily answered. Sol was a nice person, but he wasn't especially loyal, and he tended to watch out for himself. What else could he do? Austin looked at Mary. She returned his gaze and frowned. At least the Yutzys were firmly on his side.

Sol came bounding down the stairs with the quilt draped over his arm. "*Denki* for being so understanding. Raymond says that's just the way it is in business sometimes."

Mary pulled a garbage bag from the drawer. "You better put it in a bag or it will get dirty."

Sol sprouted a weak smile. "*Ach, jah.* That's a wonderful *gute* idea, Mary."

Sol stuffed the quilt into the bag, obviously not truly understanding how valuable it was or he would have treated it with more care. "Maybe my *mamm* will make you another quilt sometime. For sure and certain she will if you pay her what Raymond Glick is paying her. She likes you better, but it's just business."

Austin longed to point out that as soon as Raymond put Austin out of business, he'd decide he didn't want Erna Nelson's quilt in his store anymore. But he kept his mouth shut and resentfully watched Sol walk out the door. Erna Nelson was only one person, and her quilts weren't going to make or break him. Still, he was disappointed that Sol could be talked into turning on Austin so quickly. He took a deep breath and tried to convince himself of what Sol had said. It was only business. Nothing personal.

Of course, with Raymond Glick, it was deeply personal, and he was as mad as a wet hen.

Will Williams came in the back door about ten minutes after Sol had left. He smiled widely and brought six gallons of milk in on his wagon. "Hey, Austin. How did it go yesterday after I left? It looked like people were having a good time." Will wore a bright pink beanie, and his hair stuck out from under it. The long locks went clear to his shoulders.

"We sold all your milk," Austin said.

"That's why I brought more this morning. I could see you were running low when I left. I had three customers tell me they planned on coming today." He opened the fridge. "I'll bring cheese next week."

Someone knocked on the front door. Austin opened it to Matt Gingerich holding a shoebox. He grinned awkwardly and shook his box slightly. "I brought more ornaments. Just a few, because the paint only dries so fast."

"*Cum reu,*" Austin said. "We sold every ornament yesterday. An Englischer wanted to decorate her whole tree with them. She said she'd be back today to see if we got more in."

"*Wunderbarr,*" Matt said. His smile faded. "If she wants more, tell her to go to Glick's Market. We're selling our ornaments there too."

Austin's stomach fell to the floor. "You sell your ornaments at Glick's? Since when?"

Matt hemmed and hawed for a few seconds. "*Ach, vell.* Raymond came to me this morning. He buys our ornaments for a dollar more than you do, and he doesn't even ask us to do consignment. He pays cash."

Austin didn't try to hide his irritation. Matt was a *gute* friend. Austin should have expected better from him. "Until I opened my store, Raymond didn't care about your ornaments."

At least Matt had the decency to look embarrassed. "I'm sorry, Austin, and you're right, but he's interested now, and I'm saving up for a new hunting rifle. Every little bit helps. And Mandy needs a new pair of glasses." He tried to put a hand on Austin's shoulder, but Austin shrugged away from him. "Raymond wanted us to stop selling ornaments to you, but I told him you were my friend and I'd sell them to you, even if you pay us less for them. I'm still planning on selling them to you, though it might be hard to keep up with all the orders."

Austin was tempted to tell Matt to take all his ornaments to Raymond Glick and see how long that business lasted, but Hannah wouldn't want him to do anything unwise. He would talk to Hannah and then decide what to do about Matt and his ornaments. He shouldn't let anger and irritation rule his *gute* judgment. "I'd . . . I'd appreciate anything you can give us."

Matt didn't seem completely satisfied or comfortable

with Austin's answer, but he nodded and laid his box on the counter. "Raymond Glick is just trying to run a business, like you. I don't begrudge him for that."

Austin couldn't agree, but he wisely kept his mouth shut. Matt opened the box and counted the ornaments. Austin paid Matt for the ornaments he'd sold yesterday, and Matt left. Austin thought he might be sick. Raymond was angry. Angry enough to undercut Austin and put him out of business. And it was only Austin's second day.

Will finished loading his milk into the fridge. "Raymond Glick called me too."

Mary propped a hand on her hip. "He talked to my *dat.*"

Austin felt as if he'd been hit with two sticks simultaneously. "He did?"

Will smirked. "He offered to buy my milk and eggs and for more than I'm selling them to you."

Austin didn't dare ask if that was the last of the milk he'd be seeing from Will.

Will wiped his hands on a paper towel. "Don't worry. I turned him down."

"But why?" Austin said, puzzled but grateful.

"I've read enough about economics to know that if Raymond puts you out of business, I'll have nowhere to sell my milk because he'll drop me faster than a kid drops an anchovy pizza."

Austin frowned. He was in trouble. How many of his friends like Sol would sell to Raymond and leave him high and dry? What if Raymond set his prices ridiculously low and Austin couldn't compete? Austin couldn't afford to pay the prices he was already paying. Would Raymond squeeze him until he collapsed under the pressure? Once again he wished for Hannah. She'd know what to do. At the very least, he'd worry less if she shared the problem with him.

He turned to Mary. "What time is Hannah coming in?"

Mary concentrated extra hard on her dough. "I don't know, Austin. I truly don't know."

Austin was starting to get suspicious. He watched out the window as Mary and James unloaded dough and supplies from their buggy. Hannah had not come again. He hadn't seen her since the store opening on Tuesday, and now it was Friday morning. Austin didn't even bother to ask about Hannah when Mary and James came in the door. He always got the same answer. *She's got twenty or five or a million orders for cinnamon rolls. She's baking them at home because our oven is bigger.*

Austin was tempted to buy two extra ovens to put in his kitchen so Hannah wouldn't have an excuse to stay home. And she never brought her rolls to the store when she finished making them. James left the store every afternoon at about one and fetched the cinnamon rolls from Hannah.

For sure and certain, she was avoiding him. He was puzzled and irritated and hurt all at the same time. Didn't she know how much he needed her? The quilt room still needed to be rearranged since Sol had taken his *mamm*'s quilt, and Austin needed help figuring out what goods to reorder. Scilla didn't know how to do it, and she wasn't interested in learning. She was singularly focused on organic foods, and she didn't pay attention to anything else. He needed Hannah. He needed to see her smile. He needed her reassurance that Raymond Glick wasn't going to win. He needed her artistic touch in his store so it didn't look like a thick-fingered bachelor had decorated it.

Why had she abandoned him? He had half a mind to close the store, march to her house, and demand an explanation.

But he didn't dare close the store. It would be *deerich* to give Raymond Glick any advantage.

The store's early success should have made him wildly happy. Despite Raymond's attempts to steal his quilt makers and his milk supplier, the store was regularly packed with people looking for Christmas gifts or baked goods or even groceries. Several Amish families that used to shop at Raymond's now shopped here. Austin had found enough products that Raymond didn't sell in his store to make it worth people's while to come to this side of town. Raymond had a nice big store, but he and his sons had a reputation for being prickly, and shopping at Glick's Market wasn't an especially pleasant experience.

Mary set another bowl of dough on the counter and washed her hands at the sink. Austin already knew the answer, but he asked anyway. "Where's Hannah?" Hope springs eternal, or something like that.

Mary barely even looked at him anymore, as if she didn't want him to see the secret in her eyes. "She's got twenty orders of cinnamon rolls for Sunday dinners. She's staying home to bake them in our oven. It's bigger."

Fine. Let her be that way.

The day after tomorrow was Sunday. The store would be closed, and Austin would have time to get to the bottom of this. He'd find out what was keeping Hannah away or die trying.

There were three thuds at the door, as if someone had kicked it. He wished they wouldn't do that. They always left scuff marks. His heart flipped in his chest. Maybe it was Hannah with an armload of cinnamon rolls.

His hopes died when he opened the door. He should have realized Hannah would never kick the door. She'd painted it. Was it bad that he felt only disappointment at seeing Scilla? Wasn't he supposed to be in love with her? He was pretty sure love wasn't lukewarm, like how he felt about Scilla.

He immediately felt guilty for his lack of enthusiasm. Scilla had been so helpful with his store. She'd made bread and BM cookies and spent opening day helping him. She'd found Will Williams for him and brought Austin dinner when he'd worked late.

Scilla stood on his porch with three loaves of bread in her arms. "*Ach,* help me, Austin. I almost dropped a loaf already." Austin took all three loaves from Scilla's arms. "Don't put them on the counter. I don't want any cross contamination. They go in the organic foods section. They're gluten-free."

"Sounds delicious," Austin said, hoping against all hope that was true. He'd tasted gluten-free bread before. Some of it was pretty *gute.* But Scilla's gluten-free bread tasted like Styrofoam, with about the same consistency. He should probably put some kind of warning label on those loaves. Or maybe give them away for free when Scilla wasn't looking.

She took off her coat and bonnet. "Look what else I brought." She pulled a yarn square from her pocket. "My *mamm* crocheted a dishrag. She can make a hundred of these a week."

Unlike the gluten-free bread, the dishrag looked like something Austin would want to sell. It was purple with a pretty heart design in the center. "This is *wunderbarr,* Scilla. Let's put a price on it and put it upstairs with the other handicrafts."

Scilla seemed pleased. "*Cum,* show me where you want it."

Austin smoothed a price tag onto the rag, then walked

upstairs with Scilla to find a place for it. He went into the quilt room with the bare wall. A dishrag wasn't going to do much to improve the look of the room. "I wish Hannah was here," he said. "She would know exactly how to display this."

Scilla set the dishrag on Andrew's table. "You don't need Hannah's help. The dishrag looks nice right here."

Austin attempted a smile, even though Scilla was being especially sour today. "It does. It's just that Hannah hasn't been here for three days, and she's the one who decorated this room. I need her to figure out how to make it look nice again."

Scilla finally noticed that the quilt was gone. "Did you sell that huge quilt?"

"*Nae.*" He scrubbed his hand down the side of his face. "Raymond Glick offered Erna Nelson more money for it, so it's at his store."

Scilla drew her brows together. "That doesn't seem very nice."

Not nice at all. And it made him sick. "Raymond is also paying Matt more money for his ornaments, and Raymond offered to buy Will's milk and eggs for more than I can pay him. Mary says Raymond even talked to the Yutzys about moving their donut stand to his store."

Scilla pinched her lips together and narrowed her eyes. "He's trying to make you go out of business."

"*Jah.* But Will won't sell to Raymond, and Matt is still selling to us. And of course, the Yutzys are on my side. But it makes me a little uneasy about what Raymond is planning next."

"I'm sorry about what Raymond is doing, but you don't need the Yutzys," she said.

"Of course I need them."

Scilla sat down at Andrew's table and smoothed the dishrag in her hand. "I could take over the bakery and make it organic and gluten-free. You could build a reputation as a health-food store."

"I don't think I can go completely organic. I don't really want to. Do you know how many donuts and cinnamon rolls I sell every day? I'd lose half my profit."

Scilla stuck out her bottom lip. "Don't you have any faith in me? My *dat*'s second cousin owns a store."

Austin gritted his teeth. He refused to go bankrupt just because Scilla thought she knew more than he did. He didn't know much, but for sure and certain, Scilla knew less, despite being related to someone who owned a store. He tried to be nice about it. "Of course I have faith in you. But I don't want an all-organic store. It would be a mistake."

"You don't have to get huffy about it. I'm just pointing out that you don't need the Yutzys, especially since they're probably already selling to the Glicks."

Austin's heart froze mid-beat. "What do you mean?"

Scilla lifted her chin. "You said Hannah hasn't been in for three days. What is she doing with all that time? You've rejected her, and she's mad about it. Wouldn't it make sense that Hannah is making donuts and cinnamon rolls for Raymond? In fact, I'm certain I saw her going into Glick's Market not that many days ago. She's sneaking behind your back, and you don't even know it."

Austin wouldn't believe it. "Hannah would never do that to me."

"You saw how unreasonable she was on Tuesday night. She got irritated when people wanted my BM cookies instead of her gingerbread, and she stole your shovel right off the wall."

"James brought it back," Austin said, not entirely sure what Hannah meant when she told James that *Austin and Scilla can do whatever they want with it.* Did she simply not care anymore?

But why not?

Because she'd gotten a better offer from Raymond Glick? How could she bake cinnamon rolls for Raymond Glick when she disliked him as much as Austin did?

She had been furious about Scilla ruining her sign and about Austin letting Scilla do it. Was she baking cinnamon rolls for Raymond out of spite? Mary herself had admitted that Raymond had approached her *fater* about moving the donut stand into his store, and Scilla had seen Hannah go into Glick's Market, even though Hannah avoided that store like the plague. Or at least she used to.

Austin's heart stopped altogether. He had really messed up with the sign—letting Scilla paint on it—but that was no excuse for Hannah to sell her baked goods to Raymond Glick. Austin might have expected Sol Nelson to do something like this but not his best friend. And she was going to hear about it.

He pulled his watch from his pocket. Ten minutes to opening time. He stormed out of the quilt room and down the stairs.

"Wait for me."

Ach. In his frustration, he'd almost completely forgotten about Scilla. Lord willing, she'd understand his urgency. "Mary," he said, "I need to leave for about an hour. Could you mind the store while I'm gone?" Seeing as how Mary probably knew exactly what Hannah was doing, it might be risky to put her in charge, but he had no other choice. Hannah was going to hear his displeasure.

Mary raised her hands. They were covered with flour. "We're a little busy yet."

"I'll mind the store," Scilla said. Austin had never heard such delight in her voice before. His heart sank. Scilla didn't know how to make change or work the cash register, and she wasn't exactly the warmest person to help customers.

Austin growled inwardly. He had to set Hannah straight or at least voice his profound disappointment, but he couldn't leave the store in Scilla Lambright's hands. They closed tonight at six. He'd go after work and give Hannah a piece of his mind. And then beg her to come back. Traitor or not, he just couldn't do anything without her.

Chapter Seventeen

Austin was tied into about seventeen knots by the time he got home. He needed to talk to Hannah, but he needed to check in with Mamm and explain why he couldn't help with the peanut butter tonight. With Andrew working on his carpentry business and Abraham called out to see to neighbors' animals, Mamm had been making most of the peanut butter by herself. Austin was going to help her put up a few jars tonight before bed, but it would have to wait until he talked to Hannah.

Mamm wasn't going to be happy about it.

She wasn't happy anyway. Austin heard her yelling before he even opened the door. He almost turned around and got back into his buggy, but part of Mamm's bad mood was likely because he hadn't been around as much to help her with Dawdi and Mammi and the twins. She deserved to be a little irritated, and he'd let her take it out on him if it made her feel better.

"Pride is a terrible sin, young man," Mamm said as Austin opened the door. Benji and Alfie and Dat were sitting on the sofa while Mamm stood in front of them pointing her finger at Alfie. It wasn't likely that Dat was being scolded with the twins, but he sat just as still, his gaze never straying, as Mamm shook her finger.

"We wasn't being proud," Alfie whined. "We was just showing everybody. They wanted to see."

"Is everything okay?" Austin said cheerfully. He was always glad when Mamm was mad at someone else.

Dat sighed. "Your *bruderen* wore their medals to school today."

The mayor had awarded Benji and Alfie medals at the city council meeting on Tuesday. They were acrylic discs with "The Brett Favre Memorial Award" engraved in gold letters with Alfie's and Benji's names on them. They were attached to ribbons so Alfie and Benji could hang them around their necks. The discs sparkled in the sunlight, and Alfie and Benji loved them. Who wouldn't? They really did look impressive.

Benji scratched his ear. He didn't seem too concerned that Mamm was going to pop a blood vessel from yelling. "We just wanted to show everybody."

"You just wanted to be proud," Mamm said. "And brag that you got a medal and no one else did."

Alfie sat up straighter. "But, Mamm, we saved their lives. We deserve a medal."

"You deserve a *gute* smack on the *hinnerdale* for thinking you're better than anyone else."

"We don't think we're better, but we've got cool medals."

"What kind of a word is 'cool'?" Mamm asked.

Alfie shrugged. "Max Glick has an Englisch friend. He says 'cool' all the time."

Mamm jabbed her finger in Alfie's direction. "Don't change the subject."

"Okay, Mamm."

Mamm folded her arms across her chest. "You boys did a *gute* deed, but if you do your alms before men, you'll have your reward of men, not Gotte."

"What are alms?" Benji said.

"Don't change the subject."

Alfie wasn't one to give up a fight easily, even though it was always better to say whatever you thought Mamm wanted to hear. "You said you were proud of us for saving those people."

"I said no such thing. I said I'm *froh* you saved them and that you did a *gute* thing. But it is pride plain and simple to wear your medals to school, and you are not to do it again."

Benji hung his head. "Okay, Mamm."

Alfie kept his mouth shut. He obviously didn't want to agree to anything he'd have to take back later, but he'd be foolish to wear his medal to school after this. Mamm would find out. She always did.

"Mamm," Austin said. "I'm sorry, but I have to run an errand before I help with peanut butter."

Mamm furrowed her brow. "It can wait. I saved you some dinner, and we need to get twenty jars of peanut butter in tonight."

"But I really need to talk to Hannah about something."

Mamm's inflexible expression softened. "Hannah? Okay. Go. There's no rush on the peanut butter."

"Okay. *Denki.*"

She tugged on his coat. "Take Alfie and Benji with you."

Alfie and Benji jumped off the sofa and cheered wildly. Going with Austin meant an escape from more lectures from Mamm and a reprieve from family reading time.

"*Nae,* Mamm," Austin said. "I need to talk to Hannah alone."

"They'll send me to an early grave if I don't get them out of here. Either that, or I'll send them to an early grave. You should fear for their lives." She said it with a lift of her eyebrow, which meant she wasn't entirely serious, but serious enough. *Die kinner* always went a little crazy right before Christmas, especially since it was too cold to go outside and expend their energy in the outdoors.

Austin expelled a deep breath and draped his arm over Mamm's shoulder. "Okay, I'll take them. But only because I love you so much."

"That is the best reason of all."

Mammi came from the bedroom. "Before you go, you all need some rose water. Austin, please get it for me."

Austin didn't even blink. Mammi insisted on spraying rose water whenever one of her grandsons came in or out of the house. The sooner he let himself be sprayed, the sooner they could leave. He got the spray bottle from under the sink, and Mammi gave Austin a few spritzes on the back of his neck. Alfie and Benji got soaked because Mammi thought they stunk all the time.

Even after a spray of rose water, Alfie and Benji skipped out to the buggy and climbed happily into the back seat. Austin wasn't too worried about bringing them. This time of day, Hannah would be at her *aendi* Linda's house. The boys could play with Ruth Ann and Dinah while he talked some sense into Hannah.

Alfie's medal dangled from his neck as he leaned over the seat to talk to Austin. "Something's wrong," he said.

Austin glanced back and nodded. "*Jah.* You're wearing your medal. Mamm told you not to."

"She said not to wear it to school. It's okay if we wear them to Ruth Ann and Dinah's."

Ach, vell. It didn't matter to Austin. Mamm could scold them later, if she wanted to.

"Something's wrong, Austin," Alfie said again.

"What?"

"Matt Gingerich drove Hannah home from the gathering."

Austin stiffened like an icicle. "Who told you that?"

Alfie fingered his medal. "Ruth Ann. Eva Zook told her that Suvie said Barbara Herschberger saw them getting in the buggy. Barbara lives across the street from Yoders. That's where they had the gathering."

Austin's throat went dry, until he realized that it probably wasn't true. Since when did he believe gossip from a nine-year-old? Matt was a nice boy but not worthy of Hannah. She'd never agree to a ride home with him. Would she?

By the time they got to Linda's house, Austin had worked himself into a frenzy. Not only was Hannah selling cinnamon rolls to Raymond, but she might be dating boys who didn't deserve her. Boys who were disloyal to Austin's store. What was she thinking, and had she even considered asking Austin's advice? He was her best friend. She should talk to him about things like this.

He strode right to the back door because Hannah was most likely in the kitchen. The twins followed him up the steps and into the house. Hannah was wiping the table while Dinah and Ruth Ann washed dishes. Surprise popped all over Hannah's face when she saw him. Or maybe it was the look of a guilty conscience.

"I need to talk to you," he blurted out. He wasn't in the mood to ease into the conversation by talking about something pleasant like the weather. He turned to Alfie and

Benji. "Would you boys take Ruth Ann and Dinah and go play somewhere else."

Dinah stepped down from the stool she'd been standing on and took Benji's hand. "Do you want to see the star I made for the Christmas play?"

"Okay," Benji said.

Dinah touched the ribbon around Benji's neck. "I like your medal."

Ruth Ann dried her hands. "Teacher says it's proud."

Alfie lifted his chin. "It's not proud. It means we're brave."

"How much money could you sell it for?" Ruth Ann said.

"I'm not selling it," Alfie replied. They left the kitchen arguing about if Alfie was going to sell his medal or not.

Austin looked at Hannah. Now that *die kinner* were gone, he wasn't going to beat around the bush. "How could you sell cinnamon rolls and donuts to Raymond Glick? I thought you were a better friend than that."

Her eyes got wide. "What?"

"I found out you're selling cinnamon rolls to Raymond Glick behind my back."

She took in her breath sharply, as if he had slapped her, and the pain in her eyes sliced right through his chest. "You think I'm selling cinnamon rolls to Raymond Glick?"

That wasn't the reaction he had expected. His throat tightened, and he couldn't swallow. Had he made a mistake? "Uh. Wait. Are you?"

Hannah stared at him in disbelief until the silence became almost unbearable. "I would never do that. I. Would. Never."

"*Ach.* I guess I got some wrong information."

Hannah sank into a chair as if her legs couldn't support

her anymore. "I was once your dearest friend. I . . . I thought you knew me better than that."

He hated the way she emphasized *once.* His heart, his lungs, all his guts plummeted to the floor. He pulled out a chair and sat next to her. "You're still my best friend."

"*Nae,* I'm not." Hannah wasn't a crier, but moisture pooled in her eyes. He'd really done it this time.

Her reaction was like a punch to the gut. If there was a bigger idiot in all of Wisconsin, Austin would like to meet him. He backpedaled faster than he'd ever done anything in his life. "I'm wonderful sorry, Hannah. I shouldn't have assumed . . ."

In a flash, she blinked back any hint of tears, and a raw, angry fire flared to life behind her eyes. "Who told you such a horrible thing?"

He held out his hands as if to push her anger down. "Sol took his *mamm's* quilt down because Raymond bought it for two hundred dollars more than I offered to pay. Raymond wanted to buy Will's milk for more money. He's trying to put me out of business. Even Matt Gingerich is selling his ornaments to Raymond." Austin emphasized Matt's name. Hannah needed to know what a disloyal friend he was.

"I heard about that," Hannah said. "And I think it's despicable." She dropped her rag on the table. "The question is, why would you think that of me? Shame on you, Austin Petersheim."

Austin felt bad. He truly did, but why did she scold him like he was a nine-year-old who'd worn his medal to school? She always scolded him, and it made him feel about two inches tall. He'd made an honest mistake, and she was the one who had been avoiding him all week. He threw up his hands. "What was I supposed to believe when you stormed out of the store on Tuesday?"

"You were supposed to believe that I wouldn't give Raymond the time of day, let alone any of my cinnamon rolls. You're supposed to believe that I am a loyal friend who would never go behind your back."

He swiped his hand across his mouth. "Well, okay. You're right, but I just wasn't sure. Scilla said she saw you go into Glick's Market."

Hannah erupted. "*Ach, vell,* if Scilla said it, it must be true."

"That's not what I mean."

She narrowed her eyes. "That is exactly what you mean."

Austin cleared his throat. Maybe it was best to admit he was wrong and forget about what Scilla did or didn't see. "Hannah, please just listen to me. I'm sorry. I was a *dummkoff,* but you disappeared for three days. I didn't know what to think."

Hannah clamped her lips together. She wasn't moved by his apology in the least. "I've stayed away for that very reason."

"What reason? I don't understand."

"Because you'll always believe Scilla over me. Scilla's feelings will always be more important than mine. I know that's how it should be, but I don't have to sit and watch."

Austin pressed his fingers to his forehead.

She glared at him. "Don't do that."

"Do what?"

"Don't rub your forehead like I'm nothing more than an annoying problem giving you a headache."

He laced his fingers together. "You're still mad about the sign."

Her look could have curdled the milk in his *kaffee.* "Yes," she hissed scornfully, "because you've always known me to be petty like that."

"You're not petty, but you're still mad."

"I'm mad that you thought I would ever negotiate with Raymond Glick."

She had him there. He'd accused her unfairly. "You know I'm a little bit thick, but you've always forgiven me for the stupid stuff I've done."

She glared at him. "I'll forgive you, but I'm going to take a few more days to be mad about it."

"Then will you come back to the store?"

Her glare turned frigid. "I'm not coming back."

"Why not?"

"Mary and James are doing just fine."

"I'm not doing fine. I need your help." He sounded utterly selfish, but that was the way he felt.

"You don't need me. You've got Scilla."

He opened his mouth to argue and promptly shut it again. He did have Scilla, and she was more than eager to help, but hers wasn't the kind of help he needed. Scilla gave more wifely kind of help. Hannah's help was more useful and practical. "Scilla's not really cut out for that kind of work."

Hannah folded her arms and turned her face away. "She'd better learn right quick."

Austin drew his brows together. Scilla was pretty and appealing, but he couldn't see Scilla learning enough to be of any help to him. Those weren't her skills, and Hannah was perfectly aware of it. She was just being stubborn. "Why don't you just say what you mean? You don't like Scilla."

Hannah hesitated as if he'd caught her off guard, then

she huffed out a breath. "Of course I don't like Scilla. And I don't even care if that offends you. She's a gossip, and she's as selfish and cold as a fish."

That wasn't very nice. Hannah seldom said anything bad about anyone, and she'd just compared Scilla to a fish. "She likes children, and she's smart," he said weakly. Scilla really did like children, just maybe not Alfie and Benji specifically. Hannah refused to see Scilla's *gute* qualities.

She tossed her head back. "You don't have to defend her, Austin. The fault is mine for not showing forth more love."

"*Jah.* You should take the beam out of your own eye before complaining about the mote in hers." He pressed his lips together. He wanted to talk Hannah into coming back, not drive her away. "I shouldn't have said that."

"But you meant it."

"Okay. I suppose I did. If you would just try harder to like Scilla, we wouldn't be having this argument."

She nodded. "I know. Jesus said to love everyone, and I'm being small-minded. But I'm too old to try to change."

"You're only twenty-one."

She leaned back in her chair. "Okay then. I'm *unwilling* to change. I don't want to try to get along with Scilla. I don't like her, so I'd rather bake my cinnamon rolls at home and let James take them in for me."

Austin couldn't stand the thought of not seeing Hannah every day. "I need your help, Hannah. Sol took his *mamm*'s quilt, and the wall is bare. The whole room looks incomplete. I couldn't make it look nice if I tried."

"Emma can do it. She has a *gute* eye."

"I want you to do it."

She stood up and grabbed her rag. "You can't eat your cake and have it too, Austin. It would be a waste of my time to redecorate for you. Scilla would only rearrange my work later."

Austin ground his teeth together until they squeaked. "You're still mad about the sign. Don't try to deny it."

Pain traveled across her face followed closely by chilly anger. "Go away, Austin. I have to finish the dishes."

He stood up. She backed as far away as she could get from him. The movement made his heart ache. "Don't, Hannah."

"Go away, Austin."

He strode forward and gently touched her arm. She stared resentfully at his hand but didn't pull away. "Don't make me choose between you and Scilla."

She tugged her arm from his grasp, went to the sink, and rinsed out her rag as if he hadn't just bared his heart to her. "You've already made your choice, Austin." She turned and pinned him with a fierce gaze. "Don't you dare try to make me feel guilty about it."

"I don't want to make you feel guilty."

Refusing to look at him, she fell silent and wiped down the counters with frantic energy. He felt like a propane lamp standing in the middle of the kitchen for all the heed she paid him. His chest hurt as if she'd cleaved his heart with an ax. His feet felt like two blocks of ice. Would he be able to drag himself out the door?

Hannah stepped to the arch between the kitchen and the front room. "Benji, Alfie," she called, "it's time to go home."

Benji and Alfie appeared so quickly, they couldn't have been standing less than five feet from the door. Ruth Ann and Dinah followed right behind. Had they been listening? Maybe, but they were too young to understand what went on between grown-ups. And even if they did understand, what did it matter? They'd just heard Hannah being resentful and Austin trying to talk some sense into her.

Austin took a deep breath and scrubbed his hand down the side of his face. That wasn't what had really happened, but the thought that Hannah had just yanked herself from his life buried him in despair.

Chapter Eighteen

Alfie sat in the corner of the schoolroom and nibbled resentfully on his *dumm* cupcake that had looked like chocolate in the wrapper but had turned out to be carrot cake when he'd bitten into it. Who brought carrot cake cupcakes to a school Christmas program? No kid liked carrot cake, but someone had brought them anyway, and Alfie was stuck eating it because Mamm would give him the spatula if he threw away a cupcake with only one bite taken out of it.

It was a stupid ending to a stupid day. He'd said a *dumm* part in the *dumm* school Christmas program, and his *dumm* costume had dragged on the floor and tripped him as he got up to say his part. The big kids had laughed at him, and then he'd had to recite a *dumm* poem about a baby Christmas star that wanted to be big like the real Christmas star, and the big kids had laughed at him even more. They wouldn't have laughed if Mamm had let him wear his medal to the Christmas program.

He pinched a sliver of grated carrot between his fingers.

Who put vegetables in cake? It should be against the Ordnung.

Alfie gazed around the schoolroom. Parents and grandparents and scholars were laughing and talking and eating delicious cookies and normal cupcakes. Mamm looked like she was having a serious discussion with Bitsy Weaver. Would she even notice if he slipped his cupcake into the garbage?

The way his life was going, she probably would.

He should have been wonderful happy. Austin wasn't going to marry Hannah, but like as not, he was going to marry Priscilla Lambright. He would move out of the house and live in his store, Abraham would marry Emma and move out, and then Alfie and Benji would get their upstairs bedroom back. No more sleeping in the cellar.

He should be jumping up and down for happiness. But he was too sad to do any jumping.

He hated to admit it, but Benji had been right all along, and Alfie would gladly sleep in the cellar for the rest of his life if only Austin would dump Scilla in the garbage like a carrot cupcake. Scilla hated Alfie and Benji, and she was snippy and sour and would probably lock them in the cellar and not let them out ever, not even for family reading time.

"There you are, Alfie."

Dinah, Ruth Ann, and Benji walked to where he was sitting, stopped, and stood there looking sorry for him. Probably because he'd tripped on his costume and had to eat carrot cake.

"Aw," Dinah said, with disappointment in her voice. "You got the last carrot cupcake."

Alfie raised his eyebrows. "Do you want it?"

Dinah burst into a smile. "I love carrot cake."

Alfie would have hugged her if she hadn't been a girl. He didn't hug any girls except his *mamm.* He handed her the cupcake. "Okay. You can have it," he said, pretending he really wanted it but was doing something nice for Dinah. Ruth Ann liked it when he was nice to Dinah.

Dinah peeled back the paper, licked all the frosting off the cupcake, and tossed it in the garbage. Alfie frowned. He should have thought of that.

Ruth Ann folded her arms and glared at Alfie. "We need to talk about Austin and Hannah. The plan isn't working."

Alfie was tired of everybody blaming him all the time. "It's not Austin's fault. Hannah told him to go away."

"Because Scilla painted her sign," Ruth Ann protested.

Alfie held out his hands. "What do you want me to do? I can't help it if Austin is *dumm.*"

"My *mamm* needs that wheelchair."

Alfie didn't know how to tell Ruth Ann, but even if Hannah and Austin got married, Alfie and Benji would be forty years old before they earned enough money for a wheelchair. *Ach, vell.* He'd promised Ruth Ann a wheelchair. He'd keep that promise, even if he'd be old enough to trip on his beard before he did it.

Benji hung his head. "Austin will have to marry Scilla. No girls like him. He's too cocky."

"What does cocky mean?"

Benji frowned. "I don't know. That's what Mamm said."

Dinah licked the leftover frosting from her fingers. "Hannah pretends to smile."

Ruth Ann kicked Alfie in the foot.

"Ouch!" Alfie said.

She didn't even apologize. "We aren't giving up. I want

that wheelchair, and Hannah and Austin have to get married. We need a better plan."

Alfie shook his head. "There's nothing we can do. Austin is too *dumm.*"

"He's not *dumm,*" Dinah said. "He's handsome. And Mamm says it's not nice to say '*dumm.*'"

Ruth Ann tilted her head as if an idea had just come to her. "We've been trying to get Hannah and Austin together. Maybe we should try to get rid of Priscilla. We could put tacks on her chair."

Alfie caught his breath at a wonderful *gute* idea. "Let's set a smoke bomb in the library."

"*Nae,* Alfie," Benji said. "We'd start a fire, and they'll take away our medals."

Alfie clutched his shirt at the spot where his medal usually hung. For sure and certain they'd take away his medal. He'd no longer be "one of Bienenstock's finest and bravest citizens," like the mayor said.

Dinah's bottom lip quivered. "Jesus wants us to love everyone."

Benji put his arms around her. "Dinah is right. We don't like Priscilla, but we shouldn't be mean to her."

Alfie sighed. "And Mamm would give us the spatula." And take his medal.

Ruth Ann narrowed her eyes. "What if we're extra nice to Scilla? Maybe she'll get sick of us and go away."

Benji didn't like that idea. "Who could ever get sick of us? We're cute little kids."

"You're right," Alfie said. "And if she starts to like us, that will make her love Austin even more."

Ruth Ann scrunched her lips together. "We need a better plan."

They stood in silence until Benji spoke up. "Do you

remember when we were spying on them, and they talked about that old hideout?"

"*Jah,*" Ruth Ann said. "But how will that help?"

"Ruth Ann, Dinah, *cum.* It's time to go." Ruth Ann's *dat* motioned to them from across the room.

Ruth Ann stuck out her hand. "Secret spy shake," she said.

"What?"

"We need to have a secret spy shake."

Alfie made a face. "What's that?"

"I made it up. I'll show you." She shook Alfie's hand like normal, then let go and snapped her fingers. "Like that," she said.

That was the dumbest secret spy shake Alfie had ever seen.

Ruth Ann shook Benji's hand, then Dinah's, then snapped afterward. Alfie turned his head and rolled his eyes. He was going to make up a better secret spy shake for the next time they got together.

Benji walked back to the eats table, and Dinah ran and jumped into her *dat*'s arms. Looking very pleased with herself, Ruth Ann put her hands behind her back and leaned toward Alfie. "Do you want to give me a kiss?"

Alfie drew back in horror. "*Nae.*"

"Not even a Merry Christmas kiss?"

"I don't want to give you any kind of kiss."

She didn't seem mad. "Okay. Maybe next time."

Nope. Wasn't going to be a next time. Ever, never, ever. What was it with Ruth Ann and kissing?

Christmas had been nice. Dreary and depressing, but nice, in a sad, heartbroken kind of way.

Hannah stared out the kitchen window and watched the snow blow around the backyard. The thermometer outside the window said zero degrees. No doubt the wind chill was closer to thirty below. The new year was coming in with a deep freeze. Thank Derr Herr all the Christmas festivities were over. She could hunker down at home for weeks with a perfectly *gute* excuse. When it was this cold, everybody hunkered down.

Austin was likely sitting all by himself in the store without a soul to wait on. Few people dared brave the weather on a day like this. Mary was at the store today, but it was the first time she'd been there since New Year's. There just hadn't been enough business for her to be there every day.

According to Mary, every day leading up to Christmas at Austin's store had been breathtakingly busy. Hannah had received enough cinnamon roll and cookie orders to keep her baking twelve hours a day. It really had been better to stay home and bake. They needed the extra oven just to fulfill all the orders. But now it was January seventh and winter had truly set in.

Hannah felt a twinge of longing at the base of her throat. For sure and certain, Austin would be discouraged today. If she were there, she'd be able to cheer him up. "January is always a slow month in the retail business," she'd reassure him. "Don't worry. People will come. As soon as the weather gets better, we'll plant flowers and sell petunias and hand out free seed packets." Well. Not *we. He. Austin* would hand out free seed packets, and someone besides Hannah would have to suggest it. Austin was too focused on his accounting and inventory to come up with something like that by himself.

Hannah sighed and wiped down the table for the third time. Flour tended to stick to everything. She had to wipe the table at least three times any time she made dough. She'd made two batches of cinnamon rolls this afternoon, and they were finally in the oven. James would take them to the store later today. That was all the orders they had for the week. Hannah was going to spend the rest of the week painting shovels and milk cans for the store. Three people had asked Austin for their own decorative shovels, and he'd sold one milk can right before Christmas.

Austin had sent three notes to Hannah through James, which she had thrown in the trash, pretending that she hadn't read them first. He had been too busy before Christmas to come see her, and he probably hadn't dared after the holidays. He'd also tried to talk to her at *gmay,* but it had been easy to avoid him by being busy with the fellowship supper. Sooner or later he would have to accept the truth of what she'd told him. He couldn't eat his cake and have it too. He couldn't be friends with Hannah and marry Scilla—mostly because it wasn't appropriate for a married Amish man to have a female best friend, but also because Hannah was in love with him and if she had any chance of forgetting him, she'd have to stay away. She would not covet another woman's husband.

It really, truly might require a move to Colorado.

Matt Gingerich was a nice diversion, but he wasn't Austin, and Hannah wasn't really interested. She should probably be honest with Matt. He wouldn't find the right girl while wasting his time dating Hannah.

Ruth Ann and Dinah came barreling into the kitchen as if they were wonderful excited about something. Their cheeks were bright red from the cold. Onkel Menno picked them up after school and brought them to Hannah's house every other day, and Hannah would go to their house on the other days. She made dinner for Aendi Linda's family almost every day. On the days Ruth Ann and Dinah spent at her house, she would make dinner here and drop it off at Aendi Linda's with Ruth Ann and Dinah. Today was one of those days she was making dinner here and taking it in. Oh, how she wished she could do more for Aendi Linda. She had such a hard life.

Hannah said a little prayer of gratitude right there in the kitchen. Her heart might be broken, but she had her arms and legs and a strong back. She was extremely blessed.

Dinah latched on to Hannah's apron. "Look what we brought."

Alfie and Benji Petersheim strolled into the kitchen with cheeks and noses equally as bright as Dinah's.

"They came to play," Ruth Ann said.

Hannah didn't question the idea of Benji and Alfie playing with Ruth Ann and Dinah, even though it seemed a little strange. Her cousins and the Petersheim twins spent a lot of time together. They just didn't seem like playmates.

Alfie fished in his coat pocket. "We brought you a present." He pulled out a handful of individually wrapped candy. It was some of the old-fashioned candy Austin kept in the jars on the front counter, and it looked as if it had been in Alfie's pocket a long time. The clear paper was a little filmy and bent, and the candy inside was dusty and chipped. "It's from Austin. He really likes you and is wonderful sorry for that time he yelled at you."

"This is from Austin?" Hannah asked, cocking her eyebrow and taking Alfie's candy.

"He's wonderful sorry."

"He told you to give it to me?"

"Don't you like that kind?" Alfie said, sidestepping the question. It was one thing she liked about Alfie. He could be devious and tricky, but neither he nor Benji would ever tell a lie.

She pinned him with a suspicious gaze. "But Austin didn't really mean it for me, did he?"

Alfie made a face. "Every time I go to the store, Austin lets me choose one piece of candy. I've been saving it up for you."

Hannah smiled. Alfie had shown a lot of self-restraint saving that candy for Hannah instead of eating it himself. "That's wonderful nice of you, Alfie. *Denki.*"

Benji nodded. "I give him half of my piece of candy so he doesn't feel bad."

"And we saved the rest for you," Alfie said. He gazed regretfully at the treasure of candy he had just given to Hannah. "Austin is wonderful sorry."

"I'm sure he is, and I forgive him." Hannah unwrapped a piece of watermelon candy and popped it into her mouth. "I can't eat all this candy by myself. Do you all want a piece?"

"Yippee!" Dinah clapped her hands, then carefully examined the candy in Hannah's palm. "I don't want horehound."

"We never got horehound," Benji said. "It's disgustful."

Each of the children picked a piece of candy. Alfie didn't seem especially pleased to get a treat. He didn't seem especially pleased about anything today. "Don't you like Austin anymore?" he said, unwrapping his root beer–flavored candy.

Oy, anyhow. Children could be so nosy. "I like Austin just fine," Hannah said, picking up her rag and wiping the table for a fourth time. It never hurt to be extra sanitary.

Dinah tried to talk around the hunk of candy in her mouth. "But he likes Scilla."

Hannah scrubbed at a stubborn spot of flour that turned out to be a chip in the table. "Yes, he does."

Alfie fake laughed. "Austin likes everybody. He's so nice. And he knows how to juggle."

"He does?" Dinah said, extremely impressed.

Alfie smiled at Hannah. "Wouldn't you like a husband who can juggle?"

"I'm sure I would." That painful thought stole her breath. Did she really care that much if her future husband could juggle?

Alfie's fake smile turned into a fake laugh. "Austin is one of my favorite *bruderen.* Benji's too."

Benji nodded so hard, he fanned up a breeze. "One of my favorites. He killed a spider in the cellar once."

"He's not afraid of anything," Alfie said.

Dinah bit into her candy. It crunched against her teeth. "He's handsome. Do you want a handsome husband?"

Hannah sighed inwardly. She wanted to put Austin from her mind, not be reminded of everything she'd lost. She didn't need a husband who could juggle. Juggling was the most worthless skill in the world. And who cared if her husband was handsome? Handsome boys were selfish and overconfident and stupid. That was the last thing she wanted. "I don't want a handsome husband," she said, and she meant it. Let the handsome and pretty people marry each other and leave the sensible folk alone.

Alfie brightened. "Austin isn't handsome. He'd make a *gute* husband."

"He is too," Dinah protested. "He looks like Benji."

Benji didn't seem to grasp the significance of what Dinah had said, which was probably a *gute* thing. "I have freckles. Austin doesn't have freckles." He looked at Hannah. "Do you like freckles?"

"I love freckles."

Ruth Ann pulled a pencil and a notepad from the drawer. She sat down at the table and wrote "Hannah" at the top of the paper then "freckles" beneath it. "What else do you like?" she said.

"Me?" Hannah said.

Ruth Ann nodded. "What is your favorite color? And your favorite flower."

"Why do you want to know?"

"Just tell me."

Hannah huffed out a breath. Ruth Ann could be persistent, and Hannah couldn't always understand what she was thinking, but it was best to get this quiz over with so she could start dinner without the children underfoot. "I like blue and chrysanthemums."

"What kind of blue?" Ruth Ann said, writing furiously on her paper. Hannah was impressed. She spelled *chrysanthemums* correctly.

"I like dandelions," Dinah said. "They grow everywhere, and nobody cares if you pick them and make a bouquet."

Benji scratched his nose. "Bitsy Weaver gets mad if you pick her dandelions or even step on them."

"I like deep blue, like when the sun is about to set and the sky gets dark."

Ruth Ann seemed impressed. "I like that too. What is your favorite animal?"

Alfie made a face. "We don't have to know that."

"It never hurts to get more information," Ruth Ann said.

Hannah giggled. "Why do you need to know my favorite animal?"

Alfie glanced at Ruth Ann. "How about your favorite food?"

"Pizza," Hannah said. "Barbecue chicken with onions."

Ruth Ann wrote it down. "What kind of a husband do you want? Tall, medium, or short?"

Hannah wasn't going to answer that. The kind of husband she wanted was Austin Petersheim, and she was never going to say that out loud. "Why are you asking these questions?"

"We want to know."

"Why do you want to know?"

Dinah didn't seem to feel the need to keep it a secret. "We want you to marry Austin, and we have to trick him."

Ruth Ann gritted her teeth in Dinah's direction. "Dinah, be quiet." She looked at Hannah. "Don't listen to her. She's only six."

Hannah's heart sank. She sat down next to Ruth Ann and did her best not to burst into tears. She smoothed an errant lock of hair at Ruth Ann's forehead and spoke as gently as she could. "I'm not going to marry Austin so you might as well not bother. You should go show Alfie and Benji your rock collection."

Dinah frowned with her whole face. "But don't you think he's handsome?"

Hannah's shoulders felt heavy, as if she were carrying a great weight. These persistent, guileless children deserved the honest truth. "Austin wants to marry Scilla." According to Scilla, they were already engaged.

Alfie narrowed his eyes and nudged Benji with his elbow. "I still think we should light a smoke bomb."

Benji drew his brows together and looked at Hannah.

"Do you want us to run her off? Because we will if you want us to. We have walkie-talkies and a rope."

"And binoculars," Alfie said.

Hannah didn't even want to know how the boys planned to run Scilla off with a rope and binoculars, not to mention the walkie-talkies. "*Nae,* I don't want you to run her off. That wouldn't be nice at all. Jesus said to be kind to everyone."

Dinah pursed her lips and seemed very satisfied with herself. "I told you."

Hannah tried to keep all emotion out of her voice. "Besides, Scilla is going to be your sister-in-law. She'll be family, and you always watch out for family."

Benji screwed up his face like he always did when he was about to cry. "Alfie says she's going to lock us in the cellar."

Hannah scolded Alfie with her eyes. He had the sense to look contrite. "She *might* lock us in the cellar," he said. "She hates us."

"She won't lock you in the cellar," Hannah insisted, but she couldn't give them any reassurance about Scilla's affection. Scilla didn't necessarily hate the boys, but she certainly didn't like them very much.

Benji studied her face. "Would you marry Austin if Scilla moved to Ohio?"

Alfie sat down and leaned his elbow on the table. "How could we get her to move to Ohio?"

"Cheese," Dinah said.

Hannah sighed. "I'm sorry, Benji. That's not going to happen."

Alfie scowled at Benji. "Nobody but Scilla wants to marry Austin. He's *dumm.*"

Benji nibbled on his bottom lip. "But would you marry him if Scilla moved away?"

Oy, anyhow. Benji was as persistent as Ruth Ann. Hannah slumped her shoulders. "I don't know."

Alfie seemed encouraged. He leaned toward her eagerly. "She didn't say no."

His enthusiasm pulled a smile from her lips. "Austin and I are best friends." Or they used to be. Those days were over.

"Like me and Alfie," Ruth Ann said.

Alfie grimaced. "We are not."

A giggle tripped from Hannah's mouth. "I like Austin very much, just like Ruth Ann likes Alfie and Benji." She felt her smile fade. "But sometimes I feel like Austin ignores me. I helped him with the wood floors and did half the painting and I decorated the upstairs of the store."

"It looks pretty," Dinah said.

"*Denki.* I think it looks wonderful nice. Austin likes it too, but he takes me for granted, and I don't really want to be around him anymore. It makes me sad that he doesn't appreciate me."

Alfie frowned thoughtfully. "Like when he let Scilla paint your sign."

"*Jah.* I worked very hard on that sign, but Austin loves Scilla, so he let her paint it even though he knew it would hurt my feelings."

"She can't draw letters *gute,*" Dinah said.

Hannah reached out and squeezed Dinah's hand. Hannah agreed, but it was better if a six-year-old said it instead of Hannah. She was a grown-up. She should be more charitable. "I was happy to help Austin get his store going, but I would like for him to appreciate me, instead of treating me like . . ."

"Like he treats us," Alfie said.

It hurt Hannah's heart to hear it, but yes, sometimes Austin disregarded his own *bruderen.* His *bruderen* had risked a lot by going into Glick's Market and spying for Austin. They had spent hours at the store picking up trash, washing walls, and dusting shelves. They had offered suggestions on everything Austin should put on his shelves, and some of their ideas were wonderful *gute.* Austin loved his *bruderen,* but sometimes he couldn't be bothered with them.

That was probably how he saw Hannah now—a nuisance who was useful only when he needed a floor scraped or a sign painted or a batch of cinnamon rolls baked. And Hannah was smart enough to know it was time to move on.

Benji hung his head. "Andrew says Austin is shallow."

Hannah pressed her lips together. Austin wasn't shallow. He could be self-centered and insensitive, but he was also uncommonly kind when he took the time to notice. He wasn't afraid to apologize when he did something wrong, and he treated Hannah and every other girl like she was just as important as any boy or man in the *gmayna.*

Dinah propped her hands on her hips. "I like Austin, no matter what any of you say."

"I do too," Hannah said, though admitting it was sort of humiliating. She loved Austin, but he couldn't care less.

Benji lifted his chin. "Don't worry, Hannah. We're not giving up."

Hannah had no idea why, but Benji's determination made her feel better. There was someone watching out for her, even if there wasn't any hope. She took a deep breath. "No smoke bombs, okay?"

Alfie shrugged noncommittally. "They have really cool purple ones."

Hannah curled her lips. She'd like to see that. She really would.

Mary swept into the kitchen as if she'd been blown in with the wind. James followed, carrying a large bin and stomping the snow off his feet as he walked down the back hall.

"Mary," Hannah said. "I didn't expect you for another hour."

Mary practically ripped the mittens off her hands and tore the coat from her shoulders. She pinched her lips together and raised her eyebrows. "I didn't expect us back so soon either." Her nostrils flared. "We. Were. Fired."

"What does that mean?" Dinah asked.

"What?" It felt as if someone had whacked Hannah in the chest with a baseball bat. "What happened?"

James placed the box on the counter. "Here's our yeast and sugar. I'm going back tomorrow to get the rest of our things, but I need Dat to help me with the fryers."

Hannah stared at her *bruder* in disbelief. "But . . . but I don't understand."

Mary slapped her mittens onto the counter. "Scilla told us Austin wants to make the bakery organic, whole wheat, and gluten-free, though how he plans to do all three at the same time is beyond me. Scilla said thank you for all our help, but she is going to take over the bakery herself. We're not welcome anymore." Mary threw up her hands. "Not welcome. After all we've done for him."

Surprise nearly paralyzed Hannah. "But . . . Austin needs our bakery. The store can't survive without it. What did he say?"

"Oh," Mary said, her eyes a pair of angry slits on her

face. "He wasn't there. He had to run to the post office for something. That's when Scilla pounced."

Hannah felt sick. "I can't believe Austin would agree to that."

Mary blew her top like a teakettle. "Of course he didn't agree. For sure and certain, he didn't even know. Believe you me, this was all Scilla's doing. I could see her just waiting for a chance to get us alone without Austin in the store. She was like a cat on a mouse."

Hannah was stunned. Absolutely stunned. And angrier than Mary. "You've got to go back and tell Austin what happened."

"He'll find out soon enough," James said.

Mary grunted her disapproval. "She never would have done it if she didn't think she could talk Austin into it."

Hannah's throat went dry. Scilla could talk Austin into anything. She just had to flash those big, round eyes and make her bottom lip quiver, and Austin would melt like pink Jell-O on a hot day. "But Austin needs our bakery," she said. They were useless words. The person who needed to hear them wasn't even here.

Mary folded her arms. "I'm sorry, Hannah. I know how much Austin needs us, even if he doesn't realize it himself, but I'm not going back there. Scilla thinks she owns the store, and I'm tired of her prancing around like she knows more than I do about everything. I knew it would make you feel better if I was there, and I wanted to help Austin. I really did. But I can't do it anymore. Scilla is driving me crazy. I say we just forget Austin and open our donut stand in the spring like we always do. It will be as if his store never happened." Mary came to rest on a chair next to Alfie at the table. "He's got all that white flour in the basement.

I don't know what he'll do with it. I guess we could buy it from him."

"I guess that would help him out," Hannah mumbled. She couldn't help but feel this was somehow her fault. It was obvious Scilla resented her. Was she taking out her irritation on Mary and James?

Didn't Scilla realize that Austin was the one who would be hurt in the end?

Chapter Nineteen

Austin stared at the instructions without really reading them. He'd been sitting here for ten minutes and hadn't begun to figure out how to work this credit card reader. The bishop had approved it because so many Englischers carried only credit cards these days, and many of them didn't have anything else to pay with, even if they wanted to buy something.

All things considered, the bishop had been more than accommodating to Austin, and Austin was very grateful because Raymond Glick hadn't been making things easy for anyone.

Austin set down the instruction manual and pressed his fingers to his forehead. He hadn't been able to concentrate on anything this morning, hadn't been able to concentrate since before Christmas, and it wasn't because Raymond had stolen another one of his quilt makers yesterday.

Hannah wouldn't talk to him. She had barely even looked at him at *gmay* on Sunday. Scilla had stared at him all through the sermons, but Austin found that the more attentive Scilla was, the less he cared.

He pressed his forehead even harder. How long should

he keep trying with Scilla? Because he was beginning to think his resistance to the thought of marrying her wasn't just cold feet. It didn't matter how pretty or popular she was or how much help she tried to be with the store, Austin just couldn't feel much emotion for her anymore—except irritation. Every time she walked in the store, he felt irrational annoyance bubble up inside him. Maybe it was because she expected him to pay her three dollars for every loaf of gluten-free bread, but it sat on his shelves until it molded and he had to throw it away. Scilla meant well, but if there were people besides her who ate gluten-free bread, they didn't get it from the Plain and Simple Country Store. And it was obvious why. Scilla was no cook. She simply couldn't compete with Mary and Hannah Yutzy's donuts and pretzels. Hannah's cinnamon rolls could stop traffic. Scilla's BM cookies would only cause a wreck.

Maybe he was irritated because Scilla wasn't Hannah. Hannah was the one he wanted to see coming into his store every day. He needed to see her smile. He needed to hear her laugh. He needed her to help him figure out how to make the store successful. She'd never had a bad idea.

Austin stared out the front window. James and Mary should have been here thirty minutes ago. Where were they? It was cold out, but the roads were clear and there wasn't supposed to be any snow today. It was Saturday, so they surely had a few orders of cakes or cinnamon rolls or something else, especially since they had left early yesterday. When Austin had come back from the post office, they were gone. Scilla had been there all by herself, cleaning up the mess James and Mary hadn't bothered with. Scilla said they'd just packed up and left.

Austin pulled his watch from his pocket. If Mary and James didn't get here soon, they wouldn't have time to make donuts for the afternoon rush, if there was an afternoon rush. Business before Christmas had been *gute,* but things had slowed down in January. Would anyone come for afternoon *kaffee* and donuts today? Should he make a different flavor of *kaffee* or start selling sandwiches to attract some lunch customers?

If Hannah were here, she'd know what to do. Her absence was like a hole right in the center of his chest.

A buggy pulled up, and a sense of relief washed over him until he realized it wasn't James and Mary, but Scilla. She slipped out of the buggy, and when she spied him at the window, she motioned for him to come outside. Unfortunately, she probably had more gluten-free bread than she could carry on her own.

Austin shrugged on his coat and ran outside. He was going to have to have a talk with Scilla today. She'd be disappointed, but the gluten-free bread had to go. She'd understand. Probably. Her cousin owned a store. He'd probably told her that sometimes things just didn't sell.

Scilla seemed extra excited about something. She didn't usually smile, no matter how *gute* her life was going, but today she was beaming from ear to ear. "I made three different kinds of bread. You are going to be so happy." She reached into the back of the buggy and pulled out a box of bread and handed it to Austin. She'd written the kind of bread on each plastic bag. Some of the bread said *gluten-free.* Some said *whole wheat.* The rest of the loaves said *twenty grain.*

Twenty grain? How many grains were there? Austin could only think of nine or ten. The twenty-grain bread was roughly shaped into loaves, but each loaf looked like it had a bad case of acne. Austin drew his brows together. Someone might break a tooth on that bread. Of course, no one was going to buy it, so that was one less thing to worry about.

Scilla reached into the back of the buggy again and got another box. It was filled with bags of BM cookies and what looked like giant brown snail shells. "What are those?" he said, not really wanting to know.

Scilla lowered her eyes and fluttered her eyelashes. "Hannah isn't the only one who makes cinnamon rolls."

Ach, du lieva. Scilla's cinnamon rolls were dark brown spirals that hadn't raised properly. Maybe Austin could sell them as dog treats.

Austin followed Scilla into the store and shut the door behind them. They set their boxes on the kitchen counter. He'd better have that conversation with her now, or she'd bake him out of business within a week. "Scilla, you don't have to bake any more goodies or bread for the store."

"I don't have to. I want to. This is all for you, Austin. People are going to love this new bread, and I'll get better at the cinnamon rolls. They didn't raise well and I left them in the oven a little too long, but they still taste delicious. I had one for breakfast."

Should he suggest that doggie treat idea?

What would Hannah do?

A wonderful *gute* idea came to him. "Um, okay, Scilla. But I'll have to buy them on consignment. I hope you don't mind."

Scilla wrinkled her forehead. "What does 'consignment' mean?"

"I'll pay you for the bread if someone buys it, but if nobody buys it, I don't pay. You just take it home. It's what I've worked out with Matt Gingerich and his ornaments."

Scilla still looked confused and maybe a little annoyed. "You don't think people are going to buy my bread?"

Austin was irritated enough to be straightforward. "*Nae.* Most people don't like gluten-free bread." He didn't mention that Scilla's gluten-free bread tasted terrible. He wasn't that mean.

Scilla's right eye twitched slightly. "People don't understand how *gute* it is for them. All you have to do is hand out more samples. I told you that you needed to give out more samples."

Austin sighed. Scilla had chosen to forget that they'd given out gluten-free bread samples every day before Christmas. "Nobody takes the samples."

Scilla turned up her nose. "*Ach, vell.* They'll like my whole wheat bread. And the twenty grain is an old Quaker recipe. You'll see."

Austin forced a smile. "I hope we sell every loaf." And he truly did. "But I'll still need to sell them on consignment. That's how I work with a lot of the folks who sell their goods here."

"You don't make the Yutzys sell on consignment."

"They almost always sell out. And they're doing me a favor by being here. They attract more customers than anything else."

Scilla's face turned slightly red. "When people hear about my whole wheat cinnamon rolls and my twenty-grain bread, I'll bring in more customers than Mary and Hannah ever did."

Austin wasn't going to argue with her. After a few weeks, she'd figure out she was wrong, and quit wasting her time making bread she couldn't sell. "I hope you're right. And I appreciate how much time you've spent baking bread for the store, even with your job at the library."

Scilla formed her lips into a pretty little tease. "I quit my job at the library."

Dread grew like mold in Austin's chest. "You . . . quit your job?"

She nodded. "I've dedicated myself to helping you with the store."

Austin swallowed hard. Was she making a lifetime commitment? "You . . . you didn't have to do that."

"I didn't have to. I wanted to. I did it for you, Austin. I want to share every part of your life—your joys, your sorrows, your pain, your happiness. I've never wanted anything more in my whole life."

Austin took a couple of steps back. It sounded suspiciously like she was about to propose marriage. *Ach, du lieva.* How could he have let it go this far? The only thing to do was change the subject. He smiled widely and picked up a bag of cinnamon rolls. They knocked against each other in the bag. "Where should we display your *appeditlich* cinnamon rolls? I want people to see them, but we need to leave room for Mary and James to make pretzels and donuts."

"Mary and James don't need any room," Scilla said.

The front door burst open, and Alfie, Benji, Ruth Ann, and Dinah ran into the store as if it was the happiest place in the world. "We came to help," Benji said, as he and the other children peeled off their coats and hats and mittens.

Austin's heart swelled. He'd never been so happy to see his *bruderen.* Not only had they interrupted a very awkward conversation, but Austin realized he simply liked having them around. They were nine, so they could be silly and childish, but they were also loyal and sincere and they loved Austin even when he made stupid mistakes and said stupid things. Austin had only just begun to appreciate how important it was to have friends who stuck by him no matter what. Alfie and Benji were truly on his side.

They came to the store almost every Saturday and were surprisingly *gute* helpers. Their wages were a piece of candy and a day-old cinnamon roll. Even Austin could afford that. Benji and Alfie were both wearing their medals. They'd probably sneaked out of the house with them because Mamm didn't like them wearing their medals at all. But Austin didn't mind. The boys had done a *gute* thing. Let them show off just a little in front of the girls. No one else would see them.

Ruth Ann's expression drooped when she saw Scilla, but then she seemed to brighten instantaneously. "Scilla is here."

Benji and Dinah jumped up and down and cheered as if they were acting out a part in a school play. It was strange and somewhat comical. *Die kinner* didn't like Scilla, and watching them try to pretend made Austin smile.

Alfie hung his coat on the hook by the door. "We brought Ruth Ann and Dinah. They want to help sweep. I hope that's okay because Hannah isn't coming back until noon."

"Hannah brought you?" Austin's heart skipped a beat, and he strode to the front window in hopes of catching a glimpse of her, but she was long gone by then. His heart skipped another beat thinking that maybe he'd see her at noon when she came to pick up *die kinner.*

Scilla leaned over and whispered to Austin. "I don't know if it's such a *gute* idea for all these *kinner* to be running around your store. If you want, I'll mind the store while you take them home."

Austin contemplated the possibility of taking *die kinner* home and stopping by to see Hannah, but he also contemplated the possibility of leaving Scilla by herself. She could run the cash register but only if Austin was standing right beside her, and she tended to get sour with people who came in and didn't buy anything. Besides, he didn't really want to get rid of the children. They were always loyal to him. He should be loyal to them. "Alfie and Benji are going to sweep and mop the storeroom floor. Keeping it clean keeps the mice away. I'd be in trouble without my *bruderen*."

Benji stood a little straighter. "We know how to dust too."

Scilla's frown looked as if it was etched into her face. "Why are you wearing your medals? You shouldn't brag."

Alfie wrapped his fingers around his medal and took a few steps away from Scilla.

"They're not bragging," Dinah said. "They're brave, and we love them."

Ruth Ann pinned Dinah with a steely eye. "We don't love them."

Alfie glanced at Austin. "They don't love us, and we don't like girls. They're stupid."

Ruth Ann rolled her eyes, clasped her hands behind her back, and spoke to Austin. "We want to dust the top shelves first and work our way to the floor."

"That is very sensible," Austin said.

Ruth Ann gave Scilla a sickly sweet smile. "We can't reach. Will you dust the top shelves for us?"

Scilla stepped back as if Ruth Ann had tried to pinch her. "Use a step stool."

"We're not tall enough."

Austin might have volunteered, but there was that thing about Scilla not being left by herself with the cash register. "Leave the top shelves. I'll do them later."

"That's foolish," Ruth Ann said, as if she was the most sensible, thoughtful person in the world. "If you don't dust the top shelf first, you'll get everything below it dirty again."

Benji stunned everybody in the room when he reached out and took Scilla's hand. "Won't you come downstairs with us and help us dust? It would help Austin with the mice, and we think you're wicked cool."

Wicked cool? The boys really needed to stop hanging out with Max Glick's Englisch friend.

Even Scilla couldn't resist Benji's cute-and-adorable face. "*Ach, vell,* I suppose I can dust the top shelves for you."

"That would be helpful," Ruth Ann said, as if she meant it.

Scilla let Dinah take her other hand and lead her down the stairs. She was being manipulated, and she didn't even know it. The real question was why did *die kinner* want Scilla in the basement. Anybody could see they didn't like her.

Dinah, Benji, and Scilla were halfway to the basement when Ruth Ann poked Alfie with her elbow. "Do you have your paper?"

Alfie growled. "*Jah.* Quit poking me."

She poked him again. "Girls aren't stupid."

"I know. I just said that so Scilla wouldn't get suspicious."

"Suspicious of what?" Austin said. Maybe Scilla was safer up here.

Ruth Ann shoved Alfie in Austin's direction. "Alfie has some questions to ask you."

Austin cocked an eyebrow. "Questions?"

"*Jah,*" Ruth Ann said. "Don't mess up." She tromped down the stairs leaving Austin to wonder if he or Alfie was the one who shouldn't mess up.

Alfie pulled a piece of paper from his pocket. It had been folded about ten times, and it took Alfie a little bit of time to unfold it and smooth it out so he could read it.

He sat on one of the stools at the kitchen counter, pulled a pencil from his pocket, and wrote Austin's name at the top of the paper. He examined his paper, probably in Ruth Ann's handwriting, and read the first question. "What is your favorite food?"

Of all the questions Austin had expected, that hadn't been one of them. "Why do you want to know what my favorite food is?"

Alfie gave him the stink eye. "Will you just answer the questions? It takes too long to explain, and Scilla isn't going to stay down there very long, no matter how hard Dinah cries."

Was Dinah planning to cry? Austin couldn't begin to guess what was going on, but it was better to go along with his *bruderen* and get it over with. Like Alfie said, at most, Scilla would last five minutes in the basement. He swiped his hand across his mouth. "I like Petersheim Brothers peanut butter and Yutzys pretzels."

Alfie seemed to like that answer. He nodded his agreement and wrote Austin's answers down. "Okay. What is your favorite animal?"

Austin drew his brows together. "I don't know. I guess a horse. Or a dog."

Alfie wrote down Austin's answer as if it was the most important information in the world. Austin smiled to himself. Little kids found pleasure in the smallest things. "What is your favorite color?"

Alfie had about ten more questions about Austin's favorite things, including favorite part of *gmay,* favorite *bruder,* favorite dessert, and favorite river. That was a hard one, but Austin figured his answers really didn't matter, but his cooperation did.

Alfie wrote down Austin's response to "What is your

favorite flower?" then paused and studied the next question. It looked like there were three or four more. *Ach,* Austin really did need to get to a few chores before the store opened. Alfie lifted his paper to take a closer look. "Do you appreciate Hannah?"

Austin made a face. "What do you mean, do I appreciate Hannah? Of course I appreciate Hannah. You know that."

Alfie didn't react to Austin's answer, simply wrote it down and read the next question. "Do you take Hannah for granite?"

He sort of stuttered on his answer. "What? I don't get it."

"Hannah says you take her for granite."

Austin opened his mouth to ask what kind of a question that was anyway and had Alfie been talking to Hannah and what had she said about Austin? Did she think Austin took her for granted? *Did* he take her for granted?

"Doesn't Hannah think I appreciate her?"

Alfie squinted in Austin's direction. "I'm asking the questions."

How could Hannah think Austin didn't appreciate her? He'd told her thank you for the gingerbread cookies, hadn't he? Had he? He'd thanked her for the painting and the wood floor and the sign.

His throat went dry. Then he'd let Scilla paint over it as if it didn't mean that much to him. She had been honest with him, and he'd gotten defensive about Scilla. She'd made dozens of cinnamon rolls for the store, and then he'd accused her of selling them to Raymond Glick, like a fair-weather friend. He'd asked her to come back, then gotten annoyed when she refused to return to the store. He'd been anything but appreciative.

Austin's stomach rolled over itself.

Of course she didn't feel appreciated.

She was the most underappreciated girl in the history of people being underappreciated by Austin Petersheim. Underappreciated, undervalued, and ignored. How could he have been so stupid? And how could he make it right?

Alfie was staring at him and nibbling on the eraser of his pencil. "What is your answer? Do you take Hannah for granite?"

Austin scrubbed his hand down the side of his face. He was really starting to hate these questions. "*Jah.* I take Hannah for granted."

Alfie recorded his response. "She said you did."

Austin felt like a waterlogged worm on the sidewalk after a rainstorm. Sometimes Alfie was really a pest.

Alfie looked at his paper. "Are you going to marry Scilla?"

"None of your business," Austin snapped, even though he knew the answer. He had known for weeks, but had tried to talk himself into something different.

He wasn't going to marry Scilla. She was wonderful pretty, but he didn't love her. He didn't even like her, and he'd been trying too hard for too long. He shouldn't have to force himself to love anyone. Wasn't that why they called it "falling" in love? It was supposed to be easy and natural and *wunderbarr.* Being with Scilla had become a chore at best. Maybe it was cold feet and maybe it wasn't, but he knew one thing for sure and certain. He wasn't going to marry Scilla, and he wasn't going to try to talk himself into it.

Austin heard several feet coming up the stairs. Alfie expelled a frustrated breath, wadded up his paper, and stuck it in his pocket. Thank Derr Herr that the questioning was over. Austin had suffered enough abuse and remorse for one day.

Scilla appeared from the basement dragging Dinah up with her. Ruth Ann and Benji followed. "You're going to get blood poisoning," Scilla said, pulling Dinah to the sink.

"I won't," Dinah said. "I want to be an artist like Hannah."

"You don't draw pictures on yourself," Scilla scolded. "Do you understand?" She pumped liquid soap onto a paper towel and scrubbed at a black mark on Dinah's arm.

Austin frowned. "What happened?"

Scilla huffed out an exasperated breath. "Dinah found a Sharpie downstairs and drew a flower on her arm." She bunched the paper towel in her fist and pointed to Dinah's forearm. "You're a naughty girl. It's not coming off."

Dinah's eyes filled with tears. "I thought it was pretty."

In three big steps, Austin was around the counter. He wiped the water off Dinah's arm, picked her up, and wrapped his arms around her. She laid her head on his shoulder and sniffled, but the tears had seemed to stop. "Shh, it's okay. You didn't know."

Scilla leaned against the counter and folded her arms. "She won't learn anything if you coddle her."

Dinah lifted her head. The tears were gone, but her bottom lip quivered. "I was trying to love everyone like Jesus said."

Austin wasn't sure how drawing on her arm was showing love, but Dinah was sincerely upset, so he didn't ask her to explain. He patted her on the back. "It's okay. Just don't do it again. Those Sharpies don't wash off easy."

"You could get blood poisoning," Scilla said. "And it is against the Ordnung to deface your body."

"She didn't draw a face," Ruth Ann said, with an indignation that looked quite fierce on a ten-year-old.

Scilla narrowed her eyes. "Don't talk to me like that. I'm your elder. You should show some respect."

"I like Hannah," Dinah said.

Alfie put a brotherly arm around Benji and glared at Scilla. "Dinah was trying to be nice."

"It's okay. Let's all calm down," Austin said, before a fight broke out among Scilla and four little kids. He set Dinah on the counter. "I'm sorry you got your feelings hurt. It was just a misunderstanding."

Scilla glanced at Austin and seemed to grasp he wasn't going to defend her or even argue about it. "I didn't mean to hurt anybody's feelings. I just didn't want you to die of blood poisoning."

Austin wiped an errant tear from Dinah's face. "Okay. All better?"

Dinah stuck her finger in her mouth and nodded.

Scilla seemed to soften at the edges. She half smiled and patted Dinah on the head. "I know just the thing to make you feel better." She opened a bag of her cinnamon rolls. "I made these fresh this morning. And they're whole wheat so they'll keep you regular." Scilla handed a cinnamon roll to each of the children, who took them reluctantly. She also gave one to Austin, and while he wasn't necessarily eager to impress her, he still needed to be polite. And how bad could it be? It had glaze on top and cinnamon in the little crevices.

The children froze, staring at Austin as if waiting for him to take the first bite. He'd have to set the example. The cinnamon roll crunched against his teeth like a handful of clay dirt. It actually didn't taste terrible. It had a slight burnt taste, but the outside of the roll was the only thing that was hard enough to break a tooth. The inside wasn't soft, but it could be chewed. Once he worked at it for a while, it tasted like sugary sawdust in his mouth.

Scilla looked at him in anticipation. He wasn't going to lie, but he could try to be nice. "Not bad," he said. "I like the glaze."

"*Denki,*" she said, as if he'd just asked her to marry him.

Which brought him to an incredibly hard, incredibly necessary conversation. He helped Dinah down from the counter. None of *die kinner* had taken even one bite of their cinnamon rolls, but it had already been a hard enough day. "How about when Mary and James get here, I take you kids home?" he said. "You can dust next week." He'd take *die kinner* home, come back to the store, break up with Scilla, then have a talk with Hannah. Or should he break up with Scilla last? He could apologize to Hannah for taking her for granted, then she could give him some advice about the best way to break up with Scilla.

"Mary and James aren't coming," Benji said. He licked the glaze off his cinnamon roll.

"They didn't tell me," Austin said.

"They got burned," Dinah said, also testing a little of the glaze with her tongue. She must have thought it tasted okay because she licked off the rest.

Ruth Ann set her cinnamon roll on the counter, not even attempting to taste it. "They didn't get burned, Dinah. They got fired."

At times like these, Austin wished he could understand even a fraction of what went through a child's mind. "What do you mean, Ruth Ann?"

Ruth Ann gave Scilla a pointed look that could have withered even the coldest snowman. "Scilla fired them."

Austin drew his brows together. Ruth Ann was obviously

as confused as he was. "What do you mean Scilla fired them?"

Scilla cleared her throat in that high-pitched voice of hers. "Um, Austin. Can we have a private talk? Away from the children?"

Austin studied Scilla's face as if he'd never seen her before. "What did you do?"

Scilla laced her fingers together. "Why don't you children go outside so Austin and I can talk privately?"

"It's three below zero," Austin said, the rage rising inside him like a saucepan of boiling jelly. "They're not going anywhere. Tell me what you did."

"Fine," Scilla huffed. "If you want *die kinner* to listen in on a conversation that should be between two grown-ups."

"Where are James and Mary?" Austin said, without taking his eyes from Scilla's face.

"Well, Austin, what could I do? You wouldn't listen to my ideas for making the store better. If you'll just give my bread and rolls a few weeks, you'll have more customers than you've ever dreamed of."

"So you fired Mary and James?"

Alfie set his cinnamon roll on the counter. In a show of youthful unity, Benji and Dinah did the same. "She told them not to come back," Alfie said. "She said you didn't want them anymore."

"*Jah,*" Ruth Ann added. "They're coming later to get the fryers, and they're going to have a donut stand like always in the summer."

Dinah looked up at him with those big, innocent eyes. "Mary says, what are you going to do with all the extra flour?"

Austin looked to Scilla. "Is this true?" It was a silly

question. Of course it was true. It was exactly what he expected from Scilla.

"If you'd just give me a chance to explain," she said. "With Will's organic milk and eggs, people will come to the store for health food. You can't sell donuts and pretzels when people expect health food."

"People don't expect health food," Austin said.

"Of course they do. It says 'organic' right on the sign. Customers will get confused if you don't have an organic bakery."

Austin didn't think he could get angrier, then he surprised himself. "It says 'organic' on the sign because I let you talk me into painting it there." He ran his fingers through his hair. "How could I have been so *deerich?*" How could he have done that to Hannah? Oh, sure, he'd apologized, but he never should have let Scilla talk him into it in the first place. No wonder Hannah could barely stand to lay eyes on him.

"You're not *dumm,* Austin. Believe me, it was the smartest thing you could have done."

"You shouldn't have done that to Mary and James. They depend on this store as much as I do."

Scilla's face grew redder with every passing minute. "Can't you see, Austin. I did it for the good of the store. For your good and my good."

Austin didn't want to talk about it anymore, didn't want to argue. Scilla needed to go so he could start trying to fix the mess she'd made. He picked up the box of BM cookies and cinnamon rolls and handed them to Scilla. Then he picked up the box of bread. "*Cum.* I'll help you take these to your buggy. I'm not going to be able to sell them, so you might as well take them home. And please don't waste your time baking anything else for me."

Scilla immediately looked contrite and blinked back some genuine tears. "I shouldn't have fired Mary and James without consulting you. I had hoped you would see things my way, but I see now that I was hasty. It's freezing cold out there, but I'll go over right now and ask them to come back. I'll tell them I made a mistake."

"They won't come back," Alfie said. "They don't like you."

Scilla's mouth fell open. "Don't talk to your elders that way."

Unfortunately, Ruth Ann saw a weakness and decided to try to make it worse. "Hannah doesn't like you either."

Well, that was something Austin knew already.

But wait a minute. Maybe he didn't know everything.

He snapped his head around and pinned Scilla with an intense gaze. "What did you say to her?"

Scilla smoothed her hand down her apron and tilted her head to one side. "Say to who?"

The innocent look didn't fool Austin. "What did you say to Hannah?"

Scilla lifted her chin and looked anywhere but at Austin. "I've said a lot of things to Hannah. I don't know what you mean."

He pointed an accusatory finger in her direction. "On the day we opened. Hannah was happy. Until she wasn't."

Scilla pressed her lips into a hard line, as if she was going to be stubborn about it, then she slumped her shoulders and looked at Austin with her eyes wide. "Sometimes we do crazy things for love," she stuttered. "That's right, Austin. I love you, and I told Hannah that she couldn't be your friend when we got married. It would be wrong."

"You told her we were getting married?" Austin said, with all the restraint he could summon.

"Of course I did. And don't tell me you haven't been planning on it. I know what you've been thinking."

Austin closed his mouth. Scilla was right. This mess had been partly his doing. He'd been unsure and led Scilla to believe something that wasn't true. He couldn't fault Scilla for jumping to the wrong conclusions.

Scilla laced her fingers together. "Hannah needed to hear the truth, and you were too nice to break it to her. I simply pointed out that you didn't love her and that she was embarrassing herself by following you around like a puppy. In the long run, the truth is always better than not knowing. I only wanted Hannah to see that she isn't *gute* enough for you. The sooner she accepts that, the sooner she can find a husband suitable for her."

How could Scilla say such cruel things to Hannah? Austin was so angry, he was bound to say something he'd regret later, even if right now he couldn't imagine he'd regret anything he said to Scilla. He looked down at the four curious faces staring up at him. "I'm sorry, Scilla, but I don't want you to help me run the store. I don't want you to share my pain or joy or sorrows. I don't want to see you anymore."

Scilla blinked and blinked until the tears cleared from her eyes. "I know you're mad, but we can work this out. I'll go straight to Mary and James and hire them back. I'll apologize to Hannah for hurting her feelings, even if what I said was true."

Austin handed his box of bread to Alfie and took Scilla's box and gave it to Benji. "Will you boys take this to Scilla's buggy?"

"Okay."

Austin and Scilla watched in silence as all the children put on their coats and hats and went outside. Scilla turned to Austin. "I know you're mad, but we cannot have a serious discussion with the children gawking at us. Please, come to my house tonight after you close the store. We can work this out. All married people have rough patches."

Austin sighed in resignation. "I don't need to talk," he said, trying not to sound harsh. "I'm sorry that I led you to believe I wanted to get married. At one time, I thought I did, but I don't anymore. I don't love you, Scilla, and I never will. I'm sorry if this causes you pain."

Scilla didn't make any more attempts to blink back the tears. They trickled down her face like rain on a window. "My *mamm* and I were up all night baking bread. I thought you'd be pleased. I quit my job so we could spend more time together. Doesn't that mean anything to you?"

"I appreciate that, Scilla, I really do, but I can't marry someone who drives my dearest friends away with her unkindness."

She must have finally realized she couldn't talk him into anything. She stood up straight, and Austin could almost hear her spine snap into place. She whipped on her coat and hat as if she was suddenly in a very big hurry to get out of there. "Maybe I'll pay a visit to Raymond Glick. For sure and certain he'll be very interested in my whole wheat and twenty-grain bread. And the gluten-free. I don't wonder but he'll buy every loaf."

"I hope he does," Austin said. Nothing would drive customers to Austin's store like gluten-free bread at Glick's.

Scilla opened the door and tried to walk out just as *die kinner* walked in. "Get out of my way," she said. Benji scooted over and put a protective arm around Dinah's shoulder as Scilla shoved her way between Alfie and Benji and down the steps.

Benji waved cheerfully as Scilla climbed into her buggy.

"See you later. Come back in July. We'll have a hundred kinds of ice cream."

Alfie shoved Benji's shoulder. "Don't tell her that. We don't want her to come back ever."

"Of course we do. Everyone is welcome at Austin's market. Her money is as *gute* as anybody's. That's what Mamm says."

Austin laughed. How could he have ever considered marrying someone who didn't adore his *bruderen?*

Alfie herded the other children inside and slammed the door. "I'm never eating another BM cookie again."

"Me either," Austin said.

Alfie pulled the wadded up paper from his pocket and smoothed it on the kitchen counter. "Are you going to marry Scilla?" he read. He pulled his pencil from his other pocket. "*Nae,*" he said, writing down the answer. He looked up at Austin with a huge grin on his face.

Austin burst into laughter. "I guess that answers that question."

The children laughed as if something very funny had just happened. It *was* funny, in a way, but it was also sad and uncomfortable and confusing. Much as he was glad to have her gone, he was sorry he'd made Scilla upset. It was his fault her hopes had been so high, and he regretted it deeply. She had caused a lot of hurt to Mary and James and Hannah, but wasn't he just as responsible for that pain? If he hadn't encouraged Scilla and made her believe he loved her, she wouldn't have felt justified in treating the Yutzys poorly.

She may have said mean things to Hannah, but she'd only done it because she felt secure in Austin's affection, or perhaps insecure, and Hannah had left because of it. Because of him.

Alfie held his pencil at the ready. "I have one more question. Do you love Hannah?"

Alfie might as well have reached out and smacked him in the face.

Did he love Hannah? Austin caught his breath as the room began to spin. He felt giddy and sick and off-balance all at the same time.

Of course he loved Hannah.

After all his confusion, it was the only thing that made sense.

His heart did three somersaults and a backflip. He loved Hannah Yutzy. He loved the way she crinkled her nose when she laughed. He loved how she scolded him when he deserved it and even when he didn't. He loved how she tried to knock his confidence down every chance she got. He loved her laugh, and oh, how he missed it. He missed everything about her: her joy, her determination, her kindness. Her baking, her painting, her *gute* heart.

He'd made Hannah feel underappreciated. He had definitely taken her for granted. But he was only now realizing how much everything depended on her. His store, his happiness, his life. They were all tied up with Hannah. Her leaving had punched a huge hole in his heart. If she didn't come back, he'd be gasping for air the rest of his life.

He leaned against the counter for support. "*Jah,* Alfie. I do love Hannah."

"Then why don't you marry her?" Dinah said.

Now his heart was doing some sort of tumbling routine. Did he dare ask Hannah to marry him? Did he dare hope? He'd made a horrible mess of things, all because of his foolish infatuation for Priscilla Lambright. *Ach,* how badly he wanted to erase everything about Scilla from his life.

But if Scilla had never happened, maybe he wouldn't have come to appreciate Hannah the way he did now.

What could he say to her? "*Hallo,* Hannah. I appreciate you. By the way, do you want to get married?"

Ruth Ann looked Austin up and down as if he were an outhouse, like she refused to waste her time with him. "*Nae,* Dinah. He can't marry Hannah. She doesn't want to marry him."

Austin's hopes crashed to the ground like a duck in hunting season. "She doesn't want to marry me?"

"She said she doesn't want to be around you because you make her sad," Benji said.

"I make her sad?" Annoying her was one thing, so was taking her for granted, but Austin couldn't bear the thought that he made Hannah sad. He pressed his hand to his heart to stop the throbbing ache. Hannah should always be laughing and smiling, but even before she'd stopped coming to the store, he hadn't heard much laughter. Was that because of Scilla? Or him? He sat down, unable to support the thought of Hannah being unhappy.

Benji's mouth drooped. "We tried to tell you. Now she likes Matt Gingerich, and she doesn't like you."

Dinah gazed at him pitifully. It had gotten really bad when even the six-year-olds felt sorry for you. "Do you want a piece of candy?"

He leaned his head in his hand. "Could you get me a piece of horehound?"

Dinah made a face. "I guess. But watermelon is better."

"I don't deserve watermelon."

Ruth Ann pinned him with an accusatory gaze. "You better fix this. Other people are depending on you. Lots of other people. Even some people who can't walk."

Austin drew his brows together. People who couldn't

walk were depending on him? "I'm not sure how to fix it, Ruth Ann."

Alfie patted him on the shoulder in a kindhearted show of brotherly support. "You need our help."

Austin needed some kind of help, but a bunch of little kids weren't it. How much progress had Matt Gingerich already made? And if he'd made progress, it was only Austin's fault.

"We have a plan."

Dinah's eyes went wide, and she clapped her hand over her mouth. "*Ach, du lieva.* Look at the shovel."

Austin turned toward the front door and gasped. Sometime between last night and this morning when he hadn't been looking, Scilla had written *organic* on Hannah's shovel in white paint. It was like throwing mud on a freshly painted barn.

All regret about how he had treated Scilla disappeared. That girl was devious and selfish and vindictive. He was glad to be rid of her, but angry that he had been so blind to begin with.

He looked at the children. "Scilla shouldn't have done that to Hannah's shovel."

Dinah nodded. "She's going to be sad."

He wasn't going to let her be sad anymore. "Each of you pick a candy bar. I'm closing the store for the rest of the day, and we're going to Hannah's house."

"A whole candy bar?" Alfie said.

Ruth Ann smiled at Benji. "All to ourselves?"

"All to yourselves," Austin said, pulling his keys from the drawer, then extinguishing the lights as fast as he could go. "We're going to Hannah's."

"We can't," Dinah said. "She went to see the horses."

"What horses?"

Ruth Ann was already at the candy shelf choosing a candy bar. "She dropped us off and told us she was going with Matt to look at some ponies. Matt might buy one. He wants Hannah's advice."

Austin gritted his teeth. For sure and certain, it was a trick. Matt didn't want Hannah's advice about horses. He simply needed an excuse to be with Hannah in the first place. It was exactly what Austin would have done if he hadn't been so preoccupied with Scilla Lambright. If he'd been paying attention to anything besides his own popularity.

"Well, then, I guess I'll just go to her house and wait for her to come home."

"She's not going home. She's coming here to get us."

Austin's heart beat faster. "That's right. She'll be here at noon."

"But she doesn't want to marry you," Ruth Ann said.

"Maybe I can talk her into it."

Alfie shook his head. "*Nae,* Austin. You'll ruin it."

Alfie was probably right. He'd ruin it. Besides, Hannah knew about all the stupid, foolhardy things he'd ever done. She'd told him herself that she thought he was arrogant, self-centered, and insensitive. Who wanted to marry that?

Benji unwrapped his giant-size Snickers bar and took a huge bite, then lifted his medal and held it so Austin could get a better look. "We're heroes. You can't do it without us."

How many times had he messed things up with Hannah? He doubted his *bruderen* had any *gute* ideas, but they couldn't be any worse than his. Austin folded his arms and leaned against the counter. "What do you have in mind?"

The nutty chocolate bar crunched between Alfie's teeth. "Don't worry. We have a plan."

"What is it?"

"We can't tell," Benji said. "It's secret. But dress warm."

Ruth Ann grinned. "Hannah for sure and certain will love you after."

Austin couldn't argue with for sure and certain. And if the plan didn't work, which it wouldn't, he could always try a sincere apology, his irresistible charm, and a jar of peanut butter. Maybe he'd take a super-size candy bar as insurance.

Because if Hannah wouldn't love him back, he could go home, open his jar, and drown his sorrows in chocolate and Petersheim Brothers peanut butter.

And never smile again.

Chapter Twenty

Hannah was about ten minutes late picking up *die kinner,* but they knew how to entertain themselves at Austin's store, and Austin could give them jobs to do while they waited.

Looking at horses with Matt had taken a long time that seemed even longer because she wasn't all that interested in horses. Matt loved horses, and he and Josiah Yoder had spent half an hour debating what horses were best for pulling a buggy and a plow. Hannah wouldn't have minded the conversation, but it had taken place in Josiah's barn, and it hadn't been more than forty degrees in there. Hannah's toes still felt like icicles.

Hannah pulled the buggy into the parking lot in front of Austin's store. There wasn't another car or buggy in sight. Austin usually drove his open-air buggy, even in the winter, and stalled the horse in the one-car garage behind the house. But there was no sign of Austin either.

Maybe he'd gone to run an errand and left *die kinner* at the store by themselves. That didn't seem likely, but what else could account for the absence of his buggy?

She pulled up to the edge of the porch, hoping *die kinner* would see her from the window and come out without her having to go in. She didn't want to brave the cold to fetch the children from the store, and she certainly didn't want to lay eyes on Austin. It was too bad buggies didn't have horns, because honking for the children would have been very convenient right now.

While she waited, she peered at the foundation of the porch. A patch of petunias and zinnias would look beautiful up against the brick. Wouldn't ivy climbing up the house be *wunderbarr?* Maybe Austin could plant some evergreen bushes so the store didn't look so bleak in the winter. Such improvements wouldn't matter to Hannah though. To her, the store would always look bleak, no matter how many flowers Austin or Scilla planted.

A paper was taped to the front door with a piece of masking tape. Didn't they know masking tape would peel the paint off the door? She'd have to get out now just to remove the tape. Hannah set the brake, slid out of the buggy, and climbed the porch steps. The piece of paper had been folded and crinkled and smoothed out, rendering it thin and soft like a piece of fabric. It was a note for her, written with a crayon in a child's handwriting.

Hannah, go to the hide out behide the schoole right now. Bring warm cloths. Love, Benji.

What? This didn't make any sense.

She tried to open the door, but it was locked tight. She peered in the window. All the lights were out, and there wasn't a soul inside as far as she could tell. The OPEN sign still hung in the window, but Austin was definitely not open. Where had he gone? And where were the children? She glanced at the note again. Apparently, they were at the old hideout where Hannah and Austin used to play. But why?

She'd better get over there and make sure the twins and her cousins didn't freeze to death. Why they had gone there and asked Hannah to join them was anybody's guess.

She carefully peeled the tape off the door and the note with it. Fortunately, the tape came off without taking the paint. The other side of the note was filled with questions in one child's hand and answers in another.

What is your favrit food? Petersheim bruthers p.b. and prenztels

What is your favrit amimal? Horse or dog

Favrit rivr? Jordun, where Jesus was babtized.

Hannah smiled to herself. These were the same questions *die kinner* had asked her, but they were obviously Austin's answers. Who else's favorite food was Petersheim Brothers peanut butter? Hannah's gaze traveled down the page, reading Austin's answers. She giggled. Some questions appeared to irritate him.

What is your favrit color? Dont have 1

What is your favrit hat? That is a stoopud question

Hannah pressed her lips together. The last four questions were significantly more interesting.

Do you appreshiate Hannah? Of corse

Do you take Hannah for granite? yes

Hannah's heart pounded against her chest as she read the next question.

Are you going to merry Scilla?

She held her breath as her heart seemed to leap out of her chest and run down the road with what was left of her sanity.

Nun of your biznes was crossed out and nae was scribbled beneath it. Was this wishful thinking on the questioner's part, or had *nae* really been Austin's answer?

The last question almost knocked Hannah over on her *hinnerdale.*

Do you love Hannah? Jah.

What in the world?

Barely breathing, Hannah folded the note and stuffed it into her coat pocket. Maybe *die kinner* had made up these answers, and maybe they hadn't. One thing was for sure: She had to find out. She was going to that hideout.

Sol Nelson's hideout wasn't much of a hideout. It sat right out in the open in the middle of a pasture not a quarter mile from the school. It was a wonder the thing hadn't blown over years ago. Hannah parked her buggy on the side of the road and made her way across the snow to the old shed. There wasn't a sign of anyone. She hoped *die kinner* had the *gute* sense to go home, or at least huddle in the shed for a little warmth.

Hannah turned at the sound of horse hooves and saw Austin pull behind her buggy. If she wasn't feeling unsteady enough already, the sight of Austin sent her crashing right over the edge of a cliff.

He smiled and waved. She bit her bottom lip. There was no way the note in her pocket said anything about his real feelings for her. Ruth Ann and the boys had been playing some sort of funny game. Austin loved Scilla. He was going to marry her. Anything else was just wishful thinking.

Hannah thought of running headlong to the shed and locking herself in, but it wasn't as if he hadn't seen her, and he could outrun her by a mile—not that he would chase her or anything, but running was a stupid idea. She couldn't very well return to her buggy because she'd meet him on the way back, and she really did need to do what she could to keep *die kinner* from freezing to death, if they were even here.

So she did the only sensible thing. She stopped and waited for him to catch up with her. He jumped from his buggy and jogged through the snow to meet her. "I hope I dressed warm enough," he said, his breath hanging in the air. He seemed as cheerful as ever, if a little unsure of himself.

"You must have gotten a note too."

"Not exactly. *Die kinner* told me to come to the old hideout. Benji and Alfie are smart. I try to do what they tell me." He grinned sheepishly because they both knew how little attention he'd paid to his *bruderen* until recently.

"Do you know why we're here?"

"They said it's a secret."

Hannah raised an eyebrow. Austin knew something he wasn't telling her. He wouldn't close the store just because his *bruderen* had asked him to come to the old hideout. Her pulse raced, and she tried to slow it down by sheer force of will. No good would come of hoping for anything from Austin, even after reading that questionnaire. *Die kinner* had told her they weren't giving up, but she wasn't going to hold on to false hope. She and Austin could never be, and Matt Gingerich was a wonderful nice boy.

They got closer to the shed, and Hannah nearly jumped when Benji, Alfie, Ruth Ann, and Dinah stepped out from behind it. Thankfully, they were bundled for winter weather, and they were all smiling like big-toothed donkeys.

Hannah sighed. "It's freezing out here. You're going to catch your death of cold."

"We had to come here," Ruth Ann said, holding out her hand and motioning to the shed as if she was presenting

Hannah with a prize. "This is the place of your childhood dreams."

"My childhood dreams?" Hannah said.

Benji nodded. "We heard you and Austin talking about it."

Hannah didn't want to burst any bubbles, but this shed was where they had held their club. It had been a pretty *dumm* club, even if she and Austin had become friends because of it. The shed was the place of nobody's dreams. It was old and damp and stinky inside, and the only reason they used it as a hideout was because nobody with any brains wanted to go inside.

Benji took the medal from around his neck and handed it to Austin. "Wear this," he said.

Austin tried to give it back. "I'm not going to wear your medal, Benji."

Benji wouldn't take it back. "Girls like boys with medals, and you need all the help you can get."

"What are we doing here?" Hannah said slowly.

Ruth Ann took Hannah's mittened hand. "Austin is wonderful nice, and we want you to get to know him."

"I already know him."

"We want you to forgive him. He has some good parts about him, and you should give him a second chance."

Hannah didn't dare even look in Austin's direction. She'd give him a hundred chances, but he didn't want any. "But why are we here at the shed?"

"We want you to get to know him," Benji said.

Hannah resisted the urge to growl. She faked a smile for *die kinner.* They meant well. They didn't deserve her frustration. "We already know each other."

Alfie motioned toward the shed door. "We made supper for you."

Dinah squeaked with delight. "It's romantic."

Ruth Ann nodded. "We want you to have a romantic dinner together in the shed so you can get to know each other. There's romantic candles and stuff."

Hannah swallowed hard and glanced at Austin. He stood there with a concerned look on his face, obviously wishing he could run as far away as possible. "This is wonderful nice, but I'm sure Austin would rather have a romantic supper with Scilla. You should have invited her."

"I would rather eat with you," Austin said, his voice low and earnest.

It was *gute* the wind wasn't blowing because it would have knocked her over. Her heart jumped around in her chest like a frog in a frying pan. "What do you mean, Austin?"

He stared at her as if all the answers on that questionnaire were true, as if he really did love her. She stared back, letting herself get lost in his eyes.

"Look," Dinah squealed, pointing to the shed door. Wisps of white smoke curled out from every crack around the door, and something sputtered quietly inside the shed.

Benji's eyes went wide. "Is it the candles?"

Austin gingerly opened the door and was met with a wall of smoke. Coughing and waving his hand in front of his face, he slammed the door shut. "I think our supper is on fire and so is the tablecloth."

Alfie sprinted toward the door like he was shot from a gun. "We've got to get that tablecloth. It's Mamm's nice one for Sundays."

He opened the door, letting out more smoke, and tried to run inside, but Austin yanked him back. "It's too late for the tablecloth. If you go in there, the shed will burn down on your head."

Alfie's expression was pained. "It has lace around the edges."

"We need to put it out," Benji said. "Everybody grab some snow."

Hannah eyed the smoke pouring from the shed, then glanced at Austin. He gave her a slight shake of his head. They both knew how useless it was to try to put out the fire. Judging from the gray, thick smoke, it was already out of control. The shed, with its fifty-year-old dried wood, was going to ignite like kindling.

But that didn't matter. *Die kinner* were going to know that she had tried to save the shed. Austin was cautious and smart. He wouldn't let anyone get too close, but he encouraged all of them to grab big handfuls of snow and throw them into the shed. The snow sizzled, but once the flames took hold of the shed walls, there was nothing they could do. It was like a snowball fight with a fire monster.

When Austin could see it was a lost cause, he held out his hand and sort of nudged everybody back. The flames curled around the tin roof while devouring the shed walls. The shed held strong for a few minutes, then collapsed into itself. It ended up looking like a bonfire. They'd probably be able to roast marshmallows on the coals in an hour or so.

"There goes Mamm's card table," Alfie said.

Austin eyed Alfie reproachfully. "You borrowed Mamm's card table?"

Alfie's frown took over his face. "We wanted it to be nice."

Benji nodded. "We put two folding chairs in there so you wouldn't have to sit in the dirt."

Austin's eyes nearly popped out of his head. "You borrowed Mamm's folding chairs?" He looked at Hannah. "We should have tried harder to put that fire out."

The look on his face and the absurdity of the situation struck Hannah's funny bone. She started to giggle. Austin watched her for a stunned second, then joined in the laughter. They could either laugh or cry. Hannah preferred to laugh.

Alfie swiped his coat sleeve across his nose. "Do you think she'll take away my medal?"

"I don't doubt it," Austin said.

Dinah slipped her gloved hand into Hannah's as they gazed at the burning shed. At least it warmed the air enough so they wouldn't freeze. It was almost nice, just standing in the fresh air watching the many colors of the fire dance along the wood, basking in the warmth of the flames, listening to the comforting crackle as the heat of the fire met the boards of the old hideout. And Rebecca Petersheim's card table.

Austin sidled next to Hannah, gave her a tentative smile, and slipped his hand into hers. He had gloves on, she had mittens on, but his touch still sent a jolt of energy up her arm. Hannah jumped out of her skin and jerked her hand away.

He seemed to deflate like a balloon. "Don't you want me to do that?"

"Scilla doesn't want you to do that," Hannah snapped. How dare he play with her emotions?

To her surprise, his mouth curled into a grin. "*Nae,* she doesn't. But I don't care what she thinks anymore."

Hannah didn't have the energy or the heart to puzzle out what Austin meant, or to try to interpret that aggravatingly attractive smile. "Don't tease me, Austin. I just don't have the stomach for it today."

He grew more serious. "I'm sorry, Hannah. No one

would expect you to believe a word I say after how I've treated you."

"You've treated me fine," she said. And just to prove she didn't want his pity, she took Dinah by the shoulders and nudged her cousin between herself and Austin.

Dinah looked up at her, the fire reflecting in her blue eyes. "Are you mad about the shovel?"

The shovel? Hannah's stomach sank to her toes even though she had told herself that the shovel was Austin's gift to do what he wanted with it. She glanced at Austin. "She wrote on it, didn't she?"

Any trace of happiness fled from Austin's face. "She did it sometime yesterday when I wasn't looking. Dinah noticed it this morning."

Hannah turned her face toward the fire and shrugged casually, even though her heart ached. "You can do whatever you want with that shovel. I don't really care."

"But that's what I'm trying to tell you," Austin said, reaching over Dinah's head and placing his hand on Hannah's arm. His touch made her shiver. "I care. She never should have done that to your shovel. I didn't want her to."

"He was really mad about it," Alfie said.

Benji tapped her on the other arm. "He had us load up Scilla's lumpy bread and told her never to come back." He frowned. "I told her to come back, but only because we want her money."

Austin had told Scilla never to come back?

Ruth Ann sidled next to Benji. "He didn't even make us finish the cinnamon rolls."

"I licked the frosting," Benji said, as if confessing a horrible sin.

Dinah patted Hannah's coat to get her attention. "She called you a puppy, and Austin got really mad."

Benji looked extremely concerned. "We don't want you to marry Matt Gingerich."

"Austin can juggle," Alfie said.

Ruth Ann nodded. "And he gave us all a giant candy bar, and we didn't even have to pay."

"All right, all right," Austin growled. He palmed the side of Alfie's head and shoved him sideways.

Alfie made a very disgusted face, as if he was barely putting up with his older *bruder.* Hannah kind of felt the same way. What was going on, and would her heart ever beat normally again?

Austin pointed to the other side of the fire. "You *kinner,* scat. Go over there."

Benji scrunched his lips to one side of his face. "Where do you want us to go?"

Austin gave Benji the stink eye. "Go to the other side of the fire. I want to have a private, uninterrupted talk with Hannah. Shoo." Alfie opened his mouth to protest, but Austin cut him off. "Go away. Now. Don't get too close to the fire. And don't poke at it with sticks or throw anything in. Just go to that side and stand."

Hannah smiled to herself. Austin knew very well how fascinated children were with fire.

"Can we throw snowballs in the fire?" Alfie said.

"Just go," Austin snapped. Benji took Dinah's hand and led her around to the other side. Alfie and Ruth Ann trudged reluctantly around the fire, never taking their gaze from Austin.

Hannah studied Austin's face while a windstorm of emotions whirled around in her head. "You kicked Scilla out of your store?"

Austin turned to her and curled his fingers around her upper arms. His eyes were filled with longing and pain. "First tell me this. Are you in love with Matt Gingerich?"

Hannah sighed and leaned into him. He was just too hard to resist. "Not especially. He doesn't even juggle."

Not even a ghost of a smile touched his lips. "Please tell me I haven't ruined my chances with you."

The tenderness in his eyes made her melt like a card table in a bonfire. "Well," she said, unable to stop herself from giving him an affectionate smile. "You've been insensitive, self-centered, and *dumm.* You let Scilla paint my sign and hand out BM cookies at your grand opening. You took me for granted and accused me of selling cinnamon rolls to Raymond Glick. And you love Scilla."

"*Ach,*" he said, grimacing tightly. "That is a wonderful long list, but I don't love Scilla. I don't even like her."

Hannah thought her heart might burst with joy. "*Gute* to know," she said calmly. She gave him an arch look. "But you also helped me scrape your floor and got me into Sol Nelson's club and defended me whenever someone made fun of my drawings. You let us have a place in your store, and you never insisted we make gluten-free bread. And you always liked my baking better than Scilla's. I could tell."

He chuckled, despite his obvious distress, and his hands tightened around her arms. "*Ach,* Hannah. Can you even begin to guess how much I love you?"

"Not really," she said, her heart pounding a wild rhythm in her ears.

"Can you ever love me back?"

"Believe me, Austin, I love you even better than you love me, and I have for a very long time."

He smiled so wide, she could have counted his teeth.

"I don't want to argue with you, but no one, no one could ever love someone as much as I love you." He glanced to the other side of the fire where Alfie and Benji had started throwing snowballs into the flames. They could hear Ruth Ann scolding the boys for being so foolish. "Oh, my dear, dear Hannah," Austin said, taking off his glove and cupping his hand around her cheek. "We only have a few minutes before Alfie and Benji do something stupid, so I'm going to have to make it short. Another day, when we have hours and hours to talk about it, I'll tell you exactly how sorry I am and how deeply I love you. But since it's very likely Alfie has a smoke bomb in his pocket and my lips are going to freeze in place, this will have to do." He leaned in and planted a slow, achingly sweet kiss on her lips right there in front of *die kinner.* Hopefully, they were too busy throwing snowballs to notice that Hannah's world had just turned upside down and rolled on top of itself.

This was what she had been waiting for, this feeling of utter and complete happiness that not even the bitter cold or flying snowballs could dampen.

He curled his fingers around the nape of her neck and their foreheads met. "I love you, Hannah, and I'm going to spend a lifetime proving it."

A clump of snow sailed over the fire and hit Austin on the cheek. Somebody on the other side of the fire had a *gute* arm.

"Sorry," Ruth Ann called.

Austin put his glove back on and wiped his face. "We should get *die kinner* out of here before something really bad happens." He smiled and winked at Hannah, sending her heart to the moon and back.

"Do you think we should put out the fire first?"

"Probably, but Alfie and Benji are just trouble waiting to happen."

Hannah groaned as the sound of a distant siren met her ears. The fire department had been alerted. The good news was that by the time they got here, there wouldn't be anything to put out. The bad news was, someone's shed had been destroyed. How were they going to pay for that?

Die kinner heard the siren too and bolted around the fire to be close to Hannah and Austin. "Are we in trouble?" Benji asked.

"*Jah,*" Austin said. The question now was, how much trouble?

Hannah couldn't be too concerned. Austin loved her, and he wasn't going to marry Scilla. All was right with the world.

Ruth Ann sighed sadly. "We didn't even get a chance to light the candles. It would have been so romantic."

Austin drew his brows together. "It wonders me how the fire started if you didn't light the candles."

"I don't know," Benji said. He frowned. "Do you think it was the little fire I started in the corner to keep the shed warm?"

"Benji!" Alfie yelled. "You lit a fire in there?"

"It was cold," Benji protested, as if any reasonable person would have done the same.

Alfie gave his twin *bruder* a healthy shove. "You *dummkoff.* Mamm's going to take away both our medals."

Dinah's eyes were two big pools of tears. "We made sandwiches."

Hannah squatted and gathered Dinah into her arms. "I'm sure they would have been delicious."

A big red fire truck came down the deserted road. Its

lights were flashing, but thank Derr Herr, they'd turned off their sirens several hundred yards ago. A police car and a smaller red truck followed the fire truck. They parked in an orderly line behind Austin's buggy.

Two firefighters in heavy coats and helmets got out of the fire truck. Hannah had no idea how she was going to explain this. The firefighters hiked across the pasture, obviously aware that there wasn't any real emergency. Nothing else was in danger of catching fire, and the shed was almost completely gone.

The male firefighter hooked his thumbs in his belt and looked at Austin. "Would you like to tell us what happened?"

"We fixed a romantic supper," Ruth Ann said.

One corner of the firefighter's mouth curled upward. "It doesn't look like that worked out so well."

Hannah was used to taking charge in situations like this. "The children wanted to do something nice for us. They made us supper and built a fire to keep us warm. They weren't thinking of what could happen."

The firefighter nodded. "I see." He looked right at Benji, though how he knew Benji was the one who had started the fire, Hannah couldn't begin to guess. "You shouldn't ever play with matches."

"I don't play with matches," Benji said. "It's a rule."

The firefighter cocked his eyebrow. "I'm glad to hear it."

"I borrowed the lighter Austin uses to light the pellet stove," Benji said.

"Benji," Austin said. "You know that lighter stays at the store."

"I know," Benji said. "But it was an emergency."

The female firefighter grinned widely. "It looks like we interrupted something important." She motioned toward the burning pile of rubble. One leg of Rebecca's unfortunate table stuck out of the embers like a flagpole. "Emmon Giles has been wanting to burn this thing for years, but the city told him he had to tear it down because burning it was too dangerous. I'm sure he'll send you a thank-you note."

"Will he give us a medal?" Alfie said. Austin cuffed him on the back of the head. "Ouch," Alfie protested, though it hadn't hurt. Austin rolled his eyes, and a giggle escaped Hannah's lips.

"We'll come back in a few weeks when it's warmer and clear away what's left," Austin said.

"That would be appreciated, I'm sure."

Austin looked back at the police car. "If you need to go, we'll wait here until it burns down, then pile snow on it."

The fireman took off his hat. "Don't worry about that. We'll stand watch until it burns out, then we'll douse it."

The woman firefighter grinned. "And by stand watch, he means we'll sit in the truck and play on our phones."

The fireman made a face. "We have to make sure little kids don't play in it. That's dangerous."

"Okay," Hannah said. "We'll take the children home."

"And no more lighting fires," the fireman said. "We don't want anybody getting hurt."

Hannah patted Dinah on the head. "*Cum.* I'll take you and Ruth Ann home. Alfie and Benji can go with Austin."

Austin grabbed her hand and squeezed it. "Meet you at the store in an hour? I need you to repaint the sign."

Hannah smiled, happier than she'd ever been. "I'll bring cinnamon rolls."

Benji looked at Austin with those wide, innocent eyes. "Can we come?"

Austin groaned, then glanced at Hannah. They both knew it would be better if *die kinner* were there, no matter how badly they wanted to be alone. "Okay," Austin said. "Candy bars for everyone."

The four children cheered as if they knew something important had just happened, and it had nothing to do with candy bars.

And in their own way, they did have a hand in bringing Hannah and Austin together. They deserved a candy bar a day for the rest of their lives.

And Scilla wouldn't be around to protest.

Chapter Twenty-One

Alfie and Benji sat facing each other on the air mattress with a notebook and a pencil between them, but neither of them had any ideas and the notebook page was blank except for the word *wheelchair* written at the top of the page in big letters.

"We could give them all our tomato money," Benji said.

Every summer, Mamm let them sell the extra tomatoes from the garden and keep the money. But after they paid for the card table, the tablecloth, and Mamm's folding chairs, there wouldn't be anything left for a wheelchair.

They had to think of something. Austin and Hannah weren't getting married until October when they finished baptism classes. Emma and Abraham were getting married on the same day as Austin and Hannah, so Ruth Ann and Dinah had fulfilled their part of the agreement. Alfie and Benji would get their old room back, but now Alfie and Benji needed to help Ruth Ann and Dinah's *mamm* get a wheelchair. Fair was fair. Alfie should have thought it through better before shaking hands with Ruth Ann. He couldn't see a way to come up with that much money, even if they sold their medals, which they weren't going to do ever. As some of Bienenstock's finest and bravest citizens, they had to think of something else.

"Benji, Alfie, dinner," Mamm called from upstairs. "Wash your hands."

In spite of his dilemma, Alfie smiled. In a few months, Mamm wouldn't be yelling down the stairs to them anymore. They'd be respected members of the family with a room upstairs where the adults slept.

Benji closed the notebook and laid the pencil carefully atop it. "Maybe we can think of something after dinner."

Alfie grimaced. There wouldn't be a chance after dinner. That was family reading time. *Ach,* he hated family reading time.

He and Benji tromped up the steps to the kitchen where they washed their hands and sat down at the table. Mammi and Dawdi sat next to Benji, and Abraham was on the other side of Alfie. Andrew, Mary, Mamm, Dat, and Austin crowded around the table too. Alfie's niece, ElJay, sat in her high chair and slapped her hand on the tray.

It would be nice when Austin and Hannah moved into the store, and Abraham and Emma went wherever it was they were going to go. Then at least Alfie would have a chance at a second piece of pie every night. Of course, he had to be patient because October was still months away, but he could see the end in sight.

They joined hands and said silent grace. It was sinful, but Alfie always said a quick prayer, then peeked at everyone else while they prayed. ElJay wasn't closing her eyes either, but she'd never tell anyone Alfie wasn't closing his. Mamm always looked sort of irritated when she prayed. Dat looked like he was asleep. Austin always smiled and so did Mary. Why did people smile when they prayed? Were they telling Gotte jokes?

After the prayer, Mamm passed around the food. "Austin, when will you move the rest of your things out of your room and into the store?"

"Like as not next week, Mamm. James is going to help me with the boxes, but there isn't much."

Alfie was so excited about his room, he could nearly taste it. "When is Abraham moving out? Benji and me want to move our stuff upstairs as soon as he goes." Maybe Abraham would move out before he got married. For sure and certain, he'd have a funner time staying with Austin at the store.

Mamm served Dawdi David a clump of mashed potatoes. "What do you mean, Alfie?"

Alfie tried not to sound too eager to get rid of his *bruderen,* but he and Benji had been in the cellar so long. "Is Abraham moving out before he gets married?"

Mamm stopped passing bowls and stared at Alfie. "Where have you been, young man?"

Alfie looked around the table. Every eye was on him, except for Benji's. "What . . . I went to school today."

"*Nae,* I mean where have you been? We talked about this weeks ago. Austin is moving to the store, and after Abraham and Emma marry, they're going to live here until Abraham can save enough money to buy some land. You and Benji are staying in the cellar."

Alfie thought his tongue was going to fall out of his mouth. "What? When? We didn't talk about this."

"You were sitting right there, young man."

Andrew and Mary watched Alfie as if they felt sorry

for him. So did Abraham. "You never told me," he said. He glared at Benji. "Did she, Benji?"

Benji stuffed four green beans into his mouth. "*Jah*. She told us."

"And you didn't tell me?"

Benji frowned. "You were sitting right here."

Alfie squeezed his fork so hard, for sure and certain he bent the metal. "But . . . but what about the cellar? We can't stay down there, Mamm. We'll get bit by a spider and we'll die, and mice will eat our bodies."

Mamm raised her eyebrows. "You'll be just fine, young man. Summer's almost here. Remember how cool it is down there in the summer? It's the best place to sleep when it's hot."

Alfie scowled. "That's why all the spiders went down there."

"I thought you liked it," Andrew said.

"We hate it," Alfie shot back.

Mamm slammed her cup on the table. "You can stop that right now."

"But we're going to die, and you don't love us."

Mamm gave him a stern look. Alfie shut his mouth, even though one of Bienenstock's finest and bravest citizens should never ever get looked at like that. "You're being wonderful snippy for a boy who burned down Emmon Giles's shed, ruined my card table and tablecloth, and set off a purple smoke bomb outside the library."

Alfie pushed his food around his plate. They'd never been able to prove it was his smoke bomb, and Ruth Ann hadn't told a soul. Besides, not one inch of smoke had floated into the library. There had been too much wind that day, and Scilla hadn't even noticed it. But he wasn't going to lie, so he'd better just keep his mouth shut about the cellar and the shed and the smoke bomb.

"I could make some curtains for that window down there," Mary said. She was trying to be nice, but Alfie was too mad to care.

Benji picked up a piece of corn with his fingers. "We'd rather have a ladder so we can climb out the window."

"Benji!" Alfie said. Benji was a *gute* partner, but he didn't always know how to keep secrets.

Mamm shook her finger at Alfie. "You are not to climb out of that window ever. Do you understand?"

"Why are you pointing at me? Benji's the one who said it."

Mary covered her mouth with her hand, but Alfie could tell she was laughing. Alfie frowned. He had thought he wanted a sister-in-law, but sometimes she was a big nuisance.

Alfie didn't say another word during dinner. He was too mad at everybody, and Mamm was looking at him as if she was just waiting for him to confess to the smoke bomb. He wouldn't give her the satisfaction, not when all his hopes and dreams were dead. He was going to die in that cellar, and nobody would even care. They probably wouldn't even take his body out to bury it.

Mamm was just pulling the peanut-butter-and-chocolate pie out of the fridge when someone knocked at the door. Alfie jumped from his seat so fast, he almost knocked his chair over. Any excuse to get away from his family. Benji followed close behind, even though Alfie wanted nothing to do with him. He somehow felt Benji was a traitor, though he couldn't quite put his finger on why.

Alfie opened the door and caught his breath. The two old people they had pulled out of the motor home stood on their porch with big smiles on their faces. Their dark brown skin made their bright smiles seem extra friendly. It was nice to see some friendly faces when everyone at the dinner table was against him.

"Are you Alfie and Benji Petersheim?" the man said.

Benji's eyes got wide. "You're that man."

The man chuckled. "I'm that man. The one you saved from the motor home. My name is Don. This is my wife, Hilda."

Hilda stepped forward and shook Benji's hand, then Alfie's. Her hands were warm, and she had that look on her face like she was somebody's grandma, like she gave good hugs and never got impatient with little kids. "It's very nice to meet you. It's not every day someone saves your life."

It sounded like a herd of elephants coming from the kitchen. Everybody but Mammi and Dawdi gathered in the living room and stared at their guests. Alfie sort of puffed out his chest. Mamm wouldn't give him nasty looks after this. "This is Don and Hilda. We saved their lives."

Mamm pushed her way forward and shook their hands. "It's wonderful good to meet you. How nice of you to come over."

"We couldn't be at the city council meeting when they gave your boys the awards," Hilda said. "I had a shareholders meeting, and Don had to be at the office. So I told Don the next free day we had, we'd drive up here to thank you in person."

"Did you come from far?" Mamm asked.

"Originally from South Carolina, but we've lived in

Milwaukee for thirty years. Don is a dermatologist, and I'm the president of a credit union."

Don put his arm around Hilda. "She's very important."

Hilda laughed and pushed him away. "Not that important."

"Would you like to stay for pie?" Mamm said. It was wonderful nice of her, but that meant less pie for Alfie. He probably wouldn't even get a piece. Still, it was nice to have Don and Hilda here to remind Mamm what a brave and fine citizen he was. She forgot that all the time.

"We would love some pie," Hilda said. "But first we want to ask you something."

"Me?" Alfie said.

Hilda bent over so her face was closer to Alfie's. "Both you and Benji. We want you boys to know how grateful we are. The police told us how you came right into the motor home and dragged us out. It was very brave of you."

Alfie nodded. "We were brave."

"Show some humility, young man," Mamm said.

Hilda smiled at Mamm. "You have some fine sons here."

It was *gute* Hilda had said it, because Mamm needed to be reminded all the time.

"We want to show our gratitude," Don said. "Will you help us?"

"How can we help?" Benji said.

"We don't know a lot about the Amish, but we wanted to give you a monetary gift."

Alfie's heart raced. He didn't know what "monetary" meant, but he heard "gift" loud and clear. "You want to give us a present?"

Don squatted down next to Alfie. "We want to give you some money that you could set aside for the future. Ten thousand dollars. Maybe you could use it toward your education or save it to help with a house."

Ten thousand dollars! That would buy a lot of walkie-talkies.

Mamm looked a lot surprised. "Oh, but that's . . . but we couldn't."

"Yes, we could," Alfie said. He grabbed Don's arm. "We would like that very much."

Mamm glanced at Dat. "It's a lot of money. I don't think we could accept it."

"Yes, we could," Alfie said again, wondering if he should have Benji take Mamm into the kitchen. She wasn't thinking straight.

"Mrs. Petersheim," Hilda said. "We don't know how else to express our gratitude. We've got four kids and eight grandchildren who are extremely grateful that they still have their grandparents around. Please, won't you accept our money? You could save it for the boys when they get older. Buy them a buggy or something."

Alfie nearly jumped out of his skin as the best idea crashed into him. "Could we use it to build something?"

"I don't see why not," Don said, standing up and smiling at his wife.

Alfie put his arm around Benji. "Me and Benji need our own room because Dawdi had a stroke. We sleep in the cellar, and there's spiders down there. Could we build another room onto the side of the house?"

"That's sounds like a terrific idea to me," Don said.

Mamm folded her arms. "I suppose we could consider it."

Benji poked Alfie in the ribs. "I need to talk to you."

"Go ahead and talk," Alfie said.

"In private," Benji said.

Alfie smiled at Don and Hilda, just so they knew everything was okay, even though he was a little annoyed with Benji. Was Benji going to try to talk him out of a new bedroom? Because that wasn't going to work. No way.

They moved away from everybody and leaned against the wall. "We can't build our own bedroom," Benji whispered.

Was that all? Benji worried about the silliest things. "Andrew will help us. And Dat and Austin."

"*Nae,*" Benji said. "Dinah's *mamm* needs a new wheelchair."

Alfie's stomach felt like he'd just eaten three BM cookies. "But we need our own room," he said. "When we get our own room, it will be easier to make a *gute* plan for the wheelchair."

Benji frowned and bit his bottom lip. "Why should we get our own room when Dinah's *mamm* can't even walk?"

Alfie ground his teeth together. Benji was a *gute* partner, but sometimes he didn't use his head. "What if we get bit by a spider and die? Then we won't be able to walk either."

Benji looked down at his hands. "I'm just saying."

"But it's our money," Alfie said.

Benji blinked real hard. "But, Alfie, we can run in the fields with our dog and play tag and hide-and-seek. Dinah's *mamm* can't even fix dinner or milk the cow or make peanut butter chocolate pie for her kids."

She couldn't even walk or hug her *kinner* real tight or climb into the hay mow when she wanted to be alone. Alfie's eyes clouded with tears. He wanted his own bedroom something wonderful, but he'd never be able to sleep in it knowing Ruth Ann's *mamm* didn't get the wheelchair she deserved. It might mean they'd be in the cellar forever, but they'd buy Ruth Ann's *mamm* a wheelchair, even if the spiders did them in. His lip quivered. "Okay, Benji. We'll get her a wheelchair." Maybe he'd get another medal for being so nice.

Benji threw his arms around Alfie. "You're the best *bruder* in the whole world."

"I know. So are you."

Mamm had invited Don and Hilda to sit on the sofa, and Mary had already brought them each a piece of pie.

Alfie wiped his nose with his sleeve, draped his arm around Benji's shoulder, and pulled both of them toward Don and Hilda. "We've decided what we want to do with the money."

Don was just about to take his first bite of pie. "What would you like?"

"Well, see," Benji said, tracing his toe along the rug, "Our friend Dinah's *mamm* needs a new wheelchair. Can you buy her a wheelchair, even if it's our money?"

Hilda smiled so wide, Alfie could see most of her teeth. "What a nice thing to do with your money." She looked at Mamm. "You've got some excellent boys here."

Mamm nodded. She must have had a piece of pie stuck in her throat, because her eyes got sort of watery and she couldn't talk.

"And would there be enough money left over for a card table and a new tablecloth for our *mamm?*" Alfie said. Maybe they wouldn't have to use their tomato money.

Don smacked his lips. "Delicious pie, Mrs. Petersheim." He looked at Alfie. "What kind of wheelchair does your friend's mother need?"

Benji scratched his head. "It has to be one that goes by itself because she can't push it herself anymore."

Hilda frowned at Don. "What's the matter with her?"

Alfie shrugged. "I don't know."

Mamm finally cleared that pie from her throat. "Linda was diagnosed with Lyme disease five years ago. Nothing has helped, and she's been getting worse. She can't walk anymore, but the doctors don't know what to do for her."

Don wrinkled his forehead. "Alfie and Benji, I think there's something better we can do for Linda."

Alfie tried not to look disappointed. Ruth Ann wouldn't be satisfied with anything but a wheelchair. And their tomato money was only going to go so far.

Chapter Twenty-Two

Hannah caught her breath as Benji stepped on the petunia she'd just planted. Bless his heart, he was trying to be helpful, but he was doing more harm than *gute*. "Benji, maybe you could turn up the soil on that side of the house. You just stepped on my petunia."

Benji gingerly lifted his foot. There was a very sad and flat petunia plant underneath. "Sorry. I was looking for weeds."

Hannah couldn't be mad. *Die kinner* had come to the store every day after school for weeks, willing and eager to help Austin, even if they weren't a lot of help. They cleaned and swept and took out trash and ate day-old cinnamon rolls. Sometimes they helped Hannah in the bakery. Their help was usually more of a hindrance, but she tried to be patient and teach them. No child learned anything without making a lot of mistakes. Some days the children just ran around or played hide-and-seek or drew pictures on each other with the Sharpie and weren't much help at all, but they were so sweet that neither Hannah nor Austin could say no to that much enthusiasm.

School would be out next week, and Hannah suspected

die kinner would spend even more time at the store. She gazed at her flattened petunia plant, not sure if she was looking forward to that or not.

Hannah sat in the dirt surrounded by Ruth Ann, Dinah, Alfie, and Benji. Each of them had a garden trowel and was helping Hannah plant petunias. Dinah's job was to turn the dirt over and soften it up so Hannah could plant flowers. Benji and Alfie were supposed to pull the weeds, and Ruth Ann was digging holes for Hannah's petunia plants to go in. Alfie was pulling out weeds with one hand and grasping the medal around his neck with the other. He insisted on wearing his medal every day after school, but he didn't want to get it dirty, so he was practicing one-handed gardening.

Hannah had purchased seven dozen petunia plants for the front of the store. Austin thought it was too many, but he didn't really have an eye for what Hannah was going to do. By July, these petunias would be a sea of color around the foundation. They'd be breathtakingly beautiful, and people would stop at the store just to take a look. She was also planning on climbing roses and clematis right up against the house and a huge garden in the back. The Plain and Simple Country Store wasn't just going to be a retail spot. It was going to be a tourist destination, famous for its gardens and shovel head collection.

"Alfie, that's not a weed," Hannah said, stopping Alfie before he dug up the clematis she'd planted three days ago. Oy, anyhow.

"What is it?"

"It's a flower that will grow right up the wall of the house."

Alfie didn't seem to care much if the flower grew up

the side of the house or not. "You should grow a giant pumpkin. I seen one at the fair last year."

"That's a *wunderbarr* idea, Alfie. Wouldn't a giant pumpkin look nice growing right here next to the petunias?"

"It will smash them," Dinah said.

Ruth Ann dug another hole for Hannah. "Maybe we should plant it off to the side."

Hannah sprinkled some fertilizer into the hole. "We can leave some space for it on the other side of the porch. I'll buy a pumpkin plant tomorrow." She grimaced. Hopefully, it wouldn't be expensive, but now that the idea was planted in her brain, she simply had to have a giant pumpkin. Wouldn't that be a sight?

"More rocks," Austin said, coming around the side of the house with his full wheelbarrow. He was preparing some of the backyard for a vegetable garden, and there was no shortage of rocks in the soil. He dumped his load of rocks in the already tall pile and winked at Hannah. *Ach,* how she loved that smile. And it was all hers.

They were going to build a rock wall, one foot tall and one foot thick, between the flowerbeds and the parking lot. It would look charming, and give them something to do with all the rocks. Hannah planned to start that rock wall tomorrow, when *die kinner* were in school. She didn't see it going well unless she and Austin did it by themselves, with a little help from James.

Benji threw a weed on the pile. "Austin, I stepped on one of the petunias."

Austin grinned. "*Ach, vell.* We still have eighty-three petunias left. I think we'll be okay."

"I dropped one, and it broke," Alfie said. "And Dinah chopped one in half with her shovel."

Austin's mood was not dampened by the thought of dead petunias. "Eighty-one. That's still a lot of petunias."

"Nine times nine," Ruth Ann said.

Benji stepped back and studied a patch of bindweed growing in their flowerbed. "Hannah is going to grow a giant pumpkin."

Austin cocked an eyebrow. "Is she?"

Hannah couldn't help but giggle. She loved to surprise him. "You're going to love it."

"I'm sure I will." He gazed at her with such warmth, she couldn't help but melt like butter.

Ach. Emmon Giles's shed had burned to the ground three months ago, and she hadn't thought it possible that she could be any happier. But she loved Austin more every day, and her happiness just grew and grew. They were both taking baptism classes and would be married in October, Lord willing. It was going to be a long summer. But working on the store and garden would keep her busy, and dreaming about her new home and life with Austin would keep her wildly happy.

They were going to live at the store once they married. Austin and his *bruderen* planned to finish the entire basement, putting in a small kitchen, one more bedroom, and a bathroom. They were also going to expand the shed in back for more storage and more room for the horse. It was going to be a big project, and they'd be nicely cramped for several months before it was finished.

Hannah didn't mind. Being cramped just meant being closer to the man she loved.

Business at the store had picked up in March and continued to do well. Raymond Glick's plan to lure away Austin's vendors hadn't worked out. He hadn't sold Erna Nelson's quilt because he'd priced it too high, and the

Christmas season was over, so not many tourists were buying Matt Gingerich's ornaments. Raymond would never offer to carry Petersheim Brothers peanut butter or Honeybee Sisters honey in his store, plus Andrew's furniture or Lily Yoder's quilts. Bitsy Kiem had started selling beeswax candles at the store along with her honey, and those were things Raymond wouldn't carry. There just weren't enough ways for Raymond to squeeze Austin out of business.

With the bishop's permission, Will Williams had helped them set up a website where they sold quilts, Amish handicrafts, furniture, and peanut butter. And Will's cheese. Will had proven to be a *gute* and loyal friend. Hannah would always be grateful.

A buggy pulled off the road and into the parking lot. Ruth Ann and Dinah dropped their trowels and ran toward the buggy. "It's Mamm," Dinah squealed with pure joy in her voice. Hannah's heart swelled. Aendi Linda had never seen the store before. She was going to be delighted.

Hannah gasped as Onkel Menno helped Linda out of the buggy and she walked toward the store leaning heavily on a walker for support. Hannah laughed at the happiness of it. Aendi Linda could walk!

Hannah and Austin met Aendi Linda and Onkel Menno at the porch steps. Aendi Linda put a hand on Dinah's shoulder. "The girls have talked my ear off about this store. I decided to come and see it for myself."

Austin beamed like the sunshine. "We're still working on the yard yet."

Linda's gaze traveled to the flats of petunias in the dirt. "It's going to be beautiful. Hannah has a knack."

"She does," Austin said. "I couldn't do it without her."

Aendi Linda gave him a pointed look. "And don't you forget it."

"I won't."

Linda grinned at Austin. "I'm getting better at this all the time, but it wonders me if I could get a ride up the stairs."

"Of course," Austin said.

Austin and Onkel Menno formed their arms into a seat, Aendi Linda sat down, and they carried her up the stairs, through the small atrium Andrew had built, and into the store where Mary and James were making donuts.

"I want a ride," Alfie said.

"Your legs are *gute* enough," Austin said. "Be grateful."

Alfie shrugged. "I am, I guess."

Austin chuckled and gazed at Alfie affectionately. "Okay. Up you go." He bent over and grabbed Alfie's arm. In one fluid motion, he swung Alfie onto his back and galloped around the store, making Alfie bounce wildly with every step.

Alfie lost his grin when Austin whinnied like a horse. "I'm not a little kid, Austin."

Austin laughed and set Alfie on his feet. "Okay. Next time no horse noises."

Aendi Linda tousled Alfie's hair. "I'm the one who's grateful. You and Benji gave up a whole new bedroom for me."

Alfie touched the medal around his neck. "We're some of Bienenstock's finest and bravest citizens."

Ruth Ann folded her arms and rolled her eyes. "Don't be proud."

Alfie showed Ruth Ann a sour face. "It's not proud if it's true."

Hannah gave Aendi Linda a hug. "When did you start using the walker?"

Linda wrapped both hands around the top of her walker. "Well. Today."

Onkel Menno nodded. "We're testing to see how well she does."

"I think I'm doing well, don't you?" Linda said.

Hannah felt as if she might explode with joy. "Very well."

Derr Herr performed miracles in the Bible, and some people thought the days of miracles were past, but Hannah didn't believe that. Gotte still sent miracles every day for those who paid attention. He had brought Hannah and Austin together. He'd walked Don and Hilda Burnham out of the valley of the shadow of death, and He'd healed Aendi Linda's body when they thought all hope was gone.

After Benji and Alfie had asked Don and Hilda to buy Linda a wheelchair, Don had met with Linda and then arranged for her to see a specialist. She was diagnosed with chronic neurological Lyme disease and put on a strict diet and exercise program. She'd seen improvement in less than a week. Now she was walking again. It was truly a miracle.

They showed Aendi Linda around the store. Austin and Onkel Menno even carried her upstairs to see the quilts and the hall of shovel heads Hannah had painted. Onkel Menno bought donuts for everyone, even though Austin offered them for free. "*Nae,*" Onkel Menno said. "You'll go out of business if you give out free donuts. We want to pay so we can tell everyone we were customers at your store."

After everyone ate a donut, Aendi Linda gave Hannah a weary smile. "It wonders me if I shouldn't go home now. I think I've worn myself out."

"We'll help with dinner tonight," Ruth Ann said. "Hannah taught me how to make potato soup."

"That would be wonderful *gute.*" Hannah wasn't going to be the mother's helper forever. She'd soon have her own house and babies to care for.

"*Cum,* girls," Linda said. "We'll come back another day."

Without warning, Ruth Ann threw her arms around Alfie and kissed him hard on the cheek. "I love you forever, Alfie Petersheim."

Alfie pulled away like she'd laid a hot poker on his cheek. "Stop it." He wiped at his cheek as if he was trying to rub the skin off his face.

Dinah waved at Benji. "Bye. See you at school tomorrow."

Austin and Onkel Menno carried Linda down the steps. Her family surrounded her as she hobbled to the buggy and got in.

Austin, Hannah, Benji, and Alfie watched from the porch. "Girls are stupid," Alfie said.

Benji tilted his head. "But Ruth Ann and Dinah are nice."

"They're not nice," Alfie said, still rubbing his cheek. "They attack people."

Austin laughed and strolled down the porch steps. Hannah and the twins followed him. "You boys finish weeding the flowerbed," Austin said. "And try not to step on any more petunias. I'm going to show Hannah the vegetable garden."

Alfie and Benji each picked up a trowel. They didn't usually complain about digging in the dirt. "Okay," Benji said. "But hurry back before we ruin something."

Hannah laughed. Benji was too smart for his own good. She followed Austin around the corner of the house where he promptly grabbed her hand and pulled her close to him.

"Austin, what are you doing?"

He put his arms around her and pulled her even closer. "I can't go another minute without kissing you, and I didn't want the boys gawking at us."

Her heart did four flips. "It's against the rules to kiss before we're married."

A playful grin tugged at his lips. "Do you know how many of *die youngie* follow that rule?"

"Do *you?*"

"Zero. Nobody."

"How do you know?" she said, the laughter just bubbling up inside her.

"I just know. If I'm ever the bishop, I'm going to get rid of that rule. It's not fair to two people in love." He traced the back of his hand down the side of her face. His touch felt like heaven. "I do love you. You know that, don't you?"

"*Ach, vell,* I suppose I do. And I have found I can't live without you, even though you're self-centered and a little insensitive."

He grimaced. "A lot insensitive, but you've already agreed to marry me, so you can't back out." His arms tightened around her. "Can I please kiss you now?"

She sighed in mock exasperation. "Okay, but make it a *gute* one. You never know when we'll get a chance like this again."

One of Austin's *gute* qualities was that he usually did whatever Hannah told him. He brought his lips down on hers with a tenderness that stole her breath and made her dizzy. She wrapped her arms around his neck and pulled him closer. Not only did he make it a *gute* kiss but he made it a long one, and she had to eventually pull away or risk hyperventilating. "I love you, Austin."

"I love you, Hannah. You are my everything."

They quickly separated when they heard a buggy pull into the parking lot. "A customer," Austin said. "How nice."

They peeked around the corner of the house, and Austin's eyes flashed with amusement. "Here comes our spy."

Hannah gave Austin a wry smile. "Right on time."

Every day for the last seven weeks, Perry Glick had come to the store. He might have been spying for his *dat,* but Hannah doubted Raymond even knew about Perry's little visits, because Perry came every day at four o'clock sharp and bought three donuts.

He wasn't a very *gute* spy, but he was one of their best customers.